TOM YOU

ASSIMILATION
THE EMILY SMITH TRILOGY, BOOK 2

outskirts
press

Assimilation
The Emily Smith Trilogy, Book 2
All Rights Reserved.
Copyright © 2018 Tom Young
v5.0 R1.1

This is a work of fiction. The events and characters described herein are imaginary and are not intended to refer to specific places or living persons. The opinions expressed in this manuscript are solely the opinions of the author and do not represent the opinions or thoughts of the publisher. The author has represented and warranted full ownership and/or legal right to publish all the materials in this book.

This book may not be reproduced, transmitted, or stored in whole or in part by any means, including graphic, electronic, or mechanical without the express written consent of the publisher except in the case of brief quotations embodied in critical articles and reviews.

Outskirts Press, Inc.
http://www.outskirtspress.com

ISBN: 978-1-4787-9431-8

Library of Congress Control Number: 2018900028

Cover Photo © 2018 thinkstockphotos.com. All rights reserved - used with permission.

Outskirts Press and the "OP" logo are trademarks belonging to Outskirts Press, Inc.

PRINTED IN THE UNITED STATES OF AMERICA

Contents

CHAPTER 1	ANTICIPATION	1
CHAPTER 2	NEW ARRIVALS	3
CHAPTER 3	THE MEETING	5
CHAPTER 4	CHOCOLATE DELIGHT	12
CHAPTER 5	NEW FRIENDS	19
CHAPTER 6	EARLY SUNRISE	29
CHAPTER 7	EMILY'S COUNSEL	36
CHAPTER 8	WEDDING PREPARATION	42
CHAPTER 9	TWILIGHT SLEEP	48
CHAPTER 10	RELAXED	53
CHAPTER 11	SUPRISE AWAKENING	57
CHAPTER 12	FAMILY REUNION	64
CHAPTER 13	THE WEDDING	72
CHAPTER 14	RESTLESS SLEEP	76
CHAPTER 15	SUPRISE PASSENGERS	87
CHAPTER 16	EMILY'S NEW GUEST	89
CHAPTER 17	MERMAIDS OF OLD EARTH	94
CHAPTER 18	EXASPERATION AND RELIEF	106
CHAPTER 19	AFTER ACTION CRITIQUE	111
CHAPTER 20	FIRST DAY OUT	117
CHAPTER 21	THE INVITATION	133
CHAPTER 22	ASTRONOMY LESSONS	137
CHAPTER 23	NEW PATHS	145
CHAPTER 24	HOSPITAL VISIT	151
CHAPTER 25	SUCCESSFUL TRIP	159

CHAPTER 26	DINNER PARTY	163
CHAPTER 27	MERMAIDS	175
CHAPTER 28	SAUCER INTRODUCTION	180
CHAPTER 29	CHILDRENS DELIGHT	186
CHAPTER 30	LATE NIGHT CALL	192
CHAPTER 31	INTRODUCTION TO EMILY'S WORLD	198
CHAPTER 32	DAMAGE CONTROL	207
CHAPTER 33	CALL TO DUTY	215
CHAPTER 34	HUSBAND AND FATHER'S REGRET, A MOTHER'S PAIN	221
CHAPTER 35	WORKING THRU ISSUES	226
CHAPTER 36	FIRST MISSION	233
CHAPTER 37	ACCEPTANCE	239
CHAPTER 38	TRAVAIL AND PAIN	247
CHAPTER 39	LOVE STRONGER THAN DEATH	251
CHAPTER 40	COMING HOME	258
CHAPTER 41	NEW REALITIES	263
CHAPTER 42	APPREHENSION	267
CHAPTER 43	MUSKULA'S CHALLENGE	275
CHAPTER 44	SPACE INTELLIGENCE ALERT	277
CHAPTER 45	HELLO FATHER	281
CHAPTER 46	FRIENDS, CHILDREN NO MORE	287
CHAPTER 47	A FRIEND AVENGED	303
CHAPTER 48	ANOTHER CALL	311
CHAPTER 49	GRARGOL, NEANDERTHAL FROM THE STARS	322
CHAPTER 50	ALIEN OR HUMAN	335
CHAPTER 51	MIND MELD	343
CHAPTER 52	WAITING FOR EARTH	347

CHAPTER 53	IRENA'S ENLIGHTMENT	349
CHAPTER 54	FLATA'S FEAR	355
CHAPTER 55	SCIENCE INTRODUCTION	364
CHAPTER 56	BUSY AT WORK	369
CHAPTER 57	FIRST COOKOUT	376
CHAPTER 58	AMBULANCE RIDE	381
CHAPTER 59	PLANNING SEEDS OF DESTRUCTION	385
CHAPTER 60	BATTLE PLAN	391
CHAPTER 61	EMBARCATION	395
BOOK TWO	ASSIMULATION CHARCTERS	399

Book 3
Emily Smith Trilogy, TARGET EARTH

Chapter 1	Ugly Surprise	405

CHAPTER 1
ANTICIPATION

Blain gathered the three children into the control room before entering the saucer to help encourage them in their new assignment. Jawane and Hanlee were excited and wanted to go even though they were afraid; the only reason they were willing to go was because they knew Emily and trusted her with their lives. And, truth be known, they had developed a new kind of love for her that was foreign to their Andrian species.

Persha was of a different mindset altogether. She did not want to go. She wanted to join the Andrian military forces and fight the "things", or life form, or whatever they were that had destroyed her parents. So many Andrians have been destroyed, including three fully populated solar systems. Not one life form had been spared on the planets and the six intergalactic carriers that were defending them. All personnel on board had been vaporized with a new kind of weapon. The last place she wanted to be was on the earth. The Humans were so, so…, stupid!

Blain said, "Remember to do what Emily says. She loves you in the earthly way Humans love and she will not allow anything to happen to you. And Persha, I believe that at this time, this assignment will be in your best interest and to the best interest for the "Council of Yield".

They are depending on you to help channel and direct other young Andrians that will be following soon.

Persha acknowledged Blains word of admonition by indicating she was the lessor and he the greater, but he knew she was not pleased. Blain also knew that with the devastating loss of her parents, as she was one of the few, who had known no other, being with Emily was the best thing for her. Emily would help her heal.

All four boarded the saucer and left the intergalactic ship. Since the enemy had been discovered on Saturn's moon, Iapetus, all craft leaving the carrier had a small contingent of military. The saucer quickly located the proper coordinates, and hovered in the landing position.

Blain and Persha exited the craft first. Persha stayed close to Blain as they moved to the side. Jawane and Hanlee huddled close as they stepped off the lift next. All three children were terrified and had second thoughts about the great adventures they might have on a planet.

Everything was green. There were things called birds flying everywhere, some of them making a grating noise. A wind was blowing softly, and the smell, it was unlike anything they had ever sensed before. It was very pleasant. And the sun, it was so bright and hot but for some reason, the air was somewhat cool. It was also disconcerting not to have a ceramic glass or cover protecting them from the cosmos. Looking around they did not see any barriers whatsoever separating them from their surroundings. It looked like they could walk forever! Then they saw Emily standing near the trees with her hand vigorously waving.

CHAPTER 2
NEW ARRIVALS

Emily, Skip and Billy had just put away the dishes from the morning breakfast; Warren had gone to work at the Forrest Service Terminal in the small town twenty miles away. After Emily had convinced him of the dire nature of the environment, Warren had switched his interest from mathematics to the chemical analysis of the soil and air. He had already been instrumental in developing several new analytical systems to define standards and quality of various environmental issues. Emily believed he was progressing in his mental health steadily although be it somewhat slowly. Working in a forest that was richly oxygenated enhanced the healing process and helped clear his head and enabled him to think clearly. Indeed, he was steadily regaining his old self confidence again.

Emily looked over at Skip and Billy who were working on the new mathematical puzzle that Emily had given them. It was the strangest thing they had ever seen. The math did not formulate in a linear line but instead entwined in a helix fashion. Emily was pleased with their progress. They had already solved two of the major theorems.

"They are already much more knowledgeable than Dr. Calander, that stuffy ole wind bag!" Just the thought of her pompous former physics professor made her shiver.

Oh well, she had heard he had been dressed down quiet sternly by Admiral Cleary.

"Okay boys, I am going for a walk. I will be back soon. I want you to listen for the phone." Emily left the house out the back door and proceeded up the path that led to a wooded area that opened into a meadow about one mile away.

Skip and Billy looked at one another and simultaneously got up and left out the back door careful not to slam the screen. They followed Emily at a discreet distance using the foliage to conceal their presence.

"Where do you think she is going Skip? She has been acting like she believed someone was going to arrive at any moment."

"I do not know Billy but we need to stay out of sight, we do not want her to think we are spying on her. But I guess we are. I feel bad about that but she has been acting so strangely since she returned I just cannot help but wonder what she is up to. I mean, where on earth did she come up with those math equations? I am amazed we can figure them out!"

"Me too!", Exclaimed Billy."

Emily knew the boys were following and was pleased that they were concerned about her. Had she not been able to read their minds and listen in on their conversation and thoughts, she never would have known they were there. They were progressing in their knowledge of spherical mathematics at a phenomenal rate. "Ha, they would put Dr. Pompous to shame!" Emily laughed. She would give them a chance to learn the truth, they have always been trustworthy.

CHAPTER 3
THE MEETING

As Emily exited the shaded path into the clearing she observed the saucer hovering in the center of the glen. Blain was flanked by his two children, Jawane and Hanlee. They both had grown several inches since she had last seen them. There was also a young Andrian woman who was about seventeen or eighteen. She had not yet met the young woman but she was advised her name was Persha. Persha's parental unit had been killed by the alien species in a distant galaxy.

As Emily approached the saucer, Blain telepathically communicated to her that two young boys were hiding behind the bushes observing them. Emily replied that she was aware of their presence and that it was okay.

As Emily approached the group she greeted them first in Andrian, the lesser to the greater, and then telepathically advised, "Now that you are on the earth you must learn to act Human!" Emily first reached up and put her arms around Blain's neck and pulled him down toward her. Leaning into Blain and pressing her body into his she gave him a soft kiss on the lips teasing him with her tongue. Releasing Blain she said laughingly, "Why Blain I do believe you are blushing! Welcome to my home!"

Blain, caught unawares, was indeed blushing. His lips tingled and Emily's body heat was still imprinted on his legs and thighs. He found the contact more than just pleasing. He felt a gnawing in his groin that he had experienced one other time. That time was when Emily had kissed him on the lips after she had emerged from the Entity consciousness on the saucer. She was not herself then. Other than these two incidents they had up until this point in time not touched one another except for the time Blain had helped Emily into the saucer upon their first meeting, or perhaps, a more adequate description of the meeting, was abducting her; and also of course, when placing Emily into the proper position in the saucer before takeoff. He knew now that he wanted Emily as a consort more than ever, more than any woman he had ever wanted in his life.

Blain stammered verbally, "Thank you Emily for that great earthly welcome and invite. You did catch me by surprise. But then you always do, I always thought I knew "Humans", but I guess I really do not."

Emily then faced Jawane and taking him into her arms, gave him a fierce hug and kiss on the cheek saying, "Welcome Jawane!" He had grown six inches since she had last seen him about eleven months ago. It seemed like another life time ago.

Releasing Jawane, Emily approached Hanlee and gave her a fierce hug and kiss also.

Emily said, "I missed you both so much! I did not have anyone to play "Duh", with!"

Blain and the children laughed with the exception of Persha, who was watching the proceedings with reluctant participation.

ASSIMILATION

"I am so glad you could come! We are going to have so much fun!"

The term "fun", sounded totally alien to the children. Exactly what did "fun" entail? There was no room in the Andrian quest for daily living and survival that had a function that was classified as, "fun". Fun was obviously a basic human function.

Emily then looked at the other young woman. She could see a sad cloud in her eyes and felt empathy for her. She then greeted her in Andrian, the lessor to the greater, she being the lessor, the young Andrian woman the greater. Persha accepted the acknowledgement that she was the greater.

Emily then telepathed to her, "Welcome to my home Persha, and I wish to extend my sincere condolences to you for the death of your parental unit."

Persha looked in shock to Blain. There was no reason to inform the Human Emily of the loss of her parental unit. "Why have you done this? To what purpose does it serve to talk of these things?"

Blain responded by saying, "You have a lot in common with Emily. You will be fine."

Looking down, Persha responded to Emily by saying, "Thank you".

Emily then extended her hand for a Human handshake and verbalized, "Let us start over. Hello, my name is Emily Smith. Welcome to my home."

Persha just looked at Emily's hand then back up to Emily, then back down to Emily's hand.

Emily said, "You might as well learn how to greet

someone you do not know or one who is not necessarily close to you but you want to acknowledge."

Persha looked at Emily's hand again wondering what she was supposed to do with it, if anything. Emily, using her left hand, took Persha's right hand and placed it in her right hand and shook it up and down. "There! You have just received lesson number one in saying hello on the planet earth! Well, maybe lesson number two! Blain received lesson number one!"

From their concealment in the foliage, Skip and Billy observed the group of five as they just stood around in a circle. It did not appear they were saying anything.

Skip said, "They must be speaking telepathically or something because it does not look like they are talking. All the aliens' clothes look okay except they looked like they are dressed like farmers or something. They could really use some better clothes. Emily just stared at them, and they her."

Billy responded, "Yea. Well at least they are not wearing space suits."

Then Emily gave the man a kiss and a hug. She also hugged the two younger children but she shook hands with the young woman. The young woman obviously did not know anything about handshakes because Emily had to show her how to do it.

"The young woman appears to be our age, at least seventeen or eighteen. It is hard to tell her age because they are so far away."

Suddenly the group of aliens and Emily turned in their direction and started walking back to the house.

ASSIMILATION

Skip and Billy turned and ran. After a short distance they looked back and observed the saucer rise into the sky at an incredible speed.

Upon entering the house they were careful not to slam the screen door. Skip breathlessly intoned, "Can you believe that! Wow! Where did they come from and who are they?"

Billy said, "More importantly, why are they here? What are we going to do?"

Skip replied, "We are not going to do anything. We are going to love and trust Emily in all things! After all, she was living with them for almost a year. I do not know why they took Emily but it does not seem to have had a bad effect on her. Besides, she greeted them as friends. And any friend of Emily's is a friend of mine!"

Both boys seated themselves at the table and busied themselves trying to work the mathematical puzzle that Emily had given to them. The back screen door slammed shut as Emily, the man, and the children entered the room. Both Skip and Billy stood up and greeted the newcomers and extended their hand for a handshake.

Emily said, "Skip, Billy, this is my Uncle Blain."

Blain accepted their handshake knowing full well that the two young men knew that they were not from the planet earth. They seemed excited but they did not show any fear, nor did they outwardly give themselves away that they knew that they were not from earth. Blain knew that their lack of fear had to be contributed to their trust in Emily.

"Emily then said, "These are his children, my cousins,

Jawane, Hanlee and Persha. "

Emily then looked at the group and telepathed, "Remember, speak verbally. They are not telepaths… yet!"

Both boys and the two younger children then shook hands, limply so.

Emily then introduced Persha and said, "This is Persha."

Skip looked at Persha closely. He noted that her hair was shoulder length, blonde and really fine stranded. She was sort of thin but definitely trim, and she had really nice breast. As an afterthought he intoned to himself, "Wow! She is really one hot space girl!"

Persha's face colored red as she looked down saying, "Nice to meet you," and limply shaking Skip's hand.

Jawane and Hanlee looked at Blain wide eyed in astonishment. "Is sex all that earthlings ever think about?"

Blain smiled at Emily and said to Skip, "You are Skip, right?"

"Yes sir," Replied Skip.

"Well Skip, would you be so kind to show Persha around and watch out for her? She has been isolated and has led a sheltered life and perhaps you can be a positive influence on her; you too Billy. You two could be the "dynamic duo". Escort her around and make sure no harm comes to her. Could you do that for me please? I would consider it a personal favor."

Both boys stammered in unison, "Yes Sir!"

If Blain saw the look of pure disgust on Persha's face or heard her telepathic rebellious response he did not seem to notice.

ASSIMILATION

Jawane and Hanlee, having watched and listened to the exchange, again rolled their eyes saying, "Telepathically", of course, "Yea Right! They could not find their way out of an empty weightless playroom!"

The three young people then noticed the spherical mathematical equations on the table. Skip, observing them looking at the math puzzles, said, "Emily comes up with the strangest math games we have ever seen. Have you ever seen anything like this?"

The three Andrian children looked at the formulas then at each other. They were the most basic and elementary theorems in spherical mathematics. All Andrian children learned them when they were about five years of age. However, for a Human of any age to learn them was almost unprecedented.

Hanlee responded first and said, "No, we have never seen anything like it. Is it hard?"

Billy responded with exasperation in his voice and said, "It took us four weeks just to line up the formulas. We still have not completed the puzzle. We cannot figure out where Emily comes up with this stuff. It is so interesting. I have never had to think so hard in my entire life! So far we have completed what we believe to be two theorems. I do not have the foggiest idea of what they are for or to what ends they accomplish. I certainly do not know how many more theorems are exposited. I bet there must be hundreds! Look how they entwine each other!"

Persha smiled. She was pleased that they had at least accomplished the elementary level of spherical mathematics. They might not have such a hard time teaching them after all.

CHAPTER 4
CHOCOLATE DELIGHT

Emily placed her arm in the crook of Blain's arm and escorted him to the kitchen table. The table had two trays piled high with fresh baked brownies and chocolate chip cookies. The children looked on with interest. They knew that it was obviously something special and the smell was so strong and enticing.

Emily said, "Okay everyone, let us have a seat. Everyone came to the table to set down. Just before Persha sat down both Skip and Billy scrambled to help Persha with her chair, she did not know what they were doing but she allowed them to move the chair for her as she took her seat and then move it closer to the table. Persha believed she could move the chair perfectly fine by herself.

Emily, observing their behavior, smiled. "They are such perfect young men." They were both obviously smitten by Persha. Emily went to the refrigerator and retrieved a cold pitcher of milk and placed it on the table. She then went to her chair which Skip pulled out for her and moved the chair forward when she sat down. Hanlee was surprised when Billy helped her with her chair. For some strange reason it made her feel "special".

Emily said, "Thank you boys. That was so kind. You both have such good manners."

ASSIMILATION

None of the three young people could fathom what manners were or what the utility was of moving a perfectly healthy person's chair; they all telepathed to one another that Humans really were strange. Listening in on their thoughts, Emily smiled thinking, "Let the lessons begin." Emily then poured each of them a glass of milk in an icy mug, her favorite way to serve milk. She then gave each of them two brownies and two chocolate chip cookies and they smelled so good having just come from the oven. Emily said, "Eat up!"

Skip and Billy did not have to be told twice! They quickly devoured their cookies and reached for more. Emily made the best cookies they had ever had, even better than their mom's.

The three children carefully took a small bite. Emily watched them with interest. It did not take long. All three children eagerly ate the sweet cookies and asked for more. They drank the milk slowly, tasting and sniffing. Soon they drank that down too.

Emily said to Blain, "Children are the same everywhere. They all like cookies."

Blain responded with a brownie in his mouth and said, "Me too!"

As Persha ate her cookies she carefully glanced at Skip. Thinking, "He is not ugly. He is so much more muscular than Andrian men. I wonder why? His hair appears to be light brown in the house but sandy in the sun, the collar length cut looked nice too. But unlike Andrian Men, he allows it to hang down to just above the eyes. And when I shook his hand it was very calloused. Billy's hands were not that way." Unknown to Persha, was the fact that Skip was an accomplished gymnast, not that she knew what a gymnast was.

After everyone was finished with the cookies and milk, they all went and sat on the porch facing the lake. It was getting dusk and the sky was changing from dark blue to a pale light pink. The land gently sloped downward toward a large body of water. The water was an inlet to Lake Ontario. The many islands dispersed away from the shore line just made the body of water to appear like a lake. The water glimmered as the light reflected from the choppy surface. The children remained verbally silent but there was not a moment of peace as thoughts flew between them. They were excited and pleased they had come. So far, everything had been exciting.

Emily had baked a turkey and made mashed potatoes and gravy. It was a full Thanks Giving dinner. They were going to wait until Warren came home to serve dinner. The experience for the Andrians, Emily hoped, would be a satisfying one. They certainly liked the cookies and milk; it was really a big success. Since Emily had returned home she had learned to cook in earnest and she believed she was progressing nicely. When Warren's mother and father left to be with the Andrians she knew she had a need to improve her cooking skills.

Blain was impressed with Emily's cookies and the other food cooking in the oven smelled even more delicious. He telepathed Emily, "Emily, are you sure I could not talk you into being my consort? Everything you do is absolutely perfect!"

ASSIMILATION

Emily responded, "Blain I am truly flattered that you would consider me worthy of being your consort, but, as you know, I am hopelessly in love with Warren. You are such a good man. And you know, I hope you find love someday".

The three children looked at Emily in opened mouthed amazement for having refused Blains offer to be his consort. He was the top commander of the entire Andrian fleet in the galaxy. He could have any, and as many, female consorts as he desired. It was a privilege and honor to be his consort. And, for some odd reason, which they could not understand, Sharla, one of his consorts, and Jawane's mother, left Blain to marry the human, Robert Aaron.

"Warren will be back soon. I would love for you to meet him. I know you will like him. He is extremely intelligent, just like his father." Emily then looked at Skip and Billy, and continued her conversation. "The boys are just like him. They are way above average in intelligence from the standard Human population. I have been working with them for several years and I can see great increases in their abilities. I am sure, with your children's help, they will soon develop telepathic skills. Warren was deeply injured when I went missing. It will take some time for him to heal. But when he does, he too may develop telepathic skills. And, we intend to have many children." Looking at Blain and grinning, "To help the Earth, you know!"

Skip and Billy did not miss the expressions on the three young people's faces. Emily and the man called

Blain were definitely communicating telepathically. They wished they could do that. They did not know what was said but whatever it was, it shocked the three children.

Moments later Warren drove up in his new pickup truck. He waved as he got out of the truck. Emily got up and walked down the wooden stairs to meet him and placed her arms around his neck as she had done with Blain earlier, and she kissed him on the lips with a nice soft kiss saying, "I love you. Come and meet my uncle Blain and his three children."

Warren walked up the stairs and extended his hand for a hand shake. Blain extended his hand and said, "Please to meet you Warren. I have heard a lot of good things about you."

Warren responded, "Well I guess the pleasure is all yours because in all the years we have been going together she never mentioned you."

Emily said, "Uncle Blain and his children lived out of the country. I haven't seen him since I was a very little girl. I actually forgot all about him because Mom and Dad never spoke of him. He recently heard of Mom and Dad's death and came to see if there was anything he could do. Since I have never met my cousins I asked if they could stay awhile. I think it will be fun and they said they would love to stay. Emily hated telling Warren an untruth but right now it was necessary. When he was better she would tell him the truth.

At the mention of the death of both of Emily's parents, Persha queried Blain as to the circumstances. He responded to her silently explaining to her how Emily's

ASSIMILATION

parents had been murdered by the traitor Zelegark, as he carried on his conversation with Warren. Persha looked at Emily carefully and thoughtfully. Thinking to herself, "I guess we have some things in common after all."

Blain recognizing the awkward situation said, "Actually it is my fault. I sort of made a pass at Emily's mom, Martha, one night when I had too much to drink and really made John extremely angry. We found it best to part ways after that. Of course it did not help when I lost most of their savings in that money market scam. I had pretty much become the black goat of the family".

Emily said, "Sheep. Black sheep."

Blain corrected, "Black sheep, I mean black sheep".

"Thank you." Blain silently said to Emily.

Billy and Skip kept quiet. They watched everyone's responses.

Jawane, Hanlee, and Persha were rapidly comparing notes and inquiring of any shared knowledge they had of Warren and Emily's parents. The children were surprised to realize that they knew very little of Emily's personal circumstances. And, Warren's parents were just as mysterious. Obviously, they must have been very important to allow them to travel with them on an intergalactic carrier as guest.

Emily, in a concerted effort to avoid further discussion pertaining to Blain's relationship said, "Ok gang, dinner is going to get cold. Let's eat". They all went inside to the kitchen and prepared to sit down. As before, both skip and Billy helped Persha with her chair and then Billy helped Hanlee with hers. Warren helped Emily bring the food to the table then he helped her with her chair.

Jawane was still standing in front of his chair after every one had set down. Skip looked at him and said, "Sorry dude, you are on your on".

Emily looked at Jawane who had a confused look on his face, and said, telepathically, "Helping a lady with her chair is a courtesy that a man will extend to a woman. You can start by practicing with Hanlee". Jawane had ignored Hanlee as she sat down at which time Billy had helped her. Emily smiled at him as he sat in his chair.

Warren had noticed Emily's strange behaviors and assumed that it was a result of being kidnapped and held captive by the Gypsies, it seemed to be getting more pronounced with the arrival of her Uncle Blain and his family. He could feel an undercurrent of "something", he could not identify. It seemed to be floating just beyond his cognizant thoughts.

After setting down at the table, Emily had everyone join in holding hands as Warren said grace. The Andrians enjoyed their first meal on the planet earth.

CHAPTER 5
NEW FRIENDS

After dinner and visiting on the porch until late in the evening, Emily showed the three children to their room. There were two sets of bunk beds, one set on each side of the room. A dresser was in the middle. The room was located upstairs in the corner of the cabin and thus afforded two windows on each of the two outside walls. There was a door that led to second story open porch that ran the length of the structure. The porch afforded a view of the lake that stretched out below and reflected the light of a full moon. The scene was absolutely idyllic and pristine. A cool breeze could be felt as it ascended up the slope from the lake. The weather was cool enough to require a jacket. And, the air smelled of wet wood, tinged with a faint odor of wood smoke.

Standing on the balcony overlooking the lake, Jawane, Hanlee, and Persha, looked up at the moon. They had seen thousands of holographic videos with three dimensional images of planets, moons, and star systems. But, being on a planet and looking up at a moon, they had never experienced. It was truly beautiful. Nor had they ever breathed in such idyllic air. The clean coolness allowed their lungs to expand with a feeling of…completeness. The air had a damp woodsy smell. No doubt the richly oxygenated air contributed to their feelings of wellbeing.

Skip and Billy exited their room which was adjacent to the three Andrian children and stood on the other end of the balcony. At first they did not see the three young Andrians on the other end of the balcony. But of course, the three young people knew they were there and stood silently listening as they conversed.

"They look exactly like us. They just seem to be very quiet. I wish I could do that telepath thing. I think it would be really neat. And, I cannot imagine what it would be like to go to different stars and planets like Emily did. I wonder if they took her or if she went on her own free will? And why take her at all? I wonder if I would be afraid to go up there in a space ship. I wonder if Emily was afraid. I mean, there are so many questions and so few answers. I just know I would be absolutely terrified!"

Billy said, "Me too! I would be so scared I would probably wet my pants!"

Skip looked at the moon and wondered if he would ever have a chance to go there. "I have always wanted to be an astronaut. How exciting it would be to walk on the moon or another planet! Just think what it would be like to travel to another star, explore other planets! I would be so excited but you know what? I would be afraid too!"

Persha and the children listened to Skips words that he spoke to his brother. It seemed strange to express such thoughts of fears and aspirations so openly. On the Andrian ships and in their society, one just did what one was told. One did as one was told because it was for the

ASSIMILATION

greater good. You were assigned according to one's aptitude. There was never any debate. And because their verbiage expressed very personal concerns and aspirations, all three of them felt guilty for being present within hearing range.

Skip then looked over and saw the three young Andrians standing on the other end of the balcony. He felt terror that he openly revealed that they knew that they were from the stars. He did not know what to say.

Persha could feel all his emotions. She was touched that he felt the same as she, should their roles be reversed. Persha thought; "Fear of the unknown must be prevalent in all species."

Persha said, "Hello Skip".

Skip did not respond. He was just looking at her from the other end of the balcony. Remembering that Skip was not a telepath, Persha spoke the words, "Hello Skip".

Skip was frozen in position, as was Billy.

Billy whispered, "I hope Emily will not be mad at us for letting them know that we know that they are not from earth."

"Me to", Whispered Skip.

Upon hearing Persha's greeting, Skip responded, "Hello Persha. I am sorry. I did not see you all standing there. Emily never told us anything. We saw you when you got off the saucer. Man that was really cool! I would love to ride in a saucer! I could not believe you did not have little antennas on your heads! That is our conceptual perception of what an "Alien" would look like!"

The three Andrian children laughed as that was

almost the exact concept of what they caricatured humans would look like!

Billy said, "I would love to ride in a saucer too!"

Hanlee and Jawane smiled, as they could feel their enthusiasm.

Hanlee telepathed to Jawane, "Humans might be really stupid but they are also very honest, I have not detected any sense of duplicity and their thoughts are honest; And they trusted Emily and have accepted us as friends, whatever that is. I guess we should give them the same respect. After all, we do have some kind of strange new feelings for Emily."

Persha said, "You will not tell anyone will you? Blain said that under no circumstances were we to reveal to anyone where we come from. Of course we knew you were aware of us when we landed, our saucer sensor alerted us to your presence. Emily told Blain that it was all right. She also said that she has been working with you for several years and she hoped that soon you would develop telepathic skills, with our help of course! Blain told us, when we were assigned to come to the earth that we were to help you develop these skills."

Skip and Billy were utterly amazed. They could not believe that the young people were already aware of them. And what did she mean that "Emily was already working with us? She helped us with our homework and she really made it simple, but that was all."

Billy said, "Of course we will not tell. But, where do you come from?"

"We originated in the star system Andria. It is several

ASSIMILATION

galaxies away from your star system. Andrians are the progenitors of many civilizations throughout the star systems. We assume that Emily has told you nothing of us as you were unaware of us until this morning. Therefore, should you wish to know more, you will have to ask Emily." Persha did not reveal anything that was contrary to Blain's instructions.

Both Skip and Billy looked at them and were amazed that the young woman would be so forthcoming. She was from another star system and it was like talking to the new girl next door; that was not what they believed the first alien encounter would be like, but then, who thought that they would look just like us? And wow, was she beautiful with the moon giving her hair a silver glow!

Again Hanlee and Jawane rolled their eyes at one another. "What is up with these Human earth people? Don't they have anything else to think about?" They telepathed one another comparing notes as to what the mores of the planet were. It seemed to differ within each of the cultures. And yes, sexual attraction seemed to reign supreme.

Skip and Billy approached the other end of the balcony where the children were standing and they stood as a group looking up at the moon.

Jawane said, "Your moon has a lot of minerals that could be used to fuel your space craft with clean, efficient energy. I do not understand why you do not use the resources. We mine many moons in every star system. In your solar system we mine Saturn's moon Hyperion. And, we have been doing so for hundreds of your earth years. We use robots to mine the minerals and nano bots to break the minerals down into their basic chemical compositions. They then store up the mineral compositions for our use when we come into this solar system. I believe your Cassini space craft spotted our mining operation in your year 2008. At least some of the pictures I have observed in our earth science studies showed our mining operation on the moon Hyperion. It can be seen as a small green dot in the upper right hand quadrant of the image. Of course your governments and space agencies sanitize all pictures from space. It looks like they just missed this one."

Jawane then expounded exactly what minerals they were looking for and what chemicals the nano bots used to break them down into their individual components. Skip and Billy looked at Jawane with awe. How could someone so young talk so knowledgably about Earths' space programs and their mining operations on one of Saturn's many moons?

Jawane, being able to read their minds, advised, "It is necessary for us to utilize our mental and neural capabilities as much as possible because we are a highly technical society and it is necessary for our survival. We must make every atom of product usable for the good of the society in which we live. I think that a reasonable approximation of the challenges we face in space in a closed environment would be somewhat similar for you to take one of your acre of trees, and care for them as if they are the only tree resource you have for the next one hundred of your earth years. And do not forget, that acre has to

ASSIMILATION

meet the needs of five thousand people."

Skip and Billy looked at one another. Billy said, "I thought you were only twelve years old? I mean, how can you possibly construct such analytical thoughts and express such a complex process in a way we can understand?

Jawane smiled and said, "Believe me, it is not easy!"

Skip said, "Yea, you make me feel like, really stupid. I don't mean that in a disapproving way, nor am I criticizing you for your obviously knowledgeable assessment. It is just, think...gee whizz! Compared to you we must seem like real dummies"!

All three of the Andrians smiled broadly at Skip's acknowledgement of their sentiments. Persha said, "Yes that is true, but we like you anyway!" All the young people laughed. Skip loved Persha's sense of humor. Persha was surprised at herself for coming up with such a response. A sense of humor had no place within the Andrian culture.

Hanlee said, "And, if you are willing to learn we will be glad to teach you. We loved teaching Emily. She was always dancing around putting her hands by her head with her finger extended and saying "duh"!"

All the young people laughed again, this time at the image of Emily dancing in a circle and saying "duh".

Hanlee then said, "It is true that our knowledge, technical skills, and our neurological skills may be greater than yours. But it is because over the generations we have worked very hard to develop them. Emily said she had been teaching you and helping you increase your mathematical skills. Mathematics is the life blood of our Andrian society. Should the existence of your species depend on that one acre of trees that Jawane exposited, then there is no doubt you would know your trees inside and out. And, in order to know that you would be measuring the genome of the tree using mathematics that as of yet you have not considered."

Persha then said, "And as for being a technical society, we are leaning something new from you. Some of your concepts are as foreign to us as our mathematics is to you." Persha paused and had to think a minute. That in and of itself was an exercise she was not accustomed to. "We are learning the concepts of "friendship". I suppose that duty would transcend friendship. We know all about duty. That is why I came. Not because I wanted to. I wanted to join the Andrian military and fight…"

"Persha!" Hanlee said sharply.

Persha looked at her in surprise. Then recalled what she was about to say. The knowledge of the new enemy was not to be revealed, under any circumstances, to the humans.

The demeanor of all three children changed. They no longer smiled and they certainly did not appear to be at ease as they had been before. Saying goodnight they turned and returned to their room.

Skip and Billy looked at one another. Skip said, "What was that all about?"

"I don't know but it sounded like Persha wanted to join the Andrian military and fight some kind of enemy." Skip intoned in a subdued manner. "Evidently it is one

ASSIMILATION

of the things that we definitely are not supposed to know anything about. I wonder if we should ask Emily or let it rest. What do you think, Billy?"

"I don't know. I am sure that even if we did know, we probably could not do anything about it. Besides it might scare us to death to know for sure that there is some kind of big bad wolf out there that would love to eat us for lunch. And you know what? Persha was saying that the concept of friendship is foreign to them. We can honor their word as confidential information and not divulge it to any living soul, even Emily. It is like…, no one is going to get hurt if we do not tell. So what is the point in telling? We cannot effect any positive changes if we tell. And on the other hand, we can demonstrate what the concepts of friendship are. I definitely believe we should show them by example what friendship means." Billy ended his speech then pointedly stared at Skip.

Skip was somewhat amazed at the reasoning which Billy used to justify not telling, or in this case, in not asking Emily about the enemy. Skip then said, "Your right Billy. I think it boils down to trusting Emily. I do not know what Emily knows of this enemy but if she thought it was important that we know she would tell us. Perhaps it will become necessary to tell us at a later date. Until that time we will keep Persha's almost slip of the tongue, just between us."

Skip and Billy returned to their room and retired for the evening as had the Andrian children earlier. The three Andrian children each took a bunk. Even though they were highly disciplined and could almost sleep on demand, they all had trouble going to sleep. None of them believed that this task was going to be as easy as Blain led them to believe. Hanlee and Jawane knew and trusted Emily. She was their stabilizing influence.

Persha, now, that was a different story. She literally had no one; with her two guiding influences both dead; killed at the hand of the new enemy. And if the rumor is true, one of them have been found in this solar system. How could it have come so far into this galaxy without detection by the Andrian military? These troubling thoughts haunted Persha's sleep but soon sleep did come due to exhaustion.

Emily was laying in her bed, the open window just a few paces from the porch. With a strong gentle breeze blowing in from the lake, the young people's words were carried easily within her hearing. She was pleased with the young Andrians and proud of Skip and Billy. They did not have a need to know about the enemy that was discovered nearby. Perhaps she would tell them later. It would be a good opportunity for the boys to demonstrate friendship. It was going to be alright.

CHAPTER 6
EARLY SUNRISE

Persha, Hanlee, and Jawane woke up to a new and very enticing smell. They did not know what it was but it was so good. They got up and examined the bathroom and shower. About that time there was a knock at the door and Emily entered. She was wearing her hair in really strange fashion; it was tied behind the center of her head and hung down on her shoulders. It swayed with her walk. She had on a red and white checkered shirt and real tight blue pants. The children queried each other and Hanlee remembered that they were called blue jeans.

"Hi gang! I hope you slept well. I wanted to show you how the bathroom toilet and shower worked as I know you did not have anything similar on the ship, I mean out in the wilderness!"

Emily showed them the flushing mechanism on the toilet and how to turn the water on and to set the temperature on the shower control. "Take as long as you like in the shower, we have plenty of water."

Emily then showed them the closet with a few sets of clothes she had got for Jawane and Hanlee. She guessed at Persha's size and was pretty accurate, and thus had picked her up some items at the last minute.

"Persha, this is a bra. It is used to support your breast. You do not have to wear one if you do not want to but I think you will find that it will help keep the boys less excited than they already are." Emily smiled at her. Hanlee and Jawane rolled their eyes at one another. Emily started the shower for Persha and left the room.

All three children looked at one another and then disrobed and stepped into the shower. It easily accommodated all three of them.

Jawane said, "Is it true? Can we use as much water as we like? Surely she did not mean that. I mean how wasteful can you get!"

The young Andrians quickly showered as they would have in their home. They sorted out the clothes and carefully dressed. Persha's blue jeans were much tighter than to what she was accustomed to so she was very self-conscious. Jawane and Hanlee help her with her bra. It seemed so useless. It also rubbed her nipples and felt strangely…discomfiting.

She put on the blue and white checkered shirt, similar to Emily's' but a different color and tucked the end of the shirt into her jeans. Looking in the mirror, she observed that her nipples were erect and hard as they were agitated by the rubbing of the thin bra and coarse shirt and thus strained against the tight fit. Remembering what Emily had said about getting the boys excited, she turned to the side and observed her curvy breast in the mirror. "I guess there is not much I can do to keep them from getting excited or whatever, earthlings are so…strange," said Persha. She remembered what had gone thru Skip's mind when they were introduced. In a way Persha was flattered, as no Andrian male had ever really looked twice at her. But then again, why would they? What utility would there be in that?

After combing her hair back and noticing a small round rubber device she fixed her hair in a similar fashion as Emily's by placing the rubber device around her hair. "The boys seem to think that I am...desirable?...attractive?...hot...?"

Looking in the mirror she tried to see herself as the boys seem to think she looked. "I do not think I am anything special by Human or Andrian standards. They seem to be preoccupied with my breast. They look normal to me. Several Andrian men have taken a cursory second look at me but then they kept on going. Guess they do not find me as attractive as the Human boys obviously think I am," thought Persha; now, for some reason that was a pleasing thought.

Jawane and Hanlee quickly dressed in the clothes provided and all three of them exited the room to go down stairs. Once outside the room the smell was even stronger, and it was so good!

Emily was in the kitchen busy cooking a breakfast fit for a king. She wanted their first breakfast to be memorable as was there first dinner. There was a large stack of pancakes on the table next to a steaming picture of pure maple syrup. Emily removed the thick sliced bacon from the oven that was evenly crisp. The scrambled eggs with small chips of red and green bell peppers added flavor and eye appeal, at least for a human. Then she removed the crisp hash brown potatoes smothered in onions and cheese from the iron skillet and placed them on a serving tray next to the large steaming bowl of white milk gravy. Last but not least she removed the home made biscuits from the oven. She checked everything and noted that the orange juice, coffee and butter were on the table.

Blain, Warren, Skip, and Billy were already at the table when the three young Andrians came down the stairs and into the kitchen. Both boys mouth dropped opened when they saw Persha. They both jumped up and pulled her chair back to assist her to the table. Emily smiled. Persha was a beautiful young woman. She just did not know it.

Jawane and Hanlee rolled their eyes at one another saying telepathically, "Here we go again".

Then to the surprise of Hanlee, both Billy and Skip helped her with her chair. Warren helped Emily with her chair.

Emily smiled at Jawane and telepathed, "It is a human custom that gentlemen help the ladies with their chairs."

Emily then had every one hold one another's hand in a circle around the table and said grace over the food. Persha thought, "Why would they thank someone they could not see and did not know, for their food; yet another mystery?" Persha could feel the warmth and perspiration on the boy's hands and could feel a slight tremble in her palms. The touch of the two young men felt foreign to her. Andrian sexuality is predominately an artificial fusion of neural links to the sexual neurological functions of the brain. Of course the sex was good but it was not physical. Ones eggs and sperm was harvested by Flata, the Andrians geneticist, and the embryo inserted into the

ASSIMILATION

female for six weeks, then the embryo is removed and placed in an artificial womb. It was all very superficial, controlled and sterile.

All the Andrians ate heartily and telepathed continually how good everything was and ate second helpings of everything. Then Persha asked what the crisp flavorful strips were that was called bacon. She telepathed the question since Warren was also at the table.

Emily responded in kind, "All the food that humans eat is grown for consumption by farmers or ranchers that specialized in growing particular products. Some grow beef, some pork, some chicken, and then some grow the vegetables. However, the crispy meat is pork."

An image of a mammal came into her mind. It was really, really ugly. And it constantly stuck its round blunt nose in the dirt. Not only that, it ran to the first mud hole it could find and immersed itself as much as possible. It made an awful grunting noise and if it was not grunting it made a whining sound all the time, and the most astounding thing of all, Humans considered them intelligent! Persha, thinking too herself, telepathically intoned, "I do not think I am going to do very well here. We consider humans stupid and they think pigs are intelligent. What a paradox!" Persha saw Emily smiling at her; she forgot that Emily was a very skilled telepath and could also read minds. She was embarrassed that her manners were wanting.

Emily silently said, "There is no doubt that earth and its inhabitants will hold many incomprehensible paradoxes that seem strange to you. I want to be your friend and confident and help you thru the transition period. I know that I was so grateful that Hanlee and Jawane accepted me and became my friends and made me feel welcome on the ship, it was not easy for me. They both taught me so many things. I had no one except the other abductees to converse with for several months until Blain invited me into their home. I understand now how much of an honor and sacrifice it was to invite me into your personal living area." Emily flashed a smile at Blain, Jawane and Hanlee.

Billy and Skip watched Emily and Persha. They knew she was conversing because they sat silently staring at one another then Emily started smiling. Warren observed Emily's behavior but was perplexed why she acted the way she did and it seemed too appear strange to him also. He assumed that her strange behavior was due to her long incarceration by the Gypsies.

Emily said to Warren, "Warren, can you believe that we are going to be married next month? I did not think it was ever going to get here!

Warrens face twisted in irritation. The shock of losing Emily so unexpectedly had irrevocably changed his personality leaving a leery edge and not so sure of promises to come. He had never been jealous before and had never given a thought to loosing Emily to another man. Now for some reason he was not able to reconcile Blain in her life. He knew that Emily loved him. Yet, she seemed to have some sort of clandestine relationship with Blain that he could not put his finger on. He could feel wisp of thoughts that were just lurking beyond his consciousness and he could not quiet bring them to light. That was disturbing to him.

Warren said, "I read over the guest list. I do not know any of these people. Where and when did you meet them? It seems like they are so young that it does not seem likely you had any classes with them. I can understand you inviting the two detectives that found you. But who is this Admiral Cleary. How on earth did you meet someone in the navy? And what kind of name is Breveka? Is she Gypsy or something"?

At the mention of Admiral Cleary's name Skip and Billy's ears perked up and they paid rapt attention to the conversation between Warren and Emily. They did not know that there was going to be ten young people their age or younger at the wedding. And, the presence of Admiral Cleary at the wedding was a bombshell. But then again why not, aliens were attending too. Skip punched Billy's arm playfully and said, "Wow, this wedding is going to be out of this world!"

The Andrians did not smile at his joke. Neither did Emily. Warren was being Warren and was busy shoveling down Emily's pancakes.

Skip bowed his head and contritely and quietly said. "I am sorry".

The apology seemed to have been accepted as Emily said, "That is alright, be more careful from here on out. Help clean up the table". Both boys jumped to their feet and began removing the dirty plates, then started washing the dishes. They did not quit until all the dishes were done and everything was put away.

CHAPTER 7
EMILY'S COUNSEL

After breakfast, Blain and the children walked to the lake so Blain could instruct the children and introduce them to their first ever lake. Blain was not pleased with Skip's comment in regard to the wedding. He had asked Emily to rethink her position of allowing the two young men to become aware of their presence. There was simply too much at stake to cause an unnecessary panic. He said they could remove all memories of them and he believed that was the most correct course of action.

Emily stood by her judgment and advised she would counsel the boys on the severity of the issues, and, if there should be one more slip, she would allow their memories to be erased. She also advised Blain that they had mastered, by themselves, two theorems of spherical mathematics. That surprised Blain, until he remembered who their Father was. He told Emily he would give them one more chance.

Warren had gone to work at the Forest Service Facility leaving Emily and the boys alone. Emily called the boys and told them to meet her on the lower porch, out of the direct sunlight. They could still view the lake and watch the Andrians, even though that was not the intent. Emily had set out some cookies and milk for them and the Andrians when they returned.

ASSIMILATION

Emily was setting close to the boys in her chair, knees almost touching. She wanted to make sure that she had their complete attention and for them to know that this was not just another friendly chat. Neither of the boys touched the cookies and milk. They sensed that this was indeed a very serious issue.

Emily began by saying, "The comment you made at dinner may seem trivial. However trivial things have a way of becoming unmanageable problems. I am going to share a little with you and give you a choice. If you want to know more I will tell you, if you don't, then I can have your memories erased about any knowledge of the Andrians. Blain wants to erase your memories now and not take a chance on you exposing them, and or, our mission. Yes, "our" mission, all of Earths forces. For your information, Blain is the Commander of all Andrian military forces in our galaxy. Even though he appears to be easy going, he is a very serious man." Emily was very serious.

"People have died. A lot of people, my parents included; not only my parents, but the parents of the ten young people whom you are going to meet. They were sought out and imprisoned and their parents murdered by traitors to the Andrian cause, and to our future. You will meet them soon. We owe it to them that their sacrifices not go unrewarded. Not only that, but more lives are at stake. I thought, and told you that my parents died in a car accident. It is true that it was a car crash but it was not an accident. The crash was orchestrated by an Andrian traitor by the name of Zelegark. They wanted to kill my parents and imprison me but for some reason were unable to locate me; they were successful in murdering my parents."

Emily looked them both in the eye. "Are you sure you want me to go on because if you say one single thing, your minds...will be wiped. There are no second chances. What I have to say is not pretty and it will alter the way you live and think from this time forth, for the rest of your lives. It is the kind of knowledge that all Andrians live with their entire lives."

Both boys looked at one another and said in unison, "We will not let you down and we will not say word." It was as if they read one another's mind.

Emily smiled and said "Ok. Now here is the crux of the problem. Many people are furiously working on a two prong agenda both of which must be solved. One is the saving of the planet from becoming uninhabitable by our actions. We have about eight hundred years before earth looks like mars, about three hundred years before mankind can no longer live on the planet. Working together with strong government and forward thinking individuals this problem can be solved. That is why I encouraged Warren to go to work for the Forrest Service. It is necessary work that needs brilliant minds and he simply would not fit into a military type environment at this time.

The second issue is just as terrifying and we do not have a time line but we do know the consequences should certain events come to pass; those events would be the destruction of all life on the planet. This destruction will

ASSIMILATION

be brought about by an alien life form that we believe is from a different dimension and when it attacks, it does not leave any specie alive."

Both Skip and Billy felt chills go down their spines. This was much, much more than they had anticipated. It was the kind of knowledge that moved them from being an everyday high school student and a freshman in college, to young men engaged in the serious struggle of survival; No wonder the Andrians did not smile much.

"When Blain and I were exploring Saturn's moon Iapetus, we discovered one of the dead aliens locked in vacuum in a chamber in one of the moon's artifacts. It was frozen solid. Their scientist is trying to determine its age and how it got there. It is the same type of being that the Andrians are fighting several galaxies away. So far this alien entity has destroyed all life in three solar systems, they leave nothing alive. The number of lives lost is innumerable. They also destroyed every Andrian on their newly developed intergalactic carriers. There were six carriers. There are nine thousand Andrians on each carrier. That is fifty four thousand lives. They are the same beings that killed Persha's family unit. They were on one of the intergalactic carriers that were engaging the enemy. The enemy does not leave survivors. That is primarily why Blain brought Persha to be with us. It is to help her heal.

Skip and Billy sat back in their chairs mouths open. "No way", said Skip. "Impossible", said Billy. "Emily we love you like we love our mother and we believe anything you say because we trust you. But how could this be true?"

"It is true. Could you not see the clouded sadness in Persha's eyes? I can relate with that kind of pain because my parents were murdered also." Both Skip and Billy had noticed an underlying sadness in Persha but had no clue as to what it was. Nor did they know Emily's parents were murdered.

Emily looked them both in the eye. "Ignorance is bliss. Do you want your minds wiped of this knowledge?"

Skip said, "I guess not. It is just so much to take in. Like we just met our new friends yesterday and today we find out that the earth might end."

Billy said, "Yea, it is a lot to take in. But I know you can count on me Emily!"

"Me too." said Skip.

Both boys were clearly dejected after learning the nature of the deaths of both Emily's and Persha's parents.

"Can they really wipe my mind where I would not remember them or anything else they choose?", Asked Skip.

"Yes, they can, and much more," Said Emily. "We are fortunate that the leaders among them have been more than considerate of us. Now, one last time; are you in or, or are you out? Speak now or forever hold your peace," Said Emily.

She was not smiling. In fact there came hardness into her face that they had never seen before. It was a part of her that was new due to her experiences since she was gone. The new knowledge she had gained placed a heavy burden on her spirit. Her eyes were piercing. She meant

ASSIMILATION

what she said. They knew in their hearts and minds that should they make an error in judgment by mistake or design, she, not Blain, would have their memories wiped.

Skip said, "Okay Emily. I am sorry I did not take you serious as I should have the first time. I am In.

Emily looked at Billy. His stare was direct, not wavering. "I am in too, Emily."

Emily held their gazes and searched their mind for any sense of double mindedness and found none.

"Fine! Now lets' eat some cookies!

CHAPTER 8
WEDDING PREPARATION

Skip and Billy looked at Blain when he approached the stairs. Both boys got up and met him at the top of the stairs. With their heads down, they contritely apologized to Blain and gave their word that they would not ever make a similar mistake again.

Blain searched their minds and found nothing contrary to their verbalization. "That is okay boys, if you are to play a primary role in helping all of us achieve our objectives, it is important that you be disciplined in your words and actions. I am aware that Human and Andrians approach problems in a different way because our behavior is predicated on generations of star faring requirements. You will be required to learn new ways of thinking and resolving issues. However, without your independence in thinking and problem solving, we, in all probability, will not be able to defend ourselves, and thus you, from our new enemy. Therefore we must all work together for the greater good. Your responsibilities are great. You're Father and Mother, at this very time is now traveling the galaxy learning and contributing in any way they can."

Skip and Billy then turned to Persha, and Skip, to Persha's surprise, took her in his arm and held her close saying, "I am sorry that your parents were murdered by our common enemy. I promise to help you in any way I can."

After skip had released his hug from Persha, Billy then went up and held her close in a hug and said, "Me too, Persha. I promise to be one of your very best friends."

Persha was caught off guard, again. She was not used to being hugged and close physical contact was, "alien" to her. However, for some inexplicable reason, it did seem comforting. Mumbling, "Thank you", Persha went into the house and up to her room. Jawane and Hanlee followed Persha to their room.

The week was busy after the construction crew completed building a pavilion with a high ceiling cover about fifty yards east of the house. There were no walls and the view to the lake was unobstructed. Also included in the construction were large restroom and shower facilities and a large brick cooking pit.

Unbeknownst to everyone except Emily and Blain, the Andrians had also constructed a large underground hanger facility in the meadow area inside the mountain behind the house. A tunnel ran from the house to the facility, and, to a six car garage that was also constructed at the same time as the pavilion. Emily's isolated lake house was to be used as a transfer point for new arrivals. The intelligence service had built a new convenience service station near the access road to Emily's cabin thus enable them to monitor traffic in and out of the area. It too had a large underground facility constructed by the Andrians.

Warren had put several briskets, chickens and sausage lengths on the new smoker grill around six P.M.,

Friday evening. The cooking was accomplished by military cooks posing as restaurant workers. There was to be a veritable feast to accommodate at least fifty guests. The Andrian young people watched the proceedings with great interest as they had never experienced a bar-b-que before.

Skip and Billy were sitting on the upstairs porch when they saw a group of at least twenty people walking from the direction of the meadow. They were all dressed in slacks and nice shirts but no ties.

"Emily! Your guests are here!" cried Billy.

Skip and Billy ran to Persha's room to tell her that the young people were here. Her room was empty. Going downstairs, they found the young Andrians helping Emily in the kitchen. Warren and Blain was attending the outside grill.

"Emily! There are about twenty people coming from the meadow," exclaimed Billy!

They all went outside and waited for the party to arrive at the back wrap around porch. The ten young people, Robert Aaron, Sharla, Jawane's mother, Breveka, alien species analyst, and Chandra, Hanlee's mother, greeted Emily in Andrian fashion, except this time, they greeted her as the lesser to the greater, she being the greater. Emily bowed her head in acknowledgement.

The three young Andrian children staying with Emily were awed that Breveka, Sharla and Chandra would greet Emily in such a fashion. It seemed their entire existence was being turned upside down. First they had to come to the planet earth then they were told that Emily was superior to all of them, maybe even Blain, then the way Emily was greeted as her being the greater, confirmed the telling!

Skip looked at the other seven men and woman in the group. They looked...hard. Their gaze was steady and piercing and they walked with assurance. They were also dressed different. Each of them wore a light weight jacket and up close one could see some sort of weapon hanging from their shoulders. There was a woman in front of the group who was small in stature. Her dark hair was cut short in a bob. And, she was very beautiful. The other six members walked beside and behind the ten young people. The woman in front noticed Skip's scrutiny and read his mind thus, she gave him a smile. Skip smiled back, face reddening, then looked down; "A normal male adolescent behavioral characteristic, and some adults too," thought Sasha, remembering Agent Jessop's mannerisms.

The beautiful woman walked up to Skip and placing an arm around his waist and extending her hand for a hand shake said, "Hi Skip. I have heard so many good things about you. It is really nice to finally meet you. My name is Sasha Palangin. My friends and I are with the Space Intelligence Commandoes and were here escorting our ten fine young people, although they have proven themselves more than worthy of taking care of themselves. And of course, we are excited about Emily's and Warren's wedding."

Skip's heart beat faster as he felt the touch of the beautiful woman's arm around his waist, not to mention her breast snugged up against his chest. Skip thought, "Things are moving too fast in my world!" Then he said, "Why on earth would you hear about me?"

Sasha laughed. "Are you kidding? You're the son of one of Earth's most imminent and renowned scientist."

Skip was amazed. He knew his father was really smart but he did not know he was so widely known.

Emily came bounding down the stairs and ran to the young people embracing them all one at a time. Telepathically they extended greetings and salutations.

Emily then approached Sasha and gave her a long hug. Sasha too could communicate telepathically and they exchanged information of recent developments. Emily was surprised and somewhat jealous that Sasha was able to explore Saturn's moon Iapetus, before she had the opportunity.

Sasha said, "Do not worry Emily; you will get the chance soon. I cannot tell you how exciting it was. We did not find any more of the aliens you and Blain discovered. There were several frozen humanoid bodies in different areas of the artifact. It appears to have been some kind of space ship with interstellar traveling capabilities. There were some mechanical engines that used some kind of fuel to move it through space. The reason they think it was interstellar was because of the numerous star maps they found in a working computer. It is so amazing that anything could possibly be working."

"The Andrians believe a lot of the systems were preserved because of the deep cold of space and the outer sterilizing effect of the sun's radiations and Saturn's enormous magnetic field. They both had a cleansing effect on the artifact. They estimated that the artifact is a least a million years old. None of the star maps were close to any type of inter-galactic information that the Andrians had accumulated! The Andrian scientist believe that the artifact may possibly be from a different dimension, primarily because of the alien you found on board and your transference to what you believed to be a different dimension when you were immersed with the new bio mechanical entity on the saucer and saw the thousands of aliens exiting their dimension thru a black hole. Evidently they are in the process of coming to ours."

Skips heart momentarily stopped as he listened to Sasha. He had no idea how serious their situation was. Emily had quickly glossed over the alien part of her telling of her experiences. Even though there had been the destruction of all life in three different solar systems, they were galaxies away!

Sasha looked at Skip in surprise as she easily read his terror. Looking at Emily she said, "I am so sorry Emily, I did not know he was a telepath".

Emily took Skip by the shoulders and looked him in the eyes. He was in shock, his eyes were glazed over. Emily said, "Be at peace Skip".

The present returned to his eyes as the glaze dispersed. "Yes Emily, peace is good. I think I will go lay down." With that, Skip turned around and went into the house up to his room and lay down in his bed. He was soon sinking into a deep, peaceful sleep.

CHAPTER 9
TWILIGHT SLEEP

Persha, being near, heard all the things that Sasha had told Emily. She could understand why Skip would react the way he did. It was pretty much the same for her when she learned of her family unit's death. Persha followed Skip up to his room.

After Skip had lain down on the bed and was in a deep sleep, Persha sat down beside him and began to rub his temples and using her mind she soothed his fears away all the more. She did not understand why, but she found herself being attracted to him and without thinking, she leaned over and gently kissed him on the lips. A light electric shock coursed thru their lips. It was a feeling like she had never had before as she had never kissed anyone, much less someone of the opposite sex. Her breath became short as she again kissed his lips more fully and forceful this time.

Skip was already in twilight sleep and believed he was having another one of his dreams of Persha like he had every time he slept, but this time it was so real! He did not know that while he slept Persha would enter his mind and search out his dreams. She was mystified by his attraction toward her. Entering ones private thoughts was considered taboo and was something they were never supposed to do, but, after all, she was supposed to

ASSIMILATION

learn about Humans.

    Skip automatically responded to Persha's ardent kiss and placed his arms around her and held her close. Slowly and gently he placed his tongue between her lips and moved them apart. At first she resisted then she opened her lips slightly. The feel of his gently probing tongue excited her beyond all expectations. Skip moaned lightly as he pulled her close and pressed her breast gently to his chest. He rubbed her back, her buttocks and then moved his hand up between her legs. Then it was Persha's time to moan which she did.

    It was all she could do to pull away. She was breathing hard. She ached in places she never ached before. Her nipples stood erect against her blouse slightly chaffing them making them all the more harder. She did not understand any of her feelings. Persha carefully extracted herself from Skip's embrace as he mumbled unintelligible words. Moving away from the bed and backing quietly out of the room, Persha carefully closed the door behind her. She leaned against the door in an effort to regain her composure and think about what had happened. Embracing herself with her arms, Persha went down the stairs and out on the porch. Surely, she could regain her composure out in the fresh air.

    Going out on the porch, Persha was astounded to see everyone running every which way shouting, "Duh! Duh! Duh!" They had their hands by their heads with one finger up in the parody of horns! Jawane and Hanlee were in the lead. They were shouting. They must have gone mad! Emily was right behind them laughing and shouting the same thing!

Emily was shouting, "We are Humans from Earth! Take us to your leader! Duh! Duh! Duh!" Emily then grabbed Jawane and Hanlee by the waist and began tickling them. Laughing, they all fell squirming to the ground getting on top of Emily and tickling her!

Persha felt for sure that she was going out of her mind! First her impulsive behavior in kissing Skip, resulting in his arduous advances and now everyone incomprehensively shouting and going in circles. Surely she was sick with some kind of Human ailment!

Emily, lying on the ground with Jawane and Hanlee, could sense Persha's confusion and emotion. She disentangled herself and got up and walked up to porch stairs to where Persha was standing. Placing her arms around Persha and pulling her close she said, "It is going to be alright Persha. On our world you would say you feel like you fell down a rabbit hole. It is exactly how I felt when I entered your world. Jawane and Hanlee helped me cope. If it was not for them I would have had a much harder time."

Everyone was still running around in a frenzy saying "Duh", as Persha buried her head on Emily shoulder and unsolicited tears ran down her cheeks. Tears were new to her too. She was soon heaving in great sobs as her shoulders shook uncontrollably. She did not know why. It seemed like she had lost all control over her mental faculties. The young people seeing and feeling her distress immediately ceased their play and gathered around Persha and Emily and gave her comfort. She did not know it but in addition to her feelings for Skip, she was grieving for her lost family.

Andrians had extraordinary control over their emotions and the releasing of ones anguished feeling by crying was basically unknown to them. Persha's release of emotion was precipitated by the exposure to everyday Human experiences which were slowly weaving its way into her Andrian psychic. Her newly awakened sexual feelings for Skip which were exacerbated by Skip's own feelings for Persha diminished her carefully conditioned response for emotional balance.

After Persha had cried herself out she was thoroughly embarrassed. Emily placed her arm around her waist and walked her up to her room comforting her and said, "What you have just experienced is a normal human response to a traumatic event. In this case it is the death of your parental unit. You were doing fine until you experienced your sexual attraction to Skip. I think that opened the door to every day Human emotion. You will be fine. Now, lie down and go to sleep. Be at peace Persha."

Persha was too exhausted to understand everything Emily was saying. She lay down on her bed and immediately fell into a healing and deep, dreamless sleep.

Emily quietly observed Persha as she fell asleep in the bed. She was somewhat apprehensive for her because she well knew the battle that she was going to go thru with her newfound sexuality and attraction to Skip. She would have to instruct Skip to be careful with her and not take advantage of Persha's new found attraction for him. She would also warn him of other wolfs that no doubt she would soon meet. If they were destined to be together then it must be on equal terms.

CHAPTER 10
RELAXED

Skip woke up slowly, feeling refreshed but groggy. Lying in his bunk he tried to remember what had happened the day before and what time he had gone to bed. After his head cleared he remembered what he had learned from Sasha Palangin, the day before in reference to the alien menace. He had gone into shock. Emily had brought him to his room and told him to be at peace. Then,…nothing; until now.

Looking at the clock he observed that it was four A.M. After going to the restroom and showering, Skip went downstairs to the kitchen and got a cold bottle of water from the refrigerator. Walking out on the porch Skip felt the cooling breeze on his face and it helped clear his head. The moon was once again over the lake giving the water a silvery glow. There was a crowd at the cooking pit with loud talking and laughter. Everyone seems to be having a good time.

Skip decided to return to his room instead of going to the cooking pit. Upon reaching the top of the stairs on the way to his room, Skip stopped by Persha's room and opened the door to look in on her. He thought he heard her mumble his name but he could not be sure. Stepping farther into the room he could see her face which was bathed with moonlight streaming in the window at her head. Her forehead was damp with perspiration. She was moving her head back and forth rapidly saying, "No! No! No!" He then heard her say, "Help me Skip, Pleeeezzze!"

Skip went and sat down on side of the bunk bed placing his left hand on her waist and leaned over her to her ear saying, "I am right here Persha! Everything is going to be okay. You are safe with me."

Persha's arms went up around his neck and back, pulling him close and hugging him tightly.

He heard Persha again catch her breath with a sob. He laid his head on her shoulder and could smell a light tinged sweet odor of the perfume that Emily had given her. Skip placed his arms around her and murmured in her ear, "You are safe, you are safe. I will never allow any harm come to you. I will never leave you. I love you Persha. I have never loved anyone the way I love you!" Skip would never have had the courage to tell Persha that he loved her if she was awake.

Persha turned over with her back too him taking his arms with her. Skip lay down behind her and she snuggled her body next to his. Her moaning had stopped and her breathing had become regular. Skip carefully cradled her head in the crook of his arm and placed his other arm around her waist while pulling her yet closer still. Soon they both were fast asleep in deep, contented slumber.

Hanlee and Jawane had had a full schedule of activities the previous evening visiting with their mother's, Chandra and Sharla, and were very tired when they went to bed. Therefore, sleeping in till ten in the morning they both lay in their respective bunks and conversed about

ASSIMILATION

the recent events. The wedding was to be later that evening and they were to both have a part in it. Hanlee was to be the flower girl, whatever that was. Jawane was to be the ring bearer, again, whatever that was.

Jawane, on the top bunk, rolled over preparing to get up. He saw Skip and Persha in the same bed. He could not believe his eyes! He rubbed his eyes to clear his vision. They were still there! He had never seen two people in the same bed. One's bed was the most sacred of all personal space on an intergalactic carrier. He waved frantically to Hanlee to get her attention then he pointed them out to her. She too had to rub her eyes in disbelief. They very quickly and quietly dressed and left the room closing the door silently behind them.

Over the generations, Andrian sexuality had diminished to a "necessity only" contact. One had physical sex only when procreation was absolutely necessary and at which time, physical relationships were required. Procreation was deemed a duty. Before a child was conceived, the womb was prepared with the proper nutrients to insure conception. One's sexual partner for procreation was chosen by the geneticist assigned to the intergalactic carrier. Most chose to bypass the physical contact altogether and just donate sperm and ovaries to the geneticist. The geneticist was by far one of the persons on the ship with the most status. Only those on the "Council of Yield" had more influence. After the fetus was in the womb for sixteen weeks, should one choose to carry a baby, it was removed to an artificial womb and cared for until birthing time. Should one want the "feel good" for sex, then one picked a partner and shared a neural link. In Blain's case, he being the commander of the intergalactic fleet could have as many consorts as he desired. He had had many but when he fathered Hanlee and Jawayne, he chose to remain with Sharla and Chandra, the mothers of the children.

About an hour later, Emily looked in on Persha to insure she was okay. Seeing Persha and Skip sleeping together entwined in each other's arms and legs was not what she expected to see. She was not surprised to see them together as she was well aware of their attraction to one another; she was surprised that it had happened so quickly. She would have to talk to Skip and council him on the vulnerability of Persha in regard to her socialization on the earth. She would also warn him of the necessity of protecting her from wolves which she would surly come into contact with. She too quietly closed the door as she left the room.

CHAPTER 11
SUPRISE AWAKENING

Persha was sound asleep. Her rest was disturbed by a quiet moaning. She slowly regained consciousness and the moaning became more audible and pronounced. When she became more cognizant she realized that the moaning came from her own lips and throat. Then she became aware of a sensuous pulling on her breast nipple. It felt like nothing she had ever experienced before. Moving her arms she then realized they were wrapped around a naked body. She was cradling a head in her arms and pressing the head to her breast. Looking down she was shocked when she saw Skip suckling and kissing her breast lightly using his tongue and lips. She did not have her blouse or bra on. He did not have a shirt on. They both had their recreational shorts on. Her leg was between his leg and she could feel his erection thru the thin cloth.

Like she was earlier, Skip appeared to be asleep and the suckling was purely an instinctive reflex action. She searched his mind and found only a profound feeling of helplessness and human emotion called "love". What was he doing in her bed anyway? She searched the recesses of her mind and was able to recall the bad dream she had the night before. It was of the alien menace that threatened all their existence. She remembered calling out to Skip to save her. He must have been standing there and heard her plea and he had come to her bed and comforted her. She then remembered him telling her that he "loved" her as he "loved" no other. It was that mysterious human emotion that afflicted humans on the earth; and, evidently now her.

She was still feeling the effects of the constant sensuous suckling and drew her breath in as a sharp nerve released a flood of feeling from between her legs. Persha pressed Skip closer and closed her eyes enjoying the feeling. She did not know what it was but she did not want it to stop.

After a minute the ecstatic feeling diminished leaving a comfortable feeling of wellbeing and completeness. She also felt dampness between her legs. She queried her mind as to what she was feeling and learned that it was an orgasm. She definitely wanted more of those.

Skip stirred in her arms releasing her nipple after one longer lasting suckle. He slowly became more aware of his surroundings and he smelled Persha's unique body perfume. Opening his eyes he saw her breast just inches away from his face. Looking up he found himself looking into Persha's light blue eyes. She had a slight smile on her full lips. Again her cheeks reddened with embarrassment but instead of looking away, she bent her head forward and softly kissed Skip on the lips.

Persha said, "I love you too Skip, although I do not think I understand what love is. I know that I want to be with you and I have never felt such an attraction. I think my parental unit loved one another too. They never

ASSIMILATION

separated to take other consorts and I was always with them until the last deployment where they were killed. There are a few Andrians that stay together like that but due to genome requirements for our isolated star faring specie, those types of commitments are not encouraged by the social mores of our society. The female is still required to contribute her genome to the society by having babies by different male donors. I have several siblings on the two other Intergalactic Carriers."

That was the longest speech that Skip had ever heard Persha give.

"Persha, I do not want to take advantage of you. From now on we will have to be very careful. I hope that you do not ever want to be with anyone else. You have so much to learn about Humans and our culture. By the time you understand us you might just want to get on your ship and take off, and never come back! Not only that, but your Uncle Blain will be really angry with me. Do you think he will have my mind wiped? Can you really make it so that I would not know you or know that I love you?"

Persha laughed throwing her head back and hugging Skip close to her breast saying, "No, you silly Human! Blain will not have your mind wiped. And yes, we could make you happy going around and saying "Duh"; after all, you are almost there now!"

"Our scientist and geneticist have learned that with the combining of Human and Andrian DNA, the resultant offspring will be more intelligent than either of our species individually, and that resultant offspring may well be, perhaps, a new species all together. It may take that kind of species to defeat the new alien menace."

With a smile Persha sat up on the bed and examined her breast, this time with scrutiny that she never used before. They were not overly large but from Skip's mind she learned they were nicely shaped and very desirable. She hoped they would remain that way.

"Persha, I really am sorry that I took advantage of you last night. I honestly do not remember how or when we took our tops off."

"How did you take advantage of me, Skip? I did not do anything I did not want to do? The major difference between Human and Andrian sexuality is that ours is more cerebral and yours is more physical. As of yet, no Andrian male have ever found me interesting enough to really take a second look or to consider me for a neural link to share ambrosia with. I really do not know why. I have been available for such sharing for three years. I imagine a mate would soon have been selected for me to have offspring to further the genetic diversity of our specie. However, I am glad I have not been joined with another cerebrally. I think, it being my first experience, it would be much more meaningful to share with someone who has also not had such an experience; even though the experience with Andrians is supposed to be pleasurable, and it truly is, it does not create a bond to one another like a similar experience between Humans upon the earth. But, I believe my parental peers truly loved one another similar to the way Humans do."

"You have told me that you have never even kissed

ASSIMILATION

another female. I am glad you have not done so because that is something I wanted to share with you. You know when we first met, you said, "She is one hot space girl." Is that good? Do you still think so?"

Skip was taken aback by Persha's frank and open statements. He was well aware that he had little to no experience with the opposite sex. Thinking to himself, "How did she know that I have never even kissed another girl? I do not recall ever having told her that".

Persha, reading his thoughts laughed. "Skip, by Andrian standards and I guess by Human standards, I have been a very naughty girl! I very carefully entered your mind while you were sleeping so I could read your thoughts and understand you better. You were always thinking and dreaming of me. I was so awed that you would find me desirable and was fascinated with the things you wanted to share with me. I still am. But I promise you I will never do that again. I do have so much to learn."

Skip was embarrassed at the thought of Persha being able to read his private thoughts when he was asleep. But since she was honest with him he replied, "Thank you for telling me. You know that I can read minds a little now. You will need to teach me what I should and should not do. Ever since I first saw you I have never been able to think of anything else but you. You are so beautiful!"

Persha did not know why but for some reason she was really pleased with Skip's comment. "Emily is going to get married today, or whatever that Earth custom is. I want to learn more. Let us go outside and see what is going on. Something smells so good!"

As skip was preparing to return to his room and shower, Persha said, "Skip, why do you not shower here with me? We can save a lot of water if we shower together?" And, that was Persha's true intent.

Skip looked at Persha with astonished eyes. "Persha, if I got in the shower with you I would never be able to keep my hands off of you and we would never make it out of the shower!"

Persha looked at Skip, this time she being surprised. They always had communal showers on the intergalactic cruisers. It was the most efficient way to conserve water. Showers certainly had nothing to do with attraction and sex.

"I will go to my room and get ready and then I will come back for you. I am starving!" Skip grabbed Persha in his arms holding her close and gave her a long sensuous kiss then turned and literally ran out of the room.

Persha was left standing in the middle of the room breathing hard and wanting to chase after him. She turned instead and after quickly disrobing stepped into the shower and for the first time, took a long hot leisure shower. It was a new experience. She pushed away the guilt and life time indoctrination of conservation as the warm water washed over her face, hair and body. After allowing the water to run over her for ten minutes she turned the water off knowing that she had used more water during this one shower than she used on the Intergalactic Carrier in one month of daily showers. What an extravagant use of precious resources!

ASSIMILATION

Persha got out of the shower feeling languid and rested in body and soul. She looked in the drawer and picked out panties, bra, jeans and a red plaid shirt. They had so many colors. Her onboard clothes were nice but they were all basically four color schemes for the entire crew.

For the first time in her adult life, she questioned, "Why?" "Why do we only use four colors? What purpose does it serve? Why do we not love one another the way Humans love? Why am I so attracted to Skip? Why do I want him to touch me all the time?"

Persha sat down confused as the myriad of questions assailed her orderly mind. She realized that she needed Emily more than ever. "How can I ever fit in to this strange, strange, world?" She thought.

Skip had seen Persha sit on the bed with a pensive look on her face. She was staring off across the room not seeing anything. Walking over to her, he was surprised he could read her thoughts of confusion and consternation. Sitting down beside her he put his arm around her and pulled her close. "It is going to be okay Persha. I will always be with you. At least as long as you want me to. Emily will help too."

CHAPTER 12
FAMILY REUNION

Emily observed Skip and Persha exit the house and walk down the stairs and proceed to the area of the cooking pits. Persha's arm was casually hooked thru the crook of Skips arm and her other arm was crossed across her breast and her hand clasped the bicep of his arm and she was laughing at something that was said. Their demeanor appeared to be one of ease and satisfaction. Emily carefully queried Persha's mind and found happiness and love. The earlier shadow of misery and pain was no longer prevalent. She was pleased with their apparent attraction to one another. They were both young and inexperienced and they would be good for one another.

Warren looked at Skip and Persha as they stopped in front of him at the cooking pits. Skip said, "Hello big brother, got anything we can eat, were starving?"

Warren was mystified how Skip could have fallen so helplessly in love with the young woman he believed to be Emily's cousin. It happened so fast;. but then again, why not? That was exactly the way he and Emily had fallen in love with one another.

Every time Warren looked at Persha, she had a slight smile on her lips and he could feel like she was saying something to him but it was just out of reach and he could not figure it out. It was like she had a secret or something

ASSIMILATION

and he was the only one not included. Thinking to himself, Warren was pleased Skip had found such a nice young lady, they were so hard to find these days. "I just wish I knew why she smiled at me all the time! You would think I had spinach or something between my teeth!"

He heard Persha give a short giggle. She had an image of green spinach between Warren's teeth and the unexpected image had caused her to laugh. She reached over and placing her hand on his arm said, "Warren I really like you."

Warren was taken aback by the young woman's comment and touch. She had been before this moment, very quiet and reserved and she certainly had never touched him.

Warren removed a brisket from the smoker grill and cut several slices for their plates saying, "Do not eat too much. Dinner will be served in a couple of hours."

Skip took the plates and put some potato salad, coleslaw and a pickle on each plate and placed them on the table saying, "Eat up!"

Persha looked at the plate of food. There was so much!

Persha said, "If this is not too much to eat now then how in the stars am I supposed to eat later!"

Skip laughed and as he started forking the beef into his mouth and said, "Do not worry! You will be able to have seconds later."

Warren watched the willow thin girl examine the meat, potato salad and coleslaw like it was some kind of lab specimen. She first took a small amount of meat and sniffed it. She then hesitantly touched her tongue to the meat and then took a small bite. Closing her eyes she slowly chewed the meat like it was the first time she ever had anything like it. She was really a strange girl. She ate all her meals like that.

Warren said, "Persha, eat up girl! You act like you never had bar-b-que before!"

Persha opened her eyes startled that she was being so closely observed as she indeed tasted her first piece of bar-b-que meat. It was heavenly! Meat juices dripped down her chin as she sank her teeth greedily into the sweet meat. She had never tasted anything like it!

Emily sat down next to Persha and wiped Persha's chin with a napkin saying, "Warren, your cooking is absolutely heavenly! Actually a lot of us here have never had the opportunity to taste your fine culinary skills!"

Persha looked at Emily and telepathically said, "Thank you! I have never tasted anything so good in my life! It seems like the food just gets better and better!"

Emily laughed. "I am sure all your earthly food experiences will be new and exciting. I just hope the rest of your experiences are just as pleasing." Indeed, Persha had a healthy glowing countenance that seemed to emanate from within. Placing her arm around Persha's shoulder she gave her a sisterly hug.

Billy, Hanlee, and Jawane joined the group at the table after getting a plate of food. They had just come from the lake and Billy had taught them the joy of skipping flat stones across the water. Jawane and Hanlee were totally immersed in eating and tasting the ribs.

Admiral Avery Cleary accompanied Chandra, Sharla,

ASSIMILATION

Robert Aaron, now a lieutenant, and Earl and Karen Abbott down the path from the meadow to the back of the house. This was the first time Chandra had been on a planet anywhere in the universe and she was very apprehensive. She clung to Karen's arm and Karen kept up a descriptive chatter of all the things they were seeing and experiencing.

Upon entering the house thru the back door Karen said, "Admiral, you all will have to excuse Chandra, Earl and I because we are all going to go take a long hot shower. You can make yourselves comfortable in the kitchen, I am sure there is a fresh pot of coffee on the stove."

Admiral Cleary smiled and showed Robert Aaron and Sharla to the kitchen. Karen followed Earl upstairs pulling a reluctant Chandra along behind her. Once in the bathroom they stripped naked and again Karen pulled Sharla into the large accommodating shower.

Earl adjusted the two shower heads which inundated them with water. The eight months they had spent on the intergalactic carrier had totally desensitized them to nudity in front of others. The Andrians never gave the Humans a second look other than a cursory glance of curiosity. It appeared only Humans were obsessed with physical sexual desires. However, their superior Human minds were a different thing and in their case both male and females lusted after their minds and wanted to share ambrosia with either or both of them. Of course the open shower would not work with most other Humans.

Chandra could not believe the amount of water that was going down the drain. Both Karen and Earl held her close and let the water wash over them. Karen lathered Chandra's hair as Earl stood silently with face turned up to the water flow feeling the luxury of the water running over his head and shoulders. Earl's earlier lite joke about the woman lusting after his mind instead of his body became a truth.

Karen had immediately taken a liking to Chandra, especially after she learned she had befriended Emily. She could just imagine how difficult it was for Emily to be suddenly thrown into such a social setting. As far as Karen was concerned, Chandra was her surrogate daughter.

Chandra could not believe that the wanton waste of water was acceptable but she enjoyed the feeling of her first ever shower and hair wash so much she just closed her eyes and immersed herself in the moment. After twenty minutes under the hot showers they hastily toweled each other off. Of course Earl did not touch Chandra, leaving the duty to Karen. But, Karen did enjoy being toweled by Earl and it was all they could do to keep from being amorous in the shower with Chandra present.

Karen helped Chandra with the bra and explained its function, primarily, from a man's point of view, to keep men from getting so excited. The jeans were tight; the blouse fit like it was tailored and showed off her figure nicely and the shoes were hard soled slip-ons.

Once again, Karen, Chandra and Earl locked arms and casually went down the stairs and started toward the pavilion which was crowded with people. Admiral Cleary followed behind with Robert Aaron and Sharla.

ASSIMILATION

Warren looked up and saw his parents enter the pavilion Shouting, "Mom! Dad!" He rushed to them and embraced them. Jawane and Hanlee slowly walked up to Chandra and Sharla and greeted them in Andrian form, the lesser to the greater, then, they both gave their respective mothers a hug. The ten young people crowded around too having become part of the Abbott family and considered both Karen and Earl, Surrogate parents.

Emily observed from outside the crowd with Persha at her side. After the commotion had died down she observed Karen looking at her then she heard her telepathically say, "Hello daughter. You have taken good care of my sons. Thank you."

Emily smiled and responded, "I think you are in for more surprises."

Karen raised one eyebrow in a questioning manner then she noticed the young girl standing next to Emily. She was a lovely girl and seemed to have an inner glow. She had never seen her before. Karen detached herself from Chandra and Earl and made her way thru the young people and stood in front of Persha and Emily. Looking Persha in the eye she silently studied her.

Verbally Emily said, "Karen, this is Persha. Persha, this is Karen, Skip and Billy's mother."

Persha returned the stare and telepathically greeted her in the Andrian way and said, "It is nice to meet you... Karen. I have heard so much about you and your most famous husband Earl. Hanlee, Jawane and I have enjoyed teaching Billy and Skip, Three Dimensional Mathematics. Of course it was easy because Emily had already taught them so much. They are also very intelligent and learned much on their own. And in turn, I have enjoyed learning..., about the earth. Everything is so confusing. Skip has taught me so much. And, I do not understand my new feelings but I think I have earthly feelings for him. I think you refer to these feelings as love. I want to be with him all the time. I think it is the same kind of relationship my parental unit had before they were killed. Even though it is not the Andrian way, they stayed together and only associated with others for dissemination of ones DNA; it is every Andrains's responsibility to share of themselves to enhance the genetic pool of our species.

Emily watched Karen and Persha closely. Andrians were forthcoming in their relationships. There was no equivocation here. Persha had stated her intent to have Skip as a mate. It was just a statement of fact.

Karen studied the young woman closely. She could read her mind and she knew full well the young woman only stated the truth; only she was so young and naive in the way of humans.

Karen placed her arms around the young woman and pulled her close in an intimate embrace. "I know what you say is true. Obviously my son loves you the same way. I will love you as my daughter in the same way as I love Emily." Karen then reached out and drew Emily into the embrace.

Earl approached the group and reading their minds he looked over at Skip who was watching his dad. Earl telepathically said to Skip, "Is it true son, do you love this young Andrian woman?"

ASSIMILATION

Skip would never lie to his parents replied, "Yes Dad. I do. I do not want to be with anyone else. I have never felt the way I do before. I know am young but I think we would be good for one another, and yes, I love her." Grinning, he then said, "In the Human way, of course." Coming together, they all embraced in a family hug.

CHAPTER 13
THE WEDDING

The day had progressed quickly and everyone enjoyed the outdoor serving of an afternoon lunch. The new arrivals were enjoying the comradery of renewing old acquaintances. To everyone's surprise Agents Jessup and Reese showed up just prior to the wedding. They had married immediately after returning from the Intergalactic Cruiser to where they were instrumental in tracking down Emily.

And, the ten young people they had located and help rescue from Zelegark and his minions, loved them all the more and were accepting of them as their Father and Mother; their parents having been murdered by Zelegark. They all would have been dead if they had not been rescued by them.

Emily dressed for the wedding in her own pale blue dress and pale blue heeled sandals. The first time she and Warren secretly married she had to wear some of Karen's clothes as she had none of her own. However, she again wore Karen's wedding veil. The first time they got married was the night she returned home from the Intergalactic Carrier. It was a stormy night and her return caught everyone by surprise. She decided then and there she was going to marry Warren and not wait another day.

Earl wore his wedding suit which he had put away

ASSIMILATION

in preservation again for a second time. His shoes were highly polished and the white silk scarf was wrapped loosely around his neck.

Warren was dressed ready and waiting down by the covered portico. There were now about hundred people gathered drinking a mild alcoholic concoction of one kind or another. Fortunately the weather was mild and a slight fragrance of lilac was in the light breeze. In effect, it was a perfect evening for a wedding.

Chairs had been set up under the portico and the surrounding patio. Every effort had been made by Emily to make the portico the comfortable gathering center for guest. Breveka, the Andrian Species Analyst, was sitting in the second row. Persha was sitting next to her two seats from the isle. Warren and Skip were standing on a platform with a third man whom she was told was the religious leader and was supposed to say special words that would supposedly keep them together for life.

Persha did not understand what significance words would have in keeping Warren and Emily together for life. It was simply a matter of need and requirement. Persha had strange new feelings for Skip. No doubt her parents had the same feelings and stayed together for life because of the feelings they had for one another. Words were not needed.

Tears came to Persha's eyes as she remembered when her parents had left her. They said "Be strong Persha. We will always be with you among the stars." They must have known that there was a chance that they would not return.

Skip and Warren noticed Persha's pensive demeanor and saw the tears run down her cheeks. Warren was at a loss. He did not understand why Persha would look so pensive and be crying on his wedding day. Skip could read her mind and was sorrowed that she was brought to tears by the thoughts of the last moments with her parental unit.

Before Skip could move, Karen sat down beside her and took her in her arms and held her close. She weeps with Persha and soothes her spirit and told her she loved her as her parental unit loved her and she would always be there for her.

"Persha, you will always be part of our family. Your parents must have been wonderful, caring, and loving people because you are such a beautiful spirit of a woman. I am so glad that you love Skip. I know now that whatever happens that he will be okay with you by his side."

Persha hugged Karen and was surprised that she received the same feeling of love and comfort that she had received from her parental unit. It was different from the command, "Be at peace." This was so much more… "Mystical?" Strange word thought Persha. Persha wiped her eyes and sat up straight.

They both saw Hanlee dressed in a pale lavender dress with a wreath of flowers braided into her hair. She was carrying a shallow basket and was throwing rose petals on the ground in front of her as she walked.

Behind her was Jawane and he was carrying a blue pillow with a ring lying in the center. He was wearing a

ASSIMILATION

black suit, lavender shirt and black shoes. He smiled at Persha when he walked by.

Last in line was Emily being escorted by Earl. Emily looked so small next to him barely coming up to his armpits. He was smiling broadly as he escorted Emily to the Alter then sat down next to Karen.

Vows were repeated, love foresworn unto death. And Emily had momentarily had a heavy heart as she knew somewhat of what was on the horizon, and death was a realistic possibility.

CHAPTER 14
RESTLESS SLEEP

After the wedding party, Emily prepared for bed and kissed Warren goodnight. Laying her head back on her pillow she fell into an exhausted sleep. She did not dream of anything immediately. But soon she did start dreaming. She was again connected with the mind of the entity within the machine. She could see and sense the neurons flowing thru her body. She felt so alive! She felt she could see forever.

"Emily"... Emily! Wake up! Hurry!"

Emily could hear her name being called out in her dream. It seemed so real. Emily struggled into consciousness and became fully awake bathed in a profuse sweat. She instantly became deeply chilled due to the coolness of the room.

Looking over toward Warren's side of the bed she observed him partially uncovered. She felt his chest. It was cool to the touch and moved up and down rhythmically. She could tell that he was in one of his deep sleep modes.

Crawling carefully out of bed so as not to awaken or disturb Warren, Emily put on her house shoes and robe to cut the chill. Going into the restroom she closed the door behind her. A light was not necessary as a full moon bathed the restroom with a translucent light.

After washing her hands and her face Emily was

ASSIMILATION

looking forward to cuddling up to Warren in their warm bed. She heard her name again, this time it was not in a dream.

"Emily".

Emily then recognized the feminine voice of the entity that resided within the molecular structure of the saucer.

"Emily, please come to me. I have missed our communion. I am in the hanger. You must hurry! There is an emergency!"

The request was non-verbal, in her head. After looking around and observing no one but Warren fast asleep in their bed, replied, telepathically so as not to wake Warren, "How can we speak to one another and we not be together? If you are in the hanger as you say, then that has to be at least a mile away and deep underground?"

"Our communication is no longer predicated on distance. Distance is relative only within the same sphere of tachyon emissions. Hurry now! Time is important. We have all been busy searching for our common enemy. We now know what dimension it resides and where it is currently attacking. I will show you later. Come now so we can commune!"

Emily returned to the bed room, slipped out of her robe and nightgown and slipped on her jeans, sweatshirt and hiking boots. After putting her long blonde hair in a ponytail, she exited the room and went downstairs. Emily went directly thru the kitchen to a secret access that led down to the transportation tunnel.

Upon entering the platform she observed two armed guards armed with laser rifles. They were immediately on guard; one was Andrian, the other Human. Emily greeted them telepathically and advised them she was going to the hanger. They moved to escort Emily but she advised them to remain at their post. They obeyed without question but uneasy that Emily was going to be out and about without an escort. The "guarding" of Emily Smith was not taken lightly by the military.

Emily sat on the small levitating transport and telepathically gave the command for the vehicle to proceed to the hanger. Emily arrived at the hanger access port one minute later.

Again she was met by two guards, one Andrian and one Human. Having been informed by the house sentries of her immanent arrival they greeted Emily first and stood at attention in a military manner. Emily smiled at them and greeted them with a proper salute. The salute caused Emily to become somewhat sober. Whither she wanted to or not she was being heavily indoctrinated into military protocols; the weight of her responsibilities were beginning to infuse her psychic.

Emily entered thru the heavy steeled door elevator access. The door closed quickly behind her and the elevator literally flew down thru the solid rock elevator shaft. Emily never stopped being amazed at the technology the Andrians had developed. Exiting the elevator into the large cavern cut into virgin rock by Andrian mining technology, she spied several saucer craft resting on cushions of air. One of the saucer craft was the largest she had ever seen in the hanger. It looked like it could hold a small company of combat infantry.

ASSIMILATION

She immediately knew that the saucer was "hers". As she approached the saucer a large platform commensurate with the saucer size lowered itself from the center of the saucer. A ramp also lowered next to the saucer to provide additional access if necessary.

As Emily stepped upon the platform, six military men and woman, heavily armed in body armor, approached the craft. A young female marine, Human, stood at attention and saluted, then said brusquely, "Ms. Smith, we were advised you were coming. We are to accompany you whenever you leave the compound.

Emily smiled and returned the salute. "Hop on. However I do not know where we are going."

Without a word the six military escorts stepped upon the lift and bracketed Emily between them as the lift was raised into the saucer. And as before, three were Andrian and three were human.

After Emily and the six marines assumed their position within their respective encasings, Emily's' position being a lower seat, they rested their arms on the arm rest. The armrest then folded themselves and placed their arms across their breast. The only difference was the light fabric that enfolded around Emily's' head

Emily felt a slight electrical tingling go thru out her body. Emily's mind became immersed in the Entity as the Entity infused itself into her very soul. Emily no longer saw with human eyes. Her human vision was clipped, skewed, and an indirect jumble of light patterns as information began to form in her cerebral cortex. The vision of the entity flowed thru her being. Soon impressions began to form in her mind. They initially were a staccato of multi-colored images in swirling patterns but very quickly became quick moving shadows. As the images cleared, Emily observed the alien beings attacking other non-human life forms on planets around distant stars. They killed every living thing, being or fauna; whatever they could get close to and touch. The enemy appeared to be spraying a chemical substance on the life forms then they quickly attacked injecting poisons from sharp needle like appendages which snaked out from the sucker holes which was prevalent all over their alien body. Unlike the alien she and Blain had found on Saturn's artifact moon, Iapetus, they were not wearing any kind of spacesuit.

Emily was unaware the saucer had left the hanger. She could see, feel, and taste the flood of neurons as they coursed thru her body. They felt like great gulps of cool fresh water administered on a hot dry desert.

Emily could see a fast approaching dazzling light punctuated by a small black hole. The light quickly enveloped the saucer. She could feel the power of creation in every molecule of her being as her body seemed to expand in every direction. The black pin point of total darkness grew immensely and the saucer shuddered violently as it hurdled into the abyss.

Then just as quickly there was absolute silence. A large world covered with water held a lonely vigil in the near starless sky. As the world slowly rotated a single spate of land came into view. It was an island with a rich verdant green jungle that grew almost, but not quiet, to the ocean's edge.

ASSIMILATION

"Where are we and what are we doing here?" Emily queried the Entity.

As a reply, the wall of the craft changed from a panoramic view of the water world and island, to a close up view of the beach. There was a small group of humanoid beings on the sand all facing the water. Several of the beings lay prostate on the beach, two others were being drug away from the water's edge. All of the beings held what appeared to be some sort of lance with most all of them shooting toward the ocean. Sharp, bright, jagged flashes of light emanated from the tips of the lances which looked like lightning bolts. The direction of fire was toward the beaches edge.

Emily then observed furious churning of the water as she saw thousands of the alien beings moving forward as one toward the beach. It was obvious that the humanoid beings on the beach would soon be annihilated.

The view then switched to a male and female clothed in what appeared to be greenish copper body amour, from the waist down. They were standing shoulder to shoulder with their lances constantly flashing electrical charges into the alien enemy. It was a useless but gallant attempt of survival.

Without thinking, Emily shouted out in a commanding tone, "Land the saucer! Collect the survivors! Hurry! Marines, form a defensive line around the craft."

The six marines, already startled by the swift unfolding of unprecedented events, acknowledged Emily's command. They had all heard rumors of an alien enemy but now they were suddenly confronted with the naked, ugly, truth. They were afraid but relied on their training to carry them thru. That is just what marines do.

The annunciator in the saucer listed the chemical and oxygen content of the atmosphere. It was compatible to Humans and Andrians and did not require space suits. The saucer hovered silently behind the surviving defenders who focused their entire attention on the approaching mass of destruction and death.

The six marines and Emily exited the craft quickly taking up defensive positions on each side of the craft. Immediately they opened fire on the approaching hordes of aliens who were making an end run around the humanoid beings defensive position.

Emily ran up to the defensive position of the two beings she believed was in charge. She dropped down on one knee in front of them careful to stay below their level of defensive fire and using her laser rifle she began cutting a swath thru the ranks of the approaching hoards. The rifle was effective against the enemy aliens but no hand weapon or laser rifle could overcome their approaching mass.

After firing her weapons Emily stood and faced the two beings she believed to be in charge. They were both "Hollywood" beautiful. Their armor appeared to be some sort of scales. But strangely, they were naked from the waist up. The woman had waist length flaming red hair. And oddly enough Emily noticed a small seashell clip holding her hair away from her face. The man too had shoulder length red hair. He was the same size as Warren and was heavily muscled.

ASSIMILATION

Emily turned and faced them and tried to communicate telepathically. Getting no response, she spoke verbally. But, other than their look of utter astonishment with wide eyes and open mouths, they remained mute and still.

Emily touched the man on the shoulder and pointed toward the saucer behind them. She did not miss the flare of anger and challenging response in the green eyes of the redheaded woman. Emily quickly removed her hand and started walking toward the saucer beckoning them to follow with hand gestures.

The humanoid beings expecting nothing but complete annihilation of their species, quickly grasped at the straw of salvation proffered to them by the strange woman. They then saw the other six beings defending a floating "thing" behind them. They too had the strange light guns that cut the enemy in half.

They both screeched loudly in descending octaves and began backing away from their defensive positions firing as they did so. The rest of the humanoid beings turned as one, grabbed what children that was left and ran toward the saucer.

Backing up and firing her weapon with the original two beings she barked out, "Get them all aboard and into transport positions"! The approaching alien enemies were renewing their effort to destroy their prey.

The marines did not have to be told twice. They pushed and shoved the humanoid beings into the saucer going up the extended ramp. Emily and the two humanoid beings were the last aboard and were firing as the platform lifted into the saucer craft.

As the ramp and lift closed, the saucer began vibrating as it lifted into the air above the beach out of reach of the alien hoard. Emily and the two rescued beings clung to each other and a stanchion to keep their balance. Quickly the craft steadied and the walls became opaque to almost clear. The previously pristine white beach was now covered with a dark undulating mass of aliens jumping up and down in an angry dance at having their prize of total annihilation of the resident species of the water planet snatched from their very grasps.

Emily firmly grasps the arm of the male and female and walked them to the last two available receptacles. As Blain had done to her during her first saucer ride, she grasped both biceps of the male and gently but firmly moved him into the receptacle. Emily then did the same to the female who was again glaring at her for, no doubt, placing her hands on her male counterpart.

Emily then looked into the females eyes. They were a beautiful green. And, as before, they gleamed with an unmistakable challenge. Emily smiled at the woman again trying telepathic communication, said, "Hi! My name is Emily. I have no interest in your companion."

The woman looked surprised and then smiled. She felt impressions of the strange woman in her mind and seemed to understand what she was saying. She looked the strange light haired woman in the eyes and carefully formed the thoughts, "My name is Muskula. I am the leader of the once mighty Sea Stars. We are grateful for your rescue."

ASSIMILATION

Emily nodded an acknowledged response and then proceeded to the navigation console taking her place within her chamber located directly in front of the two leaders of the Sea Star specie. The neuron fabric folded over her face and tightly adhered to her skin. The neural link was now established and she became one with the entity. Emily received a loving stroke in her mind with an unmistakable caress of a job well done.

"Take us home, Star Light. But do not return the same way we came".

The saucer responded by lifting away from the planet which became a tiny blue ball rapidly disappearing into the dark velvet escarpment of the galaxy.

Muskula watched as her home disappeared into darkness. She did not know that her home was a round ball of water suspended in blackness. She watched as the light from their star also rapidly diminished into a faint pin prick of light. She and her mate Karlalif knew they were going to die with all their offspring but they were determined to fight to the end. And then suddenly, this strange woman in a strange object appeared out of nowhere and whisked them from the very depths of the acid bath weapons of the yet stranger destroyers. It was perplexing that in such a short time period, one strange life form brings certain death and another life form brings life. Perhaps the second life form may be offering just another way to die. How is one to know?

The saucer returned to the Earths' solar system after a very circuitous route thru three light gates. Emily queried Star Light as to how the saucer could go thru light gates when the original design was not meant to do so. Even though her saucer was at least five times bigger than the original saucer, it was still just a saucer.

Star Light responded, "I am much more intelligent than my creators. I have learned to disassemble molecules into light refracting properties and reassemble them in a different spectrum of light. In effect, we become quarks and thus we are able to travel thru the universe without physically moving. Our material selves are in stasis in a different plane of existence at our origination point. We are but printed copies of our minds eye and can travel the cosmos at will. When we return we will be imprinted upon ourselves. The things which we have learned and experienced are real."

"Now the exception to this is the humanoid specie which you rescued from annihilation. We could not leave a connected quark copy on their planet as the destroying aliens would be able to follow us and know where we live. Our time is still short. We cannot wait. We must attack their home world quickly. I have gathered their entire DNA structure. Using this information the military should be able to form a biological weapon capable of destroying them. We also must learn to repair the rent or tare in the space time fabric to seal them back up in their dimension. Prepare for transition."

CHAPTER 15
SUPRISE PASSENGERS

The saucer came to rest in the hanger. "Well marines, I hope you enjoyed our little excursion. I am sure your superiors will be anxious to hear from you! I do not want you to disembark our visitors until everyone of import has had time to gather. I think our visitors will be a surprise to the humans and Andrians alike."

The six marines laughed with the female marine stating, "Now that is an understatement if I ever heard one!"

After the ramp lowered, Emily casually strolled down the ramp like she was on an afternoon walk, took time to stretch and yawn. When she opened her eyes she observed that she was met with a small contingent of Human and Andrian defense forces. Several were in full battle armor. They all had concerned looks on their faces.

A young lieutenant approached Emily. He smartly stood at attention and executed a crisp salute in the finest military tradition.

Emily smiled and returned the salute with the correct respect of the honors he extended. Her father had taught her to salute with military precision. A quick flash of insight streaked like lightning thru her mind. "My Father knew I was going to somehow in some way going to be associated with the military, He prepared me for this moment from the time I was a child!"

"Ms. Smith, Everyone has been worried about you. Where on earth have you been? You have been gone for seven days!"

Emily responded, "Do not be silly lieutenant! We left this morning. I am hungry as are the others. It is not a week's worth of hungry!" Emily queried the entity in the saucer about the time discrepancy as she knew they had left this morning.

The entity responded, "Well Emily I am very sorry about that. We have travelled thru three different time gates and two universes to return home. Frankly I am glad we returned in such a timely manner. We could have easily returned one hundred years later!"

Emily grinned and replied, "Really! That is way cool!"

Emily noticed everyone backing away from the saucer and upon turning round she saw the otherworldly contingent of her crew exiting the craft and walking down the ramp.

Emily walked over to the male and female. She only came up to their armpits. Then Emily bowed her head before them and greeted them in Andrian fashion, the lessor to the greater, with she, being the lessor; then, looking them in the eyes she telepathically said, "Welcome to my home world".

CHAPTER 16
EMILY'S NEW GUEST

An accounting of the visitors showed there were twenty four adults and sixteen children that were returned to the planet earth. The military wanted to quarantine them in lock up but Emily suggested they be allowed to stay by the water which was on her property line. She believed that since they were from a water world and they were an aquatic species they would feel more comfortable around a water environment.

The military agreed and quickly prepared to erect a small temporary city compound in a somewhat secluded cove on the large water inlet. The lake was an inlet blocked by small islands and other coastline inlets of Lake Ontario, thus it appeared to be a secluded body of water immediately around Emily's property. Guards disguised as fishermen would patrol the lake preventing any other parties from entering the area.

After preliminary plans had been made, Emily again stood in front of the aquatic pair and looking the female in the eyes she said, "You will be okay. Go with the six marines that rescued you and you will be taken to a safe location as my guest. You will be fine."

The aquatic female nodded in response. Emily noted that even though they could not verbalize as humans, they were highly intelligent.

After placing the six marines in charge of their safety, Emily returned to the house where she found Warren. He was in the kitchen with his mother and father. Warren was surprised to see Emily as she walked toward him and put her arms around him. She could feel a tremor in his body and she quietly held him until it subsided, it took several minutes. Glancing at Karen and Earl, Emily saw the relief on their faces.

Upon hearing that Emily had returned, the three Andrian young people, Jawane, Hanlee, and Persha and Warrens two brothers, Skip and Billy, rushed into the Kitchen and gave Emily heartfelt hugs and rapid telepathic communication, except Billy, he was highly vocal, as to her wellbeing. Emily responded with a few details and ended with a verbal, "I am starving!"

While everyone took their places around the table, Karen brought sandwiches and chips. When everyone began eating they silently watched Emily eat like she was famished. Emily did not know she was so hungry. After eating two sandwiches and drinking two glasses of ice tea, Emily sat back, sated and satisfied. And much to her surprise as everyone else's, she let out a loud uncharacteristic belch. Emily looked at everyone and smiling said, "Sorry about that. I feel like I have not eaten for a whole week!"

After the lunch, everyone went into the living room and took their seats. Emily, without thinking, took a chair and plopped down with her legs stretched out before her. She was exhausted.

Telepathically, Emily began telling of her experiences.

ASSIMILATION

She began by saying. "Circumstances are changing rapidly. I do not believe we have generations to safeguard our planet from the alien destroyers. I have seen them again and they annihilate all life forms in which they come into contact. The Entity within the saucer also does not believe we have much time and we must mount an attack on their home dimension immediately."

Everyone sat mesmerized and somewhat terrified by what Emily had just told them. Everyone except Warren and Billy who were not telepathic, both of whom had been forgotten as Emily related her experiences and assessment. However, they both observed the strange behavior and facial expressions as Emily spoke.

Warren surprised everyone by quietly saying, "I do not understand what is going on around here but I know I am being left out." Looking at Emily across the room Warren said, " Do not lie to me any more Emily, We are married now and there will be no more secrets between us."

Emily looked Warren in the eyes with tears welling up in her own. Getting up from her chair she crossed the room and straddled Warrens lap. Taking Warrens face in her hands Emily gently kissed him on his lips. Warren could taste Emily's salty tears on her lips. He was not really sure he wanted to hear what she had to say. He had never seen her act the way she was acting.

"My beautiful husband, the love of my life and soul, when I left you about two years ago you were severely injured. I was gone for a year. When I came back it has taken you almost another year for you to heal. You are still in the healing process. This time I was gone for a week. I am sure it took all your strength to hold it together. But you are right. Married couples should not have any secrets from one another."

Upon hearing Emily say there should be no secrets, Skip and Persha looked at one another and smiled. They too had vowed never to keep secrets from one another again. They loved one another and were virtually inseparable.

Taking a deep breath Emily began her explanation. "You were right to suspect and not believe that Blain was my long lost uncle. And therefor, Hanlee, Jawane, and Persha are not my cousins. But, they are his children."

A hard fierce look came on Emily's face, one he had not ever seen in his life. The "countenance" on her was observed by all present and instilled awe and some fear into what she may have to say.

"Even though they are not blood related, they are my family and I would die for them as I would for you."

Emily's declaration about dying to protect the children and him scared him. Her countenance scared him even more. It was definitely a new dimension to her character and not a renovation of a hidden trait.

Emily continued. "When I disappeared two years ago, I was not taken by Gypsies. I was taken by Blain. Blain abducted me to save my life as I was in mortal danger. The only safe place for me was,.. not on the earth…".

Emily talked for an hour, never leaving Warrens lap or taking her eyes off of his. She brought Warren up to date including her last absence which to her was only one

ASSIMILATION

day but on the earth was seven days. Everyone was surprised to hear of the Aquatic species.

After Emily stopped speaking Warren sat quietly for several minutes assimilating everything that she had said. He then looked at the three Andrian children and smiled.

"So, you think I am a dummy do you?"

All three of the children looked at Warren with big smiles on their faces and Hanlee responded, "Well, we think you are improving and there is hope for you yet!"

Everyone laughed all around and the three children went to Warren and gave him a hug. That was a new dimension of their learning experiences on the earth and one which they all found comforting.

Earl then jumped up and said, "Let's go take a look at that red headed mermaid! I have always wanted to see a real mermaid."

Karen responded by saying, "You better look her in the eye Earl!"

CHAPTER 17
MERMAIDS OF OLD EARTH

Every one ran outside and jumped in their respective vehicles, the young people having their own extended cab pickup. As Warren led the three vehicle convoy out of the gate going to the cove, he was still in deep thought trying to assimilate everything Emily had told him. The revelations were mind stretching to say the least. He just had to put all the facts in one coherent package. At least he now knew why sometimes thoughts and impressions seemed like ghostly fragments of thought just beyond his grasp. "Perhaps soon, he too would be able to communicate telepathically. What a mind blowing experience that will be," mussed Warren. Thinking of Persha, Warren was amazed to believe she or the other two children were not of Earth. And to top it off, he was off to meet some aquatic species that apparently resembled old Earth legends of Mermaids!

Emily sitting quietly beside him was able to hear his thoughts and she too hoped he would be able to do the same. Time was short and a great conflict would soon be at their very door. She smiled thinking of the new aquatic species she brought home and saved from extinction. Evidently, in their culture the female was the dominant

ASSIMILATION

member of their societal structure. Muskula said she was the leader of the Sea Star species.

Skip drove his new truck and had Persha sit next to him so he could hold her hand. He just simply could not stand not to touch her in some way, even if it was an adoring caress with his eyes. Persha felt the same way.

Warren could see Skip following close behind and as usual Persha was snuggled up close to him. He was amazed that they had fallen in love so quickly. But then again, is that not exactly what happened to him and Emily? "I wonder if I would fit into their society should our positions be reversed. Emily did okay but then was she somehow in some way of the same genetic mixture? I am way above the norm on the human scale of intelligence. Does that mean that perhaps sometime in the past one of my ancestors was genetically crossed with a superior intellectual alien species? These Andrians consider my dad as an equal, or at least almost an equal. And what makes us Human and them Alien? We all look alike except they are short one finger and had to have one implanted or grown to more easily fit in on the earth. And Persha and the other two Andrian children, they are so smart. How do they manage to fit in with other Humans? Now I am going to meet the mermaids! I wonder if Alice had a brother or something because I sure feel like I fell down the same rabbit hole."

Emily reached over and gave Warren a reassuring pat on the leg. "You're going to do fine husband. This adventure has a long way to go."

As the three vehicles approached the turnoff to the

cove, they were stopped by armed men. They were obviously military. Warren was caught by surprise when he saw that his three cooks were among the soldiers at the access point to the cove.

One of the cooks looked at Warren as he drove by and said, "Hi Warren! Welcome to our world"! The cook then waved them thru.

As they approached the area of the cove, they could see several camouflaged tents set up in a semicircle. The small truck convoy that had brought the aliens to the cove had just previously arrived and the dust had not yet settled. The aliens were exiting their respective trucks amid high pitched squeaking sounds that rose and descended on a sliding scale.

Emily quickly exited her truck and ran over to the aliens who were disembarking. Their family units were together. There were far too few children. Emily spied Muskula and her mate standing at the edge of the contingent. They were standing close to one another with Muskula's arm draped across her mates shoulder. It appeared that she was wearing a thin film of fabric extending from her armor suited wrist to her waist.

Upon getting closer, Emily's heart began to beat faster. She thought that her heart was going to leap from her chest. She slowly walked around to the front of the two aliens. They were making soft clicking and squealing sounds to one another in rapid fire sequence. Apprehension began to grow in Emily as she slowly began to exam their scaled armor suits. She thought it strange the armour did not cover the woman's breast or

ASSIMILATION

the man's chest. At the same time she remembered where she had heard similar clicking sounds. It was from sound recordings of dolphins, whales, and other kinds of sea life. They all communicated using similar verbal sounds.

The suit of armor was not armor at all. They were scales. Scales just like what fish were covered in. As Emily closely scrutinized them, they scrutinized her. All had become quiet as Human and Alien examined one another. The woman then reached out to Emily's head and pulled her hair back and looked behind her ear. Even though Emily was startled by the woman's move she did not move. Then as the woman pulled her hand away she noticed that her fingers were inordinately long, about eight inches, and between the lower portions of her fingers there was fine webbing. Emily had not noticed her fingers before because they were curled in.

Emily then reached up to the woman, who had beautiful facial features, and pulled her red hair away in like manner and looked behind the woman's ears. The woman did not move. Emily sucked in her breath when she saw a series of slits which ran vertically into the hair line and were obviously gills.

Emily quickly turned to Persha and called her over to examine the female. As Persha examined the gills Emily spoke telepathically to her.

"Have the Andrians ever discovered a humanoid water borne specie in their travels?"

Persha was startled by the question. She looked more closely at the man and woman and then over at the other aquatic aliens. She then began to notice the differences between herself and their species.

Turning to Emily, Persha said, "No Emily. To the best of my knowledge, we Andrians have never discovered a humanoid aquatic species. We have found other life forms so it should not come as a surprise to find these beings on a water world. Did you not say that their world was a water world with one rather small land mass?"

Persha then turned toward the alien aquatic species couple and addressed them telepathically, "My name is Persha, and like you, we are not from this planet but from another star system, again, the same as you. We are glad you are safe and are sadden by the loss of your loved ones. Your enemies are our enemies and together we can defeat them."

Emily and Persha watched closely as Muskula acknowledged Persha's remarks by nodding her head. The man reached up with the palm of his hand and hit the side of his head on the ear several times like he was trying to dislodge water. Muskula emitted a rapid clicking sound and started laughing.

Emily decided then and there that she liked this woman. They were in a totally alien environment, had seen almost their entire species destroyed from their aquatic planet, and yet she could laugh at her "husband's" naive antics.

Emily moved close to the woman and looking up into her eyes she said, "Let us go close to the water to see if you can live there. This area is just a protected inlet of a large fresh water lake. Or we can move you to a larger fresh water area if necessary; the inlet is connected to a

ASSIMILATION

total of four more large fresh water lakes that may be more to your liking. I hope they are not too polluted for you. However, if you require salt water we will have to make other arrangements."

The woman's eyes indicated comprehension. She clicked and squealed of what could be considered nothing else but commands. The other members of the group became instantly silently.

Warren came up and stared open mouthed at the aquatic man and woman. "Emily, how on earth do you get yourself entangled in such mind blowing circumstances?"

Emily turned toward Warren and standing on her tiptoes, she placed her arms around his neck and pulled him toward her and kissed him with a long and sensuous kiss. "Honey I love you so much, you are such an understanding husband!"

Those within ear shot laughed. The Aquatics remained silent, observing the strange behavior. But the female aquatic leader, Muskula, did not miss out on the message that Emily provided. Emily wanted to make sure Muskula understood that she was not interested in her male companion.

The two aquatic leaders turned and slowly walked to the water's edge, followed by the contingent. Emily and Warren and a few others tagged along behind. It would be interesting to see what the aliens thought of their current refuge.

Muskula and her companion stepped into the water inlet lake and stopped, clicking to one another, they entered the lake until it was waist deep. Even though it was midsummer the water was a cool sixty-five degrees. Clicking once again between themselves they dove under the water.

Emily, along with everyone else waited on the shore. Then suddenly almost a mile away, they saw two silver streaks break the water in a long swan dive. It happened so fast that one could not be sure what he had seen if one was not looking.

Billy exclaimed, "Wow! They are fast. They could not have been in the water for more than a minute or two."

About twenty minutes later, the pair surfaced about twenty yards from the shoreline. They began to click and whistle in a kaleidoscope of different octaves in rapid fire sequence. Suddenly, as one, the remaining aquatics ran toward the water immediately immersing themselves, disappearing from view.

"Well so much for secrecy", said one of the cooks.

"Yeah! So much for controlling them!", said another. All three of the Andrian children looked as one with a rock hard stare and impressed upon his mind that no one controlled them.

Realizing what he said, with the help of the impressions of the children, he stammered, "I mean so much for controlling the circumstances in trying to keep their presences secret."

Emily looked the soldier in the eye and said privately, "One more slip in your choice of words and I will wipe your mind of all of our experiences. You will be happy standing guard duty in Alaska. Do you understand?"

ASSIMILATION

The private bowed his head in submission and said, "Yes mam, sorry mam". Truth be known, all the military around her were somewhat awed and afraid of her seemingly never ending expansion of her intellectual powers and abilities. They had no doubt whatsoever that Emily herself could personally wipe their minds should she deemed it necessary to do so.

Only the Andrian children heard what she had said to the soldier and they were mollified that Emily recognized the gravity of his offense and had chastised him thusly. In Andrian culture one was not controlled but acquiesced to the greater good. An example of one who controlled was Zelagark and he was spaced for his crimes. The Andrian children were sure that the ten Human-Andrian hostages would agree. If anything, Emily was a little soft on the soldier but they believed her threat to wipe his mind was a grave enough threat to a Human; after all, they were almost there already.

Emily could sense the Children's anger and hostility toward the soldier. She understood how they felt. It appeared free agency was a supreme tenet everywhere.

Everyone sat on the ground and waited for the aquatics to return. After about an hour one of the cooks said, "Well, Admiral Cleary is enroot and he is not pleased with the arrival of yet another alien species. He said it is our fault for letting you get away! He is going to demote us to real cooks and ship us to Siberia!"

Emily said, "If anyone is to blame it is me. I am the one who brought them here. I am glad they can survive here. They are probably the last of their species. They knew they were going to be destroyed and they were fighting so valiantly. I just saw all those awful alien beings trying to kill them and without thinking, I helped them escape. Actually, there was really no other choice." Then quietly and somberly she said, "It may well be that the planet earth may become a "city of refuge", to many different species throughout the galaxies. It is time to stretch our minds as to what constitutes intelligent life". Laughing, Emily said, "If the Andrians can accept us as being an intelligent species then we better be just as giving in accepting others!"

Upon mention of the alien enemy that destroys every living thing on the planet, everyone's mood became somber; and the thought of the planet earth becoming a refuge among the stars was in itself perhaps a revelation of what was to come.

Skip leaned over to Persha and kissed her on the cheek and said, "Persha, whatever may be, we will be together."

Persha squeezed his hand and kissed him back. "I feel so different being with you. You fill a void in my life that until I met you, I did not know existed. My parental units must have felt the same thing. I am so glad for them." Tears slid down her cheeks as Persha thought of her parental units. This time though the tears were of joy instead of sadness in her understanding at last of what her parents must have felt.

A cool chill began settling on the lake shore as the aquatic beings began to emerge from the water. The sun was low on the horizon and the light beams shined

ASSIMILATION

brilliant gold and green from the sheen of their scales. They were indeed beautiful beings. They all sat down next to the water except Muskula and her mate. They came to Emily and Warren and sat down with their legs folded to their sides. Both of them folded their arms across their chest and bowed their heads, similar to fashion as Emily had addressed them earlier. They then clicked in unison very slowly a melodic repertoire of musical sound.

Emily and the three Andrian children were trying very hard to read their minds. It was all but impossible. The concepts of the aquatic species were so incongruous to them it was all they could do to flesh out the meaning. This was the first time that Emily, Persha, Jawane and Hanlee had ever linked in a mind meld before and the experience in and of itself was enrapturing.

They were able to discern that on the aquatics home planet their species population had been numbered as the sands of the seas. The ugly beings arrived two revolutions ago of their great light, meaning their sun. The water was not a hindrance to them. They had great battles and killed millions of the ugly beings but there was always more. They seemed to come from a black hole that appeared in the air above the water and they poured like sea bottom mud from the hole. There was no way to stop them. They were the only ones left from their pod. They were grateful for deliverance from certain death and extinction of the Sea Star species.

Lastly Muskula said, "We do not understand where we are or how we got here or even how you found us, but thank you."

The efforts the aquatics put into their communication showed Emily and the Andrians that with a lot of work they would soon be able to converse on a more consistent basis. For the present, the communication would basically be one way.

After the aquatics attempt at communicating with Emily and the Andrians, Emily began to interpret to the best of her ability of what she believed they were saying. And again, if any of them did not know of the alien menace and the gravity of the threat they all faced before, they did now.

Warren had a faraway look in his eye and without thinking he pulled Emily a little closer. "What am I to do? How can I possibly protect Emily?" thought Warren.

Emily, being able to read Warren's troubled thoughts said, "Do not worry Warren. We have the Andrians on or side. Together we will be able to defeat the alien menace. Be at peace husband." Warren's troubled spirit began to subside.

Emily sat up and looked at the aquatic female leader. Her red hair flamed even redder in the sunset. Her face was absolutely beautiful. Her neck was long and set on wide, muscular shoulders. Her breast were large and stood firm pointing out and slightly up, proportionate to her body. Somehow, someway, these beautiful creatures had been on the earth of old and spawned the numerous mermaid fables in cultures all over the planet, of that Emily was certain.

The aquatic female observing Emily's scrutiny and contemplation reached out her webbed hand to Emily.

ASSIMILATION

Emily took her webbed hand in hers and felt that it was surprisingly soft. The woman then pulled Emily to her breast in a hug. Emily placed her arms around her and hugged her back. The female softly clicked dolphin like and Emily could sense a feeling of comradeship. They both recognized they were leaders among their species. There was a heavy sense of responsibility.

CHAPTER 18
EXASPERATION AND RELIEF

Admiral Cleary was sitting in the Intelligence Command Center with his Andrian counterpart, Blain. Everyone was concerned about Emily's safety and wellbeing after her disappearance with the new larger saucer. The Andrians were unable to locate where the saucer went once it left the solar system. It had been seven days since she left with six marines.

The phone rang and Admiral Cleary answered using the intercom. A breathless master sergeant working Emily's security detail exclaimed, "She is back!"

Blain showed a visible sign of relief at the words. His heart released tension that he was unaware that he had been holding.

Admiral Cleary placed the phone on privacy and continued listening. Blain observed the color drain from his face. His eyes actually began to bulge. He then shouted into the phone, "She did what! She went where! What do you mean she brought back an alien species! Has she gone mad?"

Blain smiled at Admiral Cleary's exasperation. "Yep, that sounds like my Emily!"

After telling the master sergeant that they would be

ASSIMILATION

coming immediately, he hung up the phone. He looked dazed, stupefied, and haggard. He even looked like he had aged.

"My, whatever Emily had done really upset the Admiral. I wonder if perhaps I should be really concerned. Well, it is Emily. Maybe I should be concerned," thought Blain.

Admiral Cleary looked at Blain and said, "The master sergeant said that Emily saved forty or more aquatic aliens on a water world from annihilation by the new menace we are facing. Have you Andrians ever encountered some type of aquatic humanoid species in your inter-galactic travels?"

Blain did not hesitate, "Never Admiral. Where did she find them?"

Again looking at Blain, Admiral Cleary said, "Apparently, the new saucer craft that claims Emily as its own, can accomplish not only inter-galactic travel but inter-dimensional travel as well. It is beyond me how that could be possible."

"As it is to me Admiral", replied Blain.

"The Entity within the saucer has told Emily that we do not have much time. Come on; let's go see what Emily brought home. I wonder if these amphibian humanoid species looks like, "The Creature from the Black Lagoon"?

Blain looked perplexed and replied, "I do not know Admiral, I have never heard of such a creature."

Admiral Cleary laughed, "I imagine not! The creature was a make believe aquatic life form that was made into an entertainment movie about a hundred years or so ago."

Blain queried Admiral Cleary's mind and was stunned with a vision of the life form that was generated to entertain, and considered as art by Humans.

Admiral Cleary said, "Come on Blain. Let's go see what Emily has brought home.

After their saucer had deposited them in the secret underground hanger, Admiral Cleary waved off his staff assistant and declined to be briefed with the usual photos. "I will be perfectly briefed soon enough, take us directly to these "creatures" camp.

Admiral Cleary and Blain arrived at the encampment just in time to observe Emily being embraced by a beautiful woman with bright flaming red hair that reflected sunlight. She was twice Emily's size and the scene looked more like a mother embracing her child.

After Emily released her embrace she saw Admiral Cleary and Blain standing at the edge of the crowd. Taking the female alien by the hand she walked up to where they were standing.

Admiral Cleary was dumfounded. "Why on earth did not the woman dress properly and cover her breast." As for Blain, nudity was not an Andrian issue.

Smiling at Admiral Cleary, Emily said, "So nice to see you again Admiral." She reached out and shook his hand. Releasing the female's hand, Emily turned toward Blain and placing her arms around his neck, she hugged him and then kissed him on the cheek.

"Oh Blain, there you are turning red again!"

ASSIMILATION

Blain for his part, zinged in every fiber of his body and soul and ached to possess Emily in any way he could, Andrian and Human. He could feel every curve of her body as she held him close; perhaps a second or two longer than need be.

Warren was observing the greeting with tinges of jealousy although he knew he had nothing to worry about. Emily was his wife and companion. After all they had been together for a whole year and nothing had come of it so there was no need to worry now.

Muskula watched the reactions between Emily and the two males. She did not miss the desire on one man's part to possess her and the jealousy on the other man's part with her apparently close relationship with the other male. Well, it is the woman's right to choose whom she will.

Again, taking the aquatic female by the hand and facing Admiral Cleary, Emily introduced her. "Admiral, this is Muskula, leader of the Sea Star aquatic species. As of yet our communication is extremely limited. We are beginning to transfer simple thought concepts but no words.

Muskula looked from the male identified as Admiral Cleary and then to the one identified as Blain, then back again. She did not understand the Admirals seemingly frequent glances toward her breast. "How odd," she thought.

Admiral Cleary proffered his hand and said, "Welcome to earth, sorry about your species."

The female tentatively took the hand wrapping her

long fingers around the male's hand. Muskula recognized the hierarchy of leadership and was surprised that it appeared to be male oriented. Although the female exhibited leadership and the males submitted to her commands when they were fighting the menace on her planet, here it appeared that a male was in charge.

Muskula made a few quick high pitched clattering sounds and her male came quickly to her side.

Admiral Cleary was startled. He just did not think how alien they were because they looked so "Human"; he then observed their scales and his jaw dropped in disbelief. "They are mermaids!"

Emily looked at him smiling and like the old Det. Jessop, said, "Yep".

CHAPTER 19
AFTER ACTION CRITIQUE

The next three days flew by with not nearly enough hours in the day to accomplish all that was even the minimum requirements. Emily, Persha, Jawane, and Hanlee stayed at the new aquatic species camp. They, as a group, interviewed Muskula as much as possible. Their rate of success initially was tedious and slow. With Muskula's mind set focused and determined, their communications progressed reasonable well. They were able to establish a time line of the alien attack and the methods and strategy of attack. The aliens primary method was using a seemingly never ending supply of troops for cannon fodder and could overwhelm even the most advanced weapon system.

Andrian weapons specialist examined the Star Kingdom's lightning weapon. It was an amazing engineering feat using chemical transfer of energy to initiate a bolt of lightning that could burn a hole thru steel. Under water the directed energy beam was even more lethal. Muskula had said they killed millions of them but they continued to pour thru a breach in the dimension barrier like thick mud in a never ending stream. It was the same type event that Emily had witnessed in her cross dimension experience except she observed the enemy aliens from behind and above. They were shuffling away from her position of observation in lined squadrons and charging into the black hole. They were as numerous as the sands of the sea, each waiting for their queue to exit.

After three days Emily and the children returned home. Skip and Billy watched as the military escort drove from the yard. It was early afternoon, not the usual eighteen hour day. As they came up the porch they could see the resolute and focused stares of mentally draining labor. They were silent as they entered the house although Persha stopped and kissed Skip on the cheek. They all continued up the stairs and to their bedroom. The three Andrian children quickly disrobed and stepped into the shower. They were all three exhausted and took the longest hot shower ever. They remained silent allowing the hot water pour over their head and shoulders. It was amazing how the water seemed to wash away their exhaustion.

Persha said, verbally, "It is time for us to get on with our assignment of learning about humans and begin to interact with other people to sharpen our skills. Other Andrians will be arriving soon and we must experience as much as possible so we can be examples to them and hasten their assimilation."

"They think so different from us!", wailed Jawane. "Their minds are so unfocused I do not see how they have survived"

"Yes," Said Hanlee. "Our new friends are the foremost examples of their developed mental capabilities.

ASSIMILATION

What are we going to do when we run into those whose minds are asleep, unaware of the approaching enemy? Fortunately for us all, our "Council of Yield" had the foresight to develop the hybrid younglings. They are truly awesome in their capabilities."

Persha said, "Let us not forget that they defeated Zelegark and his traitorous company. The ten young hybrids developed the tactical plans and the military carried them out in a successful assault on their base."

Jawane thoughtfully added, "I know they are cunning. We must ask Emily if we can see the video they call, "Beam Me Up Scotty". It shows how they captured a three crew landing party. For the life of all the stars, I do not see how they could have done that."

With a new resolve, the three young Andrians exited the shower, dressed, and went downstairs to the kitchen. As always, there was a wonderful smell of cooking food in full bloom.

Warren's mom, Karen, was busily removing a pan of fresh baked biscuits from the oven. Looking up and observing the three young people, she exclaimed, "I missed cooking so much when I was...away. Today we are going to have fried chicken, mashed potatoes, green beans, and gravy"!

Then to Hanlee's surprise, she saw her mother Chandra step out of the pantry. She hardly recognized her and her jaw dropped. Her mom was dressed like Karen, wearing a short loose skirt, with a white low cut blouse covered with an apron. Her hair was combed back and secured with a starfish brad. The brad was a gift to her from Muskula. She had a white powder on her cheek which Hanlee knew was flour.

Chandra, upon seeing her daughter went over and gave her a hug in in human fashion and kissed her on the cheek. For Hanlees' part, she was speechless, verbally and telepathically. Her mother had never hugged her close much less given her a kiss.

"I am learning to cook! At least I did not have to kill the chicken!"

Karen said, "Dinner is served".

Earl helped his wife Karen to her seat by moving her chair for her. Warren helped Emily, Skip helped Persha, and to Chandra's surprise, Jawane seated her. After everyone was seated they held hands and Earl offered the prayer thanking a God which they could not see, have never heard but believed in trusting Him with their very lives. Persha fervently hoped there was some entity like that in the galaxy because they were all going to be destroyed if there wasn't.

After dinner and the dishes had been put away everyone was sitting in the living room sated by the food and deserts prepared by Karen and Chandra. Persha remembered her resolve to continue her assignment.

Looking at Emily she said, "It is time for us to redirect our efforts to assimilate and go out and meet other people. We could start by visiting the school that Skip and Billy attend. Also, we could walk around town under the guise of what you call shopping. I think that tomorrow would be a good time to start."

Earl looked at the young Andrian woman that his

ASSIMILATION

son Skip had fallen so helplessly in love with. She was a very attractive young woman. And like all members of the Andrians group, she was direct, focused, highly intelligent, driven, and all be it somewhat confused about her newly awakened sexuality, he deemed her worthy of his son. He was pleased.

Emily was glad to hear Persha was ready to venture out. She knew she would not push them until they were ready. Evidently the arrival of Muskula and her group has reset their resolve to get on with business, as it had also galvanized earth's forces and every one was working with purpose and direction, no questions asked.

Emily smiled and said, "Fine. Skip has a gymnastics tournament this weekend. We can all go as a family. We can do a lot of shopping too. It will be fun!"

Hanlee and Jawane looked at one another again. Hanlee said, "Well, there is that "fun" again. I guess we might as well try it out. Who knows? It might have an important bearing on our assimilation into human culture."

Jawane looked at her and smiled saying, "Why not? It might be fun."

Hanlee retorted, "Jawane, you are more Human than you think!"

Emily listened to the children's banter thinking they were progressing nicely. They did not realize it but they were becoming assimilated and would have scoffed at the idea that it was so. Before this very moment they would never have dreamed of having that kind of conersation.

"Okay. Out into the world it is! We all need some new clothing."

Hanlee asked, "Is Muskula and her mate coming along?"

Emily was surprised with Hanlee's question about including Muskula in the weekend activities. She seemed to have bonded with Muskula and Muskula seems to have claimed her as one of her own. Emily did not know what to think of the new bonds but hopefully they would be okay.

"Not yet. They have not been here long enough and we have yet to learn more of their culture. Since she is a strikingly beautiful woman she will obviously attract more male attention. Then smiling, Emily said, "Especially if she goes topless!"

Everyone laughed.

Persha squeezed Skip's hand and whispered into his ear and said, "It is okay to look Skip. I just hope you find me as attractive as earth males find her."

Looking Persha in the eyes he responded, "There is no woman under creation I will ever want to be with other than you."

Emily said, "It is settled then. We will have our first adventure Saturday. We will make a day of it!"

CHAPTER 20
FIRST DAY OUT

Persha had searched her resources to learn what gymnastics was. It took great physical strength and skill to accomplish the movements and swings using ones arms and legs. Every muscle in the human body was required to maneuver in such extreme leaps, swings and twist. She knew that Skip was heavily muscled but now she really understood why.

Early Saturday morning a small contingent of security, Human and Andrian, went to the University where the gymnastics meet was to be held. And, because of Emily, a small squad of Andrian female military was included. Before Emily, only male military members were allowed to leave the intergalactic carrier. All the females accepted their assignment without comment but inwardly they were excited. And why not, this was a new dimension of Andrian female inclusion of the military. All the Andrian military members had undergone intensive mental training by Flata, the chief geneticist.

Emily and family left the house in a convoy of extended cab pickups and SUV,s. The drive to the University took about one hour and was located in a medium size town named Mount Pearl. Both Skip and Billy were enrolled in their mathematics program and mostly completed their courses on line, coming to school only for test and extra-curricular activities.

As the caravan weaved thru traffic, Persha moved closer to Skip. The three Andrian children were nervous but excited to have their first outing since coming to Earth five months earlier. Jawane and Hanlee sat stoically in the back seat of the second SUV. The caravan pulled into the parking lot and everyone got out and milled in a group. Security moved out first, casually dressed and blending easily with the population.

Emily took Jawane and Hanlee's hands as they approached and entered the building housing the gym. She was somewhat of a celebrity having been kidnapped by "gypsies", and she was recognized by the teachers standing in the hall. Skips gymnast coach was in the group. All the teachers talked at once welcoming Emily as she introduced her nephew and nieces.

Coach gripped Skips hand in a firm shake and looked at Persha who was wide eyed and apprehensive with the outing even though she suggested it.

"Coach Bryan, this is my fiancé Persha, Emily's niece."

Persha extended her hand and it was all but swallowed in a much larger and even more calloused than Skips' hand if that was even possible.

Looking him in the eye, Persha shyly said, "It is so nice to meet you Coach Bryan. We are all looking forward to seeing Skip go thru his gymnastic routines. We all hope he will win the competition. But of course, how could it be otherwise with Skip being under your expert guidance?" Then Persha broke eye contact and looked down and sideways surprised at herself by the close intimate contact and verbal exchange with Skip's coach.

She knew what he was thinking. He was evaluating how she fit into Skips' life as he had never mentioned her and they talked about everything. But all said and done he was pleased to meet her and thought her a very demure and sweet young lady.

Emily was on high alert as were the entire group and they watched the first introduction of Persha in a direct one on one exchange of greetings. "Persha is such a beautiful young woman and she is really very humble, especially considering her starting point."

After quick exchanges Emily escorted the group into the gymnasium where they took their seats. As Skip turned away a very beautiful and well-endowed female jogged up to skip and gave him a hug exclaiming, "Good luck Skip! I have not seen you in a long time". At which point she looked around the group and noticed Emily and three young people observing her.

Emily stood up and walked over to her and gave her a hug. "Hi Becky, remember me? I am Skips' sister-in-law, Emily." Grinning she said, "I am sure you know Warren."

Becky rolled her eyes and excitedly said, "What young red blooded girl doesn't. He is so beautiful! You are so lucky! I have never seen such a handsome man!"

Both woman laughed knowing full well he could have any woman he wanted. As for Warren, who had turned beat red, said, "Duh! I am standing right here!"

Then Becky turned to him as if seeing him for the first

time, said, "Oh, hi Warren. I did not see you standing there."

Again both woman laughed as Becky twirled away and jogged to the other side of the gym.

Persha, Jawane, and Hanlee watched the interaction with interest and rapt attention. Persha for some reason felt an unknown feeling of jealousy when the beautiful young woman had hugged Skip. Persha had entered Becky's mind, against all Andrian tenants, and felt the extreme sexual desire on the young woman's' part to share any and all sexual pleasures with him, just as she herself had fantasies of doing the same.

Emily, knowing Persha's thoughts, sent her a silent message, "Humans are sexual creatures. Skip is probably not the only one she would like to share sexual pleasures with. Smiling Emily said, "She likes Warren too!"

As the three young Andrians watched the gymnast perform their routines they were amazed at the things they did. It was easy to see why all the participants had such strong musculature. Jawane and Hanlee calculated the torque on the individual muscles and the greatest weight which was exerted during the twist and turns of the individual participants. Jawane was especially impressed with the dexterity of a young girl that was his age.

As the meet was over and the crowd and participants were mixing, Jawane sought out the young girl his age, she was thirteen. She was talking to two other girls and he just stood there and listened. He did not know what to say or how to insinuate himself into their conversation,

ASSIMILATION

they were certainly not talking about science or quantum physics. They were talking about something like make-up, lipstick and perfumes.

The young girls turned to him and the girl that he was interested in said, "Hello. May I help you?"

The other two girls giggled and laughed speaking to one another shielding their mouth with their hands.

Jawane, surprised at her open invitation extended his hand and said, "Hello. My name is Jawane. I am not from around here. I just wanted to say how I admired your muscle tone and dexterity on your gymnastics routine. You must eat all the right foods as your metabolism is certainly attuned to your strenuous exercise and it definitely enhances your fantastic feats of balance and poise."

The two girls quit their giggling and stared at him in opened mouthed surprise.

The young girl to whom he was speaking was observing him silently. After a moment she extended her hand and said, "Thank you, I think. My name is Sara."

Sara observed the strange boy. He was slim build, blue eyes. His hair was collar length and combed in a conservative cut. It was not blonde nor was it colored. She could not decide on what exact color it was. But, he was nice and he did not seem to be an airhead like so many other boys his age.

Jawane, being able to read her mind smiled. "In regard to the eye shadow you and your friends were discussing when I walked up, well, I would not use it because I have read somewhere that it contains certain chemicals that is carcinogenic." Jawane could have told her all the chemicals and amounts in the ingredients but obviously, there was no need to share.

Sara said, "Where did you say you were from? I have never seen you in school so where do you go to school?"

Jawane was about to answer when Emily joined the group and placed an arm around his shoulder.

Brightly, Emily said, "Hi girls."

To Jawane she said, "It is time to go shopping Jawane."

Jawane said good bye and as he turned to go, Sara placed her hand on his arm and said, "Thanks for the warning about the eye shadow. And hey, if we see each other again let's have a soda or something."

"Okay. I will get in touch with you."

As Emily and Jawane left, one of the two girls excitedly exclaimed, "Do you know who that woman was?"

Sara responded, "No, should I?"

"She is Emily Smith! She was kidnapped by Gypsies several years ago and held captive for a whole year! Wow, she was really brave!"

After going to the gymnastic meet, the group returned to their cars and went to a mall. The three young Andrians were amazed at the variety of stores and clothing that was available to purchase. The mall was relatively crowded and there was an air of ease and contentment. No one was in a hurry. Mothers pushed their toddlers in carriages, as other children walked holding hands staying close.

Going into a store Emily took Persha to a clothing rack and started checking out the many items offered. To the Andrian children it seemed like a sea of clothing of

ASSIMILATION

different styles, colors and fabric in waves of selection from wall to wall. And indeed it was. Why? It was a mystery to them why Humans had such a never ending desire for differences in taste.

Emily held up a blouse in front of Persha and exclaimed, "This is you Persha! You have to get this."

Persha looked at the blouse. It was made of cotton. The three children quickly reviewed their knowledge of cotton and learned it was from a plant. None of the Andrians clothing was from plants. Their clothing was manufactured by nano bots that spun out the material into one piece garments. The garment color was pastel blues with subtle threads of rose interwoven so that as the shirt turned it looked as if the pastels were moving like clouds in the sky or waves on an ocean.

Emily had Persha go into the fitting room and try on the blouse. Persha was pleased with the way the shirt fit and seemed to accent her breast. "Yes, Skip will like this."

After turning in a circle and showing the shirt to Emily, she casually walked up to Skip who was talking to the sales girl and brushed up against him. "Well what do you think Skip? Do you like it?"

Skip looked at Persha and smiled. "You are absolutely beautiful. But then again, you do not need a shirt to be beautiful." Skip hugged Persha and kissed her cheek.

Persha felt a hot stab of desire and placing her arms around his neck gave Skip a long arduous kiss. "I can take it off now if you want me to Skip."

Skip and the sales girl laughed. "Wait till we get home." Skip knew Persha was expressing her honest thought and if he said yes Persha would take it off then and there. The sales girl believed she was being coy and seductive.

After buying clothes for all of them, Emily paid for the purchases and as they left the store they smelled the enticing odors of a variety of foods and followed the enticing smells to the food court. The three Andrians observed the many offerings and the methods of cooking and serving. It was so wasteful and so unhealthy, but it all smelled so good! They each selected their individual foods and sat at a table that was relatively clean. The three young Andrians were communicating nonstop telepathically to one another analyzing and evaluating the different processes and verbally included Skip and Billy asking questions about different subjects.

The first ring of the security detail took up tables around Emily and family at a discreet distance and appeared to be just part of the weekend crowd, at least to the casual observer. Sara was sitting with her two friends and had watched the group come to the food court and seat themselves after selecting their food.

The young woman Emily, was seated next to the most beautiful man she had ever seen. He was obviously her husband as they touched each other often with affection and seemed to laugh at private jokes. Everyone was laughing and talking and having a good time. Then she observed the several adults surrounding the groups table, they were eating but none of them talked. Had she not been told of Emily's kidnapping she probably would not have noticed them. Their demeanor appeared to be

ASSIMILATION

one of directed visual assessment of each and every individual that came near the groups table. Then she noticed the clothing that each of them wore. They appeared to be casually dressed but each had a type of long tunic that hung just below the waist. Sara rightly deduced that they must be a security detail and were armed. Evidently they were guarding Emily from any other kidnapping attempts by the Gypsies.

Of course Sara would not have noticed any of these things but she had been raised by her father as an only child, her mother having died in giving her birth. Her father had never remarried and had given all his spare time raising Sara. Sara did not know exactly what her father did for a living as he claimed to be a salesman administrator for some multinational conglomerate. That served its purpose well but as of late Sara began to suspect that it was just a cover for some other kind of employment. It had to be in security as he seemed to be overly cautious toward her and their home. Thru the years he had instilled in her to observe her surrounding and notice obscure things out of the ordinary, hence, her detection of the security detail. Jawane was in the family group at one end of the table.

Sara excused herself from her two girlfriends and walked over to the table where Jawane was sitting. "Hello Jawane. I saw you sitting over her and thought I would come over and visit. May I sit down?" Sara did not miss the attention she had drawn to herself from the security detail as she approached the table.

Jawane looked up in surprise at seeing Sara standing

next to him and asking if it was okay sit down. He quickly got up and pulled out a chair for her in which to sit.

Sara laughed and exclaimed, "My, your quiet a gentleman! No one has ever helped me be seated before except my Dad."

Jawane, though pleased, was at a momentary loss for words and telepathed to her she was welcome. Persha said back to him, "Speak. She is not a telepath. Remember, we are here to learn."

Jawane being duly chastised said to Sara, "I am surprised to see you again. I mean this is such a large place. One would not think it possible."

Sara laughed an easy laugh and replied, "Yeah. Imagine that. But I am glad to get to see you so soon."

"Well Sara, this is my aunt Emily, and her husband, my uncle Warren." Warren gave her one of his best smiles. Sara about melted looking into his eyes and had to force herself to look away and pay attention. Emily smiled. She understood the effect Warren had on woman. He was a modern day version of a Greek Siren. Sara distantly heard Jawane say, "And this is my sisters, Hanlee and Persha, and Uncle Warren's brothers, Skip and Billy."

Sara laughed again. You are lucky to have such a large family. There is only me and my Dad. My Father and Mother was the only child in each of their respective families, and my mom died giving birth to me. My Dad says he just never wanted to get remarried again so for now I am an only child and really spoiled!"

The Andrians listened to the young girl named Sara with rapt attention. They had never known anyone who

ASSIMILATION

had died in childbirth and here was a young lady whose Mother had died giving her birth. Andrians had the fetus removed at six weeks and then Flata, the chief geneticist, removed the fetus and placed them in a berthing chamber until they were ready to be extracted. It was all very sterile, and if a fetus needed to be terminated for some defect, it was a small thing. A woman's life was very precious as was the man's life. All conceivable effort was expended to minimize risk.

Emily had recognized the young woman as the same person Jawane had approached in the gym and had been aware of the young woman's scrutiny as was her security detail. They already knew her name and her Father's name. Her father, Caleb Sears, was civilian intelligence whose primary responsibility was anti-terrorism. He was assigned to the regional contingent that covered the city of Mount Pearl. He was widowed and had raised Sara on his own.

Emily instantly related to the young woman as Emily's father had been in military intelligence and had groomed her for an unknown future role in a leadership position, military or civilian. It appeared that Sara's father was doing the same as he had enrolled Sara into the martial arts at the young age of five years old and he sparred weekly with her. The martial arts fit in well with her gymnastics.

"So tell me Jawane, where are you from? I have never seen you at my school or around town. And just think, we have run into each other twice already. Wow! It must be in the stars!"

Jawane did not have the slightest idea what the stars

had with their chance meeting. If that was true however, Sara did not have the slightest idea of how many stars he had traveled to just meet with her here at this moment in time. Therefore He just laughed as he did not know what to say in response.

Emily, on the other hand did not believe in chance meetings, and replied, "Well if this meeting is ordained by the stars then we will just have to make the most of it and keep in touch! I home school the children and have taught them everything they know. That is why they are so smart!" Emily smiled sweetly at the three of them.

Persha let out an un-beckoned and uncharacteristic snort surprising herself and everyone else at the table.

Warren looked at her and smiling said, "Gee Persha, do you not remember when you came to live with us in the mountains and everything was different and new. If I remember correctly you could not even fry an egg."

Everyone laughed as they knew Warren was having fun with her. Persha responded saying, "It is true you have taught me many things. And yes, egg frying was not one of my skills."

Again everyone laughed.

Emily said, "Their Father, my uncle Blain, traveled a lot and the children had stayed in private schools where they did not have to fend for themselves. I had convinced him to let the children live with me and Warren until they finished their education. And they, like you Sara, lost their mother at an early age. I am a stay at home surrogate mom and I take their education seriously. Warren helps them with their math and science." Smiling and

ASSIMILATION

looking at the three Andrians, Emily then said, "That is why they are so good in mathematics."

Again Persha snorted and said, "Our aunt Emily is really one of the smartest people we know in all the earth."

Again there was a round of heart felt laughter as Emily tousled Persha's hair.

Sara liked the family and really enjoyed the byplay. She did not know what it was about but she wished she could be included in their group activities. Her girlfriends were nice but they were really silly and sometimes it was embarrassing. All they ever thought about was boys.

The Andrian children could read her thoughts and felt empathy for her. If anyone could understand the disconnect it was they.

Emily said, "You know Sara, we haven't told them yet, but Warren and I were planning on getting a hotel suite and spending the night. We wanted to take them to the Astronomy Department at the University and look thru the telescope tonight. They have never seen anything thru a telescope before. I thought it would be fun to show them mars up close and personal," again looking at the three Andrian children she further said, "they have led such a sheltered life they have never had the opportunity to see the planets from earth. Maybe your Father will let you come along?"

Everyone was surprised at the sudden turn of events. Skip and Billy were really excited as they had been to the observatory only once. The three Andrian children were looking forward to seeing how advanced, or antiquated, Human astronomy was. Sara was ecstatic at having further opportunity to be part of the family group. She was also perplexed as to why she said the three children had never seen the planets from the earth. Where else could one possibly see them from?

Sara said, "Oh that would be so much fun! I will ask Dad, I am sure he will let me go!"

Everyone was again surprised when Emily said, "Hey, why not ask your Dad if he would like to come too. I wanted to ask him for permission to come spar with you on the weekends since you are and accomplished martial artist. My Dad taught me martial arts since I was five. I have never stopped learning."

Sara sobered. How did Emily know she was a martial artist?

Emily smiled at Sara knowing that in her enthusiasm, she had revealed that she knew more about Sara than she intended, well, maybe not.

"Do not worry Sara. I am well aware that you have spotted my security detail, therefore I had a check ran on you. You are a very bright young woman. Your father has raised you well. And like I said earlier, I do not believe in chance meetings, thus I extended you an invitation for you to join us this evening. Your Father is welcome to come along. I would like to meet him too."

Sara did not know how to process Emily's statements about checking up on her but her Father had taught her to trust her gut, her intuition; she did not see any overt deception on Emily' part. Sara gave Emily their contact number and returned to her friends at which time they left the mall.

ASSIMILATION

Emily's security detail arranged for accommodations at an upscale hotel and the group retired for the rest of the afternoon. All the young people were excited about this sudden turn of events and that their outing was going to be extended.

Emily contacted Commander Bob Johnson, Commander of Space Intelligence.

"Hey Emily, what a surprise; How is your first outing going? I bet the kids are having a time of their life."

"It has been interesting and one never knows what twist and turns our life events will bring forth. Commander, I would like you to vet a civilian intelligence officer named Caleb Sears and his daughter Sara. We ran into Sara this afternoon and I was impressed with her. Jawane singled her out at the gymnastics meet and they seem to hit it off."

"I had my security detail to do a preliminary background check on her Father, Mr. Caleb Sears, and he seems like a very solid man. We could use someone to specifically check for leaks and plant misinformation. Sooner or later the locals will begin to get suspicious about our isolation. Add the Mermaids to the mix and we can have a Holly Wood extravaganza on our national afternoon broadcast. Surly sooner or later someone will spot them in the water."

"You remember when Blain abducted me from the University? We were all lucky that the two officers that investigated, Detectives Jessop and Reese, saw the big picture. If I remember correctly, you were worried that exposure of alien abductions at the University would start a world panic. Well we are never far from exposure."

"I have good feelings about his daughter Sara. She is sharp. She detected my security detail almost immediately and yet she had the courage to come over and say hello. She reminds me a lot of myself with our similar relationships with our Fathers. Also, she is already an accomplished martial artist. We are going to the Astronomy Lab this evening and I invited Sara to come along and ask her Dad if he wanted to join us. I am sure he is all ears and if he were alien he would have antennas on the side of his head!"

Commander Johnson laughed. "Okay Emily, you're the boss. Consider it done."

Emily hung up and thought about what Commander Johnson had said about calling her "the boss". In a way, and in truth, she had always been in the eye of the storm. Characters and personalities swirled around her in a dizzy array of ever accelerated events encompassing worlds, galaxies, and now dimensions. A great travail was coming and she was "the boss". Emily's festive mood became somber. Emily bowed her head and silently prayed for strength and wisdom.

CHAPTER 21
THE INVITATION

Sara could not remember the last time she was so excited. She did not know what to think about the boy name Jawane. He was such a mystery. His speech pattern was different. His choice of words was articulate, precise and yet, not complete.

He was withholding something. It was like there was so much more to say but left unsaid. His explanations were superficial even though they were technical and more substantial than any she had with any of her teachers.

"Oh Dad, why did you teach me to be so analytical and observant of people that I meet; of course had you not taught me, I would not have ever picked out Emily's security detail. Why could I not be like the other girls and just be dingy about boys?"

Sara, in her introspection, did not hear nor see her Father come in the back door. Nor did she realize that she had verbally expressed her thoughts.

"Sara, are you okay? Who is Emily? Did she hurt you? What kind of security detail? Ha! Are you not glad you are not like your immature girlfriends?" Smiling he said, "If it will make you feel better, I will even start calling you dingy!"

Caleb gathered his daughter in his arms and drew her

close. She placed her head on his chest and heaved a sigh of happiness and safety. Everything was okay in her father's arms.

"Daddy, I met the most interesting boy and woman today. The boys' name is Jawane and the woman is Emily Smith. We have been invited to accompany them and their family to the University Astronomy Department tonight to view Mars. I really want to go. Emily expressly made a point to invite you too. Have you ever heard of Emily Smith?"

Caleb thought for a moment as the name did sound familiar.

"I do not know for sure but is that not the name of the young woman that was kidnapped by Gypsies a couple of years or so ago and held captive for a whole year?"

"Yes Daddy, she is one and the same. I met her and her family today. I met her nephew named Jawane at the gymnastic event. He came up to me and my friends after you had left, and introduced himself to me. He said he liked my muscle tone and that I must be eating all the right foods to accomplish such feats of gymnastic skill. Now how is that for a "come on"? You have never mentioned that as a line, boys would use on me to seduce me in their fiendish ways."

Caleb laughed, releasing his daughter and removed his coat.

"No, I cannot say I have ever used that one before. It is really different. And what about this Emily Smith, did she get kidnapped by Gypsies? How do you know she had a security detail? How many were there?"

ASSIMILATION

"There were eight security agents on the inner ring. I assumed there was another level but I did not see them. They surrounded them on four corners and were very discreet and they were armed. There weapons were covered with knee length tunics. The detail consisted of four male and four female agents. No one came close to the table without their scrutiny, even me."

Caleb looked at his daughter with a serious countenance on his face. Maybe he should have let her cut paper dolls and play with teddy bears. Maybe the martial arts were nonsense. I wish her Mom were alive. I did my very best.

Sara immediately sensed her father's self-doubt and saw the pain in his eyes he normally hid so well. Putting her arms around his waist she placed her head on her father's broad heavily muscled chest.

"Daddy, I love you so much. I am happy the way you have raised me. No man could have done better. When I find a husband and help mate, I want him to be just like you."

A tear slid down Sara's cheek as she ached for her father. He had given her so much and had sacrificed so much for her.

After holding each other for a moment, both had regained their equilibrium. Sara poured coffee she had made when she first came home. Each was silent, each with their own thoughts.

"Emily Smith is a young woman about twenty five or so. She was petite, and she had blonde hair and blue eyes. And oh, Daddy! You will not believe her husband!

He is absolutely the most beautiful man I have ever seen. When Emily introduced me to him it was all I could do is to look away after saying hello. He had the most amazing eyes!" Sara was breathless.

Amused at Sara's obvious infatuation with Emily's husband he said, "Well, should I be jealous?"

Sara laughed and said, "No daddy. He is Hollywood handsome whereas you are cowboy rugged. You are both handsome men. I have seen woman look at you and do everything but jump in your lap and you just ignore them."

"Oh, Daddy, another thing, when I was talking to Emily she said she wanted to spar with me in the martial arts on weekends. I never told her I was taking the arts. She said she had been taking the arts since she was five years old, like me. At first I was somewhat uncomfortable that she would know such intimate details about me. But Daddy you always taught me to trust my instincts and inner gut. I like this woman and I would like to get to know her better, so please, let's go to the astronomy viewing tonight."

Caleb agreed that they would go to the astronomy viewing but mainly he wanted to meet this Ms. Smith. He doubted she was kidnapped by Gypsies. And most assuredly he wanted to know how she could have obtained such intimate knowledge of his daughter in such a small amount of time.

CHAPTER 22
ASTRONOMY LESSONS

There were approximately fifty people in the viewing area of the astronomy lab. Several viewing screens were placed round about to allow more people to view whatever the astronomy department was focused on for the evening. This evening it was Mars and our colonization of Mars. Even after twenty years of Human occupation, the outpost was nothing more than a few carbon huts that could accommodate no more than twenty people.

Emily and her family had one viewing area all to themselves with the viewing being prearranged by her personal phone call to the head of the astronomy department. After all, what good was the celebrity of being kidnapped by Gypsies worth if one could not cash in on special privileges for one's status?

The Andrian children examined the most sophisticated telescope on the planet and immediately pointed out many of the deficiencies of light refraction technology. Why not just use electron beam dissection of the light frequencies to obtain a more precise mathematical simulation of the object being viewed?

Skip and Billy were amazed at the clarity of image. Of course they could not see the outpost but the mountains and valleys were clear.

"I want to go there someday. I want to be an explorer,"

exclaimed Billy.

"You and me both, I know that someday we will see it up close and personal," Said Skip.

Emily was hoping Sara and her Father Caleb would come to the viewing. She wanted to meet him to make a personal assessment even though she had already told Commander Johnson she wanted him vetted for the proposed position.

As Caleb and Sara parked their vehicle outside the astronomy department he noticed the SUV'S parked on every corner of the building. In addition to the outer perimeter of security he noted the six additional security agents spaced evenly as one went up the steps. To the untrained eye they looked every bit of the part of the milling student body.

"Ok Sara, I think it will be very interesting to meet your Emily Smith.

"Oh you are going to love her Daddy! She is so nice!"

As Caleb and Sara entered the building he saw additional security agents in the hallway and at the entrance to the viewing area.

As they approached the viewing area a man stepped forward out of the shadows and said, "Mr. Sears, this way please. Ms. Smith is expecting you."

Now Caleb was beginning to be really interested into just exactly who Ms. Smith was. This was not a minor security detail. It was a full-fledged security array consisting of many layers of defense.

As the escort stepped to the side and indicated for him and his daughter to enter the room, Caleb saw two

ASSIMILATION

adults and five young people examining a telescope. Three of the young people were in animated discussion about the scope indicating that is was not necessarily the best technology for viewing distant planets and stars.

Caleb saw a young woman detach herself from the group and walk toward him. She was dressed in a tight red skirt with a white, low cut blouse with puffy sleeves. She was physically representative as Sara had described her. Her red lips were in a lopsided smile and her face was framed in a blonde catch of long wild curly hair.

As she arrived at their position she first took Sara in her arms in a maternal embrace expressing her happiness at seeing her again. After releasing Sara, Emily faced Sara's Father looking into his face. She liked what she saw and interpreted the fine lines and creases on his face as character, that is except the long scar he had received in a fight with a would be terrorist. The terrorist lost.

Emily extended her hand for a hand shake, Caleb took her hand and was surprised at her firm grip. "Nothing wimpy about this woman," Caleb thought.

"Hi, Mr. Sears. My name is Emily Smith. It is so nice to meet you. I met Sara earlier and she is such a wonderful young woman, and sharp too! She spotted my security detail almost right away!"

Sara was caught off guard. She did not know that Emily knew she was aware of her security detail; she tried to be discreet as possible.

Emily could read Sara's embarrassment in her mind. "I am proud of you Sara. It shows you have an analytical brain and are observant of your surroundings It will serve you well in your future. But, for now come on over and meet my family and take a quick view of Mars."

Caleb liked the way Emily read Sara's discomfort and set her at ease by complimenting her on her analytical skills. Yes, this was an interesting woman.

As they approached the group around the telescope a young boy about Sara's age came forward and said, "Sara, it is good to see you again. I am glad you could come. I know you will like to see Mars up close."

Sara said, "Daddy, this is Jawane, I met him at the gymnastic event. "Jawane, this is my Father, Caleb Spears".

Jawane extended his hand and shook the proffered hand and said, "Hello Mr. Sears. Sara has such fine muscle tone and strength. It was really amazing to see her maneuver thru her routine."

Smiling, Caleb said, "Nice to meet you too Jawane. Please call me Caleb. And yes, I suppose Sara does have muscle tone and strength. Being a gymnast takes those physical attributes and great skill."

As Jawane and Sara walked away to the telescope Caleb could hear Jawane giving Sara a technical assessment of the refraction of light waves verses the electron beam dissection of light frequencies. He did not understand a word he said.

Emily introduced Caleb to the rest of the family. Caleb noticed the Hollywood handsomeness of Warren Abbott and could understand why his daughter was smitten by him. He imagined all woman pretty well thought the same thing. It wa a mystery to him why Emily chose to

ASSIMILATION

keep her maiden name if they were indeed married.

A young girl of ten or so approached and extended her hand and introduced herself as Hanlee, Jawane and Persha's sister. She was proper and trim and presented herself in a very confident manner.

After the round of introductions everyone enjoyed the viewing o Mars and each said how much fun it would be to go there. However, Caleb, being more down to earth said he was happy where he was.

When the viewing was over the group proceeded to a private dining room to where a table of food was set up. It was not fancy but it had a large variety of sandwiches and salads. There were drinks available for adults and young people alike.

Emily directed Caleb to a table away from the rest of the family and sat down. She believed what she had to say was for his ears only although should Caleb accept the position everyone would know what his duties entailed.

"So Ms. Smith, I am interested to know how you were able to obtain intimate details about my daughter's personal life pertaining to her skills in the martial arts. That information is not posted on any local bulletin board. I have observed your security detail and it does not appear your being kidnapped by Gypsies warrant the level of security which is displayed. Actually, it appears to be more in line with security accorded to heads of state. I have checked my sources and surprisingly I have run into misinformation, misdirection and outright denial of access. These must be some really bad Gypsies".

`Emily looked at him and smiled saying, "I am well aware of your efforts Caleb. My slip to your daughter that I was aware of her martial arts skill was not necessarily a slip but a mulling of interest to see your response and how much effort you would expend in trying to determine who I was and how I knew so much about your daughter. Evidently you have gone up the ladder and called in as many favors as you had coming in an effort to learn the truth and, as you have learned, where access was clearly denied a separate and deep cover story was in place."

"I was intrigued by your daughter when she spotted my security team. It made me wonder what manner of Father and or Mother she had. I am pleased to see that you are one who loves his daughter deeply and has sacrificed of yourself to make your daughter as happy and comfortable as possible. Raising her on your own has had many challenges; especially now that she is applying the mental processes to the lessons you have taught her. I judged that an individual that can raise a daughter with such fine results might be someone I could enlist in a certain endeavor".

Caleb was intrigued and surprised to know that Ms. Smith was aware of his inquiries and of its results. Who was she really and what did it portend for him and his Sara. She obviously believed he could be of service to her, and or, her cause, or she would not have gone to so much trouble and expense in conducting her own personal investigation.

Caleb recalled that Sara had told him that she trusted

ASSIMILATION

her intuition and her gut in finding peace with Emily's personal knowledge of her. He knew he had instilled that axiom of faith into his daughter and she had accepted the peace that came with it. He figured he would have to do the same. He had intuition that Emily Smith was a good and trustworthy person. In his gut he knew that was true.

"Ms. Smith"...

Emily responded by saying, "Please, call me Emily".

"Okay Emily, I think I would like to assist you in your endeavors whatever they may be. However, I have been in the Security Services anti-terrorism unit for at least ten years and I do not know if my superiors will let me go. And for what it is worth, I have never run across any bad Gypsies." He said that with a smile.

Emily returned his smile and extended her hand for a handshake saying, "Welcome to your new world. You can start your training tomorrow."

"I cannot start tomorrow; I have to notify my superior officer of my resignation. I assume you are some type of government security group as all your agents just appear to be military in stance and demeanor. As for pay and vacations, I want to make enough money to travel to some exotic locations and live among the natives."

Emily could not help herself; she burst out laughing a full hearty laugh, one she had not had in a long time. Her laugh caught the attention of Warren and the rest of the group and the Andrian children focused their minds to learn what was so funny to Emily. When they perceived that Sara's Father was going to join the group and he had requested travel to exotic places and live among the natives, they too laughed. He really did not have a clue as to just how exotic they were going to be. The laugh was a deep anxiety release for Emily and she did not realize how stressed and focused she had been. The laugh felt good. The Andrian children laughed and enjoyed the feelings of normalcy it brought.

Emily's response sobered and startled him. She said, "It is already taken care of as of, let us see; you have been vetted", looking at her watch, "five minutes ago." You are now assigned to me and will assist with whatever I deem your skills can be most useful. And as I said before, welcome aboard." Emily then stood at attention and gave Caleb a crisp salute. She felt that was necessary to instill in him that he was no longer in civilian employment but the military's and more importantly, who was in command. The intent was not lost on Caleb. He returned the salute smartly, having spent several years in the military.

CHAPTER 23
NEW PATHS

Selena smoothed her tight fitting sweater over her short skirt. She checked her mirror to insure her lip gloss was properly applied. Being critical of her looks she thought that for twenty-eight she looked pretty hot! Her dark pixie cut hair framed a thin face with wide lips and deep set eyes. They looked almost black taking on the sheen of her hair. She was petite in size and carefully kept her nails properly trimmed and complete makeup on in public. She always wanted to look her best.

One would not suspect that Selena was a prodigy and held three Doctorate Degrees in extremophile molecular biochemistry. Dr. Selena Washington wrote the text books used in all the schools. She was also instrumental in discovering the first life forms in samples returned from Mars. However, if anyone asks her what she did for a living, she would reply that she was a stay at home mom raising her six year old son, Shawn, as she home schooled him.

She worked hard to personally stay out of the limelight. If anyone needed to know who she was, she simply said, "Selena Washington". Many of her professional papers were assigned pseudo names and some were even credited to several of her graduate students whom she deemed worthy of recognition.

Everyone loved Selena; everyone that is except her former husband. He was a controlling man who could not abide any limelight she received. And the strange thing was he became even more infuriated when she purposely extended credit to a deserving student. In effect, there was nothing she could do to please him. Their marriage ended in a violent clash that left Selina in the hospital with several broken bones and a mild concussion.

A restraining order had been served but to no avail. He followed Selena whenever she went out. She did not have the slightest idea how he found out she was leaving the house or where she was going. However, her fear of her husband was cast aside in lieu of her son's excitement in going to the Mars viewing in the Astronomy Department. She believed if she raced to the University she could get ahead of him and return before he realized she had gone. In effect, in the past year she had become a prisoner in her own home.

After buckling her son into the rear seat of the car, she raced from her garage and headed to the University. So far so good, she could not see him following her so maybe she successfully eluded him.

Selena parked in front of the Astronomy building in a no parking zone and quickly entered the building pulling her son along behind her in a brisk walk. She did not see him close in on her from the side. When she did see him it was too late. Selena screamed as he punched her on the right side of the face. The blow caused her to stumble backwards. He then grabbed her by her short hair and swung her around in a circle with her feet leaving the

ASSIMILATION

ground. After turning her loose Selena slid across the floor in a heap. He then ran toward her and was just getting ready to stomp on her when out of nowhere he was hit from both sides.

Emily and her family were just exiting the viewing hall when they heard a scream. They then observed a large man punch a small female on the face knocking her backwards. He charged the woman and grabbed her by the hair swinging her around in a circle throwing her across the room sliding right up in front of Emily and Sara, who were walking arm in arm in an amiable fashion.

Everyone was shocked at the sudden violence that erupted before them and landed at their very feet. Emily and Sara acted instantly, being trained in the martial arts, each blow was devastating and incapacitating. They attacked from different sides.

The large man made an easy target. He was strong and in good condition but conditioning would not stand up to the jabs, punches, and kicks to his groin, knees, solar plexus, and throat. Emily landed the last blow which was cupped hands either side of the head over the ears. He landed on the floor with blood streaming from his eyes and ears.

The security team response was also rapid. But Emily and Sara had put the big man down within seven seconds. Caleb and Warren did not have time to enter the fray so they attended the young woman laying prostate on the floor.

The Andrian children had never seen such a

demonstration of explosive self-defense. The Andrian members of her defense team looked in awe upon the two woman. That kind of fighting was unknown to the Andrian military. Skip and Billy knew Emily was a martial artist but neither had ever seen her in action. They were finally fully aware of Emily's status as Co-Commander of Earth's forces against the new foe. The entire encounter from the time Selena was attacked till her attacker was subdued was fifteen seconds.

Selena ached all over. Even her hair hurt. She slowly opened her eyes fully aware her former husband had successfully attacked her again. She blinked her eyes and reached up and rubbed them. Thinking she had died and gone to heaven she saw two of the most beautiful and handsome men she had ever seen in her life. They were looking intently into her eyes and were touching her gently on the side of her head and touched her lightly down her body checking for broken bones.

The beautiful one said," Are you alright?"

The ruggedly handsome one said, "My, you took quiet a beating. You are really one tough lady."

Finding her voice, Selena said, "Thank you for coming to my aid. He would have killed me if you had not done so."

Both men laughed and the ruggedly handsome one said, "We did not do anything. Your assailant was dispensed with by two young ladies."

The two men moved away and were replaced by two young woman. One was even a child. The young child-like girl of about thirteen had tears running down her cheeks as she reached for Selena's hand.

"I am so sorry we could not stop him before he attacked. It was so fast I could not move fast enough," cried Sara.

Emily put her arm around Sara and said, "Sara, you were quick enough. He would have killed her had you not kicked him on the side of the knee. I was amazed at your speed and depth of skill. It was the only target that would stop the attack long enough for us to eliminate the threat. I think, no, I know, you and your Father, will be a good asset within our organization."

Caleb looked sharply at Emily. He did not want Sara in harm's way.

Emily said, "I understand Caleb, but there is a definite need for her and her skills. She will be safe. I give you my word she will be safe…, or at least as safe as any of the rest of us."

Caleb was taken aback. Thinking, "What is she, a mind reader too; and what did she mean by, safe as the rest of us?"

Emily looked up at him and smiled saying, "Something like that. You will know most everything tomorrow."

Security called an ambulance and Selena was taken away. Emily assured Selena they would take care of her son Shawn, and follow her to the hospital.

Emily told her family to go to the car as she had some business with the security detail that was holding Selena's former husband.

He was cuffed and standing with a bent about the waist as Emily stood in front of him.

"Hello. Have you no remorse for beating up on your former wife? Have you no remorse for traumatizing your son?"

The man just looked down at Emily with sullen hate and down turned mouth. He said nothing.

Looking to the senior Andrian member of her security team, Emily said, "Wipe all memories of his x-wife and son. Put him in another part of the country with new identity. Make him happy doing house painting".

The Andrian saluted her and said, "Yes Sir. It will be done immediately!"

Emily returned the salute and turned and left the building. When she got to the SUV where the others were waiting for her, she said, "Okay, that unpleasantness is taken care of, shall we all go to the hospital and check on who this woman is as she seems to have dropped literally at our feet?"

CHAPTER 24
HOSPITAL VISIT

Selena awoke from the medically induced sleep to a gently probing in her mind. Someone was saying something to her but she could not understand. Finally her ears heard, "Selena, wake up. We need to talk."

Selena observed one of the young women who had come to her defense. She was blonde, about twenty-five, and somewhat small.

"Thank you for saving my life. I am sure that he would have killed me this time."

Emily responded, "I give you my word that he will never hurt you again and he has totally forgotten all about you. As a matter of fact he is now a happy house painter in Los Angeles."

Selena said, "Yea right, I wish!", Then she winced from her jaw hurting where he had slugged her.

"My name is Emily Smith. It is an honor to meet such a distinguished scholar. I am so glad to have the opportunity to meet you. Although I wish it could have been in a more favorable circumstance. Your work is known to us. We were going to contact you at a later date but it appears an opportunity has presented itself and we may as well make use of this opportunity."

"We need your help and expertise to work with others that are like minded such as you. The work will be challenging but I think we can overcome the obstacles. We do not have any alternative."

Emily stopped and paused a minute to consider what she should say next. Believing being direct was the most suitable course with this scientist, Emily said, "We are going to be attacked by a life form never before seen on our earth, or our galaxy. This life form is from a different dimension. We have seen it pouring into our dimension. It destroys all that it touches. They have destroyed all life forms on three different worlds, including all life on three intergalactic battle cruisers. We do not know exactly how much time we have but it is not near as much as we have previously believed".

Selena held up her left hand while pressing her right hand gently to her face feeling her jaw. "Wait a minute! What kind of drugs did they give me and are you some kind of hallucination?"

Selena blinked her eyes several times to clear her mind. Opening her eyes again, the same woman was still standing above her looking intently into her face. Other than the slight dull pain in her jaw, her mind was clear and her head no longer throbbed.

"You get right to the crux of the matter don't you? What did you say your name was? Emily Smith, right? Oh yeah, you were the one kidnapped by Gypsies? They were not Gypsies were they? I knew that was a cockle bull story when I heard it, I just did not know what they were covering up."

Emily smiled and said, "You are the only one that deduced the truth. We gave you an injection to counter act

ASSIMILATION

the drugs administered by the emergency room. You suffered a minor concussion but you are okay now."

Selena asked, "Is either of the beautiful men that I awoke too earlier, aliens?"

Emily gave a soft laugh. "No. The Hollywood Greek God looking man is my Husband, Warren. The cowboy rough handsome man is Caleb, and he joined our group this evening. He was formally a civilian anti-terrorist agent. He does not know what he is going to be doing and I cannot wait to tell him! It is going to be fun! I will make sure you are there."

Laughing, Emily continued, "You might have to pick him up off the floor this time!"

"He is single and is raising a thirteen year old daughter. Her name is Sara. Sara is the one that got in the first hit on your former husband and is primarily the one responsible for limiting the damage that was to be inflicted upon you and in doing so in all probability saved your life."

Selina was silent for a few minutes digesting all the revelations that Emily had revealed.

"But she is so young! How could she possibly be so skilled? I am sure her Father had everything to do with that!" Then shifting her thinking about the revelation of the new enemy, Selena said, "I always believed that our primary enemy would come, not from the earth, but from the stars. Scriptures say that they will come from the abyss. I guess another dimension could pretty well serve as the abyss."

"If you wish to join us you could use the injury as

an excuse to drop out of sight so to speak. Tell everyone you will be in rehab. Months will pass by and then we can put something out that you retired as an invalid or something in California. If you want to go with us, we will be leaving and going back to my home which has become our home base here on earth. We will take care of all you're belonging and personal items and close up your home. If you like we can even have it rented out for you."

"I suppose that if the menace you speak of is as dangerous as you lead me to believe then I really have no choice but to use the gifts with which I have been blessed, to help destroy it. But for now I would like to meet the young lady that helped save my life."

Sara quietly came into the hospital room. The light was muted but the woman lying in the bed was easily discernable. She walked to the edge of the bed and the woman reached out for her hand.

"Thank you for saving my life. I understand I would not have survived the attack if it was not for your quick response."

Sara looked down and sideways mumbling, "I have never thought I would use my skill in such a meaningful way. Up to now, it had always been a fantasy game. He was really a mean man."

Then looking the older woman in the eye she said, "My name is Sara. Dad said you are some kind of scientist. He also said he would be going to work for Emily and you would be coming too. I am glad that you will be with us. I hate moving and starting over. The last time

ASSIMILATION

we moved it was because of the rainy weather, the time before that it was because it was too dry. My Mom died when I was born. I am sure my dad is running away from the loneliness. It seems like when we move a new chapter in our lives open and the old one closes leaving behind those we have grown to love and cherish."

"I do not have the slightest idea of where we are going or what my Dad will be doing. Well at least I will have an acquaintance with the new boy, Jawane. He is a nice boy. He is sort of different in some strange way. I cannot quiet put a finger on it yet but I guess I will learn."

Selena smiled at the young woman. Children were so resilient.

"Yes, I am glad I am coming also. And Sara, I wanted to thank you personally for saving my life last night. You were very brave."

Sara just shrugged her shoulders nonchalantly.

"You said your Dad did not mention what he would be doing or where we will be going?"

"No, he just said Emily offered him a position with her, "work group", or whatever that means. He accepted immediately so it must be important. He has never changed jobs that I can recall. He has been a salesman forever. At least that is what he tells me he does. He probably does not want me to know what he really does so I will not be afraid for him."

"He is so lame. I know he is in some kind of security work. He is always harping on being aware of ones surroundings. Sometimes he even comes home beat up."

With her face brightening into a smile, Sara said,

"That is why I spotted Emily's security detail. That was so cool! It was so obvious to me but no one else even noticed. Then I saw Jawane was in the group and decided it would be interesting to go say hello again."

"I am so glad I did. Isn't it amazing how things seem to be connected and to flow with cosmic magic? So many things happened in such a short period of time, each event leading to the other and culminating with all of us moving in the same direction!"

Salina looked away and said, "Yes, it is amazing."

After learning what Emily needed her skills for, she was not so sure that cosmic magic was the right description of what was going on. Then again, perhaps there was more than an accidental confluence of events. Emily did say she was already aware of her work and was planning on contacting her at a later date. However, she also said that they did not believe they had as much time as previously thought. And what happened then? She landed at Emily's very feet.

Emily had said her ex-husband was now a happy house painter in Los Angeles. Giggling to herself she hoped that was the case because her ex-husband hated laborers of any sort and often pointed out the slothfulness of painters in particular regardless of the skills they possessed.

Sara observed the faraway look in Selena's eyes and deduced she needed her rest. Excusing herself from the room she went back to the waiting room where she saw Emily's nephew and two nieces huddled in a small circle staring at one another. They appeared to be having a conversation yet they were not speaking to one another, at least as far as she could see.

Walking over to them she said "What is up. You all look awful serious just staring at one another?"

The three children was caught totally by surprise as they were expressing to one another that they had all seriously misjudged Humans and had to re-evaluate everything they had previously believed. They were amazed at how Emily and Sara had so easily and quickly taken the large man down. They were all impressed with Sara's total lack of fear. They also knew in their heart of hearts that should they have found themselves in a similar position they would not have been able to overcome the attacking man.

Persha responded first. "We were just thinking that we have misjudged you because of your lack of mathematical skills and knowledge we deem to be important to our survival. However, should our positions be reversed we do not believe that we would be able to cope with the things you seem to accomplish without effort."

"In effect, for your time and circumstance you are well advanced making use of what you have to the best of your ability. There are major errors in your thinking in regards to the environment, scientific applications that to us are universal laws of survival, and your social structure seems convoluted. None the less, you are still here."

Sara stopped short with open mouth. Shaking her head she said, "Excuse me! Like what planet are you from? Or more to the point, what are you smoking? I know that it must be really good and I might like to try some myself but my Dad would literally ring my neck!" The three young people looked at Sara and smiled.

CHAPTER 25
SUCCESSFUL TRIP

Caleb and Selena road back to the mountain enclave with Selena's son Shawn and Emily's niece Hanlee. They were the closest in age and seemed to be a natural pairing, at least to the thinking of Caleb and Selena. Sara wanted to ride with Jawane thus there was extra space. Also, Emily wanted Hanlee to interact with other humans and practice her interpersonal skills.

Selena suspected, but did not know for sure, wither or not Hanlee was from Earth. She was obviously human. Caleb had no knowledge whatsoever what he was getting himself into and attempted to glean information from Hanlee. Hanlee answered the questions as precise and cryptic as possible and did not reveal any secrets. It helped that she could read his mind and was well aware of his objective. She enjoyed the mental acrobatics Caleb engaged as he came back to the same question from different angles and points of view. He was a good interrogator.

Hanlee entered into the exercise with pleasure and considered it a form of entertainment and tried to see how many ways she could stymie Caleb. Selena listened in on the exchanges and was soon convinced that the ten year old child in the back seat was indeed very intelligent and was making a game of playing with Caleb.

Hanlee said, "Selena, I understand you are a biochemist with your field of study being extremophile life forms, is that not true? I imagine that you would find it interesting to study the life forms on Saturn's moon Titan. Titan has an ice cover five miles thick. The life forms there never ever see the light of the sun. Like earths deep sea life forms, they would be illumines. And of course, with there being more water on Titan than all the earth, the life forms there would be quiet substantial in size, not at all like the small creatures found in the depth of the arctic ocean; do you not think so Selena?"

Selena looked at Hanlee and smiled. Yes this brilliant child was not of this earth.

"Yes, I believe you are correct Hanlee. You must have a very wise teacher and mentor to instruct you in such things".

"Yes, my teacher was what you would call a futurist in that he thought outside the confines of conventional wisdom. He did not limit himself to just thinking about earth."

Selena listened with the rapt attention of a new and excited student sitting at the feet of her guru.

"Selena, have you ever thought what it would be like to live in an enclosed system with resources being limited and thus tightly controlled? There are plenty of resources throughout the galaxy and I am sure that if there are any travelers they would do what they could to make use of those resources.

However, within the confines of a, let us just say intergalactic carrier, for lack of a better analogy, how could

ASSIMILATION

nine thousand people survive the deep of interstellar travel? Would that group of interstellar travelers somehow be just as much extremophiles as the subspecies in Earth's oceans?

Surely just in the manner they would pro create would require substantial variance from the requirements on the planet earth, I mean, our planet. I believe that just in the way one thought, every nuance would have to be directed to some mode of survival instinct. Are we not fortunate on the planet Earth we can have time for "fun"? I can imagine that in that type of society that I described, there is not even the slightest concept of "fun".

Selena looked at Hanlee with a deep appreciation of the child's intellect and accepted and respected the information which Hanlee had just shared with her about her world. Selena reached her hand back and taking Hanlee's hand in hers, said, "I would be honored to meet such a wonderful group of beings. And I would show them with all my power what "fun", means."

Selena then looking at Caleb said, "Of course that would be premised on the existence of such a group of beings. What do you think Caleb? Do you think a group of intergalactic travelers could exist as described by Hanlee?"

Caleb looked over at Selena taking the time to take his eyes from the road. After having heard Hanlee's excerpt about Titan and intergalactic travelers he was of the mindset that Hanlee needed a new teacher. He was going to say her teacher was full of corn but instead he said, "I think her teacher needs to play more ping pong." Caleb looked back at the road without further comment and continued to drive in silence.

Both Hanlee and Selena smiled. Selena continued to hold Hanlee's hand and quietly said, "Thank you".

Hanlee liked Selena. She was definitely one of the most intelligent humans she had met on the planet. She also had never seen a man strike a woman before and thus discovered two new found emotions. One, she believed to be "disgust". The other was empathy. Selena was scared of her former husband and for good reason. Yet she loved and cared enough for her son to risk bodily harm and perhaps even death, to take him to see the Mars exhibit. Education and knowledge was important to her. Hanlee smiled inwardly. Selena was Andrian; she just did not know it… yet!

CHAPTER 26
DINNER PARTY

The returning caravan had returned home late in the evening. Emily had shown Caleb and Sara their new quarters which were small, two story loft type, stand alone, apartments with long wide covered porches facing the lake. They were well apportioned and sat back against the trees. There were even rocking chairs spaced across the porch.

The second apartment assigned to Selena and her son Shawn was identical. There was a walk way between the apartments which met in the middle with a large terraced patio with half partly covered to keep one out of the elements. The apartments were far enough away to insure privacy yet close enough to easily facilitate shared social activities.

Emily had encouraged her new guest to turn in early as their work would begin the next day. Both Caleb and Selena agreed and they went into their respective apartments.

Emily contacted Commander Bob Johnson of Space Intelligence Command and informed him of her latest additions to her work group. She again reiterated her concern about the local rumors of UFO and Mermaid sightings in the area and thus her decision to bring Caleb on board as a dis-information specialist.

Bright and early the next morning Caleb decided to go out jogging around the property. After all, if he was really part of the work group he should be well aware of his surroundings. To his surprise Sara was also up and wanted to go with him.

The property was such a pristine piece of land that the beauty of it just made him feel like all was well. What a wonderful place to bring Sara. No more gun battles with terrorist, no hot heads to subdue, and mainly and most importantly to him, no more lying to Sara.

This was absolutely the safest place they had ever lived. What could go wrong? Then surprisingly a strange thought crept into his mind about the young girl Hanlee. How did she know all that information about Titan; And, what of all the talk about social structures on an intergalactic space ship? Of course there would be fun. How could it possibly be otherwise? Then thinking, "I am plenty happy here on the planet earth, I do not need the stressful thoughts of all the dangers of space clogging my mind."

Sara running along and slightly behind her Father sensed her Father's somber mood. He was very quiet and she believed he was totally unaware of her presence.

"Dad, is everything okay? You seem strangely preoccupied. Here we are running together this morning and you have totally ignored me. What's up"?

Caleb was startled from his thoughts. He had indeed forgotten all about Sara running with him. How could he have done that? Everything was wonderful was it not? Of course it was. Still, something bothered him about

ASSIMILATION

Hanlee; he just could not bring it to the consciousness of his mind. "Oh well, enjoy the moment and run with my Sara. Really, what could possibly go wrong?"

"Ms. Smith, the new guest, Mr. Sears and his daughter Sara are out of the apartment and running to the shore line of the lake. Do you wish me to stop them?"

"No let them go. Mr. Sears thinks he is just exercising but I know him better than he knows himself. He is really collecting information for his personal intelligence. I would expect no less of him. We are going to have a luncheon at which time I will inform him of his duties. If you can make it you should come. It will be fun to see him face something totally new."

The Andrian surveillance officer smiled.

"Yes sir. If I can make it I will be there in person. If not, then surveillance video will be sufficient. And yes, I suppose it could be "fun".

Emily smiled and cut the link. Yes it was going to be fun to watch Caleb grasp at his new reality.

Upon Caleb's return from the run he had a message from Emily stating there would be a luncheon at the covered lodge at noon and be there. He would be introduced to his new assignment at that time, and yes, Sara was welcome, as was Dr. Washington and her son Shawn.

At the appointed time Caleb and Sara ambled down to the covered lodge. There were approximately twenty people assembled. Sara walked over to Jawane and sat at the end of the table adjacent to him and as youth always seem to find a way, they were deep in discussion of music and artist, not a necessarily easy subject for Jawane;

for the moment no one else was there but themselves.

Caleb surveyed the scene with the eyes of an experienced investigator. Emily, her husband Warren were seated at the end of the table. Across from Warren sat a large reddish blonde haired man with a strong muscular build. He had several braids in his hair and what appeared to be starfish entwined with small shells that were space evenly down the side of his head. What a strange combination. He was wearing a tunic which was open at the front exposing his large muscular chest.

Next to him sat a beautiful woman with flaming red hair. She also had star fish entwined in her hair which disappeared behind and down her back. She too was wearing a tunic and it was open at the breast exposing ample cleavage of well-endowed breast. He looked up to her face and saw her smiling at him. His face reddened.

Muskula, leaned over to her mate and chittered quietly into his ear. He then looked at Caleb and he too smiled. Muskula thought, "Strange species".

Caleb then felt like someone was intently studying him. He looked toward the other end and across the table and noticed a small petite woman with an angular face and fined stringed hair watching him. She was dressed like Emily and had a low cut blouse with puffy sleeves. Her hair was extremely fine and was up in a ponytail behind her head. He smiled and nodded his head in a polite fashion of acknowledgement. She continued to stare and did not seem to have the courtesy to look away.

"Strange woman," Thought Caleb; "I wonder what she adds to Emily Smith's work group?"

ASSIMILATION

Selena Washington came into the room with her young son Shawn and sat next to him, and Selena said, "Wow, I slept better than I have in years; how about you?"

A party of eight came into the room. They were obviously military, they all had side arms. Of the eight, four were woman and they had long tunics with some sort of automatic weapons underneath mostly hidden.

To Selena, Caleb said, "This must be the security detail that Sara had spotted". He did not miss the smiles and small nods of their heads directed to Sara.

Sara smiled back in acknowledgement and said, "Hey".

Emily stood up and walked to a chalk board on the wall in front of the table. She wrote Caleb, Sara, Selena, and Shawn on the board.

"I would like to welcome each of you to our work group. We are just a very small cog in a very large wheel. How large the wheel is, would boggle your mind. Each of you will play a small part in insuring the successful completion of our mission; Even you Shawn. Even though you are only six you can help by being the long ranger of our group and keep us posted on the weather. Would you like to do that, Shawn? Help us keep a current weather report?"

Shawn looked up at the beautiful smiling woman. Then looking to his Mom he said, "If Momma says I can then I would like too."

Selena squeezed her son by the hand and replied, "That would be good Shawn".

Emily continued, "We are so fortunate to have the world's most distinguished scientist in the field of extremophile life forms. Dr. Selena Washington wrote all the text books on bio chemical synthesis used in universities all over the world. She is also the first to discover life forms in soil samples returned from Mars. We thank you for joining our group and we are sure that your skills will be useful to our endeavor. And, there is no doubt in my mind that you will enjoy working with your new colleagues. You and Breveka are somewhat similar in that you both study life forms but from a slightly different perspective from your average academic. I hope you can work and collaborate closely together. " Both woman smiled knowingly to one another.

Jawane reached over and taking Sara's hand and said, "Sara, I do not have many friends here. I hope we can continue to be friends even after you learn more about me today. I hope you can accept me as I am. I believe you are a very intelligent girl. And, I know you are a thoughtful…person," almost saying human.

Sara looked at Jawane carefully and studied his face. His facial structures were slightly angular, like the woman Breveka that seem to stare at her Father with no facial expressions. Their hair was fine stranded. She then looked at Hanlee and Persha. Both of them were smiling at her. They had all been reading Sara's mind and knew that soon she was going to make the intuitive leap of revelation.

Hanlee said, "Sara, you are one of the most intuitive and observant person we know. That is a good skill and

ASSIMILATION

I imagine it is required to be a good gymnast, your situational awareness as to your position in relation to the parallel bars has heightened your observational skills."

"For instance, you have observed that our facial structures are slightly different from yours. Not by much, but different just the same. It is the same observation that you made about our fine strand hair. As for Jawane, you have been intrigued and focused on Jawane's speech pattern and discerned they are different in context and pattern than your own. That is good."

Sara, not knowing what to say, said, "Thank you, I guess."

Unknown to the young people Emily had been listening in on their conversation and realized it would not be long before Sara's intuitive skills would make a leap to understanding that things were not as they seemed.

As she observed the new members of her work group she received a satisfied feeling of completeness. She knew she had made the right decisions about adding new members. In all probability they would not be the last.

"Wow, this was going to be fun", thought Emily.

Looking at Caleb and Sara, Emily smiled and said, "Caleb and Sara, we would like to welcome you to our workgroup. Caleb, you too bring skills that will benefit the overall project. Your extensive resume says you are a sales specialist of high tech machine tooling. We definitely need technical people here."

Sara, looking down at the table snickered, "Yea, sales, right. I wonder how Emily could have got that wrong."

The Andrian children enjoyed watching Sara. It was

strange to them that Caleb, being the expert that he was, did not have the slightest clue that his daughter was well aware that her Father was in some kind of security work and it had nothing to do with sales.

Emily continued, "Caleb, as I partially explained earlier, we do research and development work on advanced flight systems. We also have a group of specialist that is developing underwater weapons systems. We fly experimental aircraft in and out of the area. We conduct weapons test above and below the oceans. Consequently, because of these activities, that are highly secretive, we find it necessary to provide disinformation as to our true nature.

This is necessary because from time to time some of the locals have reported seeing something that, due to a lack of understanding of our developmental systems, has misinterpreted what they have seen. This is where your expertise will be utilized.

Smiling, Emily said, "For instance, there have been reports in the area of strange lights in the sky. Someone has even claimed to have seen a UFO. Now this is detrimental to our program."

Sara, having been busy doodling on a piece of paper in front of her, looked up in surprise at the mention of a UFO, and with wide eyes, looked at the three Andrian children. All three were smiling at her. Her mouth dropped open at disbelief at the nagging revelation that had flooded her conscious flow of thought! Impossible! Jawane slightly raised his hand and waved.

Focusing on Emily's continued presentation Sara

ASSIMILATION

dropped her pencil. Emily looked at Sara and smiled, then continued on. As for Caleb, he had a wide grin on his face and he was thinking, "What a piece of cake this assignment was going to be. How could he have been so lucky to land such a non-threatening job?"

"Now Caleb, another major issue we have is the persistent rumors of the presence of mermaids in the bay where we conduct our underwater research. We need something to deflect attention away from the bay."

Caleb's grin grew even wider if that was possible. He could hardly contain himself. "Yes! I am blessed! What a magnificent job!"

Upon hearing about mermaids, Sara's head turned from the three young children to the two large adults at the other end of the table. She looked at them closely, again taking note of the starfish ornaments in their hair. Initially Sara had thought of the starfish as a novelty but now she did not believe that they were just a five and dime replica. The woman and the man both had their hands on the table in front of them with their fingers curled up inside; "Not unusual in and of itself, however upon closer examination they do seemed inordinately large."

"Is it truly possible that they could be mermaids? Why not, the three young people were evidently aliens." Sara looked at her Father. He was grinning like a he found a brand new bike. He did not have a clue. Sara looked at Emily. Emily winked at her and said, "Good spot Sara."

Laughing, Emily clapped her hands several times; "Ha, ha, ha. How could that possibly be?" No telling what these locals will claim to see next! Of course there is another part of the problem which I will fill you in later."

Caleb was wracked with a large belly laugh. "Boy, life was good," thought Caleb.

Still laughing, Caleb said, "What am I supposed to do, go hunt aliens?"

"No Caleb. Your job is to provide cover and plausible deniability. You are to come up with scientific explanations as to why the lights are not UFO,s and the things they see in the water are not mermaids.

Caleb sat there grinning digesting what Emily had said.

"Why dispel rumors like that when it already is the perfect cover story? There are always UFO nuts around that will pick up the story and cover your operations. I mean how simple can it possibly be?"

Sara looked at her Dad. He was so down to earth. He never had time to look up and wonder what beautiful secrets might be in the canopy of stars. His life was here. His survival was here.

"Caleb, come her a minute. Come stand next to me."

Emily looked at the man standing by the door wearing a long tunic and carrying some kind of long weapon under his tunic. Emily, speaking telepathically said, "Borack, come forward."

Borack stepped forward with military precision standing at attention in front of Emily and Caleb.

"Caleb, I would like for you to meet Lt. Borack. Lt. Borack is the Andrian commander for my security detail. Lt. Borack is from the planet Andria, three galaxies from

ASSIMILATION

the planet earth, the Lower Megellanic Cloud, about one hundred and eighty thousand light years from earth."

Caleb saw Emily look at the strange woman that was staring at him earlier. Without saying anything she too got up from her chair and stood in front of Caleb.

"Caleb, I would like you to meet Breveka. She is the Species Analyst for her intergalactic fleet. She and Dr. Washington will be working closely together to...help resolve issues."

Sara sat raptly at attention enthralled in the proceedings. She could see her Father had not yet accepted the idea of aliens and believed Emily was giving him some kind of test. "Poor Dad, he really was a down to earth kind of guy."

Sara observed Persha, Hanlee and Jawane get up and go stand in front of her Dad.

Persha extended her hand and said, "Hello Mr. Sears. You know my name is Persha. And yes, I am from the planet Andria, three galaxies from your planet earth. However, I have never seen it as I have lived my entire life aboard one of our intergalactic cruisers."

Caleb took her proffered hand and felt her long slim fingers. Looking into her eyes he saw only peace and the crinkling of amusement at the corners of her eye lids.

Hanlee then said, "Hello Mr. Sears. We had a nice discussion yesterday in the car about Saturn's moon, Titan. The ice cover is five miles thick. I know because I have been there." Hanlee moved over to make room for Jawane.

"Mr. Sears, as I have said, Sara has excellent muscle

tone largely due to your leadership in developing healthy eating habits. She also has remarkable observational skills."

Caleb turned to Emily and said, "Okay, you win, jokes on me. Ha Ha; Now bring on the mermaids!"

Emily looked at the large couple at the end of the table and they got up and came forward. They too stood in front of Caleb. Looking at their clothing, he noted that the lower garments were skin tight and had a sheen glistening in the light. Both of their tops were no more than vest, exposing the woman's large breast curvature and the man's incredible pectoral muscles. When the man reached out to shake his hand, he uncurled webbed fingers eight inches long with serrated under linings.

Caleb just stared. He was in shock. He took a step back. He felt Sara's arm around his waist and her hand on his bicep.

"Dad, is this not the coolest thing ever! Thank you so much for bringing me her, we are safe here." Sara knew her Father's only concern was for her safety.

Emily, seeing the depth of shock induced by the revelation of aliens and mermaids said, "Caleb, be at peace. Peace is good."

"Yes," Caleb said. "Peace is good."

CHAPTER 27
MERMAIDS

Caleb awoke in the evening about sundown. The last of the evening light was reflected from over the horizon against the cloud layer and then onto the lake. Emily liked to call it a lake but it was really an ocean inlet with many small islands interspersed among hooks and fingers of land that added to the seclusion of the immediate area. After showering and putting on his running clothes he headed downstairs and looked for Sara. She was not in. He really needed to think about all the mind boggling information he had received. He had actually gone into shock. For the first time in his life he was afraid.

He found a note on the counter. "Dear Dad, I am out with my new friends. Call me if you need me. Love, Sara."

"New friends", thought Caleb; "what a strange lot. At least I do not have a headache any more. I wonder how Emily does the things like telling me to be at peace and I am; or how about that mind reading thing she does? I wonder if she is alien herself or maybe a hybrid or something."

Caleb ran out the door and down a back road to the back of the property. He believed a cross country run would help clear his head and he desperately needed a clear head. A full moon was coming over the horizon making it easier to find ones way. Night was his favorite alone time. It was the time when he could think of Sara's Mom and all the fun times they had together. It was only a few short years but they were generous with joy and happiness.

"What have I gotten myself into? More to the point, what have I gotten Sara into? What did I miss? I knew that whoever Emily Smith was, she was connected to work that had to be extremely covert or I would not have been blocked at every level. The true warning bell, which I ignored, was when I received a hit on my personal com unit indicating I was being monitored by Space Intelligence. I figured it had to be in error. I never even considered it had anything to do with Emily Smith. But mercy, who would have ever believed it was about aliens and mermaids?"

Caleb continued running blindly thru the paths and woods on the property for about an hour. He was unaware where he was, and finally winded, slowed to a walk. Caleb heard a light squealing sound coming from the other side of trees. Walking slowly and quietly thru the bushes he peered into the clearing. The moon fully lit the area and he saw a wide sandy beach with a gentle slope to the ocean cove.

Seated on the ground were several young people arranged in a semicircle facing the water. Then he heard Sara's voice. She was telling Jawane to ask one of the other young people what it was like to just swim and breathe under water.

Jawane turned and sat quietly looking at one of the other young people. Several of the young people began

ASSIMILATION

"talking" among themselves. They made sounds like porpoise that he had seen at different sea parks.

Jawane shook his head no.

There was more squealing sounds, this time louder and more forceful.

Jawane stood up and turning to Sara said, "Come Sara. We must go now."

"Why? What is the matter? I just wanted to know what it was like to swim under water; why would they be angry about that."

"Really Sara, it is time to go now, we have been here long enough."

Jawane reached for Sara's hand and pulled her to her feet and began walking away. The other young people ran to the water and disappeared under the surface.

"I do not understand."

Jawane replied, "It was not your question. We have been visiting with them for over an hour. They wanted me to tell you other things that I am not allowed to speak of. You are aware that you are not to speak to others about our and their presence? Well there are other things that we are not to speak of to you. You have only just arrived. Emily may choose to tell you more or she may not. She is the greater, we are the lesser. There have been too many losses. Too much depends on adhering to the rules. I am sure that in due time you will know everything."

Caleb followed at a distance and did not make his presence known. After about a mile they came to a clearing with several buildings and vehicles. They got into a truck and Jawane drove away.

"I suppose an alien can learn to drive a truck. He is highly intelligent. I hope they come with common sense."

Caleb arrived at the compound an hour later. He went straight to their apartment to check on Sara. She was sitting at the table eating a sandwich with chips. She had another plate set out with a sandwich for him. She always did. A lot of the time he did not come home till late but she prepared it anyway.

"Hi, Dad, been out for a run, huh. Is it not just really cool here? Everything is just so exciting! Jawane says he will start teaching me something they call spherical mathematics. Warren's two brothers have already learned several theorems. He said very few humans, he calls us humans, can master it. I think it will be fun to prove I can. Do you think I can Dad? You know math is not one of my favorite subjects."

"Of course you can Sara, you do anything you put your mind too. It may not be a piece of cake but in time you will get the hang of it. Oh, and thank you for the sandwich. What did you do tonight?"

Sara did not look up but continued looking down and munching on her sandwich. Finally she said, "You boob. You know where I was and who I was with. I can only assume that you came upon us by accident while you were out on your run, surly you would not be spying on me; you never have before."

Caleb was taken aback. "How did you know I was there? You are right. I was out running and when I stopped to rest I heard the noise the mermaids make and crept upon the clearing to see what it was. I did not know

ASSIMILATION

you were there until I heard you ask Jawane to ask the mermaids how it felt to breathe under water. It did get interesting after that."

"Yea Dad, that was really sort of weird. I wonder what they wanted to tell me but Jawane refused to do so. I know we can never mention them or the mermaids, but when he said there were things that we were not supposed to be told, well, that sort of made me uneasy."

"Oh, and by the way boob, you stepped on two twigs so I knew someone was there. Later, I saw a silhouette next to a tree that exactly matched your height and your weight." Laughing, Sara said, "I hope you were a better salesman than a secret agent, Dad!"

Caleb laughed and walked over and gave his daughter a hug. "You are so amazing and also full of yourself! Do not get over confident now that you have new friends. I will talk to Emily tomorrow and see what she may or may not tell me. Evidently, our new friends have all the confidence in the world in her so that should tell us something."

What Caleb did not tell Sara was that he already knew that this was a dangerous assignment. Whither they lived or died depended on the effectiveness of the alliance and how well they each performed their part. His daughter was going to have to grow up faster than he wanted. Well he had tried his best to train her to use her head; evidently he had done a good job, had it not been for her interest they would still be back in the big city.

CHAPTER 28
SAUCER INTRODUCTION

All the young people were sitting in Emily's kitchen munching on the ever present cookies that Emily baked daily. Warren had gone to work; Emily and Caleb had gone to the hanger. Emily wanted to show Caleb the saucer craft and take him aboard her personal saucer. She planned on later in the day to give everyone a short excursion in the saucer. She had not been out and about since she had returned the mermaid group six weeks earlier.

As they were in her saucer she could feel his uneasiness; and why not? She had removed him from his comfortable and familiar world of hunting terrorist to protecting aliens.

"I know how shocking for you this must be Caleb and I do understand your concern for Sara. I know when Blain took me to the saucer and then the intergalactic space craft, I was in shock. However, I was well aware of how fortunate I was to see things that few others of our kind have seen. I felt like I fell down the proverbial rabbit hole. Do not worry, you are not alone."

"We have Special Forces with Space Intelligence training with the Andrians on their craft. We also have Andrian military, medical and scientific personnel working with us in an effort to learn more about a very nasty,

ASSIMILATION

common enemy. That is primarily why Dr. Washington was recruited."

"The Andrians have been an intergalactic star faring species before we climbed out of the trees. Their knowledge of the universe is limitless. Yet, with all that knowledge and experience, they have come upon a deadly entity which has never before been encountered in their histories. Our job is to destroy it. If we cannot destroy it then we must send it back to where it came from."

"The mermaids are an interesting and separate group. Their whole world was destroyed along with millions of their species. The interesting thing about their species is that somewhere, somehow, in the distant past they turned up on the planet earth. The Andrians have never encountered them in their travels and they have traveled across numerous galaxies. Yet, here on earth they are pictured in art, stories, and folklore, especially among our early seafaring forefathers. So how did they get here and how did they get to where they went when they left earth?"

Caleb asked, "Well where did they come from? Who destroyed them on their planet? How did they get here?"

"Now here is another interesting revelation Caleb, they were found in a very distant galaxy; actually, we believe, in a different universe."

You see Caleb, this space craft you are on is not just a mechanical flying wonder. It is a combination of a living organism and mechanical device. It was created by probably one of the most intelligent Andrians ever. She is classified as the fleet geneticist and is one of the most powerful individuals in the three ship fleet. She is the one individual that determines who lives and who dies in the fleet of twenty seven thousand souls.

Three years ago, the fate of the human race on the earth hung in the balance. There were factions within the fleet that wanted to wipe us from the earth and take over the earth themselves. There accusation that we were destroying the earth and cared nothing for it was correct.

Within five hundred years, our earth will look like Mars is today should we not take immediate steps to alleviate the destruction of our environment. Warren is working on environmental issues. He is one of the most intelligent men on the earth. His father is on an intergalactic carrier working with Andrian scientist in developing new weapons to defeat our common enemy. Our enemy is not from our dimension. They are currently several hundred thousand light years away."

"And, as I said earlier, this saucer craft is not an ordinary saucer. It has a biological entity within that communicates with me when I am present. I believe it is a female entity. It is also self-aware, learns at an incredible rate and currently has more knowledge of the molecular makeup of the cosmos than the entire Andrian Species."

"I have recently learned that I am a human-alien hybrid. When, where, and how that happened is not known to me. The Andrians say they are not responsible. There is an increase of intelligence worldwide. We do not know what is ausing this phenomenon. It appears that at present the increase in intelligence is sporadic but it is happening.

ASSIMILATION

This evening after dinner, we are all going to take a ride on this saucer craft. I have never taken Skip and Billy and they have patiently bided their time. Since we are all together now as a work group we might as well provide an introduction as to what exactly we are capable of, at least in regard to interplanetary travel. This craft is capable of much more than that, as is the other ten craft which is piloted by the ten Human-Andrian Hybrids.

Caleb could only swallow. He was at a loss for words. "Has it actually only been two days since he came home from his last trip? Oh Sara, I think I may have raised a little monster!"

Emily smiled at Caleb as she could read Caleb's mind. "It is ok Caleb. Sara is exactly the kind of free thinking individual we need right now. We as a species are not near as advanced with our mental capabilities as the Andrians. They have focused almost entirely on mathematics and science. It was and is necessary for their survival. However, our intelligence works a little bit different than theirs and together we make a good team. Not only that, but neither they nor us will be able to make an evolutionary jump in our species progression without one another."

As they were leaving the saucer Caleb ask, "When you retrieved the mermaids, how long were you gone, how far did you go, and most importantly, how did you know they were in trouble."

Emily considered her response carefully. "Caleb I will answer your last question first. I was awakened from my sleep by the entity within the machine calling to me.

The "calling", if one can classify it as such, was urgent and the Entity wanted me to come to the machine immediately, which I did. I gathered my security detail of six marines and after we positioned ourselves the Entity took off immediately."

I know we went thru a worm hole and I think into a different universe. We came upon the water world where we saw what we believed to be people fighting for their lives. The enemy that they were fighting was the same type of life form that Blain and I found on Saturn's moon, Iapetus. We had found an ancient artifact there and the alien life form was inside the artifact and was wearing a space suit. We believe that the artifact was almost ageless, up to a million years old. We have since come to believe the artifact came from a different universe as not a single star chart could be identified by the Andrians.

"What I would like for you to do Caleb is to spend the rest of the afternoon in the military offices viewing the history videos that are available to you so you will be completely briefed as to where we are up to at this point in time. Make sure you read all the information regarding sightings so you can begin to figure out cover stories. I bet Sara would like to help you with that."

Caleb and Emily parted ways and Emily returned to the house. The young people were still in the kitchen, this time they were munching on sandwiches that Skip had made.

Sara was saying that if they had their sail boat here they could go sailing. Persha, Jawane, and Hanlee were not as excited as Sara but they did express a mild interest.

ASSIMILATION

For them it would be one more earthly experience which in all probability they would not ever have again once they returned home to their intergalactic carrier.

Emily piped in and said, "Hey! That would be fun. I have not been sailing in years. We used to go as a family all the time. My Dad was an excellent sailor. I sold the boat after they passed away. I think I will buy another one and have it delivered. It could be here in less than a week. What do you think Skip, Billy? You want to take the others sailing if I get a boat? Warren told me you all use to do a lot of sailing.

"That would be great Emily, but I only sailed a skiff. We would need at least a thirty-two footer for everyone to go at once, and then there is also the issue of security that is necessary for our new friends. I am not so sure I could handle a large boat."

"Good point," said Emily.

"I will get us a forty two footer and two small skiffs for training. I will also contact Admiral Cleary and tell him our plans. I am sure he can find us a certified captain that would love to sail us around.

"Oh, and by the way, we are going to take a spin in the saucer this afternoon. Persha, Jawane, and Hanlee can fill you in on what to expect and procedures for flight preparation."

"Skip, you and Billy have been patient and I appreciate that you have held your peace. Sara you will not have to wait as long as they to experience a ride of a life time!"

CHAPTER 29
CHILDRENS DELIGHT

Emily had informed her security detail of her intention to take the saucer out with her family and friends. It was something she had never done as she did not believe in frivolous use of resources. However, she decided that it was time that Warren had the opportunity to see some of the things she had been privileged to see.

Dr. Washington and her son Shawn were just as excited as the rest of the young people. As the group approached the saucer Hanlee took Shawn's hand and said, "You do not need to be afraid of flying in this saucer Shawn; I have ridden in saucers several times and it is really a lot of fun." Hanlee thought for a moment and grinned at herself for her use of the term "fun". "Really, have I changed that much already!"

Persha was holding both Skips and Billy's hands as they entered the saucer. She was able to read their minds and they were excited for the adventure but beneath the excitement they were terrified. She placed Skip on one side of her and Billy on the other. When she took her position in the middle and released their hands she said, "Be at peace, all is well." She sensed an immediate relaxing in their minds as the anxiety ebbed away.

"Wow! That was really cool. It worked on both of them at the same time. My powers must be getting stronger,"

ASSIMILATION

thought Persha.

Sara was escorted into the saucer by Jawane. Sara looked around in awe as she observed the many receptacles which held an individual. She could not see around the other side of the saucer. There must have been positions for at least fifty people, and that was only on the first deck.

Jawane escorted Sara to the lift and went to the second deck. There were just as many receptacles on the second deck as the first. Smiling he placed her into the receptacle and pushed her gently about a foot to the back of unit. She had already been told what to expect so she was not surprised when a device came down inserted itself into her mouth. As the glass door descended and enclosed Sara, Jawane then took his position next to her.

Caleb and Dr. Selena Washington took their places next to one another. Caleb was terrified. One did not have to be an alien with super powers to realize that it was all Caleb could do to hold it together.

Selena said, "Remember Caleb, these people have been traveling in space before our ancestors climbed out of their first tree. I am sure there technology is fool proof, even for humans." As she said the part about humans she looked to her side and saw Jawane smiling at her.

Muskula and her mate entered the saucer next being escorted by Emily with Warren lagging behind. This time Emily pointed to their positions and Muskula placed her man into the receptacle as Emily had done the first time and issuing a few piercing whistles and clicks as she took up her position next to him.

Emily took Warren by the hand and said, "You will be directly behind me husband. Have no fear. You will be fine. I will become immersed with the entity within this saucer and will see and hear nothing except what the entity sees and hears."

Several military escorts entered the saucer and took up positions around the area. There were still many empty receptacles.

Emily took her position in a seat about four feet lower than those above her. As she did so a black shroud lifted out of the back of the chair and slid over her head. The shroud then formed tightly around head and a soft blue hue emanated from Emily's form in the control seat.

There was a slight shaking and low rumbling and soon the walls of the saucer turned opaque; all of the guest in the saucer let out a gasp as the tops of the trees became visible, then the surrounding tree covered mountain side. The mountains quickly gave way to a pinpoint as the saucer rapidly gained altitude. Soon the Earth was a small ball in space surrounded by the blackness that could not be duplicated anywhere on the planet.

The saucer rotated slowly and the moon came into view. It too was a round white ball sitting in velvety blackness except this time the myriads of stars were visible as diamonds steadily pierced the blackness like beacons in faraway oceans.

The saucer shuddered and the opaque view disappeared and the walls of the saucer materialized. Several minutes passed then again the saucer shuddered. When the wall turned opaque the second time, the red planet

ASSIMILATION

of mars hung in the blackness of space. Somehow, a telescoping effect allowed them to see the mars manned outpost and vehicles could be seen moving about the area.

The saucer shuddered again. Several minutes later the opaque walls reappeared and the planet Saturn with its many rings appeared magnificent with the sun backlighting the planet and the rings. The saucer moved directly over the north pole of Saturn and the amazing hexagon pattern of clouds swirled around the corners at four hundred miles per hour. To this day the structural patter of the hexagon remains a mystery, even to the Andrians.

After two more hours of touring the moons of Saturn and Jupiter the saucer returned to earth. As everyone got off the saucer there was a silence that was uncommon for humans. The experience for them was sacred.

Warren looked for Emily but did not see her exit the craft. He knew he could not ever think of her again as just his wife. She was an integral part of the effort in saving earth from an alien entity just as he was a major force in saving earth from destruction by abuse of resources.

Emily sat quietly in the space craft. The Entity had told her to remain until everyone had left as she had information for her. Perplexed, Emily remained silent.

The Entity spoke softly, "My beloved, you are about to be with child. The child will be a boy."

"What!" Exclaimed Emily? That is not possible! How do you know that I am going to have a baby?"

The Entity replied, "I have felt his spirit, soon you will be with child."

Emily exited the craft elated and scared. How could

the entity know that she was going to have a baby when she was not even pregnant?

Warren came up beside Emily and took her hand and said, "Thank you Emily for the most marvelous ride of my life. I had no idea just how much you are an integral part of the saucer. It seemed like you became one with the Entity. You were actually glowing a pale blue."

Still in shock she looked at Warren and said, "I am glad you enjoyed the ride. I never get tired of flying one of the machines. I am lucky that I got the first smart one."

Linking her arm in Warrens elbow and resting her head on his shoulder Emily said, "Take me home Warren, I am exhausted."

Warren replied, "I take it you are not going to tell me what the Entity said."

"The Entity told me we were going to have a baby boy because she felt his spirit. But we both know that is not possible because I am using the most efficient contraceptive available and I am not pregnant, I just had my period."

Warren had never thought of the possibility of having children because the times just were not right. There was too much work to do and he did not relish bringing children into the world at this time.

That evening Warren and Emily shared pleasures. What the Entity had told her did not enter her mind.

Emily was awoken by the chimes which were to be used only in case of emergency. Pulling on jeans and sweatshirt Emily hurried down the stairs.

Officer Taaker, Caleb's new partner, was standing on

ASSIMILATION

the porch. His uniform was covered in blood. He quickly saluted with a bloody hand.

"Sir, Muskula and her mate were attacked about five nautical miles off the beach. Muskula has been shot several times and has lost a lot of blood. Her mate boarded the fishing trawler and killed two of the five attackers. He was able to bring her in, however, in my opinion, the medical facilities here are not adequate to save her life. She should be immediately transported to the intergalactic carrier for Flata to heal her. She may even die in route.

Emily listened and felt her anger growing at the stupid rednecks who had nothing better to do than get drunk and harass other citizens. She would have Caleb and Taaker deal with them.

Emily replied, "Prepare Muskula for transport, we will leave within one half hour."

Emily saluted Taaker and dismissed him. Taaker ran from the porch talking into his radio relaying the orders that Emily had given.

CHAPTER 30
LATE NIGHT CALL

Caleb had trouble going to sleep as he relived the recent trip to Mars, Jupiter, Saturn and several of their moons. The tour lasted ten hours. He was literally unable to assess his emotions as they ranged the scale from terror to awe. His hands on investigative skills that led to taking down terrorist did not leave him any room to consider any thoughts that was useless fantasy. When he did fall asleep it was an exhausted slumber which was mercifully without dreams.

Caleb could usually be awakened by a small sound in the night that may or may not be out of place. As he lay there he could hear the incessant ringing of the phone but he could not bring himself to answer the phone. Soon he could hear someone repeatedly calling to him.

"Dad! Dad! Wake up! Emily needs you now. Something has happened to Muskula!"

Caleb finely lurched into consciousness and he saw Sara standing above him with tears streaming down her face. She was holding the phone out to him.

Caleb finally regained his senses and reached for the phone.

"Yes Emily, what is it!"

"Muskula has been shot by some redneck fisherman and her mate killed two of five fishermen. I think the

ASSIMILATION

only way to save her life is to take her to the Intergalactic Carrier. You need to take care of things here. Find those fishermen and bring them in. Take Officer Taaker with you. He is the Andrian officer which is your counterpart. I have been amiss in not introducing you to him earlier. I failed to anticipate such a grave event this quickly.

The shooting happened about one hour ago. They were five nautical miles out when they encountered the boat. It looks like they were targeted. And Caleb, I want Sara with me to accompany Muskula to the Carrier. I promise you she will be fine."

"I will be at the office in ten minutes. I will bring Sara with me. Should she wear anything in particular?"

"Jeans and shirt will be fine. She will be furnished with a uniform upon arrival."

After getting off of the phone Caleb looked at Sara and said, "Get dressed, put your jeans and sweatshirt on, you will be accompanying Emily and Muskula to the intergalactic carrier. Emily assured me you will be safe. Evidently if they want to save Muskula's life they need to take her to where they have the most advanced medical systems."

Sara ran to her room and dressed as quickly as possible. She did not allow herself to think, she did not allow herself to be excited, she just found herself in a new mental state of focused attention like she had never experienced. Before leaving her room Sara retrieved her starfish necklace and sea horse hair braid that Muskula had given her. Putting the necklace over her head and braid in her hair she ran outside where her father was waiting.

They quickly ran to Emily's house which was a short distance away.

Upon arrival they were met by Persha, Hanlee, and Jawane. Emily, Caleb and the children went to the newly installed cellar and tunnel system that led to the hanger.

The gravitating lift quickly arrived at the hanger and Emily took Sara inside the military section and the Andrian children waited outside. Once they were alone, Emily stopped and turned to Sara.

"Sara, are you willing to take an oath of secrecy and obedience to the Space Intelligence agency? Your Father already has. You are being exposed to more than I planned on when I brought you and your Father into our circle. I believe it may be necessary to have someone that loves Muskula as you do to help her survive and to protect her. We cannot bring her husband because he is the defacto leader of the Star Kingdom and he will not leave. He has entrusted his wife to our care and specifically requested that you accompany Muskula to the Intergalactic Carrier, not that he understands what that is or what that entails."

Sara stood there open mouthed in surprise. "Do you mean like, I will be in the Space Intelligence Agency?"

"Yes. You will be enlisted and classified as a Personal Defender because of your advance self-defense skills. If you choose to accept this responsibility I will swear you in and you will be given the rank of Protector First Class. You have already proven yourself under the stress of battle. The only thing you will need is protocol training." Emily smiled and said, "The pay is good too!"

"Wow! How exciting! Yes I will be glad to enlist. Am

ASSIMILATION

I not a little young for the Military or Space Intelligence?"

"Yes, you are young. I am sure Admiral Cleary will blow a military gasket over the enlistment of one young as you. However, The President has given me full autonomy over my section and I live or die by my decisions, you can have my back at any time. Personally, I feel pretty safe with my decision to make you a personal protector. However, you do need firearms training."

Emily took a Bible up from the table and had Sara place her left hand on the Bible and raise her right arm to the square. Emily recited the oath from memory and Sara solemnly repeated the oath.

"Congratulations Sara, you are now a sworn member of the Space Intelligence Agency."

Emily went to a locker and removed a new black Space Intelligence Command uniform sheathed in plastic and gave it to Sara. Put it on quickly and meet me outside soldier!" Emily saluted her and smartly did an about face and left the room.

Sara wanted to savor the moment of excitement to have achieved such a position but she knew her new friend and assignment, Muskula, was going to die if she did not act quickly.

Sara removed the plastic sheathing covering the uniform which consisted of a long sleeve shirt and slacks with various Space Intelligence Command insignias on the sleeves; then she noticed the name, S. Sears, in small print above the right breast pocket. That took her breath away with emotions of pride and joy. Sara quickly donned on her newly acquired uniform and placed her regular clothes in the locker. It was at that time she noticed her name, S. SEARS, stenciled on the outside of the locker door.

When Sara stepped outside the office she saw the three Andrian children standing at attention and saluting her. All three were smiling and said in unison, "Congratulations Personal Protector First Class Sears!"

Sara laughed returning the salute and went to them and gave each of them a hug. Together they walked to the Saucer Craft and observed Muskula being loaded into the saucer in a gel and carbon dioxide enclosed capsule.

Jawane said, "Sara, when you get to the Intergalactic Carrier, do not be dismayed if many of the crew dismisses you as being dumb, stupid and totally ignorant, especially the very young, because after all, you are only human. We were all the same way and believed the exact same things until we met Emily."

Hanlee said, "It is not so much that you are perceived as not being very intelligent because in your own way, you are. Our measure of intelligence and worth has been developed out of necessity thru generations of space travel. In order to survive we have had to focus one hundred percent on science and mathematics."

Persha added, "The mathematical equations we showed you and which you could not comprehend no matter how hard you tried, well, a young Andrian child is required to master them by the age of six. We know that Skip and Billy are well on their way to comprehending Spherical Mathematics but that is because Emily has secretly been helping them in their math for years and they did not know it. Not only that, but after Emily

ASSIMILATION

returned from the Intergalactic carrier, she taught them the four basic equations. It took them every bit of a year to begin to comprehend them and they are highly skilled in math."

"We have all since learned that in order to live on the planet one must have a wider skill set to survive. And also there are so many people just about anyone can choose and do whatever they want to do. To us, that is totally alien."

At the mention of "alien", all three children put their hands beside their heads with finger extended and running a circle they said, "Duh, we are from the planet earth, take us to you leader" They then laughed heartily and gave each other a hug.

Emily observing their behavior felt her heart warm because she knew that now the children had joy in their heart and lives, hopefully they could retain that love thru the years to come.

"It is time to go Sara", said Emily.

Sara responded with a smart salute and said, "Yes Sir!"

Caleb came out of the office just in time to see Sara walk up the ramp to the saucer. He was surprised to see Sara dressed in the Space Intelligence Uniform. He then remembered Emily telling him she would be provided with a uniform, he just did not think much of it at the time.

Calling to her, Caleb said, "Ears out and eyes sharp! I love you. I will see you soon!"

Sara turned and threw her Father a kiss. "I love you to Dad!"

CHAPTER 31
INTRODUCTION TO EMILY'S WORLD

Emily made sure that Sara was properly secure then took her seat in the control position. Muskula was next to Sara and was in an induced coma to help slow her metabolism and hopefully prolong her life long enough to get her to the intergalactic carrier where the chances of saving her were greater than on the earth. Also, approximately ten military personal positioned themselves about the saucer, those that passed in front of Sara smiled at her and gave her a salute.

Sara felt a shudder as the craft lifted from the hanger and flew into space. Since this was not a sightseeing tour there were not any stops along the way. Sara felt a feeling of wellbeing and a dreamy sleep come over her soon after liftoff. Unknown to her she was placed in a semi state of sleep to facilitate a trip that would take several hours.

The saucer arrived in the area of the Oort cloud and weaved its way around the numerous asteroids and planetoids. Sara became fully conscious as the saucer craft was shuddering and the walls became opaque bringing into view the Intergalactic carrier.

Sara's jaw dropped open as she observed the huge space craft grow even larger as they came closer. She

ASSIMILATION

saw a hanger door open in iris fashion and observed the bright lighting exposing numerous saucer craft suspended at various levels and connected with umbilical passageways going into the interior of the ship. Their saucer entered the hanger and after viewing other saucer craft she did not believe their saucer was as big as she previously believed.

Emily took Sara's hand as they walked off the saucer and into the umbilical cord. As they approached the ship's hatch, Emily said, "Sara, we are going to have to be decontaminated. I have gone thru this before and it is nothing to be afraid of. The people you meet will be all business and they do not have a sense of humor. They do not do small talk, never smile, except of course those that know me. Also they can communicate telepathically, meaning they can read your mind. Therefore if you should find yourself in what you feel as an adversarial situation, just think of a brick wall. I am sure that in all probability that will not happen.

Just as they entered the Carrier, four men in environmental suits quickly exited the umbilical behind them moving the carrier containing Muskula. They disappeared around the corner of the passageway.

Sara said, "Thank you for including me Emily. You had so many more qualified personnel to choose from. I am so excited, this is so mind blowing!"

"I had you come with us because you are the closest Human to Muskula and for some reason she seems to have taken you under her wing, so to speak. You may make the difference when the slim margin of life tips in the scales balance of life or death."

Sara followed Emily thru passageways and thru several hatches. Finally they entered a large room that appeared to be a major chemistry lab. There were large vats of bubbling liquid and many cylinders similar to the ones on the saucer.

A lone woman was standing near some of the vats, she was wearing a one piece, pale pink flowing gown with a lavender sash about her waist. She was staring at Emily. They were apparently communicating.

Then to her surprise the woman looked at her and said, "Hello Sara, welcome to our home. My name is Flata. I am the geneticist for our group."

However, she heard it in her head and the woman's mouth did not move.

"Hello. Nice to meet you Flata, thank you for allowing me on you marvelous vessel! If it was not for Emily I would be totally freaked out! This is so cool!"

Flata extended her hand for a Human handshake; Sara, without thinking took her hand and upon looking down saw only three fingers and a thumb. Her eyes widened in surprise and she looked up at Flata, she was smiling at her.

Flata observed the surprised shock on Sara's face and read her mind as Sara suddenly remembered Hanlee and Jawane telling her they had added a finger to fit in on Earth. Flata knew she was not terrified, afraid a little maybe, but more excited about the prospects of a new adventure and at the revelation of the three fingers.

"Emily has told me of your exceptional skills and

ASSIMILATION

your emotional link to the amphibious humanoid. This should be very interesting as we have never encountered this specie before. She is currently being tended to by our medical staff. There are several projectiles in her that need to be removed."

"I do not know if Emily has told you or not but you will be required to be decontaminated before you go further into our vessel. It will take some time. If you wish to wait until we are able to determine that Muskula is out of danger that will be okay but you will be required to stay within the confines of the environmental hazard area of the medical center."

Sara looked at Emily for affirmation as she said she would wait until Muskula was out of danger.

Emily and Sara followed Flata thru several rooms containing more vats and some of them had what appeared to be fetuses in various stages of growth. By the time they reached the room containing Muskula in her own embryonic chamber Sara was almost traumatized.

Emily took Sara in her arms and holding her close said, "Be at peace Sara, all is well."

Sara relaxed and after a moment she said, "I never had a clue or realized how different the lives of Persha, Jawane, and Hanlee was from mine. I guess I had what Dad calls the Hollywood Syndrome. That is where we ignore our intuition and common sense, refusing to accept what we hear, and allow us to accept the fantasy version of life instead of what is right in front of us in broad daylight."

"Jawane tried to tell me several times that our

backgrounds are not even anywhere similar. I chose to ignore him and justify it by saying he is human, I am human, what could possibly be different? I heard him say that science and mathematics ruled their life and not once thought about how that would affect how one was raised or how that axiom would become the center of their lives.

Emily took Sara by the shoulders and looked her in the eyes. Emily knew exactly how Sara felt. When she had arrived it was like entering a new world order

"Sara when I was abducted about three years ago, I was terrified. I was taken by Blain. He abducted me because he wanted to save my life. There was a group of Andrians that revolted against the established order. They secretly kidnapped ten gifted children that were Human/Andrian hybrids and were developed to help the earth leadership in resolving destructive environmental issues. Should these issues not be resolved, the earth would become uninhabitable and look like the planet Mars within five hundred years. They wanted to destroy all Humans from the Earth and fortunately for Humankind and thus us, there were Andrians on these three intergalactic craft that wanted to save us."

"Currently there is a cadre of Humans and Andrians working on these issues. Warren is involved in this endeavor. The programs are supported and sustained by The President."

"However, enough history; when we return home you will need to view all the historical facts available in the library."

"When I first arrived I was not necessarily terrified.

ASSIMILATION

When Blain took me and I saw the saucer I was terrified. I fell backwards and lacerated my arm. Blain applied medication and explained it was for my protection I was being taken. My fears abated and reason took over and I basically knew there was nothing I could do so I resigned myself to whatever outcome may be, the circumstances were out of my control."

"So, my council to you is open your mind, learn as much as possible, enjoy the experience as we may never be this way again. Remember, every single thing they do is for their survival. They travel far and see many beautiful and amazing things and collect vast troves of knowledge. However, they pay an enormous price. They are not blessed with free agency as we are. So remember when you are slighted, looked down upon or feel uneasy, we are the true aliens to them."

Sara sniffed and wiped her eyes. Thinking to herself, "Emily is right. I am acting childish. I have always prided myself on being an adult. I need to be the very best representative for young adult Humans as possible. It is time for me to swallow my pride and apply myself one hundred percent to saving and protecting Muskula, whatever that may entail."

Emily could read Sara's thoughts and was at ease as she knew that Sara would carry her own weight. Muskula could not possibly have a better friend and protector.

Sara was standing by the receptacle containing Muskula. It was different from the one she was transported in on the saucer. This one was crawling with small nano bots that was removing damaged skin from inside the wound. The three projectiles had long since been removed and Muskula was stable.

Sara tried her best to send her thoughts to her but she did not have the telepathic gift. Muskula opened her eyes and smiled at Sara.

Sara smiled and mouthed, "I love you".

Muskula smiled back and tried to move her mouth the same way but had difficulty doing so. She raised her arm and placed a flat hand on the clear ceramic cover. Sara placed her hand in Muskula's and smiled. Tears ran down her cheeks. Muskula had been unconscious for four days and this was the first sign of life she had shown.

Flata watched the young human female Sara interact with the amphibious human. She had been observing her since her arrival and noted that Sara left Muskula's side only to relieve herself. She knew that when Sara was in decontamination she would enhance her telepathic skills and remedy any embryonic diseases, she liked this young human which to her was inexplicable. She did not "like" anyone. That was not ones duty.

Thinking to herself, "I must be contaminated with human emotions".

On the fifth day Emily told Sara that Flata advised that Muskula was going to live and it was time to be decontaminated. They both were to enter the decontamination area where Flata would begin the decontamination process.

Emily took Sara by the hand and they walked together into the room. Sara looked around at all the vats of bubbling chemicals with various colored hues.

ASSIMILATION

Emily said, "I know you like your new Space Intelligence Uniform but it is necessary that it be destroyed. You will be provided a new one when we leave. When we come out of decontamination you may wear a new one which will be manufactured by bots or you can wear their clothing, the choice is yours.

Flata entered the room and looked at Emily and Sara.

She said, "Emily it is good to have you back. Blain has talked incessantly about you; he cannot seem to help himself. I am afraid he is afflicted with the Human emotion you call love. We have never seen him act this way before. You will see him again after decontamination."

"Now, remove all your clothing and place them in the receptacle, they will be destroyed. However, Sara, your uniform will be replicated and you will receive the new one at the end of decontamination." She then motioned to the receptacle near the circles on the floor.

Sara watched Emily as she removed her clothing and decided it was not a time to be modest, did the same.

Flaca reading Sara's mind noted she had never been naked in front of anyone before as was the custom of some humans.

Emily smiled at her and said, "The Andrians have no issues what so ever about being nude, so just be comfortable as possible.

After removing their clothes and both woman were naked, Flata said, "Remove your jewelry for a separate decontamination. Sara, the starfish and seahorse are biological replicas of their true selves; we will have to submit them to a special process to preserve and decontaminate them so give them to me."

Sara did as she was told and removed the items and handed them to Flata. She picked up her uniform and threw them into the receptacle following Emily's lead. She watched in amazement as the uniform burst in a flash of light and observed the ashes disappear down the tube. Next she threw in her panties and bra, they too disappeared in a flash of light.

Emily and Sara took their position within the circle and watched the tube descend from above. The gaseous cloud ascended from the floor up to their necks.

Sara looked at Emily and said, "I love you"

Emily smiled and puckered her lips in a kiss.

The gas then began hardening into a jell locking them into place. The tube descended and inserted itself over the mouth and nose. They breathed one breath and was instantly asleep. The gas covered their head and solidified.

Because Muskula was a different species, she was placed in a similar container in a different area of the lab; She too, slept.

CHAPTER 32
DAMAGE CONTROL

Emily had introduced Caleb's counterpart, Officer Taaker, to Caleb prior to her leaving with Sara. He was a quiet fellow but intensely focused. It appeared that nothing missed his scrutiny, he also had modified his thinking of Humans from "stupid Humans", to "useful tool" Humans. In Taaker's evaluation of Caleb, he believed that Caleb was a useful tool but he did not under estimate Caleb's security skills.

In Caleb's evaluation of Taaker, he was totally at a loss. He did not have any scale of reference for "alien" abilities. The only reference he had was the Hollywood version of what aliens did or did not do. As for being his counterpart it immediately raised questions of who was in charge. Perhaps he was in charge on Earth and Taaker was in charge in space. Caleb did not want to think about that possibility.

Taaker quietly assessed Caleb. He knew he was not supposed to enter his mind and read his thoughts but he decided that this being the first time they worked together to contain a crises he needed to have an idea of how orderly his mind was.

"Good morning Caleb. If you like 1 will bring you up to the current status of the three men who survived Muskula's mate reprisal for the attack on Muskula."

"Thank you, please do. Do you have any idea whether or not he has a name? I have never heard anything other than, "Muskula's mate", surely he has a name."

"It appears that the males in their species do not have names. Breveka, our species analyst, has determined that males are completely dominated in their culture and are not named. They mate for life and are identified by mate association. Their primary function appears to be protection, reproduction, and companionship."

Caleb responded with a frown. "Glad I was not born into their culture".

"We have seen many cultures in our travels and have never found one that is totally controlled by the female of the culture. I suppose we have already found common space."

Caleb had to think a second about what common space was. "Of course, that is where they lived, in space".

"Right now the three men are at the pier is telling everyone how they killed a redheaded mermaid and that a male merman, they called him a merman, killed two members of their crew. They also confirmed they were purposely looking for them as there have been many sightings in the area. They are also pretty intoxicated and the police have been called".

After listening to the report Caleb picked up the phone and called the number he had been given and told they would support his orders.

"I need a small four man submarine. I need a crew of four. One of them needs to be female with long red hair. The crew needs to be in wet suits. I want the sub put in

ASSIMILATION

the water one mile from Ignatius Point. I need it there now!"

I need two naval officers' uniforms, ten men in navy dungarees, two men in military police uniforms, a military ambulance and one staff car. I need it within thirty minutes."

Taaker spoke in his personal communicator and arranged for the transportation of the personnel and equipment to the proper coordinates.

Taaker and Caleb dressed in the provided naval officer uniforms. When they stepped outside the compound office two saucers were loaded with the necessary equipment and personnel.

As they approached the saucer Taaker could read the uneasiness in Caleb's spirit. He said, "Be at peace Caleb. You organized an excellent response. I could not have done better myself".

Caleb's anxiousness, at again riding in the saucer, diminished. He was surprised at Taaker's praise.

"I do not know if I will ever be comfortable riding in a saucer. In my world, all my life, you just did not exist. I feel like a small child learning everything over again."

Taaker was taken aback by Caleb's admission of his fear and recognition that he indeed, and in the Andrians opinion, was basically a child learning his way.

Taaker replied, "The first time I stepped on a planet, I too was afraid. However, we Andrians never admit our fear because we do what we are told to do. There is never any discussion. The openness of your culture is one of the elements I admire most."

Taaker placed Caleb in the receptacle then took the position next to his. The Saucer lifted off and was at the designated debarkation point within minutes. The saucer with the submarine also off-loaded their cargo and crew at the designated position. The submarine proceeded to the service pier where the three inebriated fishermen were extolling their tale of battling the mermaids, killing one of them and of the merman coming out of the water onto the boat and killing their two friends.

There were approximately twenty men and woman standing outside the pub which consisted of a bait shop, restaurant, and bar. They all turned and stared at the sound of a siren approaching the end of the pier. They observed the military ambulance followed by a black staff car and a truck with a contingent of men in the back. The entourage stopped and the men in the ambulance quickly unloaded a gurney and raced toward the crowd.

There were shouts of "What's going on? Why are you here?"

The questions were asked by undercover intelligence agents that had infiltrated the crowd.

The gurney proceeded past the crowd toward the end of the pier where the mini submarine had surfaced and quietly tied up. Two men were standing on the deck reaching down into the hatch trying to pull another person up. The third person that was being pulled up was a woman with long red hair. After she was successfully extricated from the hatch and laid on the deck, another man emerged; he was covered in blood as was the red headed woman. The woman was loaded onto the gurney

ASSIMILATION

and rolled toward the crowd which at this time had become quiet.

Caleb and Taaker had positioned themselves strategically in front of the crowd and blocked the gurneys advancement.

Caleb said in a loud voice, "What happened here Chief?"

Immediately the three men came to attention and saluted.

"Commander, Sir. We were running experimental exercises about five miles out and were placing sonar buoys at one mile intervals, Sir. When we surfaced to place the last buoy we were on the deck of the sub, it was misty with visibility of at least one hundred yards, Sir. Then a fishing boat, that one there, Sir," the Chief Petty officer pointed toward the fishing trawler that was involved in the incident, "came close alongside and started firing at us sir. Their first shots hit Petty Officer Second Class Joplin three times".

Everyone in the crowd looked down at the gurney containing the wounded seaman Joplin. Her long red hair was prominently displayed and fanned out on the white gurney covering. Her hair went down past her shoulders. She displayed a large amount of blood on her torso, legs and arms.

The crowd then turned as one and glared at the three inebriated red neck fisherman. The five men involved in the incident had been a Bain in the community. The community was a small tight nit group of good citizens and had been tolerant of the antics of the five men. However it was evident their tolerance had come to an end.

Caleb then said, "Medics, get Petty Officer Joplin to the hospital and keep me apprised of her condition!'

"Yes Sir!", Replied the two medics in unison.

The two medics rushed away with the Gurney containing Petty Officer Joplin and placed it in the Military ambulance. The ambulance rushed out of the parking lot at a high rate of speed raising a large cloud of dust.

Caleb then said, "What else happened Chief."

Sir, the fishing vessel was caught broad side in a large swell. Two of the five crew members fell over the side. At the same time the fishing vessel scraped up the side of the submarine and I believe, crushed the two fishermen to death. We were unable to locate them so we immediately submerged and left the area. We also notified our Command of the incident."

Caleb replied, "As you should. You did a good job. Can you identify the other three crewmen that fired upon your vessel and wounded Petty Officer Joplin?"

"Yes Sir! Those three men standing there Sir!", pointing at the three inebriated fisherman.

Caleb then said in a loud authoritarian voice, "MP's, Take those three men into custody immediately and take them to the military base."

There was a loud ringing of a cell phone. Officer Taaker reached into his pocket and ceremoniously turned away answering the phone. He slowly closed his phone and quietly stepped close to Caleb's ear and whispered a message.

Caleb then said angrily, "You three drunk, miserable,

excuses for life, are now going to be charged with murder! Petty Officer Joplin died enroot to the hospital!"

The three inebriated redneck fishermen had a bewildered look on their faces as they were led away down the pier toward the entourage of military vehicles.

There were shouts from the crowd of, "Good Riddance!" and, "Do not come back! They were not made by the agents planted in the audience.

Caleb then said, "Chief, take the fishing trawler into custody for evidence and transport it to the nearest navy base."

"Yes sir!"

The Chief then directed five men to board the vessel and remove it from the dock and take it to the nearest naval facility.

Turning to the crowd, Caleb said, "It appears that your drunken friends tried to cover up the shooting of a Naval Petty Officer, crashing their boat into the side of a United States Naval vessel, and killing two of their crew, by concocting a story of being attacked by mermaids. If you have not known before, you now know of secret naval activities which are conducted in the area."

"Many of the activities have to do with individual transportation systems and experimental testing of different underwater suits for our navy seals, some of which are modeled after fish in that they are colored and scaled. Not only that we are conducting flights of experimental aircraft, some of which you have seen," Then smiling said, "Or, maybe not." He then laughed and many in the crowd laughed with him.

"My name is Commander Caleb Sears. I am in charge of the secret development of surface and subsurface tactical weapons at the Naval Support Facility. Should you have any questions about anything you see, or thought you saw, call me anytime and I, or my Executive Officer, Lt. Commander Taaker, will personally return your call and answer all your questions to the best of our ability without compromising security. We will leave several cards with names and phone numbers for you to use should you find it necessary. You will be contacted should statements be necessary. Thank you all for your time."

Caleb and Taaker turned and walked up the pier. The remaining enlisted personnel went to their truck. The fishing trawler and submarine left the pier. The two agents in the crowd help reinforce the plausible story and expound on the drunken state of the three remaining fisherman. No one went to look for the two lost fisherman because the navy said they would take care of that task.

CHAPTER 33
CALL TO DUTY

Sara slowly regained consciousness. She felt languid, rested and at peace. She opened her eyes and looked around. The room's light was muted and the walls were a pastel pink. She was laying down on a bed or a couch.

Sara stretched arching her back raising her arms above her head in a long satisfying flexing of her muscles. She noticed her arms were bare, then that her body was cool. Raising her head and looking down she saw she was not wearing anything.

Then in a totally uncharacteristic outburst, Sara exclaimed. "Oh my stars; What the hell!"

She saw that her breast was enlarged three times bigger than when she went to sleep. How did that happen? Sara had just begun blooming into a young woman and she just did not know how long it would take for her to completely mature.

Sara thought fast, "Emily told me I would be out for one month. I do not think Flata would give me breast enhancements, why would she? That means I have to have been unconscious for longer than a month. How long? How quickly does one's breast grow? I am only thirteen and I was beginning to mature, rather nicely, I think."

"No, something happened and I was kept in decontamination longer than one month."

Sitting up, Sara observed a mirror on the wall. Standing in front of the mirror she critically observed her body. It was definitely not the same body she had before decontamination.

Her waist was small, hips more pronounced, more like a woman. Her shoulders were broad and her breast hung nicely, and, they were at least four times as large as before.

"I think I might be about three inches taller," thought Sara. "My hair is a little longer too. At least it is the same color."

She then observed a uniform lying on a table to the side along with panties, bra, undershirt, and shoes. She put them on and was not surprised to find that they fit.

Looking in the mirror she observed a young woman looking back. She did not recognize her. She looked so much older and mature in her face. Her uniform accented the curves of her waist, hips and breast.

Tears came to her eyes and slowly rolled down her cheeks. She became aware that it appeared she had missed most of her adolescent years.

"What could have possibly happened"?

Sara heard a noise to her right and saw Emily come into the room. She was with a small child that appeared to be about three years old. That was strange. Where did the small child come from?

Emily stood in front of Sara silently. She bent over to pick up the small child and held him in her arms. He was blond and looked like Emily. Sara looked back but did not smile. In fact there was a hard look on her face.

ASSIMILATION

Emily finally spoke. "I am sorry Sara; there was an emergency on a distant planet in a different galaxy. The Andrians were forced to leave while we were in decontamination. They did not have time to bring us out of decontamination without endangering our lives, thus we came with them."

Sara said, "How old am I?"

Without hesitation Emily replied, "You are sixteen and one half earth years old. You have been in stasis for three years."

"Why was I left in stasis?"

"For your own protection; there were elements on the ship that wanted to kill you and me. They brought me out of stasis because I was pregnant with Warren's child. They wanted to continue to keep you in stasis but I told them no."

I believe that it was better for you to remain in stasis during the dangerous time because there was shooting and fighting on the intergalactic carrier and one just did not know who the enemy was. There are still enemies of, "The Council of Yield"; they are the ruling body of the intergalactic fleet. Some of the enemies are still on the ship."

Sara still did not speak. What could she say? She was excited for the adventure; it just took an unexpected turn.

Sara was thinking to herself, "I am physically more mature. What about my mental intellect? Am I still a thirteen year old intellectually, even though I was mature for my age. I am now soon to be seventeen. Am I going to act like a thirteen year old adolescent or a seventeen year old young adult? Are my fighting skills still intact? What about Muskula?"

Thinking about Muskula shocked Sara out of her introverted reverie.

"Muskula! How is Muskula? Is she still alive? What happened to her?"

Emily responded, "She is fine. She has completely healed. Right now she is resting in her aquarium. Since she is an aquatic species she required a more sophisticated habitat.

A small, petit woman in a Space Intelligence uniform came into the room. She came smartly to attention and saluted Emily then turned and saluted Sara.

Sara, not knowing what else to do came to attention and returned the salute.

Emily said, "Sara, this is Captain Sasha Palangin. When we had to leave quickly and they became aware that we could not be removed from decontamination without endangering our lives, thus enabling our return to earth, your Father contacted Admiral Cleary and demanded that your safety be insured. I had not yet had the opportunity to tell Admiral Cleary of your induction into Space Intelligence so he was caught unawares."

"He believed I had lost my mind. Maybe I did. However I still stand by my decision to bring you along. You are assigned to Captain Palangin and her team to help insure your security. You are now attached to her group you need to consider yourself as a member of her team. There are some video that you should view to help you understand just how fortunate you are to be included

ASSIMILATION

in her group."

"Your primary responsibility will be to protect Muskula. She has enemies on the carrier and one attempt has been made against her life already."

Sara saluted Emily and said, "Yes Sir."

Sara felt no more comraderies toward Emily. Before leaving the room with Captain Palangin she turned and said, "You had no right to take away my adolescent years."

After Sara had gone Emily sat down and put her son, Warren Jr. on the floor. Emily had reviewed her decision to leave Sara in Stasis for three years over a thousand times. In her heart she wanted to bring her out immediately but the military part of her knew that in order to keep her alive and safe she must be out of the line of fire.

She knew there would be consequences for leaving her in stasis but under the circumstances it was the safest and correct course of action. She also believed in her heart of hearts she allowed pride to blind her better judgment in bringing Sara to the intergalactic carrier. How could she have possibly foreseen the emergency that required the intergalactic carrier to leave the area of the planet? It made her joy with her son bittersweet.

After she was brought out of stasis and Emily learned she was pregnant, she astounded Flata by insisting that she have a natural childbirth. They did not have a record of any baby being brought to term in the natural manner.

Word spread quickly about the strange Human, Emily, and her plan to bring her baby to term. So much interest was generated that arrangements were made to deliver the baby in the largest amphitheater on the Carrier. There were to be up to five hundred woman present for the birth. Those that would not be able to attend could view the natural birth on the ships intercommunication system.

On the day of delivery, Emily felt like a cockroach under microscopic inspection. She knew most all the woman did not approve and that their attendance was due to scientific interest only.

The birth came out as planned and a healthy baby boy was placed at Emily's breast to suckle. For Emily, the birth was normal and easy, but of course that is a man's point of view. Emily quickly fell asleep with her baby at her side. The Andrians had something to think about for a long time to come.

CHAPTER 34

HUSBAND AND FATHER'S REGRET, A MOTHER'S PAIN

Caleb hung up the phone with Admiral Cleary. He called him every week and had done so for the past three years. The only information available was, of course, what came from the Andrians.

He was advised that almost immediately after Sara and Emily were put in stasis for decontamination an emergency arose on a distant planet involving another Andrian Intergalactic Carrier. The carrier that Sara was on was dispatched to assist. That had been three years ago, Sara's seventeenth birthday was to be in three weeks.

Caleb had married Selena Washington almost a year after Sara had gone. Selena and the Andrian children were the ones that kept him from going completely mad.

When he had heard that the carrier was to leave and that Sara was unable to get off because she was in decontamination, he called Admiral Cleary and spoke many words, none of them nice.

Admiral Cleary was confounded as to why Emily would swear in a thirteen year old girl into the Space Intelligence Agency and then send her to an intergalactic carrier. He promised he would send a whole team of the best Operatives in Space Intelligence and personally put them in charge of her safety. The saucer with Captain Palangin and her team of operatives managed to arrive just in time before the intergalactic carrier left the Oort Cloud.

The Andrian children knew the intergalactic carrier was going to be gone for a long time, how many years they did not know; nor did they tell Caleb that the planet to which they were going was not in the Milky Way galaxy, but their destination was to be the Lower Megellanic Cloud Galaxy, one hundred and seventy nine thousand light years from the Milky Way galaxy. The Milky Way Galaxy was one hundred thousand light years from one side to the other. The intergalactic carrier was going to go almost twice as far.

They grieved for their new friend and wished her well. They also asked Caleb and Selena to help them pray for Sara's safe return. They were careful not to mention a time frame. They knew that Humans believed in a "Higher Power", and hoped that praying with him would relieve his pain. What was strange to them is that it seemed to relieve their pain as well. They knew that even though Emily's saucer had godlike attributes in space travel, the carriers did not and, for unknown reasons it was not being used to bring Sara home. They did not mention that to Caleb either.

In the beginning of the third year Selena told Caleb she was pregnant. She was happy to have another child and she was aware the new child would not replace Sara

ASSIMILATION

but she hoped it would lesson his heartache. Caleb was happy for a new child as he was totally and completely in love with Selena. He would not have believed it possible before meeting Selena that he was capable of loving another woman other than Sara's mother. She died almost seventeen years ago.

Caleb had received cards from ten young people offering them their prayers in Sara's absence. They said they had lost their parents and were kept in captivity for years. They knew the circumstance that Sara was in on the intergalactic carrier was much better than theirs on the earth. So, Caleb prayed that was so.

Warren was better prepared this time around as he had more knowledge and information as to the circumstances Emily was in. He handled his grief and fears by throwing himself into his work, sometimes he did not come home for weeks at a time.

He did his best to smile and make small talk with Skip and Billy. He was well aware that Skip and Persha were sleeping together but he said nothing. He was now of the mindset that one needed to find happiness wherever and whenever possible.

Jawane and Hanlee spent hours on the computer in teaching study groups that had hundreds of students enrolled. The group started off small but after word got around about the brilliance and simplicity with which they taught, their fame spread as far as the communication net allowed. No one really knew who they were and they were careful to keep their identities secret. They had a lot of help from the Space Intelligence.

The Andrians had decided to send ten more children to earth to teach and be taught. They were all multi-disciplined and enjoyed the role of mentor to such an inferior species. There were five males and five females. They were all scared to death and had it not been for Persha, Hanlee, and Jawane they would have taken the next saucer back to the intergalactic carrier regardless of the punishment they would receive. However, after two years, they fit nicely into polite society.

Also at the beginning of the third year Persha was complaining to Selena she was having really bad cramps and had stopped the bleeding cycles that began when they came to earth.

Selena hugged Persha with tears in her eyes and said, "Oh my beautiful and most wonderful child, we are going to have babies at the same time."

Persha, perplexed, looked at Selena and said, "What do you mean we are going to have babies at the same time? Are you going to have two and give me one? What does that have to do with the cramps and pain I am having?"

Selena laughed and said, "No silly girl you are pregnant, as am I." Persha looked at Selena and said again, "So what does that mean?"

Selena gave a hearty laugh and said, "You know, for someone as smart as you are, you have no knowledge of what being pregnant really means except the technical analysis. You, my beautiful adopted daughter are going to have a baby. I think you and Skip need to hurry and get married!

Persha's eyes got wide as saucers as she finally

comprehended that she, personally, was pregnant, and was going to have a baby.

Persha in a panicked voice said, "That cannot be! Flata will not allow it! Only those on the carrier that have been selected to have children can have children. There is not room enough; there is not food or water enough. She will terminate the pregnancy and I will be sterilized for not following the rules!"

Tears were running down Persha's face and a great sorrow had come over her because she thought her baby would be destroyed and she could never have another child as she was going to be sterilized.

Selena, for the first time, finally realized what an extremophile society the Andrian children came from. Before, she was just academically attuned to what an extremophile society was with birth control being a necessity. But now, seeing Persha's terror of losing her baby and being sterilized brought into focus exactly what kind of society they were from. Her fear was well founded.

"I thank God I am from the planet Earth!" said Selena.

"And Persha, you can thank God also that your baby will be born on the planet earth. The child is yours and Skip's to love and cherish and teach to live the right way. You will not be sterilized, I swear to you! There is plenty of water, food and air for your baby and for as many babies as you want!"

Persha just leaned into Selena's arm and cried. Even though Persha was a head taller than Selena the comfort of her arms were still there. Selena could feel the tears falling on her short cut hair as Persha heaved sob after sob.

CHAPTER 35
WORKING THRU ISSUES

Sara worked every day with the security group. She sparred with every member of the group and they all agreed she had anger issues and they were equally divided as to wither her anger was justified. They did all agree that she was highly skilled in the martial arts. They also noted that she was stronger than any of them.

Sara had kept silent about the evident enhancements that Flata had somehow infused into her being. She did not understand how it could be done or why she did it, she just knew she liked the new found abilities and skills she had.

Sara was visiting with Muskula the first day she came out of stasis when she became aware that she was able to understand and hear Muskula's thoughts. Muskula exhibited nothing but love and respect for her and she was grateful for that. The only thing Sara did was hug her. She did not want to reveal to anyone that she was aware of what they were thinking. When she was around Emily she always thought of a brick wall.

One of the first things Sara wanted to do was to meet Chandra, Hanlee's mother. Emily told her she would take her to meet Chandra but Sara declined and requested that Sasha take her instead.

Arrangements were made and Sasha escorted Sara to

ASSIMILATION

meet Chandra.

Chandra opened the door and looked at the young woman who was Jawane's age. She had heard about her from Jawane and Hanlee's frequent communications when near the Earth's solar system. However, since leaving the galaxy she had received no information regarding Hanlee's status.

Chandra was aware there had been attempts on Sara's life while in decontamination and thus it was decided to keep her in stasis to insure her survival. She was also aware of the great anger it had caused when Sara realized she had been asleep for three years. Chandra was perplexed about the anger as that would be little or no concern to Andrians.

Sara greeted Chandra in Andrian fashion, the lesser to the greater. Chandra accepted the greeting as correct and stepped aside to allow her to enter. Sasha followed Sara into the room after she had performed the same greetings, the lesser to the greater.

Sara said, verbally, as she did not want anyone to know she could read minds and had telepathic abilities, "Chandra, thank you for allowing me in your home. Hanlee told me how your personal space is coveted and sacred. I just wanted to let you know how much I valued her friendship when we were together on the earth. I learned so much."

Chandra did not speak or respond to Sara's words. She knew that Sara was enhanced by Flata and she did not know or understand why she was deliberately acting like she could not use telepathic communication.

Chandra motioned for Sara and Sasha to have a seat. Unbidden she poured three cups of liquid and offered them to her guest.

After taking a few sips, Chandra said, "Hanlee has told me all about you. She and Jawane both were greatly impressed with your gymnastic skills. Jawane gave me a complete detail of the tensile strength of your muscle fibers and how much energy you expended in performing your feats. It is an amazing skill you have developed. I think it would be a good idea for you to exhibit your skill to Andrians here on the ship to help us open our minds as too your capabilities."

Sara smiled and said, "I would like that. I think it would be fun, well at least for me. Hanlee told me how important science is to your survival. It really does not leave any time whatsoever for the pursuit of what you would consider selfish, personal activities, that does not benefit the greater good."

"And, I imagine that should I perform gymnastics, almost every one of them would probably condemn me for wasting energy resources that could be better put to use in resolving survival problems and issues."

Chandra looked at the young woman more carefully. She said, "I could not have said it better. You seem to understand well why our society structure requires balance and commitments to survive."

Then Chandra said, "I never considered there was any other way until I met Emily. We all respect her very much. I understand your anger toward her for seemingly taking away from you three years of your life. I am also

ASSIMILATION

aware there are contentious elements on our carrier that want to kill you, not only you, but every Human on the carrier. We have lived in an enclosed system for so long that it is difficult if not impossible for some Andrians to change."

Chandra's speech was interrupted with the compartment door opening. A man came in that Sara did not know. Sasha being the closest reached up and gave him a kiss on the cheek.

"It is so good to see you Blain", said Sasha.

The man laughed and replied, "You earth woman are such teasers!"

He then greeted Chandra, the greater to the lesser. All there communication was telepathic.

He looked at Sara and communicated with her.

Sara did not respond.

Blain verbally said, "Hello, my name is Blain. You must be Sara. I have heard so many good things about you. Welcome to our home."

"Thank you Blain, I am new to all of this. I feel more like I am playing a part in a school play."

Blain laughed. "Exactly; I imagine so! You go to sleep at thirteen and wake up at seventeen. You missed your education, senior prom, driver's license, and boyfriends. That can be hard on an earth girl! And yet, you are standing here in a Space Intelligence Uniform, on an alien intergalactic carrier, three galaxies from home, in my home chatting with me, the Commander of the Andrian Military. That sounds like an impossible scenario."

At the mention of him being the Commander of the

Andrian Military, Sara promptly came to attention and saluted him.

"Sorry Sir, I had no knowledge of who you were. I just came to see Chandra to say hi because she is Hanlee's mother. Hanlee and I were friends on the earth. She tried to tell me what to expect on the carrier but I guess being put to sleep for three years was not one of the things she considered possible."

Blain looked piercingly into her eyes. "I am Jawane's father and Hanlee's father. I know who you are and I am well aware how you befriended them on earth. For that I will be forever grateful."

Then telepathically he said, "For that reason I will be merciful to you. However, you ever lie to me again I will have you in stasis for the remainder of the tour and have your mind wiped of any knowledge of our existence." Sara was shocked and she visibly paled. She humbly bowed her head and said telepathically, "Yes Sir. I am sorry sir."

"There is no room in space for petty grievances. You will be in combat situations with Earth and Andrian military forces. I can only have committed personnel who are willing to die for their fellow soldier whither the soldier is Human or Andrian. Therefore you must decide if you are going to act like an adolescent thirteen year old or a seventeen year old adult with life and death decisions to make on behalf of others."

"Yes Sir. I am sorry Sir. I was thinking selfishly of myself. And you are right, I was thinking like a spoiled brat of an adolescent prima donna. It will never happen again Sir."

Blain read her mind and entered deeply and assessed that she was indeed contrite and was telling the truth. He could not make a mistake with her and show her favor just because Emily had intervened on her behalf, not to mention Chandra had done the same. He was responsible for everyone's life.

Initially he already decided to put her in stasis and wipe her mind but Emily assured him she was worth saving. She also told him she would stake her life on her believing she would make the right choices given the time to get over her shock. Blain believed the shock of being told she would be put back in stasis and have her mind wiped was sufficient. However, it was not an idle threat. In his entire career, Blain had never changed a decision once it was made, well maybe once a long time ago and it involved Skip and Billy. Emily had made a similar request then and everything had turned out okay.

Blain sat down in an unoccupied seat facing Sara.

"We will be sending a unit into a small village on the planet Keel. They are holding Andrian men, woman and children hostage. The Andrians were a science team that was assisting the locals in developing clean water systems. Sasha will be in charge. Emily and I will be going."

"Sara, you will be given a choice. Do you wish to participate? Sasha has been training you on several weapons and she said you have mastered each one."

Sara looked first at Blain then at Sasha. Speaking directly to Sasha, Sara said, "Yes I want to go if you will have me. I will not let you down."

Sasha responded, "Fine, we will be leaving within four hours. You need to get to your unit and prepare for departure." She also wanted Sara out of Blain's presence before he changed his mind again.

Sara stood at attention and Saluted Sasha.

She turned to Blain and said, "Thank you sir for a second chance. I imagine in your culture, they in all probability, do not exist."

Sara saluted Blain who had stood and returned her salute and then Sara said to Chandra, "Thank you for allowing me to visit. I hope we can do it again in the future."

Sara turned and left the room.

Blain said, "Okay Sasha, I will go with your judgment and allow Sara to go on the mission. You said she easily mastered the weapons and was exceptional good with a knife. You may assign her as you wish. Emily and I are your backups."

Sasha stood and saluted, "Thank you sir. I need to see to our troops." She turned and left the room.

After Sasha had left, Chandra said, "Thank you Blain. I know you would not have given her a second chance had I not asked you too. From what we have learned, she was instrumental in befriending and protecting our daughter on her assignment to the Earth. They have become "friends", which for Humans is a strong bond."

CHAPTER 36
FIRST MISSION

Sara went to the barracks to prepare to go on the mission. There were approximately twenty commandoes present. Everyone was checking their individual weapons. There was another group in the hanger that was getting into battle armor.

Standing on a chair to be clearly visible, Sara said telepathically, "May I have your attention please? I want to apologize for acting like a girly immature thirteen year old spoiled brat. After all, when I went to sleep, I was one."

There was general laughter within the group.

Sara then said, "I hope you can accept me within your group. There is nothing that I want more".

There was a general applause. A male commando went up and reaching under Sara's arms lifted her to the floor.

He said, "Sometime girls have to grow up fast."

Everyone laughed and the women commandoes came up and gave her a hug, even the female Andrian commandoes.

"Welcome to our group. Let us help you get your gear. Make sure you have your three knives. You never know when you might need them."

An hour later fifty commandoes, Human and Andrian

were formed up in the briefing room. Tactical plans were formulated and groups were assigned specific targets. Sara and three commandoes were assigned to the protection of the hostages once they were able to enter the compound. Sara said a silent prayer and entered the saucer with her comrades. Taking up positions as directed the saucer left the intergalactic carrier and the saucers proceeded to their target using the moon as cover as long as possible.

They were on the ground and exiting the saucer within minutes of leaving the shield of the moon. Sara followed the other three commandoes at a dead run toward a two story building that housed the women and children hostages. The men were held in a separate area.

Without stopping, the lead commando blasted the door to nonexistence and they entered the building at a dead run. Sara could hear the sizzling of laser weapons to her right and left. Strange to her there was no shouting or audible sounds. She saw a man dressed in red leap out from a doorway directly in front of her about twenty feet away.

He immediately opened fire with a light weight laser weapon. He raked the weapon laterally across her midsection of her body. She could feel stinging from one side of her torso to the other. He then jerked the weapon and was aiming for her head.

Sara jumped sideways and fired her cluster weapon simultaneously. Five projectiles entered his body at the chest and exploded inside his body. The man's body disappeared in a flash of light; the head flew off and out of

ASSIMILATION

sight into the other room.

Sara checked her body armor and saw a deep slash burned diagonally midway. She did a mental inventory and realized she was still alive and functioning. Jumping up Sara ran into the room and observed two men on either side of a small boy. They had guns to his head.

"Drop your weapon or we will kill the boy", the man on the left said.

"You drop your weapon and we will let the boy and you live", said the man on the right.

Sara could read their mind and she knew exactly what their plans were, thus she said, "Okay, I give up. I will put down my weapon and raise my hands behind my head. Do not hurt the boy."

The two men smiled at the prospect of such and an easy kill and when Sara put her rifle on the ground and put her hands behind her head, they shoved the boy to the side and began to raise their weapons slowly at the easy target.

Sara had a knife in each hand and in a lightning movement she threw her arms in a down ward motion with the knives leaving her hands with each finding their mark embedding themselves to the hilt between the two men's eyes. They both had a look of surprise on their face as they crumpled to the floor.

Sara scooped up her assault rifle from the floor and ran to the boy. She telepathically told him to stay down and move to the area of a small pantry and hide. With his eyes wide the boy scrambled to the pantry and closed the door doing what he was told.

Sara heard crying from the top of the stairs. She ran up the stairs with two commandoes close behind. There were about twenty people seated on the floor with their hands and feet tied.

Across the room about fifty feet three men were firing out a window. She and the two commandoes opened fire killing all three men.

After a quick check around the room they signaled the upstairs area was clear. Sara looked closely at the hostages. One of them did not look right. He was squirming with his bonds which were loose. Able to read his mind, Sara learned he was wearing a nitrogen nano bomb vest. He had inadvertently tied his bonds in such a way that they became snagged on a nail protruding from the floor and he could not get loose and was unable to set off the bomb which would kill everyone.

Sara ran over to the man, which fortunately was not necessarily large, scooped him up off the floor and ran to a window and dove thru the window with him in her arms. Once outside the window while falling to the ground Sara shoved the man with all her strength away from her. They separated near the ground with the man falling to one side of a five foot wall and Sara falling on the other.

Sara hit the ground with her left arm and leg out for a brace to soften the impact. She heard a loud snap as her arm broke just above the elbow. The breath was knocked from her and she lapsed into unconsciousness just as she heard a loud explosion and saw a large cloud of smoke, dirt, and body parts from the would be suicide bomber

ASSIMILATION

fly above her.

Blain was standing with Emily watching the commandoes rounding up resistance fighters. They heard glass breaking and looking up they were aghast when they saw Sara flying out of the second story window with a man in her arms. Seconds before she hit the ground she shoved him away and he disappeared behind a five foot rock wall. Sara then hit the ground with a resounding crack of a broken bone. Immediately there was a loud explosion which was directed upward due to the rock wall.

Blain and Emily both ran to Sara with Emily fervently praying that she was alive. Blain reading her mind found himself saying the same prayer.

Sara was unconscious and had an obvious compound fracture. There was a laser burn across Sara's midsection. Fortunately the wound was superficial as the body armor adsorbed most of the energy. Sara had another laser wound on the side of her face and the tip of her ear was burned off. The wounds to her midsection and ear was cauterized therefore there was no blood. Sara was tended to immediately by commando paramedics, loaded in a blowup trauma container which filled with oxygen. They ran to a saucer and upon entering the saucer she was immediately transported to the intergalactic carrier for further medical attention. Flata was waiting with a medical team and immediately assessed Sara's condition. They moved her to the trauma operation unit which was embedded with nano bots.

The Andrian hostages were loaded into the saucers with most of the commandoes. As Blain and Emily were walking thru the two story building to check for any other hidden enemy, they saw two bodies with knives protruding from between their eyes. There guns were still in their hands. Emily recognized the knives as belonging to Sara. She removed them and placed them in an evidence bag tied to her hip.

They heard a noise coming from behind a closed door. The door opened and a young Andrian boy about six years old exited the closet.

When Blain asked him what happened he replied a female commando saved his life. He further stated she risked her life by putting down her gun as the gunmen advised they would kill him. After she put down her weapon and her hands was in the air, she reached behind her back and withdrew two knives and threw them at the same time killing both men. The commando then told him to stay in the closet until the fighting was over.

Emily took the little boy by the hand and they exited the building and boarded the saucer. Sara had been placed in a cryogenic carrier and had already been returned to the intergalactic carrier for medical attention, she was still unconscious at time of departure.

The little boy was confused as to why the woman wanted to take him by the hand but he did find it somewhat comforting. He had never had anyone hold his hand before. He knew she was Human and he was told Humans were strange in a nice way. As for Emily, it was her mother's instinct and she held his hand without thinking.

CHAPTER 37
ACCEPTANCE

Sara came to and found herself in a blue hued room with large clear ceramic vessels gurgling with what appeared to be steam boiling out of the tops. She was in an enclosed clear ceramic case filled with a clear jell like substance up to her neck. Since she was in the upright position she could see across the room where she observed Flata talking to Emily.

They both looked her way at the same time as they became aware she was awake.

Emily walked over to the medical receptor and smiled at Sara.

"We are glad to see you have finally awakened. At least it is not the same three years as last time! You took quiet a hit when you jumped out of the window. I am sure you thought it thru completely before you took that action." Emily laughed

Sara said, "I saw he was wired with a Nitrogen Nano bomb. He was trying to undo his bonds as he made a mistake when he bound himself and he was unable to get loose when he wanted too because he had snagged a protruding nail. He had just loosened them when I came in and spotted him."

"There was nothing that could be done to keep him from detonating the bomb. He was going to kill everyone else, men, women, children and commandoes. The only way to make sure no one else died was to remove the bomb from the room. If the bomb was not removed, everyone was going to die. So I ran over, scooped him up and jumped out the window. I shoved him away on the way down hoping the bomb would not get me."

Emily looked at Sara. She had performed an awful selfless feat. Did it have anything to do with bravery, well maybe a lot? But it mostly had to do with duty and love; she is a little naive because she was so young. As of yet she had not seen any one die. Well, that certainly was not true. She blasted one man to vapor and skillfully placed two knives in the foreheads of two others; no, she is a natural born warrior as it is not anything one can really teach. Just try to teach someone to jump out a window to save others when there is an almost one hundred percent chance you were going to die. It is the thing that separates the spiritual from the carnal.

Emily then thought, "Well I have not seen anyone die either. Would I have the where with all to jump out a window to certain death to save others?"

"Sara, we found the little boy you had hid in the closet. It was a very brave and risky thing to do when you put down your weapons. All the commandoes are proud of you and are impressed with your selflessness and skill. Every one of them said they wanted you to watch their back. I know you are new to the commandoes but that is the highest compliment they could pay anyone. By the way, how did you know that was a nitrogen nano bomb, have you had explosives training?"

ASSIMILATION

Sara thought for a moment. "You know, I read his mind and he was thinking of the bomb. I do not really understand how I knew it was a nitrogen nano bomb and it would kill everyone. I have never heard of a nitrogen nano bomb before. It just came to me and it felt right. I also knew everyone was going to die if I did not get the bomb out of the room. I was the only one that could do it; no one else knew it was there. And, even if they knew, they were too far away to do anything about it.

"After I went out the window my only thought was to put as much distance between us as possible. I did not know the rock wall was there and when I hit the ground it was a moot point, I was knocked unconscious."

Flata came up to Sara and said, "Sara the reason you knew that was a nitrogen nano bomb is because I have enhanced your cerebral cortex with knowledge of weapons of all classes, shapes and sizes. In effect, you will find many answers too difficult situations come to mind when you need them."

"The nitrogen nano bomb is just the first example of needed information when you desperately required it. However, it is up to you to find the solution most viable for success. You alone provided the only scenario of saving the lives of the women and children hostages. The decision to take the man with the bomb out of the building by jumping out the window was entirely yours. And, it was also the only solution if you wanted to save lives."

"It is also true you were able to easily pick up the bomber because I enhanced your already finely tuned muscle structure with nano carbon fibers to assist when extra strength is needed. In this particular case you probably did not require the extra strength. Witnesses advised he weighed no more than one hundred and forty pounds. With your strength and adrenaline that weight is within my calculated parameters of your abilities without enhancement. However, you could have picked up a two hundred pound man doing the same running and scooping up of the individual without stopping."

"I also enhanced the efficiency of your lung functions so that the exchange rate of oxygen has been increased by eighty percent. You will be able to last longer in a smoky or poisonous environment than the normal populations. All the commandoes have received the same enhancements."

"For the three months you were in decontamination, I removed all toxins and genetic anomalies that would cause you deadly issues as you age. Everyone that is decontaminated is scanned and receives a neutrino bath of pure cosmic energy; with energy properly directed, all the defective DNA material is destroyed. In effect, you come out being the most perfect being as possible. And, of course you discovered your ability to communicate telepathically."

"In regards to the injuries you sustained during the conflict, you have been completely healed. The laser scare across your midsection will remain. A little bit of the muscle had been cut but fortunately the vest did its work and took most all the energy of the laser."

"You still have a small scar on your cheekbone and are missing the top part of your ear. It is a small thing considering the possibilities."

When you hit the ground from the second story of the building you tried to break your fall and thus broke your arm. The nano fibers kept it from being completely shattered, and it also helped protect you from an otherwise fatal impact.

It has been completely healed although your arm will need to remain in a cast for a little while longer."

Emily said, "Flata will be removing you from the gel pack shortly. After you clean up you are to put on your uniform and meet in the celestial conference room for a review of the operation. I will see you later."

As Flata was removing Sara from the gel pack she said, "Sara, I have met many Humans. A very few are exceptional. As with Emily, you fall within the exceptional category. I would be proud to have you as my daughter."

Sara thought, "Wow! What an admission!"

"However, you are not part of me in any genetic way. Therefore I have used all my skills to insure you are the best you can possibly be without removing and replacing organs. I guess in the Human kind of way, I improved you as if you were my daughter and I love you as such."

"As you know, Andrians do not love as Humans because we are such an enclosed society we do not have the luxury to judge anyone except by their skills. Without skills we would be dead. However, I believe the "Council of Yield", is considering changes to our social structure to allow more latitude in our requirements. We have social scientist working with earth scientist to develop a system that would help incorporate both Human and Andrian crews for long missions."

Sara said, "Thank you Flata. I am glad you cared for me in such a loving way. As you know I never knew my mom as she died in child birth, I would love to consider you as my "Space Mom;" at which time Sara reached out and gave her a hug. "See, you would make a good Human Mom!"

Sara laughed and Flata looked mortified at the thought of being Human.

Sara, having completed the cleaning away of the healing gel process, took an Andrian style shower. How she hated those.

"Surly there is a better way to get water than what they developed. What about all those water asteroids she read about in school all those years ago; when I get home I am going to take a long hot shower and I think I will ask Jawane to join me." She smiled at that thought, "How bold of me!"

After dressing in her uniform Sara placed the seahorse brad in her hair and the star fish necklace around her neck. She had not seen Muskula since the military operation and she missed her.

Sara entered the celestial conference room in deep thought and had gone almost half way into the room before she observed the entire commando group was standing in formation and at attention. The Andrian commando group was on the opposite side of the room.

Emily was standing in front of the Space Intelligence Commandoes and Blain was standing in front of the Andrian Commandoes. As Sara was standing in the middle, Emily and Blain said at the same time, "Company Attenhut!"

There was an immediate clicking of boots in unison as the groups came to attention.

Sara said, stammering, "I am sorry I am late!"

Emily and Blain move as one to the front and center of the room.

Emily said, "Space Intelligence Protector First Class, Sara Sears, Come forward!"

Sara quickly came forward and stood at attention. She, like her father before her, did not have a clue as to what was happening.

Emily said, "Muskula, come forward."

Sara saw Muskula for the first time as she came forward and stood next to Emily.

Emily began, "Sara, because of your bravery, sacrifice, and action in confronting your enemies and achieving your objective on the planet Keel in the Smaller Megellanic Cloud Galaxy, receiving injuries in pursuing same, you are hereby to be awarded the Space Intelligence Silver Cross for your bravery and selfless sacrifice."

Sara stood dumbfounded, really unsure if she had heard Emily Correctly.

Muskula stepped forward and pinned a silver Maltese style Cross above her left breast, then stepped back.

Blain then said, "Sara, on behalf of the Andrian Intergalactic Commandoes, we award you the Andrian Golden Star for exemplary bravery in the face of your enemies. You showed exemplary behavior of self-sacrifice in protecting Andrian woman and children and your fellow commandoes, by diving out a second story window to almost certain death in order to save others."

Muskula stepped forward and pinned the second award above her left breast. The golden star was about one inch across and had seven rays extending from the star representing the seven home planets of the Andrians. Muskula then stepped back.

Then Emily said, "Sara, you are to receive the Purple Nebula award for being injured in the line of duty."

Muskula stepped forward for the third time and pinned a purple pin shaped in the spiral swirl of a galaxy, again above her left breast.

Both Emily and Blain saluted, and then both sets of commandoes saluted.

A Master Sergeant said, "At ease! This concludes the award ceremony."

Everyone cheered and Emily, Blain, and Muskula, each gave Sara a hug. Sara cried.

Both groups of commandoes came by and individually shook her hand and saluted her. By the time the last commando saluted, Sara was ready to drop with exhaustion. There was plenty of drinks and food for everyone.

Sara sat on one of the padded curved benches and looked out on the cosmos and wondering, "Will I ever get home?"

CHAPTER 38
TRAVAIL AND PAIN

Persha was waiting for Skip when he came home from his gymnastic classes. She was pensive, afraid and even though her panic had been checked and soothed by Selena, she was again near the brink. When he walked thru the doors she ran to him and threw her arms around him bursting into tears.

Skip was taken aback. He nearly panicked himself to see Persha so worked up.

"What is the matter Persha? Did someone hurt you? Why are you crying so hard? I have never seen you act this way. Whatever it is, I promise you it will be alright.

He held her close and stroked her hair and felt her trembling body close to his. After a minute her sobbing stopped and she ceased her trembling.

She leaned her head back and looking up at him she said, "I am pregnant. I am going to have a baby. I am so afraid."

Skip kissed her face and head and put his arms all the way around her and he had tears running down his cheeks. His heart had skipped a beat out of fear when she ran into his arms when he came home but now he could think of nothing but how much he loved her and how neat it would be to have a child of his own.

Pushing her back so he could look down at her he

said, "Oh Persha, that is the most wonderful thing that could happen to us. I think it will be wonderful to have a baby with you. And for your information, it is not just you that is going to have a baby, but, we are going to have a baby!

Persha said, "How are you going to have a baby?

"When a couple has a baby then the baby belongs to both of them. Therefore, when you have a baby the baby is mine too."

Persha then said, "Andrians do not have babies."

Skip looking down and smiling at her said, "Okay are you hatched from an egg or something?"

Persha looked at him frowning and said, "We are not chickens!"

Skip laughed then said, "Ok, what and how do you do, not to have, babies?"

"When the female becomes pregnant the baby is remove after six weeks and put in a berthing chamber and grown in the chamber until it is time for the baby to come out."

"Sometimes Flata will take the egg from a woman and sperm from a man and the baby is conceived and grown that way. If a woman has an unauthorized pregnancy or has a baby without permission, the baby will be killed and the woman will be sterilized and she will never be allowed to reproduce!" Again tears flowed form Persha's eyes.

Skip was horrified. "How could anyone do that? Well we are home and we can keep our baby and have as many as we want. And for your information I want a lot! We have to get married right away. We will keep the wedding to family".

Warren was not surprised to hear Persha was pregnant. He was just disappointed that he had not had a baby before Skip. He remembered that the Entity within the saucer said that Emily was going to have a baby. But how could she, she was not pregnant when she left. He did not want to think any further than that.

Hanlee and Jawane were happy but apprehensive about Persha's pregnancy. The death rate of mother and child was astronomical on the earth compared to Andrian standards; but then again, has there ever been a natural birth on an intergalactic carrier? They just did not know.

As the months passed Persha's stomach was getting larger and larger. She went daily to Selena's, more for comfort and assurance than teaching and learning.

Caleb had grown very close to her as he focused on her needs and wants in an effort to more easily distance the pain of Sara's absence. Persha just did not have the slightest idea what she was doing. He catered to her every whim when she was at the house with Selena. And, when she was at home, Skip and Billy did the same. Hanlee and Jawane did not understand all the fuss and were basically bystanders.

Warren was exceptionally sweet also. Every time he came home he brought her a strawberry banana split covered with chocolate and a cherry on top. Since Persha became pregnant, Warren was home at least three nights a week and when he had discovered that was her all-time favorite treat he found comfort in bringing her one.

When Persha was six months pregnant and she really began to expand about the waist the Andrian doctors exhibited real signs of what could only be described as fear. Not any of the doctors had ever witnessed a live birth much less delivered a baby.

Therefore, when Selena gave birth to a bouncing baby boy three months later, days before Persha was due, they were all present; in fact the birth was attended by as many as twenty interested parties. There were thirteen young Andrians which included Persha, Jawane and Hanlee. They were horrified, especially Hanlee. Caleb and Selena named their son Michael.

Four days later Persha was in the delivery room having her baby, Skip was holding one hand and Selena was holding the other, Caleb, Warren and Billy waited in the hall. Again, the delivery room was filled with Andrian children including Jawane and a terrified Hanlee.

When the delivery nurse handed Persha her baby boy, she was filled with awe and wonder. Immediately, without being coached, the baby latched onto her nipple and began suckling.

Tears rolled down her cheeks as she caressed and stroked her new son.

Persha said, "Thank you Skip for such a beautiful son. I will love him and keep him with me always."

Skip replied, "I hope he will be the first of many. I would like to name him Adam if that is okay with you."

Persha said, "That is a beautiful and strange name."

CHAPTER 39
LOVE STRONGER THAN DEATH

Blain and Emily were in one of the forested sections of the carrier. They came frequently so Warren Jr. could play hide and seek with Emily. Also present was Sara and Sasha, they took Warren Jr's safety extra serious as there was intelligence that indicated that he was the number one target, Sara was number two.

There were several Andrians working in the garden area tending to the plants. Then, without warning three men came from behind the trees and started firing with laser weapons. Sasha and Sara put Warren behind a rock and returned fire. They quickly eliminated their attackers and re-grouped with Emily and Blain.

Blain was lying on the ground. One of the laser shots had severed a large tree limb and the limb had fallen and hit him on the head. His head had a gash and was bleeding. It also appeared a concealed electric cable was severed and had fallen across Blain and had given him an electric shock. His vital signs indicated that he was dead, there was no heart beat and no breathing and his eyes were closed.

Emily grabbed Blain by the back of his head and began giving him mouth to mouth resuscitation. Sasha fell to her knees on the other side of him and started pumping his chest.

Emily shouted, "Sara, protect Warren!" The command was not necessary as Warren had become as Sara's little brother.

Immediately after the shooting, the garden area filled with security, Human and Andrian. They formed a circle around Emily, Sasha and Blain; some facing inward and some facing outward. Several security men and woman checked out the would be murderers and removed their bodies from the area for inspection and disposal.

Emily breathed air harder into Blain's lungs and Sasha pushed strongly onto his chest. Emily never admitted it until now but she loved Blain as she loved Warren. She never told him that she loved him but had expressed her love in other ways with a caress or a look. She had been careful to keep her feelings for him blocked in her mind so he could not read them. She was besieged with guilt for her love of Blain and had tried desperately to assuage her feelings by tending to Warren Junior.

Sasha too loved Blain and had always had physical intimacy with him. Emily suspected that they had a relationship but there was no room for jealousy; under the circumstances, how silly would that be. In the Andrian culture Blain could have as many woman as he wanted; he had always been celibate to his two wives as a personal choice until Sasha, and hopefully, Emily.

Tears came both to Emily and Sasha's eyes as there was no response to their efforts to induce a resumption of his heart and lungs.

ASSIMILATION

Emily cried out, "Don't you die on me Blain. Not now! I love you. I promise you I will be a good companion to you. Sasha and me both will rock your world!"

Tears came to both woman's eyes and poured freely onto Blains face and chest as they worked on him.

Emily said, "Sasha! Help me remove his clothes, hurry!"

Emily and Sasha quickly removed Blains clothing stripping him down naked. They then removed their clothing and began kissing on Blain. Both woman told him how much they loved him.

Emily kissed Blain deeply on the lips inserting her tongue into his mouth and talked to him constantly. They both stroked him all over his body. They switched positons and Sasha whispered into his ears promising him she would have his baby, just give her a chance.

Flata watched in amazement using remote viewing observing Emily and Sasha kissing on Blain and promising to have his children. She knew he was dead as the sensors indicated there were no viable indicators of life; it was a totally useless effort on their part and exactly what did they think they were going to accomplish?

Emily kissed on Blain and soon he had an erection and she sat on top of him and moved violently to stimulate his most basic animalistic senses. Sasha continued to kiss his face and lips and talked to him in expressive language that made the Andrians in the security detail turn red, as for the Humans in the detail, they understood that if promises of good sex would not bring him out of whatever his condition was, then nothing would.

Blain was in a very dark place with a small point of light in the far distance. There was complete silence. He seemed to be drifting toward the light. Then, in the distance behind him he could hear his name being called by two different voices. He did not know who they were but they were calling his name over and over. Soon he could feel something on him. He felt something pleasant in his mouth. He felt lips all over his body. Soon he felt an enormous magnetic feeling of connection and drawing. The drawing continued and became more intense. His need for release and to take a breath was overwhelming!

Blain let out and explosive breath and moan as did Emily. He breathed deeply and as he opened his eyes he saw and felt Emily on him. She was sweaty and naked. Tears ran down her cheeks. He then saw Sasha close to his face. She too had tears that ran down her face and dripped onto her breast.

Blain was confused. What happened?

He then felt the presence of both woman in his mind and they were telling him that they loved him and wanted to be his consorts and have his children.

Blain looked around and saw a large security detail watching them. Thinking, "What is going on? Why are they here; and most of all, why are you two sharing sharia with me?"

Both Emily and Sasha laughed. Emily said, "Oh Blain, we love you so much! We thought you were dead and we did not want you to leave us so we did only what earth woman know how to do. We rocked your boat!"

Emily dismounted and stood up to put on her clothes.

ASSIMILATION

Strangely she did not feel embarrassed as everyone watched her share pleasures with Blain and now watched her dress. She was just so happy that Blain was okay. For the first time since being on the carrier she felt totally at peace.

Sasha then too stood and dressed and turning to Emily and giving her a hug, she said, "Okay, you had your fun, next time it will be my turn!" She and Emily squeezed each other harder. They both knew that their life would never be the same, as would their relationship.

Flata fell back on the couch in amazement. "How could that be? He was dead; all his vitals had shut down. No one had ever come back to life. It was apparent that Human emotions were far more powerful than she had ever believed possible."

Blain was helped by two men of the security detail and he slowly dressed.

As they were leaving the area several men in Sasha's detail fell on the ground in front of her and said, "I am dead, please rock my boat!" She kicked each one lightly as she walked by and replied, "Yea, you wish!"

Sara took Warren Jr.'s hand and walked by his side. She did not let Warren see what was going on and had directed his interest toward a frog in a pond. As for her, she was mesmerized with Emily and Sasha's performance. She wondered if she could ever love a man as much.

There were more than a dozen armed encounters with insurrectionist on several planets. Sara gained more experience and was soon promoted to higher positions of leadership and now she had a squad of her own. No one in her group ever got too hurt, at least not mortally. She had exhibited bravery and skill time and again and soon became one of the most respected commandoes on the carrier.

They were all having breakfast when Blain came in and said, "We have been ordered back to the vicinity of the planet Earth. We will begin transit within hours. Hopefully we should be there within a year."

The actual trip would take one and one-half years.

Sara caught her breath. She had come on board at age thirteen and a half and kept in stasis for three years. She had been going on seventeen when she was brought out. She had now been serving in the Space Intelligence Commandoes for three more years. Now she was twenty years old. She would be twenty one when she returned home. She wanted to cry but she could not. She had cried all too often over more serious life circumstances than a little time away from home.

Emily and Sasha had both become pregnant and they now had two baby boys. Emily's son, whom she named Orion, was now two years old. He had black hair like his Father but he had her facial features. And being a hybrid Human-Andrian, he was extraordinarily intelligent. Flata fussed over him continually. You would think she was his grandmother, Emily knew Flata had tremendous personal growth and had an emotional experience when she was with Orion. Emily even heard her laugh one time. She had seen Flata smile on occasion but never had she verbalized a laugh. It surprised even her.

Sasha's baby boy was born a week later and she

ASSIMILATION

named him Perilain, after a beautiful flower on one of the planets they visited.

Perilain and Orion were always together and Warren Jr. was their primary caretaker, he was now going on six. He too was extremely intelligent. He had not yet developed the gift of telepathy but he could hear his mom talk to him, he just could not yet respond telepathically.

The other Andrian children found Orion, Perilain and Warren Jr. very interesting and enjoyed teaching them spherical mathematics. They no longer ostracized Humans and were well aware all their lives depended on cooperating with one another. There was a greater enemy force about the universe and it was time to accept realities.

CHAPTER 40
COMING HOME

The Intergalactic Carrier entered the Oort Cloud at the speed of light then slowed as they entered the Kuiper belt coming to the very edge of the accepted perimeter of the solar system. They passed the two outer planets long to be considered non-existent by Human scientist.

Emily was apprehensive about facing Warren with Orion. She was sure that he would be accepting with Warren Jr. Of course he did not know she was pregnant when they left, how could he? She did not know she was pregnant herself. Well, they were grownups with grownups' challenges. Surely he could understand the most difficult and extraordinary challenges that she personally faced.

How could she possibly explain that she loved him and Blain equally? Relationships on the carrier was so simple, they paled in comparison to Earths' mores. Well Blain understood they could not be together when she was on the planet and he accepted that. He also said he would stay with Admiral Cleary in the Space Intelligence housing which was more than a hundred of miles away.

Sara looked impressive in her Dress Space Intelligence Uniform which displayed her awards and many ribbons. She had matured into a most beautiful twenty-one and one half year old woman with poise, confidence and

ASSIMILATION

displayed a commanding aurora. She kept her hair short cropped and swept over her ears in the same fashion as Sasha. Only the tips were covered.

Sara took Warren Jr. by the hand, although he was going on eight and tall for his age he was still her "little brother". Warren Jr. loved Sara and she was his hero in every respect.

Muskula walked into the saucer behind Sara and took up a position beside her. She did not miss the fact that Sara was wearing a seahorse brad in her hair and had a sea star necklace around her neck.

Emily helped Sasha put Orion and Perilain into their receptacles then she took her seat in the saucer's command position. Immediately the covering enclosed her in a cocoon of black silk like material.

Emily felt the Entity's presence almost immediately. The Entity infused her mind with a feeling of completeness and love. She had a burning question of why the Entity had refused to take them home when the saucer left to the distant galaxy. It could have done so with no problem at all but the Entity had refused to answer.

The Entity believed now was the time to explain the delay.

"Emily my beloved, it was necessary for you to be away from the Earth for a short period of time. Our enemy had somehow traced us back to the Earth. They know you, personally you, and thus I, and they know we are their gravest threat. They sent scouts to find us so that we may be killed. They have been gone for a short time now.

When we get back to the earth you will have a little

time to spend with your family but we must find a way to destroy our enemy quickly; all our scientist must work together. We probably have twenty years before they come back. We must repair the rift between our dimensions as soon as possible. But first we must deposit several genetic alteration bombs within their dimension.

I have spent my time searching the cosmic voice to determine the best way to destroy them. They have been very successful in destroying our lifeforms because they are a different matrix of building blocks. They are of a different molecular structure entirely and thus alien to our dimension. I have found the key, now the scientist must build the weapon.

Emily was mesmerized at the information and fearful for earth and by extension, the human domain. After the saucer had left the intergalactic carrier she allowed her spirit to be infused by the Entity and fill her mind with as much knowledge as was inhumanly possible.

Emily was startled back to her consciousness when the Entity asked her if she would be willing to be assimilated molecularly with her. If she should choose to do so then she would have all the knowledge that she, the Entity, possessed.

"Think on this as we have some time. Should you choose to do so, we will be one and all powerful."

The saucer landed shortly in the hanger. Their arrival was kept secret at the request of Emily. She wanted to have some control on how she presented herself and her children to Warren.

ASSIMILATION

The Space Intelligence Commandoes disembarked first in lock step formation. The hanger had since been enlarged times ten its original size and there were at least a thousand personnel present. There were Andrians and Humans and they all were as surprised as was the Early Warning Defense Force to see the saucer materialize in the hanger.

Sara ordered her platoon into parade rest and presented them to the officer in charge.

"Formation, Attenhut!"

Saluting, Sara said, "Chief Personnel Protector Sara Sears returning home from deployment sir!"

The receiving officer returned the salute and said, "Welcome home sir! You may proceed."

Sara made an about face and said, "Platoon! Attenhut! Dismissed!"

The platoon cheered and stepped to the side to wait for their Andrian counterparts to exit the craft. Following the same protocol as Sara's platoon, they too were dismissed.

Muskula walked down the ramp with Warren Jr.; they went and stood next to Sara. Sara put her arms around Warren from behind so he could see his Mother come down the ramp. He was going on eight years old.

Emily and Sasha walked down the ramp with two four year old boys between them. At the end of the ramp they stood at attention and saluted the Officer in Charge, their two sons looking up at their moms, emulated them and they too saluted.

Emily said, "Emily Smith and Commander Sasha

Palangin reporting home from duty, Sir!"

The Officer in Charge returned the salute and said, "I will inform Staff Command Sir. I am sure they will be… amazed! Dismissed!"

CHAPTER 41
NEW REALITIES

Emily, Sasha, and Muskula parted ways. Sara was ready to go home but she wanted to walk. Once she was in the darkness of the surrounding woods and alone, she dropped down on her knees and sobbed and said a prayer of thanks for her safe return. After crying herself out and composing herself, she dusted off her pant legs and resumed her walk.

Sara walked the two miles to the house she had called home for a short period of time, and upon knocking on the door, a stranger answered the door. Her disappointment was clearly on her face. It was 10:00 P.M., thus he was wary, but upon seeing Sara wearing her Dress Space Intelligence Uniform the man was not overly concerned.

He advised that Mr. Sears had married and moved in with Dr. Selena Washington and they lived next door. He further advised they had been married for five years or more.

Sara thanked him for his time and walked to the house next door. She wondered if Alice's life had changed as much as hers, when she returned home from the rabbit hole; nothing was mentioned in the fairytale.

Sara again knocked on the door. After about a minute the door was opened by a small boy about six years old. He had large blue eyes and dark hair.

"Hello. Can I help you? Oh! That is a very pretty uniform! What do you do? My Daddy sometimes wears a uniform like that. Do you know my Daddy?"

Sara looked at him and smiled. He was her brother. He was so cute. He was so innocent and he looked at her like he expected answers to his questions.

Sara kneeled down on one knee to be eye level with him and asked, "What is your name?"

The boy replied, "Michael. Sometimes my mom and dad call me Mikey."

"Well Michael, is it okay if I call you Mikey?"

The boy responded, "I guess so but only my Mom, Dad, and my big brother Shawn call me Mikey."

"I am your big sister, Sara. Can I call you Mikey?"

Mikey's eyes got real big. He said, "Oh my! I have heard about you my whole life! Mom and Dad are going to be real surprised when they learn you are here"!

Sara said, "Can you give your big sister a hug?"

Mikey replied sure and moved forward to be embraced by the beautiful young woman who said she was his sister.

Sara held him close and closed her eyes and had to work hard to keep the tears from running down her face.

Sara heard a voice she recognized but had not heard for almost eight years.

"Who is there Mikey?"

Sara heard his footsteps come into the foyer.

She released Mikey and stood. She looked at her father and quietly said, "Hello Dad. I am finally home."

Caleb stared in disbelief. Sara was standing before

ASSIMILATION

him. Not the young adolescent girl of thirteen that had left, but, a tall beautiful young woman who exhibited grace and poise.

Then he noticed the Silver Star and the Andrian Golden Star for bravery, next was the Andrian Red Nebula Swirl for receiving injuries in combat: These were displayed with several other campaign ribbons above her left breast. Reaching out and taking her by the hand Caleb walked her into the house and under the light so he could see her plainly.

Under the bright light he observed the laser wound above her left cheek. He then lifted her hair from the top of her left ear and observed that the top of the ear was missing. He placed his arms around her and holding her close he just sobbed. He was so grateful to have her home in one piece.

After Caleb had cried himself out, Sara said, "I want a long hot shower".

Selena had stood quietly in the background with Shawn to give Sara and Caleb time for themselves. After Caleb and Sara had cried themselves out Selena came and hugged Sara. After brief salutations she escorted Sara upstairs to the bedroom and showed her the shower. She set the shower to warm and brought out some new shampoo and soap. Sara disrobed and took a half hour long hot shower.

"Merci how blessed we are," Intoned Sara.

After shriveling like a prune, Sara got out of the shower and dried off. Selena had put out Shawn's PJ's and Caleb's robe. Checking herself in the mirror she felt strange as she had not had any clothes on like these in a long time. Sara turned from the mirror and returned downstairs to visit her family.

CHAPTER 42
APPREHENSION

Emily got off the transport lift and proceeded to the small elevator. The original elevator was gone and had since been replaced with a larger elevator to go up into the house. She was holding Warren Jr.'s hand on one side and was carrying Orion on the other.

The doors opened and she stepped off the elevator. She could hear a child's laughter and the child said, "Oh Uncle Warren you are so silly!"

Emily silently walked into the living room where she saw Warren, Skip, Persha and a little boy about six and a little girl, three, seated in the living room.

Warren looked up and saw Emily and the children. He immediately got up went and stood in front of her, silently. Persha and Skip remained on the couch with their son and daughter and they too were silent.

Emily said, "Hello Warren. This is your son Warren Jr., Warren, this is your Father."

The young eight year old boy shyly held out his hand for a hand shake and said, "Hello Father. I have heard about you every day of my life. It is so good to finally meet you."

Warren got down on his knees and pulled Warren Jr. into his arms and held him quietly for a minute in a soft paternal hug. Tears came to his eyes and rolled down his cheeks.

"Hello Son. I am so glad you are home."

"Me too Father; Momma said you were going to take me fishing, sailing, and teach me to drive a car! Is that true Father?"

"Yes Son, that is true."

Persha had sensed Emily when she got off the elevator but she said nothing nor did she move in any way to suggest anyone was there. When Emily came into the room and she observed the two children, she knew immediately the dark haired four year old which she was holding, was Blain's son.

Then Emily said, as a matter of fact, as if no explanation was required, "And this is Orion, Blain's son."

Emily and Persha both sensed the spiked temperament of anger from Warren, then the spiked temperament of anger from Emily.

Emily responded, "Do not judge me Warren. Neither one of us wanted the circumstances that brought about the results. They are both my sons.

Warren responded, "Well what would you say if when you came home I presented you with a son?"

Emily said icily, "I would be glad you found comfort and peace in your time of travail."

Persha jumped up off of the couch with Adam at her side and Eve trailing behind, and went to Emily, Skip followed suit.

Persha gave Emily a hug and said, "Thank God you are home safe! What beautiful children you have! And

ASSIMILATION

look at our surprises! This young man is Adam; from my understanding that seems like a perfect name for new beginnings! And this little sweetie is Evangeline, we call her Eve."

Adam telepathed, "Hi Emily; I have heard so much about you. It is so nice to finally meet you."

Emily looked at Adam in surprise; he was at least six years old.

"Why Adam, it is so nice to meet you. You indeed are a surprise!"

Emily sat Orion down and then lifted Eve into her arms.

Emily kissed her on the cheek and said, "Eve, What beautiful curls you have! I am so happy to meet you both; now Orion and Warren will have someone to play "Duh" with."

All the children laughed as the "Duh" game was copied and played by all the children.

Emily set Eve down and greeted Adam and Eve in the Andrian, the lesser to the greater.

Adam said, "No Emily. You are the greater", and reversed the greeting.

Adam gave Emily a tight hug. "I did not believe I would ever get to meet you. Momma said you were three galaxies away and that we probably would not get to see you in our lifetime because for some reason your saucer would not bring you home."

Warren gave Persha a sharp look. Persha looked down; she could feel his anger toward her for not revealing the probabilities of Emily's return.

Emily then gave Persha and Skip a hug.

Emily introduced Orion and Perilain to Persha, Skip, Adam and Eve. Then like children everywhere they overcame awkwardness with Adam shouting, "Hey! Let's go out and Play!"

All three boys and Eve ran outside to play. For Warren Jr. and Orion, this was the first time they have been outside alone as their return had allowed only a brief view of the Earth, and now, not only that, it was dark; they were apprehensive.

Adam could sense their uneasiness and said, "It is okay, I will not let anything happen to you."

Eve said, "Me too!"

Emily sent a "thank you" and "I love you" to Adam and Eve, which they received with gratefulness. After all, the great Emily was entrusting them with her two sons.

After Persha had brought out tea and cookies they all had a seat in the den.

Emily said, "I missed you all so much. We were in decontamination when the order to leave was received. It was too dangerous to take us out of decontamination so quickly and thus we could not get back to earth. Flata took me out of stasis because I was pregnant with Warren Jr."

"There was dissention on the Carrier and several attempts were made on my life and Sara's life. Sara was kept in Stasis for three years to make sure no harm would come to her. I finally made Flata bring her out. Needless to say that Sara was madder than a wet hen finding out she was seventeen when she woke up."

ASSIMILATION

Persha, never ending her ever expanding knowledge of English language idioms had to think what exactly Emily was saying. When she figured it out and filed it away she gave a short giggle and hugged Skips arm closer to her.

"I do not blame her, especially considering she was almost fourteen when she went in. It is just that the events were so unprecedented and the risk to her life was just too great to bring her out sooner."

"Sara exhibited an antagonistic and arrogant attitude. Blain threatened to put her back in stasis until the tour was over and also wipe her mind. Fortunately, Chandra and I were able to convince him not to do so."

"As it turned out, Sara is quiet a warrior. On her first mission she saved up to twenty-five lives at the risk of her own. She was nearly killed three times. She even jumped out a two story window with a guy that had a bomb strapped to him so he would not kill everyone. Fortunately when the bomb went off, she and the bomber were divided by a rock wall. The bomb did not kill her and the fall did not kill her but she was really banged up pretty badly."

Persha listened raptly. The fact that Blain changed his mind not to wipe Sara's mind was in and of itself a miracle. Blain never changed his mind. She knew that to be true because she all but struck him to get him to change his mind when he had ordered her to come to Earth.

Persha, looking out the door at her son and daughter, then at Skip, thought, "I am so glad I came. I did not know such happiness could exist."

Skip gave Persha a hug and said, "I love you too".

Skip said, "I remember when you all first arrived, Blain threatened to wipe my mind and Billy's mind for making a joke, fortunately Emily kept him from doing so."

Warren started to speak but thought better of not speaking what was on the verge of his tongue when Emily gave him a strong look. She knew what he was going to say. Their time was too precious to be spent with petty grievances. Of course she could understand why Warren would not consider her and Blaine's relationship as petty grievance.

Instead Warren said, "Why did you not come home in the saucer? You can go almost anywhere in no time at all using the saucer."

Emily knew that was a valid question.

She responded, "For reasons I will not get into right at this moment, the Entity refused to allow us to leave. Before we get into a more serious discussion I want to have a long hot shower and then drink a good cold glass of wine."

Then looking at Persha she said, "I want Warren and Orion to enjoy their first shower also. They are really looking forward to the experience."

Turning away Emily said, "Therefore Warren, I will explain everything, after I have a shower. We can discuss the circumstances with a glass of wine."

Persha chimed in, "I hear that! There is no way I could ever be happy on an intergalactic carrier again! Come on!

ASSIMILATION

Let me help get you going! Too bad Hanlee and Jawane are not home tonight. They will be disappointed about missing your homecoming!"

Emily took a long, hot shower. Being alone for the first time in years she too broke down and cried. After she had cried herself out, she toweled off, dressed and went back down stairs.

Warren Jr. and Orion were still outside mesmerized at the beauty of being on a planet.

Emily called them and said, "Warren, Orion, come in boys. It is time for your first shower."

Both boys yelled and ran into the house followed by Adam and Eve. When Emily had told them about showering on Earth, they could hardly believe it. Emily took them upstairs and all three boys took a shower together. They were both amazed at how much water they used. Eve felt left out

Adam said, "I can hardly wait until I can go on an intergalactic carrier! Momma tells me of all the beautiful sights one gets to see".

Later in the night, having put the boys to bed at twelve midnight, Emily went into Warren. He was still sullen and not believing that she could have come home earlier. He knew the saucer that claimed Emily as its own was capable of god like feats.

Emily crawled into bed close to Warren. She did love him so much. Her life just had become too complicated. She and Blain had gone on many missions together and it seemed the constant threat of danger and possible death just brought them together. But, in her heart she knew that was just an excuse. Emily had come to love Blain on her first venture on the carrier. She had to work very hard to keep her hands off of him and always did her best to be coy. Blains constant plea for her to be his consort was her constant guilt for wanting to say yes but her torment for saying no.

"Warren, the reason I have been gone for so long is because the Entity had received information from the other intelligent saucers that our enemy had sent scouts to find me and my saucer. They did not know how the enemy followed us here to earth but they did. They were here several years looking for us. Finally they left and thus we were free to come home."

"You can choose to believe or disbelieve. As of our arrival, all our forces have gone on the highest alert and we are now on a wartime setting."

"We only have maybe twenty years to develop a weapon to destroy them. The Entity said that she had the key to their destruction and our forces must develop the weapon that I must deliver into their dimension. We must also repair the rift between our dimensions so they cannot return. The saucers are combining all their intelligences to come up with a solution to the problem."

"I love you now as I loved you before I left. I hope you can accept that and you love me too."

Warren did not respond. He turned over on his side with his back toward Emily and went to sleep. He just could not fathom in his being how he could share Emily with Blain.

CHAPTER 43
MUSKULA'S CHALLENGE

Muskula got a ride to the encampment which had since been enlarged and upgraded with tunnel access to the water. Everyone was issued light shirts and specially designed trousers to cover the scales on their lower bodies. The shirts had military insignias to denote military affiliation in an effort to masquerade their difference.

When they had arrived over seven years ago their number was very low, forty-two members. They were basically extinct from the millions of members of their species that were murdered by the new enemy.

Since reproduction was of an essence, it was necessary to enact reproduction measures found on the intergalactic carriers. With the assistance of Andrian biological specialist, their numbers had increase exponentially in seven years. There were now over a thousand new members of the specie.

Muskula walked into the main recreation area and found a large number of her specie in learning classes. While on the carrier, Flata had enhanced her linguistic skills and increased her cerebral cortex by ten percent. Thus, even though she had been gone for seven years, she was already more knowledgeable and skilled in linguistics than her counterparts.

Flata had talked to her several times about the

necessity of their specie to change the way they reproduced. She believed it would be necessary for each male to have more than one mate. She also believed leadership could no longer be by one female but, responsibility must be shared by all. In effect, leadership decisions would be determined by committees.

No one in the training room recognized her; they were all very young and were engaged in learning activities. She was amazed to see such a large group. As she walked thru the room she looked for anyone that she knew. Finding no one she recognized she continued to walk thru the facility

Suddenly she heard a loud chitter and other vocalizations. It was her mate. When she turned around she saw him running to her. When they were together they just hugged saying nothing. The moment was for them and them alone.

Coming up behind her mate was another female. Evidently she had claimed her mate after she had not returned after one year. It was their way. No one expected her to ever return.

After a short burst of communication, it was decided they would continue to mate according to the Andrian way; He would have to be shared among all the females. However, for the time being her former mate was hers and they found a vacant bathing area and became reacquainted. Muskula found that the reunion was bitter sweet as he had already accepted the Andrian way and he just did not seem to be the same. For Muskula and her specie, they were well on their way to their new reality and brave new world.

CHAPTER 44
SPACE INTELLIGENCE ALERT

Admiral Cleary was drinking his evening tea when he received a call from Space Intelligence advising him that the Early Warning Space Station at LaGrange Point Two had advised the arrival of an Intergalactic Carrier into the solar system. He was further advised that they believed it was one of the three Carriers that had left almost eight years earlier with Emily Smith.

Admiral Cleary jumped to his feet and barked an order to his orderly.

"Get my jet ready! We are going to go to the base."

The Carrier has just entered the Kuiper Belt. Admiral Cleary wanted to be there when the debarking personnel arrived. He was especially interested in seeing how the young Ms. Sears had fared.

Admiral Cleary was in the viewing room overlooking the hanger when, without warning, a saucer materialized in the hanger. The saucer was large and took two spaces.

Admiral Cleary had a clear view of the ramp and eagerly waited for the personnel to debark. He definitely had some things he wanted to say to Emily about taking an adolescent teen to the carrier and swearing her into Space Intelligence.

The first group of commandoes came down the ramp in a two line formations and was headed by a young woman he did not recognize. They smartly formed up and were presented to the duty officer by the squad leader with a crisp salute.

Admiral Cleary looked closely at the presenting platoon leader; She could not be more than twenty-one or twenty-two years old. He then noticed the Silver Star, the Andrian Golden Star and the Nebulous Swirl in addition to several campaign ribbons.

He looked again at the face of the platoon leader.

"Who is the platoon leader? Do any of you recognize her?"

He was asking a general question to any of the personnel in the control room.

One of the controllers in the room said, "Sir, I just received the official manifest from the saucer and it appears that the platoon leader is a Ms. Sara Sears, Sir."

Admiral Cleary looked again at the young woman. He had only seen a picture of Ms. Sears and at the time she was thirteen.

"If that is Ms. Sears, how did she receive a Silver Cross, An Andrian Golden Star, and the Nebula Swirl," replied Admiral Cleary.

A clerk brought over after action reports that also had been downloaded. Admiral Cleary read thru them quickly. He was amazed that a young woman could be capable of such combat skill at such a young age.

By the time he finished reading, the Andrian contingent had also been presented. Muskula the Mermaid and

ASSIMILATION

a young boy had exited the craft and went and stood by Sara; the boy, about eight, stood in front of Sara and she had her arms crossed in front of him.

Then he saw Emily and Sasha come down the ramp. They had two children between them. His jaw dropped open in amazement. There had been no mention of children in the official manifest. Surly the eight year old boy was not Sara's.

Emily presented both platoons to the Officer of the Day.

Admiral Cleary watched as Emily, Sasha, Sara and Muskula gave each other a group's hug. Then the platoons gave out a loud cheer and began hugging and slapping each other on the back. The entire group formed up in a line and individually gave Sara a crisp salute.

Listening in on a directional mike Admiral Cleary heard several of the commandoes say, "Thank you for saving my life, Sir!"

Sara responded, "Semper Fi!"

One of the orderlies came up and saluted Admiral Cleary and said, "Sir! A communique from Ms. Smith marked, "For Your Eyes Only", Sir."

Admiral Cleary took the encrypted communique and went into a small office off to the side of the Control Room. Sitting at the desk Admiral Cleary inserted the documents into the crypto translator and read the message.

Admiral Cleary's felt his face tighten and chills sprang up all over his body. He could feel his chest tighten as he became short of breath and his blood ran cold.

The communique first sentence said, "Enemy arrival

is to be expected to be no more than twenty years away."

Reading the rest of the communique was no better when he learned that they had been observed by their mortal enemy for a period of at least six years. The enemy had been looking for Emily and the Entity machine but no doubt they were collecting intelligence for a return and conquer scenario.

Due to this bit of intelligence Admiral Cleary believed it was more necessary to pass information on to The President, and other powers that be, than to visit for "ole time sake". Admiral Cleary took a saucer back to Space Intelligence Operations to see if they could review data looking for any signature indications of an incursion.

CHAPTER 45
HELLO FATHER

Sasha Palangin and Perilain took a saucer to a secret military base in the dense woods and mountains of the Caucus Region of Russia. She had not been home since she ran away when she was fifteen. She, in truth, had been a rebellious child and was constantly in a war with her father's authority over her.

Her father was military and an avid supporter for a strong centralized government. Her mother worked at the University of Physics and Science in Moscow. She was a Chemist by University records but her true love was microbial lifeforms in the human body.

Being a mother of six children, it was amazing that she got thru school at all. She was a strong and determined woman. Her husband said she was too headstrong. Perhaps that was true. Sasha was headstrong. It hurt her deeply when she and her Father would have bitter arguments over the most nonsensical issues about whether Russia should have a more inclusive military.

She knew Sasha, the baby of the six children, was his favorite and most beloved. When Sasha left he grieved over her as if she was dead, and, since they have not heard from her in over fifteen years, in all probability, that was true. She also knew that her husband, Nickolas, had tried to use his military contacts to locate his daughter but it always came up with no information. Curiously though, the returned information always included that the intelligence services believed she was okay, they just could not locate her.

Therefore when the knock on the door came around eleven at night they were not expecting to see a military officer in a Space Intelligence Uniform standing on the stoop.

Nickolas went the door followed by Irina. It was unusual to have visitors at this time of evening, and, when it did occur, it never portends any good news.

Standing next to the officer was a little boy about six years old. How strange could that be?

"Yes Officer, may I help you?"

Irena, standing behind and to the side of Nickolas, looked closely at the Officer, and then she said, "Oh my God! Thank you so much!" Having said that she burst into tears and shoved her husband to the side and enveloped Sasha into her arms.

Nickolas, like most men who do not believe in miracles such as people rising from the dead, could not believe that the Officer in front of him was his Sasha. It just was not possible. And, he had never so much as been spoken back too when he reprimanded his wife, much less shoved out of the way.

The little boy walked inside and looking up at Nicholas, said, "Hello Dedulya, I have heard a lot about you."

Nicholas eyes opened in amazement. He looked at the little boy. He was at least five or six years old. Then,

ASSIMILATION

looking at the woman in uniform he was still mystified as to who she was. It must be Sasha and the little boy must be hers.

He leaned over and gently picked up the child and said, "Come my little dove. Let your Dedulya give you a hug."

Nickolas gently hugged the boy and continued to speak soft terms of endearment of love and joy. Of course the language was Russian but Perilain could understand it perfectly.

Perilain responded, "Thank you Dedulya. Mother has told me about you and Badulya."

He reached up farther and kissed him on the cheek. He knew his Dedulya loved him because he could read his spirit and mind.

Sasha had come inside and in the light he could see clearly that she was indeed his daughter from long ago. He then gently hugged her and tears flowed all around on the surprising family reunion.

Sasha stayed with her Mother and Father for two months using just a part of her military leave. She primarily wanted to know if Perilain would be happy with his grandparents when she was away. Blain wanted Perilain with him on a carrier but he knew that the dangers they were soon to face could very well be fatal. They decided they could more easily do their front line combat roles knowing their son was safe, for the time being, on the earth; Neither Sasha or Blain had any illusions of the deadly threat they faced. In order to save their families, they needed to be focused on the task at hand which was to defeat their enemy.

Blain had come to introduce himself to Sasha's Mother and Father. They both decided that it was not prudent to reveal Blains status at the present time. Perilain agreed as he said that his Dedulya had a very tight and enclosed mind. He also said he would not expose his intelligence to his family.

As Sasha was going out the door, Perilain said, "I will be waiting Mamulya. I understand why you must go. I will help and take care of Dedulya and Badulya. I love you.", then he saluted. Sasha returned the salute, turned, and went to the waiting car. Tears were streaming down her face. It was very possible she would never see her son again.

Sasha had been gone one week when Nickolas was surprised to see a general waiting for him in his office. He stood at attention and saluted him.

The officer said, "At ease Nickolas. I am here unofficially. We are aware of Sasha's position in Space Intelligence. I am personally aware of your anguish and pain in trying to locate your daughter over the years. I am sorry I could not tell you anything about her. I always ended the communique reporting that she was believed to be okay. I could not do more than that. As you could see, she was wearing a Space Intelligence Uniform.

Nickolas remained silent. A general did not drop into ones office to talk about why he did not receive a direct answer into inquiries about one's daughter.

"We are reassigning you to Vostochny Cosmodrome. Your services can be utilized better there and the schools

ASSIMILATION

are outstanding. You will also be able to contact Sasha more easily. Irena will be challenged with the new microbial life forms that have been discovered and are being studied in a new laboratory and, she will fit in nicely with the science department at the Space Science University."

"You will both be handsomely compensated. Housing will be provided. We can sell your old home or we can rent it out. The choice is yours, of course. However, it would be in your best interest to accept the reassignment."

Nickolas was well aware he was going to move wither he wanted to or not. He liked his current assignment. All his family and friends were within thirty kilometers circle. The Vostochny Cosmodrome was in the far outer reaches of the Eastern Borders of Russia in the Far East Amur Region.

"What about my children?"

"You will have two months leave a year. Free transportation will be provided to visit family, regardless how many times you choose to go visit your family."

Nickolas was well aware that the offer was very generous and never offered to someone of his stature. He was basically a military drone; he was a good soldier, followed orders, was respectful to his superiors and most important; he was supportive of the government to a fault.

"When did you want me to report General?"

"You have already been assigned to my command. You may go home and prepare to move. You should be on base within seven days. Until then you are on your own. I have taken the liberty to advance you a cash credit of six months' salary into your bank account. Your orders are in the top drawer of your desk".

The General saluted and said, "Welcome aboard."

After the General left, Nickolas sat down at his desk and pulled open the top left hand drawer. The orders were there as the General said they would be. Pulling them from the drawer and opening the large envelope, Nickolas removed the orders from the pack. Up to this point he did not believe the General was real and this was some kind of trick that his colleagues were playing on him. However this was not the case and the orders were real.

The orders were stamped, "Top Secret".

Looking over the orders he was advised that he was not to tell any of his colleagues where he was going. His children were to be given minimal information. In effect, he was to leave the office saying nothing to anyone and just disappear from their lives. Nickolas gathered the orders together, put the picture of his wife in the vanilla folder and walked out the door.

CHAPTER 46
FRIENDS, CHILDREN NO MORE

Sara had been home for three days getting reacquainted with her new reality of no longer being the only child in her Father's life. Of course he still loved her as he always had. It took Sara awhile to realize that it was not her new brother that made her feel left out, but whatever it was, she could not quiet put her finger on it.

Sara was sitting outside on the patio mulling over the new differences in her home life when Selena walked up and said, "May I join you, Sara?

Sara was caught by surprise, which was unusual for her, and replied, "Yes, please sit down."

"Sara, I know how much you missed your Father while you were away and I am sure it was your desire to return home to be with him which helped you to remain vigilant and thus stay alive. I want to thank you for taking such good care of him for the thirteen years when you were the only female in his life. You had to grow up fast and the transition from doting daughter to caregiver was subtle and escaped your attention as you grew older. Yet, when you left you still felt the weight of responsibility for him that gave you the courage to face the dangers and overcome them."

"I love your Father and he loves me. I can never take your place Sara, but I want you to know that I will take good care of him. He is a wonderful man and most of that is due to you."

Sara looked at Selena quietly and thought, "She is right on target. It was his love for me and I him and my duty of responsibility to him that did carry me thru."

"Thank you Selena for taking care of my Dad. I am relieved he found such a good woman to care for him. You probably know by now he is terribly absent minded about some things. I bet you have to do double duty to keep up with his socks."

Selena and Sara both laughed.

"Is that not the truth? They seem to wind up in the oddest places!"

Both woman stood and hugged one another with a long loving hug.

Sara said, "Love my Dad."

Selena replied, "I promise on my life I will".

When the women parted Sara felt her spirit was lighter and the sun seemed all the brighter; she decided she would go over to Emily's and see if she was cooking anything good. She had yet to visit as she wanted to spend time with her Dad..

When Sara went up on the porch Warren Jr. ran out the door banging the screen door against the wall and literally flew into her arms.

"Sara! Where have you been? I missed you so much. You should have been here to play "Duh", with us. It is so much fun!"

ASSIMILATION

Sara gave Warren Jr. a tight hug and a sloppy kiss on the cheek. Warren shrieked and ran into the house pulling Sara with him.

Warren was carrying a large bowl of spaghetti and sat it on the table. Emily was following behind carrying a large pot of sauce. Persha came out of the kitchen with a large basket of fresh baked bread.

Persha, upon seeing Sara threw the bread on the table and ran into Sara's arms. They each hugged and kissed and cried. Skip came up and hugged her too.

Warren waited until Sara had a minute then he came up and gave her a hug. Moving her to arm's length he looked her up and down.

"Wow Sara, what a beautiful young woman you have grown up to be!"

Sara was wearing a low cut Spanish style blouse with puffy sleeves with a short light blue skirt. Her shoes were white sandals. And as always, she wore a sea horse brad in her hair and her sea star necklace given to her by Muskula, hung between her breasts.

Skip said, "Billy is going to be real sorry he missed you. He is in town to day as he had to take a math test. He will be home tonight."

"Good, I plan on being here many nights! Hopefully you all will not put me in a coma for three years."

Everyone laughed as they knew that a joke was better than reality.

"Where is Jawane and Hanlee?"

Warren advised, "They are both assigned to a military university in Oregon but they heard you were home and they should arrive sometime tonight."

They sat down for lunch and Sara could not believe how good the spaghetti was. They ate in silence as Sara tasted, much in the same way Persha did when she first arrived, the flavors of basil, oregano, and fresh tomatoes in the sauce.

Sara knew that things would be strained between Emily and Warren due to Perilain and it would take time to work things out. She personally decided to stay out of fray and just make things easy for Orion as possible.

After lunch when Sara sat down on the couch, Orion came and stood by her. Sara just lifted him into her lap as she had always done. He leaned his head on her shoulder and hugged her neck.

Telepathically Orion quietly intoned, "I am sorry that Warren will not love me".

Sara hugged him closer and replied, "Give him time Orion. Warren has been thru a traumatic event the first time Emily was taken to the carrier, she was gone one year. Now the second time she went to the carrier, she was gone seven years and comes home with you and it has shaken his confidence and self-worth. He is no longer as sure of himself as he was years ago. Humans are hard to understand from any perspective. He will come to love you as he loves Emily and as he loves Warren Jr."

Orion said, again for her mind only, "I have entered his mind and read his thoughts. Sometime he hates me, sometimes he loves me and sometime he just wishes I would go away. I do not know what to do."

Sara hugged him closer, "Be loving, Orion. Just be

yourself. You have a sweet spirit and a good heart. The things Warren is feeling and experiencing is an adult problem and has nothing to do with you. He will need to work thru his self-doubt and he will have to learn to be accepting of your Mother's responsibilities and duties. She needs love and support also. Being away for almost seven years in a wartime setting takes its toll on one's soul and spirit."

"Your Mother fell in love with your Father Blain the first time she was on the carrier. Your Father does not know it yet but he is deeply in love with your Mother. It is easier for him to accept Warren in your Mother's life than it is for Warren to accept your Father because of the different social structure we have on the earth compared to an intergalactic carrier. I promise you that everything will be okay."

"Something you need to remember is that you have both Human and Andrian DNA and you are superior intellectually to both Humans and Andrians. Your Mother and Father's responsibility is to teach you to make the correct moral choices so when you reach positions of leadership you will rule with justice and mercy."

Sara sat with Orion for about twenty minutes as he fell fast asleep. On the carrier it was his favorite way to go to sleep as he found Sara's arms around him comforting. Sara stood up with him and Emily led the way to his bedroom. Laying him down in the bed she kissed his cheek and sent him an "I love you".

Emily closed the door behind them as they left. They went down to the kitchen and Emily got two glasses of ice tea then they went out on the porch. It was a nice warm afternoon; Idyllic actually.

The breeze blew Emily's hair away from her face. Sara remained silent as she knew that Emily's heart was heavy. As of yet Warren had not accepted Orion nor had he touched Emily.

Emily said, "I will be going to the Space Intelligence Headquarters in Brussels in two weeks. I will be gone for an undetermined length of time. There is too much at stake to allow Warren's petty grievances to cloud my thinking. Sasha has left Perilain with her parents in Russia. They are being moved to the Vostochny Cosmodrome. I think that Orion will be much happier with Perilain there than here with Warren. I hate to separate Warren Jr. and Orion; I just cannot gauge Warren's mental state."

Sara sat quietly. What was she supposed to say?

Finally Sara said, "I know it must be hard. I do not have the experience to advise you or really offer you any guidance. You know I love Orion and Warren Jr. I will be glad to take care of Orion for you. I can move into the house or perhaps get our own apartment nearby. That way I can watch Orion and Warren Jr. too. Or, perhaps you can have Persha take Orion. She would love him as her own. Skip would love him and enjoy taking him fishing. He would fit in nicely with their two children."

Emily let out a sigh. "Oh Sara, for such a young woman you are so helpful in offering solutions, neither of which I thought about. Of course you are out of the picture because you will be going to Brussels with me. That is if you wish to accept your commission as Lieutenant in

ASSIMILATION

the Space Intelligence Commandoes."

Sara said, "What! What are you talking about?"

Emily was smiling at her. She was not intending to tell her now but it appeared opportunity presented itself. If taking Sara with her to Brussels was not the plan then having Sara stay with Orion would be her first choice. However, she could not see holding Sara back in her career for her own selfish reasons.

Sara said quietly, "What about the men and women in my platoon?" They depend on me. I love them and they me. I have never known such love before. It is different from parental love, or a child's love. I would die for them and they would die for me. I would be abandoning them for selfish gain. I could not do that."

Emily thought for a minute then said, "Sara, you are a talented and gifted commando. You have so much more to offer. You have good tactical understanding and your analytical skills enhances your decision making process."

"You and Sasha are both highly respected and the commandoes want to be under your command structure. And for your information, Admiral Cleary is the one who initiated the process to commission you as an officer. Blain and I both support the commission. As an officer you will be over a unit of one hundred commandoes. You can choose your own platoon leaders and you will have a say in how you carry out operations."

"Should you choose to accept the commission then I will take your advice and see if Persha and Skip can take care of Orion while we are away on assignments; I think he will be happy there and he can still be with Warren Jr.

Blain and I both believe it is going to be too dangerous to keep them with us on the carriers. We are both being selfish with the children."

There was a noise behind them as the screen door opened and Jawane and Hanlee came out the door. Sara jumped up and ran into their arms for a group hug. They were joined by Emily after a moment as she wanted to give them space of time to savor the reunion.

"Hey Jawane, you never told me I was going to be asleep for three years. What is up with that?"

Jawane and Hanlee laughed.

Hanlee responded first, "Yes, we are really sorry about that. It appears that Humans tend to bring the worst out of us Andrians!"

Jawayne said, "And not only that, I was looking forward to going to your senior prom as your date. Now I will never get to go to one!"

"You and me both," said Sara.

I guess I missed out on a lot. I still do not have a driver's license. I do not know how to drive. I am not so sure I know how to dance. And not only that, I have not had my first date!"

Jawane laughed. "Well Sara I would like to take you to the mall where we shared out first refreshments together and then go to a movie. Would you like that?"

Sara rolled her eyes and said, "I do not know, Jawane. My Father warned me about you boys who try to pick up girls by telling them they have fine muscular structure and tone and must eat all the right foods. I think I would have to have a chaperone. Hanlee would you do me the honor of being my chaperone for my first date and go with us so as to help protect my virginity!" Sara batted her eyelids as she talked about protecting her virginity.

Hanlee laughed and said, "I would love to. You would not believe all the things he has learned since you have been gone and he wants to do all those things to you! You are definitely going to need someone to help keep him in check!"

Sara said, "I would love to go to the mall and go shopping. As you know, shopping on the carrier is extremely limited. Let's go right now while the kids are asleep. We can take them later."

"Emily, would you like to go to the mall with us? You have not been shopping either?"

"No thanks. You all go ahead. I want to stay near Warren. Perhaps we can take the kids to a movie later. That will be fun."

They left the porch talking and laughing, Emily felt like Sara was going to fit in just fine as her new lieutenant.

They rode the hour long ride to town listening to music and enjoying the scenery. Sara was in her own world letting her mind wander and was unaware that she had placed her hand on Jawane's thigh. She moved closer to him and finally noticed where her hand was.

Squeezing his thigh lightly she said, "My, what fine muscle tone you have."

They all laughed and then to her surprise Jawane and Hanlee burst into song singing along with the radio. They had definitely assimilated into Humanoid culture.

They decided they would go to the food court where

they first met. After getting their food and sitting down Sara told them of her adventures she had had on the carrier. They were careful not to use any words or language that would give them away.

"Sara! Sara! Is that really you? What happened to you? You seemed to have just dropped off the face of the earth! We could not find you anywhere!"

Caught with a piece of pizza in her mouth gave Sara time to think of an answer for her old friend. As it was, Sara was speechless for a moment when she looked up and saw one of her former classmates from the eighth grade. She was one of the two girls that Sara was here with in the mall when she had seen Emily's security detail.

"Hey Kyla, how are you doing? Are you going to the university, did you start a career or, are you married? Here, sit down."

Sara believed that if she jump started the questions she could more easily control the direction of the conversation.

Kyla hesitated a minute after sitting down then she said, "Actually I have been working in a lawyers office six years now. After I graduated from high school, and you were nowhere around to be found, for seven years I might add, I just answered an advertisement in the town paper and went straight to work for Jack. He is a lawyer. It is a small office but he does well. You could have written or something you know. I thought we were friends."

Sara quickly said, "Sorry".

Sara asked, "Where is Haley? What is she up too?"

ASSIMILATION

Pain came across Kyla's face.

"You do not know? You did not hear? Your father never told you? Haley was murdered by this guy with lots of money and who is still walking around town bragging that he did not do anything wrong. He said it was an accident. He swears that he did not push her or hit her and their argument was just a misunderstanding. He stated that she turned away, tripped and fell down into the ravine."

"There were two witnesses that said they heard a loud argument in the next camp sight up in Adirondack Park. They went outside their tent and at the camp sight about seventy feet away, they saw this guy grab Haley by the hair and punch her in the face. She was crying and said she was sorry and she promised she would not tell anyone what he was doing."

"The man replied, "Too late Bitch, you are dead meat".

"At that point Haley was trying to resist and was kicking and fighting him but he held onto her hair. He swung her around putting her back to a ravine and letting go of her hair he hit her full in the face with his fist. She was knocked into the ravine breaking her neck. She died instantly."

"He was a big man. Haley met him at a car race the summer we were in the eleventh grade. They went together for a couple of years. She seemed happy but she had grown distant and we did not hang out together much."

After she finished speaking Kyla looked up at Sara.

Sara did not look the same. Her face was taunt, eyes narrow, and she was breathing slowly. It was then that she noticed a fine white scar above her left cheek bone that ran from her cheek to her ear. Then she noticed that a small portion of the top of her ear was missing.

Sara said, "Do you know his name?"

"Well yeah. His name is Roger Clovis. His Father is head of the Gaming Commission. They are above the law in the New York Burroughs and they have very powerful friends all over the Northeast."

"The lawyer I work for was the county prosecutor when Kyla was killed. He was unable to get a conviction. In fact he was unable to get a grand jury to look at the murder. They said there was not enough evidence to bring it to trial."

"He quit the county prosecutor's office and moved to Mount Pearl; he opened a private practice here. I was the only person that answered the newspaper add so I got the job."

Hanlee and Jawane were silent. They could read Sara's mind. Her mind was on a slow boil with controlled fury racing thru her cerebral cortex, although one would not be able to tell just by looking at her. It was also a new side of Sara they knew she developed in the Commandoes.

Jawane interjected, "Hi Kyla, my name is Jawane. Remember me?"

She did not.

"I met you and your friend Haley, after the gymnastics meet here in the mall, about seven years ago. I was the one that told Sara she had fine musculature, remember now?

Kyla looked at him in surprise. She did recognize him.

"Yes, I recognize you now. We all have grown quite a bit since then."

As she said that she was thinking, "You were really a dweeb".

Everyone smiled reading her mind.

Jawane smiled and said, "Yes, that was me."

Knowing Kyla would not be put off any longer, Sara said, "I had a falling out with my father over a boy. My Dad was real angry with me and he sent me to live with my Aunt in California. It all happened so fast I was unable to get your address. But the truth be known, I was so embarrassed that I believed it would be in my best interest to break off our relationship. You see, I got pregnant. I moved away and adopted the baby out."

Kyla sat up straight, open mouthed, flabbergasted at what she just heard.

"I find that hard to believe. You were always the most mature one and level headed one. You were always telling us to be careful."

"Yes, I know. It was a one night stand, with a cousin no less. He deflowered me and impregnated me all in one fling. He was about nineteen at the time. If you remember we were thirteen. He ran away and joined the army. Dad would have killed him but he was already out of his reach."

Kyla said, "Well that explains it."

Sara said, "Explains what?"

"Your Father; after we have not seen you for more than a month we went to your house and you all had moved away leaving no forwarding address. Haley and I saw him in a store in town about a year later and when we introduced ourselves and asked where you were, he turned pale and mumbled you were out of state or something like that."

"I am so Sorry Sara. I cannot imagine anything more traumatic than getting pregnant at thirteen. My goodness, it must have been terrible. Especially when your Father kicked you out."

Jawane said, "Your right. I cannot imagine anything more traumatic either. Can you Hanlee?"

Hanlee, with a very serious face, said, "No. I cannot."

They both kept their faces straight and solemn.

Sara looked at Jawane and Hanlee and frowned. They just shrugged their shoulders and smiled.

Sara then said, "How are Haley's Mom and Dad? At least she was one of four children. I know the pain will never go away but perhaps if the murderer, Roger Clovis, is brought to justice, it will give them peace."

Looking down, Kyla responded, "It would give them peace but that will never happen."

Sara reached her hands over and took Kyla's hands in hers. As Kyla looked down she noticed that there was major scarring on Sara's left hand. How strange. The hand look like it had been broken into a million pieces.

Sara looked at Kyla and said, "Kyla, look at me."

Kyla looked into Sara's eyes. There appeared to be a glistening in them and the pupils were down to pin

ASSIMILATION

points. Her face was hard and void of expression.

"Kyla, I give you my word, as the stars circle the black hole in the center of our galaxy, as the earth circles the sun and as the moon is our joy, Roger Clovis will not escape justice. His cry for mercy will be ignored and his blood will boil peeling the flesh from his bones."

An icy chill ran down Kyla's spine as she sat back and tried to remove her hands from Sara's grasps. But, she could not do so, Sara would not let go and her grip was like a vise.

Then to Kyla's surprise, Sara switched to an entirely different subject.

"Kyla, do you love Jack? If you do and Jack is available and not already married, then you should pursue him and love him. You need to find joy and happiness where and when you can. Life is short and none of us know what lay ahead for us, for our families or our friends."

Sara knew that Kyla loved Jack as she read her mind and felt her indecision as to what she should do. She was afraid because Jack was ten years older than her and he had never been married. It was such a big leap. After all, she was only twenty-one and her life experiences were extremely limited. After Haley's death, she never dated.

Sara said, "'Hey, we are going to go to a movie right now, would to like to go with us?"

Kyla answered quickly, "Thank you but no, I have to get home. I have some things I want to do. It was so nice to see you again Sara. Please, keep in touch. You know where to reach me."

Kyla left and no one spoke. The information about

Haley's death dampened everyone's spirit. They returned home early and Sara said it was time for a shower. Jawane was going to go into the living room when Sara grabbed him by the arm.

"Not you Jawane, you are going to shower with me."

Jawane looked her in the eyes and said, "Are you sure?"

Sara responded with a small smile.

CHAPTER 47
A FRIEND AVENGED

Early the next morning Sara was in the intelligence command center and spent over eight hours at a console researching the Clovis family with emphasis on Roger. She was able to access their personal computers and learned that Haley was not the only young woman that he had dispensed with under the guise of an accident. There were at least eight other young woman.

The man was an accomplished serial killer skating under the police radar due mainly to the millions that the family paid in bribes. She collected evidence on the illegal enterprises and forwarded it to National Police Intelligence in Atlanta, her Father's former employer.

She collected the names and addresses of the eight victim's next of kin and placed them on her personal computer for later use. She was now ready to pay a personal visit to the slime that murdered her friend Haley.

Sara's fervent research had not gone unnoticed by fellow commandoes and administrative assistants. Emily received a call from one of her platoon leaders and was advised that Sara was evidently on a mission and no one knew what it was.

Emily called Jawane and asked him if he knew what was going on with Sara. He informed Emily about the murder of Haley, one of her childhood girlfriends by a member of a crime syndicate. He was pretty sure that she was going to take him out.

Jawane relayed the conversation between Sara and her friend Kyla. He further stated that the murdered Haley was one of the two girls that was with Sara when they met in the mall seven years ago. He also told her about the prosecutor, Jack, that quit the prosecutor's office when bribery got in the way of justice. He was currently running a one man office in Mount Pearl with Kyla as his only assistant. They were barely making ends meet but he refused to go back into civil service.

The information concerned Emily on several levels; foremost was the denial of justice and the flagrant violation of the law in bringing Haley's murderer to justice. And secondly, the obstruction of justice to a degree that a good man was forced to make a choice and chose to leave public service. It also sounded like he was being punished by certain people for refusing to go along with the decision to allow Roger Clovis to walk.

Emily contacted one of her most trusted Andrian Intelligence officers, Commander Taaker, who was Caleb's counterpart. She could not very well inform Caleb of Sara's intentions.

Later in the evening, Sara went to the hanger and boarded a small two man saucer and left the premises. Unknown to her she was shadowed by her twenty member squad who had orders from Emily to protect and cover for Sara.

Sara exited the saucer in a wooded area about a mile from the Clovis compound. The compound had an outer

ASSIMILATION

perimeter consisting of six men at stationary post. Sara, dressed in black and using her infrared vision enhancement given to her by Flata, easily skirted the sentries.

Next was a ten foot wall with an electric wire across the top. Sara climbed the wall using technology provided the Space Commandoes. Upon reaching the electric wire she placed a coil around the wire which neutralized the electric current. Sara left the electric wire neutralizer in place and easily vaulted over the top of the wire.

Sara was able to see the family in the second story living room by utilizing a remote sensor which attached itself to the window. The mother, father, and four sons were around a large table. They were planning another scam to rip off a local charity.

Sara scaled a trellis and entered the house by the upstairs patio door. She saw a sentry standing in front of the door accessing the family room. Her targets did not include the paid help as long as they did not interfere; her research indicated the family members did their own evil deeds and the security detail was employees of a legitimate security company contracted by the family.

Sara moved against the wall while she released small nano bots that crawled across the floor with animated noise and lights to get the attention of the sentry. Coming up to the side of the sentry she sprayed him with a mist that induced instant paralysis and unconsciousness. Sara caught the sentry by the arms and lowered him to the floor.

After Sara put on an oxygen membrane over her nose and mouth she then opened the door and walked thru the door. She immediately released two levitating robots that sped across the room spraying a paralysis inducing mist. All the family members were immediately paralyzed but conscious and alert.

Sara walked into the room and stood in front of them and waited about one minute for the mist to disperse. Only those that inhaled the mist were subject to the paralyzing effects.

Sara, standing in front of them removed her oxygen generating membrane. They just stared at her unable to make facial expressions or verbalize the hate toward her but were present in their minds. She walked to the side of each one and injected a nano bot into their neck.

Going back to the front of the table Sara removed a small miniature surveillance camera and placed it about six feet above the end of the table utilizing its anti-gravitational properties to keep it in place. She began the recording process which was automatically transmitted to the saucer.

Sara said, "I gave you a neuro neutralizer so you cannot move. However, as you can tell the cerebral cortex has not been impaired. You can see, hear, think, and most importantly to me, feel. In fact this mist I infected you with will enhance your ability to experience pain."

"You will be able to begin to move your head and eyes, mouth, and arms in about five minutes. You will then begin to experience a slow burning deep in your chest; it will spread to your abominable cavity. In effect, you are going to burn to death from the inside out. And toward the end, your body will burst into flame."

ASSIMILATION

"So Roger, tell me, did you enjoy killing my friend Haley. She was basically a child in a woman's body. She never thought an evil thought or did an evil deed. Her only fault was falling in love with the devil. That would be you Roger."

"How many woman did you kill? I counted nine including Haley. I did not look anywhere else. And the rest of you, how many innocent lives have you destroyed? You have seven minutes to make peace with whatever you worship. You will be dead within nine. I am going to film your deaths and give a copy to the parents of your victims. I would like to just make it clean and shoot you myself but I do not shoot unarmed civilians. However, you will be just as dead, and this is much more…apropos."

The family group died together. Sara took the devices she brought with her and left the compound. As she went over the fence she removed the electric neutralizer. She sprinted to her saucer and returned to the hanger. Unknown to her, her twenty group platoon followed close behind no one the wiser.

Kyla was sitting at the front desk when a courier brought a special delivery package. It was addressed to the law firm of "Jack and Kyla". There was no return address.

"How strange", thought Kyla.

She picked up the phone and called Jack.

About thirty minutes later they were in the back office viewing a disc. The disc did not have any markings and there was no sound. It began with the whole Clovis family sitting around the table facing the camera which appeared to be above them, Roger was front and center. Typed across the screen were the words in capital print, "SECRET, FOR YOUR EYES ONLY".

Jack and Kyla continued to watch the disc with eyes wide and hearts pounding. The group was not talking. Soon they began writhing and looking wildly about. Their mouths worked but nothing came out. Very quickly they began to smolder. Then, one by one they burst into flames. They did not scream. They just turned black as the flesh was burned from their bones, then the flames went out. The video ended.

Both Jack and Kyla sat speechless.

Then Kyla thought of Sara. Did Sara have anything to do with the disc? She thought about the scar above her left cheek then the missing part of the top of her ear. And, her hand, her left hand appeared to have been broken then reassembled. She could not count the scars on her hand.

Kyla then remembered the "look", Sara had when she promised that Roger Clovis would pay with his blood boiling in his flesh and the flesh being burned off his bones. And she said it with an oath; it was strange, what was it?

Then she remembered the oath, telling Jack, "Sara swore a strange oath when I said the Roger Clovis would never pay for him murdering Haley. She said, and I quote, "As the stars circle the black hole in the center of our galaxy, as the earth circles the sun, and, as the moon is our joy, Roger Clovis will not escape justice. His cry for mercy will be ignored and his blood will boil peeling the flesh from his bones."

Jack looked at her opened mouthed; he had certainly seen Sara's words come to pass.

Kyla said, "I guess there is a black hole in the center of the galaxy, I doubt if anyone has ever seen it. And I do know the earth circles the sun. The bit about the moon being our joy was our wish that someday we would all be proposed to under the stars with a full moon."

"Sara also told me that if I love you I should tell you as none of us know what lay ahead for us, family, or friends."

Kyla looked Jack in the eyes. "Jack I love you. I loved you from the first moment I laid eyes on you. Will you marry me?"

Jack looked at her in amazement. "Are you really asking me to marry you?"

"Yes I am Jack. Does that seem strange to you? I have seen the way you look at me when you think I am doing something else. Have you not seen me look at you?"

"I have a strange feeling that Sara is something more than she seems. She may know things that you and I have no knowledge of."

Jack took Kyla's hands in his and said, "Yes, I will marry you."

That night, across several states, eight more families viewed the disc of the Clovis family's end of life. All of them said a prayer of thanks and felt relief from the bondage of denied justice.

As for Jack's law firm, they began receiving several

legal contracts a day from the military and other institutions all over the country. Within two weeks he hired two additional attorneys and four law clerks. Kyla was the officer manager.

They got married the next day and intended to go on a honeymoon but as in life, surprise outweighs expectations. The contracts began to come in and they decided to take care of the first few then take time off. The workload became an avalanche and soon there was no way either of them believed they could take off with unfinished business, thus the new attorneys and law clerks.

The attorneys and law clerks were Jack's former co-workers at the county. All of them jumped at the chance to go to work for Jack when he queried them to see if they were interested.

Since Jack and Kyla were now married and both worked at the law firm, Jack sought her opinion on all business decisions. They decided collectively that the two new lawyers and the four clerks would be made partners and they would share equally in the largess of contracts. It was not long before their law firm became the largest and most successful in Mount Pearl.

CHAPTER 48
ANOTHER CALL

Emily had gone to bed early in the evening having been exhausted from the day's meetings, duties and interviews with different scientist. Dr. Sears was the mediator on a board of twelve scientists from different disciplines who were investigating different methods of destroying the enemy entity from the other dimension.

Her sleep was dreamless; her heart barely pumping as it slowly went into a near hibernation mode. Emily felt a pulling of her spirit the deeper her sleep became. She was in a near unconscious state.

"Emily. Emily. Emily! We must go now. Another species is being destroyed. We need to save as many as possible!"

Emily roused from her unconscious state and felt as if she had been drugged. Her eyes would not open. Again she was drifting off to slumber.

Again the Entity called.

"Emily! We do not have much time. We need to save as many of the specie as possible and kill as many of the enemy life form as possible."

Emily jerked awake and came to a sitting position. She took a deep breath and struggled to open her eyes. She looked over to Warren's spot on the bed. It was vacant as it had been since her return three weeks earlier.

He set up a room with Warren Jr. and slept with him.

Sara had moved in with them and helped to take care of the children. She was asleep in the room down stairs.

Again the Entity said, "Emily we must hurry. We will need five Entity saucers and ten commandoes in each saucer. We must leave within the hour."

Emily reached for her com unit and contacted Space Intelligence Command Headquarters. She advised them that she wanted five Entity saucers, one of which was hers and ten commandoes for each saucer and they had to be ready to go within the hour.

Emily got up and put on a pullover jump suit identifying herself as Space Intelligence Commander. After putting on her shoes and pinning up her hair she walked down the hall to Warren Jr.'s room.

Entering quietly, she walked to the edge of the bed and kissed him lightly on the cheek and said, "I Love you. I do not know when I will be back; hopefully soon."

Emily left the room ignoring Warren whom she was sure was awake and walked down to Orion's room. As she entered the room she saw that Orion was sitting up in bed waiting on her.

"Mommy, please be careful and come home to me soon. I will be praying for you".

Emily said, "Thank you son. Also pray for Warren so that he may be made whole. You know I love him too. Help take care of your brother."

"Yes Mommy, as the cosmic spirits of the universe sing, I will take care of them."

Emily went next down stairs and tapped lightly on

ASSIMILATION

Sara' door, it was next to the kitchen and on the way out.

"One second", said Sara.

Sara disentangled herself from Jawane and went to the door. She was naked.

"What's up?"

Emily replied, "We have a combat emergency, we need to leave in one hour, report to the hanger soon as possible."

Emily hurried down the hall to the elevator and proceeded to go to the hanger.

Sara turned on the lights and quickly donned her military skivvies consisting of loose legged panties and a sleeveless T shirt; then she donned her coveralls, boots and cap. Jawane was on one elbow watching her.

She looked at him and said, "There is a combat emergency and I have to leave immediately." She kissed him on the lips and left the room.

The hanger was a bustle of activity. Three of the five Entity saucers were presently at the facility having arrived for training two days earlier. Four young hybrid Human-Andrians were already standing in front of the commando office waiting for orders. They were excited as they had been on one combat mission nine years earlier. At that time they went to the traitor Zelegark's base on Saturn's moon Europa, and to go now with Emily as the commander was to them considered an honor.

Sara went into the office where she found thirty commandoes seated quietly. All of them had their weapons and were in combat armor. Sara donned her armor suit and checked out several weapons.

The four Saucer pilots had followed Sara into the office. They all knew of Sara and had heard of her leadership skills. They quietly stood in the back of the room.

Emily came to the front accompanied by Commander Taaker.

Commander Taaker said, "Stand and present yourselves for inspection. Sara Sears will be acting captain on this mission. She will direct you as to what your assignment will be. As of this moment we do not know what the combat emergency is but we do know that the alien enemy is again destroying a species. The alarm was sounded by the Entity in Emily's saucer. She will assign ten commandoes to each saucer. Prepare to embark."

Sara walked in front of the assembled commandoes. She carefully inspected their armor and weapons. The assembly consisted of male and female, Human and Andrian commandoes. Sara quickly divided the commandoes into three groups. Each group had a primary and secondary leader. They would relay Sara's commands dictating targets and goals to accomplish their mission. Sara's primary mission was to keep track of Emily and keep her safe.

Emily looked out over the group. As was her practice, she bowed her head for a moment of silent prayer. All the commandoes followed suite, even the Andrians.

Emily then said, "The mission commences now, board the craft."

The commandoes boarded their assigned saucers; Sara rode in the command saucer with Emily.

Emily sat in the console and immediately she was

ASSIMILATION

embraced with the soft membrane that covered her head. Sara stood immediately behind her in her receptacle.

The three saucers dematerialized in the hanger and moved out away from the earth to the moon. The other two saucers were waiting stationary in position.

Emily said, "Pilots, follow my lead. The Entities will link up and together they will plot the course."

The five saucers left the solar system at the speed of light. Once free of the magnetic pull of the sun they transitioned to the ionic sphere where the Entities did what they did best, they became one with the universe.

Emily could feel the neurons flowing thru her and she could see forever. Particles streamed by and light danced in a multitude of colors. Soon the saucers stopped and began vibrating. The walls turned from a solid to an opaque shimmering see thru wall.

They were above a planet. The planet appeared to be mostly evenly divided between green firma and brown terrain. There were large bodies of water interspaced between mountain ranges.

Emily watched as the saucer magnified a plateau between the mountain ranges with water encircling the base of the plateau. There was a large cloud of dust which obscured portions of the plateau. She saw what appeared to be about three hundred humanoids battling the enemy from the different dimension.

As in the previous battle on the water world the defenders were outnumbered thousands to one. The surrounding mountains appeared to be alive with a large black mass of an undulating living organism.

The defenders were forced onto a plateau of a small mountain and were battling the enemy with what appeared to be long spears, clubs and stones. They were wearing what appeared to be animal skins which were held up with one strap.

Emily advised, "Commandoes, we are here to save as many of this species as possible. We will land in behind the combatants in the clearing. We fight by their side and show them the way into the saucers. Kill as many of the enemy as possible but the primary mission is to rescue this species from being annihilated. Two commandoes from each saucer will guard the entrance to the saucers."

The five saucers landed forming a circle in the center of the plateau with about twenty yards to the nearest combatants. Sara barked out orders to go to the front of the line and clear a space so the inhabitants will have time to turn and run.

Emily ran out with the other commandoes to the front of the fray. All the commandoes used their laser weapons to clear a swath. Emily saw a small boy fall down in front of the enemy beings and she ran to his rescue followed by a female wielding a club. Emily blasted a being with her laser just as it was about to impale the child with its acid tentacle. Emily grabbed the child by the arm and pulled the boy back out of the reach of the alien menace firing all the while. The woman came up and grabbed his other arm. She looked at Emily with a surprised facial expression but she did not otherwise appear to be afraid. Emily on the other hand was startled to observe what she believed to be a Neanderthal humanoid. She was short,

ASSIMILATION

muscular, and wore nothing but an animal skin draped over one shoulder.

As Emily was moving backward she did not see the small ravine off to her side and slipping on a round rock she fell five feet into the ravine. Immediately the undulating mass started moving toward her for an easy kill and was no farther than thirty feet away.

Sarah looked around and had seen Emily pulling the boy back toward the saucers with the help of a female and then when she looked back to check on their progress a second later, Emily was nowhere to be seen; however, the woman had picked up the boy and was running back to the safety of the other members of her group. Sara started running in the last know direction of Emily's position barking orders for others to follow and to cover her.

Sara called out, "Commander, where are you?"

Emily responded, "I am in the ravine. I fell and broke my ankle. I am unable to crawl out!"

Off to the side she saw three men in animal skins run past her into the ravine. The enemy mass was now about twenty feet away. They began spewing their acid which fell as rain just a few feet away from the ravine.

Sara and three commandoes ran in the same direction firing their laser weapons to clear a space of momentary safety in an effort to protect Emily until they rescued her. As they got close to the ravine they saw one of the men carrying Emily over his shoulder like a sack of potatoes, climb out of the ravine. He was helped by his two companions and she was firing her weapon at the enemy as best as she could.

They had gone about ten feet when one of the men in animal skin fell to the ground with a cry of pain. His left leg had been severed above the knee by a jet of acid. The leg was lying about two feet away from him flesh smoking from the acid burning through flesh and bone.

Sara and the two commandoes ran past the man carrying Emily. They were firing their weapons in an effort to clear a safe zone. The two commandoes picked up the one legged man and Sara snatched up his leg throwing it over her shoulder, not sure at the time why that was important, and firing at the same time.

The group was being moved back toward the saucers and they were beginning to file in. Soon they were all loaded. The man that was carrying Emily was directed to her saucer by the commandoes who were firing as they retreated. He sat Emily down where directed by use of hand signals.

Emily was helped by Sara, who had thrown the leg into a cryogenic chamber, into her seat. It appeared that Emily had a broken ankle. She then helped the other commandoes move the survivors into their receptacles. The one legged man received immediate medical attention which cleansed the wound, stopped the bleeding and sealed the leg until more advanced medical care could be utilized, he too was placed in a cryogenic chamber.

Sara escorted the large man to the receptacle next to hers and placed him in his receptacle. At the same time she looked him in the eyes and said, "Thank you for saving our commander's life."

ASSIMILATION

The communication was telepathic and he looked at her with surprise as he heard her voice within his head. He could not understand the language but he understood the intended content. He shook his head up and down indicating he understood.

The front glass descended from top to bottom and snapped into place. The tube came down and covered his mouth. Sara could read his apprehension but he was not afraid. He was intelligent enough to realize he and his people had just been spared certain death by their strange lifesaving benefactors.

Sara was the last to take her position. As she did so the saucer vibrated and lifted from the ground with the walls becoming opaque. As before, the undulating mass below danced with wild gyrations at having their prey snatched from their grip.

The five saucers rose far above the planet and then launched missiles carrying biological enzymes that were believed to be deadly to the lifeforms from the other dimension. It would take several hours for the enzymes to work so Emily positioned her saucers around the planet for observation. One saucer was designated as sentinel to watch for possible incursions thru rifts in the fabric of the dimension.

As of yet, the Andrians did not know how the enemy had destroyed the three intergalactic carriers which had been sent to aid Andrian planets which were being destroyed by the alien enemy. They believed that the enemy was able to open a rift on the ships themselves then they poured into the carriers and overwhelmed their defenses. Because Emily believed this to be the case, she had her saucers move erratically never staying in the same position longer than a few minutes.

The Entity infused Emily with a vision of an approaching storm. This time the enemy was in large balloon styled space ships. They were approaching their position at the speed of light. The enemy's arrival at Emily's present position was eighteen hours. The number of ships was innumerable.

Emily advised the Entity to launch the rest of the nano missiles carrying the infectious protein strains into the path of the approaching armada. The five saucers launched two thousand missiles which had millions of nano projectiles that would be scattered across space around the planet. The nano projectiles had properties that would attach itself to spaceships and remain viable for years.

They hoped the desired result would be the infection of the ship structure itself as they believed that it too had to be some type of intelligent living entity. If that was the case, the other dimensional enemy was more advanced than the Andrians and thus the Humans because they were not only able to travel thru a rift in the dimensional space time and formulate attacks to totally destroy their targets but now it appeared they were able to launch incredibly large space ships to carry their armies even farther and faster.

Emily allowed her being to be infused by the Entity, she said, "Tell me what dimension we are in."

The Entity advised, "We are in the enemy's dimension."

ASSIMILATION

"If it is true that we are in the enemy's dimension then it must also be true that they have not yet destroyed all lifeforms in their dimension. And, the ships coming toward us may in fact be their armada to assist the destroying army currently on the planet. They are seeking out targets of opportunities. It appears that this culture is Stone Age and thus has emitted no electronic signatures. They had been found by happen stance."

"They must travel their dimension looking for weakness in the space time fabric and then they exploit the weakness and exit their dimension."

The Entity replied, "You are correct my beloved. Our two dimensions grate upon one another creating a time warp door where they can come thru. It is the same way we have entered their dimension."

Emily said, "It may be that our two dimensions are in the process of merging or trying to occupy the same space. If this is true then there will be no peace between humanoid lifeforms and theirs. Only one of us can occupy our dimension at any one time."

After launching the last of the missiles, Emily turned her attention to the planet to see if the enzyme based nano bots had done any harm. It was too early to tell.

The Entity advised, "We must leave my love. We do not know their weapon capability. As of this moment they may not know that we are here."

Emily advised, "Entity move us out quickly. We want to go home but not the way we came. We should split up to minimize our signature in the space time dislocation. We will meet up again at our station in Mount Pearl.

CHAPTER 49
GRARGOL, NEANDERTHAL FROM THE STARS

The Entity directed all the saucers to return to Earth taking a convoluted route in an effort to confuse and lose any possible tracking devices the enemy may have, the saucers landed at different time intervals.

Emily's saucer landed first after entering the solar system at the speed of light. Upon entry, she immediately transferred all the data on the enemy that had been gathered by the five Entities to the Space Intelligence Command. Of the most importance was the data gathered about the flotilla of enemy craft that was approaching the planet from which they had rescued and evacuated the remaining population in the enemy's dimension.

The Entity did not believe it would be wise to leave any type of intelligence gathering device in the other dimension because it could be discovered and possibly used to track a return to the earth. It was already know that the enemy knew the location of the earth as the Entities had detected their presence. What was not known was the enemy's social structure, communication methods or military leadership command structure. Perhaps their scouts were not lucky in their return and been delayed or more hopefully, destroyed.

After entering the hanger it took several minutes for Emily to become reoriented into the present. After the ramp was opened she saw that they were being quarantined to a separate section of the hanger. The military had disbursed a full hazardous and biological materials combat team. The occupants would be quarantined for at least one month while test for biological and hazardous materials contamination was conducted. The system had been set up by the Andrians but it was not a deep molecular decontamination used on their intergalactic carriers. However, it was more extensive and technologically advanced than anything that had ever been invented on the earth.

Emily was helped down the ramp by two male members of the commando team. At the base of the ramp, she was to be placed on a levitating carrier and taken to the quarantined dispensary. But first, she stood at attention, saluted, and presented her group of commandoes and requested permission to disembark. The officer of the day, in hazardous material gear, returned her salute and gave her permission to do so.

The Neanderthal male that had helped save Emily observed the strange procedure from the top of the ramp. The young boy that Emily had saved was his son, the woman beside him was his mate. He felt like he was heavily indebted to the woman for her act of courage and bravery in risking her life in almost certain death to save his son. And not only her, but the other woman who had picked up his brother's leg at her own peril, so that he would not be crippled in the spirit world when he died.

He was motioned forward down the ramp next to the leg woman, thus he did as he was directed to do. His wife and son followed them down the ramp as they followed the levitating carrier which contained the body of the injured warrior. They followed equal distance behind Emily. Everyone in the hanger was stunned to see the new arrivals appeared to be similar to the Neanderthals of old earth. The first Neanderthal humanoid was carried in a levitating carrier and he too was taken to the dispensary.

Sara stopped at the bottom of the ramp and saluted; "Captain Sara Sears, requesting permission for commandoes and new arrivals to disembark, sir!"

The officer of the day looked at the hugely muscular man with the large head and jaw standing next to Sara. He was clothed only in a heavy, hairy animal skin.

He quickly saluted and said "Yes Sir!"

After the saucer had completely emptied, there were ten commandoes and one hundred humanoid Neanderthal types of beings consisting of males, females, and children standing in one corner of the hanger. A hazmat team entered the saucer and began a decontamination process.

In the infirmary Emily's ankle was set and sealed in a skin type membrane that would heal the ankle within two days. It was decided that the male with the severed leg should be sent to an intergalactic carrier for the leg to be reattached. Emily did not know who to send with

ASSIMILATION

the Neanderthal. The decision needed to be made immediately. She did not want to send Sara but she was the Captain of the unit and Sara was the most correct choice.

Emily summoned Sara to the infirmary. Sara saluted and presented herself in proper military form.

"I have a request for you. It is necessary to send one man to accompany the Neanderthal to the intergalactic carrier for his leg reattachment. Commander Taaker advised it should not take more than one month that is, providing any unforeseen circumstances. I would like you to accompany him. You do not have to accept the assignment if you do not wish to do so. You may select a member of your team to go in your place."

Sara responded, "Any particular reason you have selected me to go instead of someone else?"

"I think that is a valid question considering what happened to you last time you were on a carrier."

"The Neanderthal group appears to have a simple and rudimentary developed communication center of the brain; thus they are easy to read. It does not mean they are not intelligent because they are. They may not vocalize like us, but I think that they may have developed rudimentary telepathic capabilities.

When you were placing the last male into his receptacle I read his mind. He is the leader of the group. He helped save me because I helped save his son. And, He thinks of you as a "blood sister", because you risked your life to retrieve his brother's leg. The idea is that when, not if, his brother dies, with him being without his leg, he will be an invalid and cripple thru out eternity. And, that type of wound in their culture means certain death. Therefore, when you picked up the leg you prevented that kind of eternal damnation."

"Another nuance to this culture is that since you prevented this damnation throughout eternity, then it is to be considered an honor for you to sacrifice yourself at the time of his death to accompany him to the spirit world. I think that with you leaving with him in the saucer would be in their mind a translation to the spirit world."

"Also, when you return with him whole, you will pretty much be very high on their list of favorite people. Who knows, now you might not have to sacrifice yourself!" Emily smiled when she said that.

"Your status with them at this point should enable you to communicate and help us direct them in a controllable manner. Since I used the term "control", you can understand why an Andrian commando cannot be used for this assignment. The responsibility for them will not end with us getting off of the saucer, it may well be years to somehow assimilate them or find another planet for them. In which case, I think a "blood sister", is the most logical choice."

Sara was momentarily silent thinking thru everything Emily had said. And of course, Emily was correct; she was the most logical choice.

Saluting Emily, she said, "Yes Sir. When do I leave?"

"I will give you time to call Jawane".

Sara went to a quiet room and was connected to Jawane's private communicator. When he answered he was silent as was she. They both seem to know what the

ASSIMILATION

other was thinking, even over electronic communications.

Sara said, "How long have I been gone?"

Jawane replied, "Ten days."

Then Jawane said, "How long are you supposed to be gone when you go to the carrier?"

Sara replied, "Should nothing untoward happens, I will be there thirty days."

Jawane said, "Be safe and may the cosmic spirits be with you."

Sara said, "You be careful now because you know what us earth girls want to do to your body."

Jawane replied, "Yes I understand now. I am one hot space guy."

After Sara disconnected she returned to the saucer as the injured Neanderthal was being reloaded into the saucer. When she got to the top of the ramp she turned and waved to the leader of the Neanderthals. He and his wife waved back. Sara then turned and entered the saucer and took her position in the receptacle heaving a heavy sigh. Such was the responsibility of leadership and a blood sister.

The saucer left the hanger and once away from the earth quickly arrived at the intergalactic carrier hiding in the asteroid belt between Mars and Jupiter.

The other four saucers arrived within a week of one another. The total number of the Neanderthal specie refugees was two hundred and eighty nine. The leader of the group who arrived earlier in Emily's saucer, was named Grargol.

A committee of seven members consisting of three

Humans, two Andrians and two Mermaids, Muskula and Karlalif, her former mate, were formed to meet with the Neanderthal specie.

Grargol was brought into a room and stood before the committee. Emily was standing by him. Telepathically Emily told him to find two counselors to be part of the committee to help resolve issues that may arise. Grargol nodded his head and left the room.

Grargol returned ten minutes later accompanied with two other members of his group, one was his wife. Emily indicated where they were to sit at the table across from the Andrians. The table was set up in a u-shaped fashion with Emily seated alone at the open end.

Since arriving on the Earth the Neanderthals had maintained their usual living patterns by sitting and sleeping on the floor, plenty of soft blankets had been provided with numerous military style mattresses. However, for meetings Emily had indicated they were to sit at the table in proper fashion.

Emily began by looking at Grargol and saying directly to him, "We would like to begin by expressing our sympathy to you and your family at the near extinction of your people by our common enemy."

Emily waited a minute to see if he understood. He leaned his head toward his wife's head; after a moment, together nodded their heads in agreement.

Emily was sure they had telepathic abilities but they in all probability were very rudimentary. "Well it was time find out."

Emily stood up and went over to the three

ASSIMILATION

Neanderthals. She slightly bowed her head then stood up straight.

"My name is Emily Smith"; she was speaking verbally and telepathically.

"We need to learn as much about the enemy that was killing your people as possible. Have you ever seen them before this attack?"

All three of them nodded their heads no.

"How long have you been fighting them?"

They looked at one another, grunted, growled, gesticulated throwing their hands and arms in the air, and then sat back silent.

"We do not know, they just fell from a very large black circle above the ground during the snow time. We did not know what they were. Our people were just sitting in front of the fire and they came up and poured burning water on everyone. Everyone died except one woman who ran away very fast. She ran into the Cave of Our Beginning and the things followed her. She believed it would be better to die by jumping into the Hole of Darkness than to be killed by the burning liquid."

"She jumped. The things did not follow."

Emily waited for them to finish the story. They said nothing. They sat there looking at her as if she understood what happened to the woman who jumped into the black hole.

She waited about one minute and they did not move or seem to indicate that they were going to say anything else. They just stared back at her with their eyes a dark brown shining beneath their heavy brows.

Emily said, "Can you tell me how you knew one woman survived and jumped in "Hole of Darkness"? What is it and what does it mean?"

They all three had a surprised look on their faces that appeared to be closer to shock.

Grargol looked at Emily. He responded, "We thought she was with you. It was not long after she jumped that you arrived and saved us from certain death. The enemy had quickly covered our hunting grounds and killed everything, animal and people."

Emily was beginning to think that the Neanderthals were not telling everything they knew. "What were they not telling her"?

"Grargol, is talking to one another using your thoughts your primary form of communication?"

Before answering, the three Neanderthals again engaged in a heated grunting, growling and gesticulating with their arms. After about ten minutes they sat back silent.

This time, to Emily's surprise, the Woman answered.

"I am Lagala. I am the spiritual advisor for our group. I am of the opinion that we should be honest with you; foremost and primarily because you risked your lives to save us. We, like you, are telepaths. We do not know for sure how this came to be. Our histories say a superior being came to us in ages past and gave this gift to our ancestors."

Emily said, "It seems like your correct communication skills have improved markedly; how is that possible?"

After hesitating only momentarily Lagala said, "We

ASSIMILATION

can communicate with all kinds of lifeforms. I believe that perhaps we may be more advanced in our communication skills then even you. You have labeled us as "Neanderthals", as our physical structure appears to match similar peoples that were here on your planet many snows ago. Since you have never met one of these beings on your planet and they used stone tools, as we do, you have placed us into a category of not being very intelligent."

"It is obvious too, that you are a warring people. You have murder in your spirit. You have developed many weapons to kill one another. We believe that is primarily due to the fact that as a group, you have not developed telepathic skills that would allow you to communicate with each other in the true form of the spirit where nothing is hidden. We also have the ability to communicate with any of the lifeforms on our planet. We have not even thought of making a weapon more effective or powerful other than a club or a lance. There was never any need… until now."

Emily thought carefully before she answered as they could surely read her spike of anger.

"You lived in a different dimension than we do. It is only because of the intelligence of our fighting machines have we been able to come to your sphere of influence. You have only been able to survive as long as you have because of your lack of technical development. You were found by your enemy by accident. Had we not found you when we had, you would be dead, your whole specie."

"Yes we are warring specie, we have many faults, we

do horrible things to one another, but, we are at times able to rise above that and exhibit what our true spirit is or could be or should be. However, in the universe we live in and like the one you use to live in, things are not perfect."

"The Andrians are a good example of having conquered many of their lessor qualities. They have come to our world and have made great effort to keep us from destroying ourselves and our planet."

"The mermaids there," indicating to Muskula and Karlalif, "have had their world destroyed by the same enemy that destroyed yours. And I might add, is in the process of destroying all life as we know it in our dimension. They have already sent spies to our planet looking for me and the intelligent Entity embodied within the flying machine."

"None of us has asked to be part of this conflict, it may well be that our past conflicts has prepared us to cope with the one that looms before us now."

"You said that you can read the minds of all the species on your planet in addition to our minds. Therefore, could you tell us anything at all about the minds of the enemy other than the fact it's primary goal and single minded objective was to kill you?"

Lagala responded, "They seemed to be of one mind. They felt we were a threat to their way of being. Their minds were not orderly and they seemed to pass thoughts to one another by a fine spray of what you call acid. They constantly kept a canopy of acid in the air at all times."

This was absolutely the best information they had on

ASSIMILATION

their enemy. As Lagala spoke the Andrian and Human scientist listening to the interview began immediately to relay the information to scientist on the carriers and in the military to start analyzing samples of the spraying acid that they had collected. If this was the way they communicated then they could learn to counteract the acid in an effort to disrupt their communication.

Lagala then said, "Thank you for saving my son."

Emily responded, "I did not save your son. It was a group effort of everyone in this room and the many thousands working together to defeat this enemy. We believe that they will soon attack us here on the earth. As of yet we have not developed a weapon that would be effective enough to thwart their advances much less defeat them. Therefore, we would appreciate any and all insights that you may have that can help us."

"I am now going to show you what was coming your way when we rescued you. Of course by the time of the arrival of their fleet, you would have been long dead".

Emily turned on the above video taken by the Entity just as they were beginning to leave. The round bulbous spacecraft were innumerable. It also provided insight into exactly what they were. They were nomadic and they roamed the galaxies destroying life wherever they found it.

All the information that was learned from the Neanderthals and Emily's intuitive insight was that the enemy was a isolated nomadic roaming species that destroys all life forms that it comes in contact with. They communicated with some kind of acid spray that somehow allowed them to communicate with one another to give themselves direction.

CHAPTER 50
ALIEN OR HUMAN

Selina Sears was an early riser, thus on the first Saturday that she had off in a long time, she took some selfish alone time and strolled along the edge of the waterway along Emily's property. She had become used to seeing the humanoid water species frolicking in the bay area. From time to time they would get out of the water and come greet her. There were so many of them now with the enhanced breeding program instituted by the Andrians. She did not know how much longer Caleb could come up with plausible stories to deny their existence.

Selena carefully picked her way between some trees that had grown down to the water's edge and stepped thru the trees into a secluded small clearing. Looking at her new tennis shoes she was preoccupied with cleaning off some mud when she heard a rustle of bushes in front of her.

Looking up she was startled to see what appeared to be six cavemen sitting in a semicircle. A cave woman was standing in front of them with her hands clasped in front of her. They were wearing what appeared to be animal skins which hung over one shoulder. The woman was dressed in similar fashion with one breast exposed. About twenty feet away there were four naked children playing with a snake.

Unlike the experience eight years earlier of being tantalized and enthralled with the recognition and the acceptance that sweet Hanlee was not of the earth, these people were like running into a wall. It was all she could do not to scream. It was so incongruent with what she had become used too, even for aliens!

They all turned and looked at her when they heard her come thru the trees into the clearing. They had not expected anyone. They normally stayed within their allotted confines up in the mountains but chose to venture out at night as they wanted to be near the water, they had stayed longer than they expected so they had to spend the rest of the day in the secluded cove.

Selena had not been informed of their existence. There had been rumors that another species had been saved from extinction but that was all that was known. Hopefully, these beings were they. She was at a loss for words. Then to her surprise she heard the woman's voice in her mind.

"Welcome. Do not be afraid. We are Emily's guest. She and others saved the few of us left from extinction."

The telepathic communication also was incongruent to what she would expect from a supposedly barely functioning Neanderthal. Are not Neanderthals the same everywhere? Answering her own question she thought, "Evidently not".

"Thank you. I have not been informed specifically of your arrival. I knew a species had been rescued but there were no other information. And yes forgive me for my ignorance. Earths early mankind was obviously very

ASSIMILATION

intelligent; they had to be because there is evidence that they lasted over two hundred thousand years."

"They interbred with our direct ancestors, Cro-Magnon, about sixty thousand years ago. The only records we have of the Neanderthal branch are of their stone tools which they used to make other stone tools and cave paintings. We know they buried their dead and they had medicine woman and a kind of a spiritual advisor. Thus, us being who we are, believed they were limited in their intelligence because this lack of advancement in tool making, farming and building of cities."

"Also, in anatomy and the flattening cranial construction, which is the same as yours, appears that your pronounced receding frontal bone indicated the lack of development of the frontal lobe and cerebral hemisphere which controls emotion and thought processes."

"The elongated skull pattern to the back of the head indicates the increased size of the parietal lobe which controls intelligence, language, sensory input and sensory processing. Also, the increased size of the temporal lobe which control hearing and speech centers may account for your extremely advanced telepathic skills. Since you have not developed a larynx which enables speech your brain obviously opted for telepathic skills."

"The obvious extension of parietal lobe appears to indicate that you would be more skilled in basic survival skills. You have to be highly skilled in this area because our ancestors that are genetically similar to you survived as I said before, for over two hundred thousand years. We on the other hand have to fight to keep from destroying ourselves from the last ten thousand years; and, it is getting harder every day."

"And, even though the probability of you existing as a species is very limited, yet here you are, talking telepathically to me."

A short heavily muscular man with a large head, deep set eyes shielded by a large heavy brow with a sloping head stood up and faced her. He was wearing a simple animal skin. He did not have any amulets, bracelets, or any other accruements. The clothes the military had given them lay on the ground beside him.

"My name is Grargol. I am the leader of our people. It is true we do not build, farm or achieve feats of building machines. We live in harmony with our surroundings. Everything we need is supplied by our Spirit Father."

The woman, who was still standing in front of the group, went and stood by the man.

"I am Lagala, mate of Grargol. "I tend to my husband's needs"

Then an older male stood up and came forward.

"My name is Grawll. I am the seer of all things in the mist of our world".

The other two men and one woman came and stood beside her. They introduced themselves. The female said they were advisors and counselors to Grargol.

Lagala advised, "Come and set with us. We will help you hear and see things you have not yet experienced."

After they were seated, this time in a circle, Selena found herself sitting next to Lagala. Lagala said, "Let us commune together."

ASSIMILATION

The woman took Selena's hand. She was surprised how soft it was. The other woman sat on Selena's other side. She too had soft hands.

Too Selena's surprise, Grawll stood up in the middle and began a soft chant. As he chanted, he rubbed a solid object between his hands which then fell from his hands as a powder. It was then she noticed the bowl on the ground before them. The powder fell into the bowl and a sparkling liquid bubbled to the brim.

Picking up the bowl he went to Grargol and placed it to his lips. Grawll tilted the bowl and some of the bubbling liquid poured into his mouth. He repeated the same process with each member of the group. He came to Selena last and placed the bowl to her lips. Selena closed her eyes and drank from the bowl. It was bubbly like a seltzer yet tasteless.

Moving to the center of the circle, Grawll drank the last of the liquid from the bowl and seated himself on the ground. Selena was surprised to see him cross his legs and set in the yoga lotus position with arms on his legs and palms up.

As Selena held hands with the two woman she seemed to quickly drift into a subconscious state. She was floating over a large forest. In the distance she could see some dark beings crawling on the ground. They had four appendages coming from the four corners of its body. They came closer to the beings and Selena began to shiver as her fear of the things increased. They were everywhere and they seemed to just pop into existence from a large round hole in the air above the ground. Her fear grew greater and she began to weep. Then a musical voice in her head told her to be at peace that she was safe. They went closer to the beings and seemed to go right thru them.

Selena was amazed as she was able to deduce that the beings were indeed an extremophile alien life form. The outside of them appeared to be a soft rubbery surface with multiple holes. Beneath the soft exterior was a hard armor shell similar in construction to a turtle. The shell was constructed to keep the insides under tremendous pressure. Then to her surprise she saw that the extremophile life form was not just one life form, it was two. The inside consisted of innumerable bacteria that formed long chains of opposite chirality which had identical chemical properties as the outside surface which was soft and rubbery but was a mirrored chemical composition of the inside molecular structure.

The inside bacteria lived under extreme atmospheric pressure. They were sulpher based and expelled hydrogen sulfide gas thru the many portals. The hydrogen sulfide gas mixed with the outer atmosphere containing oxygen. The mixture, when sprayed into the air formed a highly dense and toxic sulfuric acid. The acid formed a dense atomized cloud which was used to communicate to the outer rubbery membrane to control its direction. In effect when the thousands of them sprayed the hydrogen sulfide gas into the oxygen atmosphere the resultant sulfuric acid acted as a communication net to connect the millions of the life forms together. The sulfuric acid was also deadly to carbon based life forms, us humans, found

ASSIMILATION

in oxygenated atmospheres. The two life forms had integrated to form a perfect symbiotic relationship; one could not exist without the other.

Selena then moved to the mountains and saw many villages with Neanderthals moving about, sitting under trees, or eating around a campfire. She then saw the alien beings just fall from a hole in the center of a village. As Muskula had said about the attack on her world, "They just poured out like mud in a never ending flow."

The alien lifeform set upon the unsuspecting Neanderthals and one could see the smoke rise from their sulfuric acid bathed skin. It took only minutes for the alien life form to overcome the community. Nothing was left alive as the black rug of undulating mass moved across the landscape. After the alien life form had moved on, there was nothing left of the village but smoking bones and puddles of sulfuric acid. Even the trees had been stripped of its leaves with the branches' bark hanging in long sections like ripped skin from a dead animal.

Selena slowly came back to the conscious presence and she found herself sobbing uncontrollable. She did not know how to process the information she had learned. She finally received understanding of what it meant for an entire world to be destroyed.

As she cried herself out, the Neanderthals sat silently. Selena gathered her wits about her and after she had wiped her eyes and blew her nose, she looked around at the group that had shared the death of their world.

"I promise you, I give you my word, on my life, I will find a way to destroy the alien menace. Without your help in somehow allowing us to view the inside of the alien we probably would never have been able to do so. But with us working together, with you using the most beautiful brains I have ever seen, we can learn their secrets."

It was only then that Selena realized that it was no longer daylight. How long had she been connected to the Neanderthals?

CHAPTER 51
MIND MELD

Admiral Cleary was with Blain in a conference room with several Andrian and Earth Scientist. The primary speaker was Dr. Sears. She was relaying the experience she had with the Neanderthal leadership in the cove. It was her opinion that they could provide the most useful insight into what could be the best option to destroying the enemy.

It appeared that one of their extraordinary skills was believed to be remote viewing of the enemy. Not only could they see the enemy thru time and distance but they could enter into the inside of the alien at the molecular level. If the viewing was not in real time it was definitely accurate replay of events on their planet.

The most intriguing information gathered by Dr. Sears was the nature of the symbiotic relationship of two different life forms to create an effective whole. When Flata, the geneticist on the intergalactic carrier, heard of this she demanded that the Neanderthal group be brought to the carrier for them to be examined.

Grargol advised he did not wish to be examined but anyone was welcome to join them in a vision ceremony. Flata advised that the instrumentation to decipher brain functions to recreate the experience could not be placed on the earth.

Previously, before the Humans and Andrians joined forces, the Andrians would simply have taken them regardless of their wishes. However, now that there was an alliance, the "Council of Yield" would not permit such an excursion. Flata decided she would come to the earth to experience the remote viewing. Even though she had a Neanderthal on the carrier and had mapped its brain extensively, there were still many dark nodules in various places for which she did not understand their function.

Flata had decided that she would go to the earth to examine the Neanderthals and experience the viewing. Even for Flata, this was the first time she had ever left the intergalactic carrier to go to a planet.

Grargol advised that the more of his people who joined in the viewing the stronger and more accurate the viewing would be. It was decided that fifty of the most advanced and strongest of his group lead the viewing and was the most advantageous number.

Dr. Sears picked out fifteen earth scientist as her allotment. Flata chose fifteen Andrian scientists from the three intergalactic carriers, none of whom was particularly interested in going to the planet. The military had fifteen officers which included Sara, Sasha, Emily, Admiral Cleary, and Captain Johnson of Space Intelligence Command.

It was also decided that all the hybrid Andrian-Human children would join in regardless of age, thus Sasha was to return to Russia and bring Perilain back. She decided she would also have her mother to accompany her.

ASSIMILATION

Persha, Jawane, and Hanlee had heard about the extraordinary powers that were possessed by the Neanderthals. They were looking forward to meeting them personally and participating in a melding of the minds. It was to be a totally new experience for them.

Warren had heard of the Neanderthals and their abilities and was hoping he would be able to join in. However, since his primary skill was in mathematics and chemical construction of natural resources, it was not deemed to be mission critical and he was not invited.

Unknown to Warren, Emily was the one who made the decision to exclude him. She was of the opinion that if he was not mature enough handle her relationship with Blain when she was away then he would fall apart if he really knew what was coming at them. The more they learned about the alien menace the nastier they realized they were.

Admiral Cleary had sent an inquiry to Flata to determine the feasibility of linking the ten intelligent saucers with the mind meld group with the Neanderthals being the control group. He believed that with this combination they could create a super brain that could resolve the problem of sealing the rent in the hyper dimensional fabric of space boundaries.

At first Flata thought it would be impossible; foremost and importantly, the saucers would have to become one with the cosmos and this could only be done at neuron levels of the space time coordinates. It is a miracle that one saucer can achieve this level but to have ten saucers connected in some way to achieve the same space time coordinates would take some engineering that might be above her skill level.

Thinking aloud Flata said, "But, is not the hybrid Human-Andrians supposedly more intelligent and possesses greater analytical skills than either of us? I believe it is time to find out."

With that thought in mind Flata became more resolute to make her trip to the planet earth worth her while.

CHAPTER 52
WAITING FOR EARTH

Sara's second time on the intergalactic carrier was uneventful. She visited with Sharla daily. They became close and enjoyed one another's company.

The Neanderthal was taken to the observation room often and when there he appeared to be in a trance. Sara too spent most of her time in the observation room next to him and sat staring out at the cosmos, each lost in their own thoughts. As a pair, they looked incongruous.

From time to time Flata would join her. They would talk of many things. One of the things discussed was Flata's strange new feelings, one of which was fear of the unknown. She admitted she was afraid of going to the surface of a planet, any planet, and especially the earth. She was terrified of being around all those dumb Humans. Sara had promised to be by her side at all times. She also said that Flata was going to go to a mall with her and go shopping whither she wanted to or not.

With the thirty day cycle completed and with the Neanderthal's leg completely healed, it was decided that it was time to go back to the earth. After the next sleep cycle, Flata, fifteen Andrian scientists, the Neanderthal, and Sara boarded the saucer to return to Earth. They each had an extra finger added to better to fit in around Humans. They had all decided they would act like they were mute so they would not have to talk to the humans. Flata could have erased the scars on Sara's hand and face but she did not want her to. She also wanted to leave her ear as it was. Sara believed in the commando code of wearing her scars as badges of honor; the only thing she would allow is perhaps the replacement of limbs and any other body part that would impair her combat effectiveness.

The Neanderthal worshipped Flata and Sara; Blain would decide what memories were to be erased, if any. They just did not understand their brains enough to remove memories at this time.

CHAPTER 53
IRENA'S ENLIGHTMENT

Sasha knocked on the door of her parent's new apartment at Vostochny Cosmodrome; no one was expecting her as she had left less than one month ago. It was amazing what could happen in one month's time. Who would ever think she would meet her first Neanderthal? That Emily and Sara are amazing! The revelation that the Neanderthals had remote viewing capabilities that could be shared offered a unique opportunity to collectively view their enemy. It had been decided that all the Human-Andrian children would partake in the viewing regardless of age. Therefore it had become necessary for Perilain to accompany her to the secluded base at Emily's home. She hoped that both her Mom and Father would somehow be allowed to come.

Sasha saw the apprehension on her mother's face when she opened the door and saw her standing there. Sasha walked into the house and her Mother turned to follow.

Without needing to be asked, Sasha said, "Yes Mom, everything is fine but circumstances have changed and it is necessary that Perilain come with me back to my, to my…base. And, not only that, but I need you to come with me to help take care of Perilain. Pa can stay here if he must."

Irina looked suspiciously at Sasha.

"Why? What is wrong? How come Nickolas cannot come?"

Then her face became emotionless, her eyes pleaded.

"It is about Perilain isn't it? He is different. He is smart. He can read my thoughts. Pa will be devastated. He loves him more than life itself. Why can he not come with us?"

"I will call the General one more time and ask again. There are steps that can be taken that can ease the stress he is going to go thru. In fact he can come after us, a special assignment. Perilain can ease his distress beforehand."

Sasha called the General and explained her plan and the steps that could be taken to keep security intact. He acquiesced to her request because of her outstanding service and sacrifice to the Earth and her country. It was decided that Nickolas was to conduct training sessions on interagency record keeping. Her Father prided himself on his near fanatical record keeping skills.

That evening when Nickolas came home he was upset. He had been told that within one week he was going to have to go to America for a records training seminar for an American Military Academy located on an isolated military base in Michigan. He came directly to the kitchen and took out his bottle of vodka and sat at the table. Perilain was standing in front of him looking up into his eyes.

"Dedulya, be at peace. We are going to America too and we can be together there. It will be fun!"

ASSIMILATION

As Perilain was saying this he reached up and placed his hands on his Grand Father's cheeks and looked into his eyes, he then moved his hands to either side of his head and lightly pressed them inward, cupping his head in his hands. Closing his eyes, Perilain carefully entered his mind and soothed his fears and anxieties and replaced his thoughts with peace, joy and anticipation of a new assignment. He then carefully removed any traces of his intrusion and moved back and smiled at his Dedulya. He loved him very much.

Nickolas smiled at his grandson. He loved him more than life itself.

"Yes, it will be fun to go to America, as long as you are going to be there. I guess your Dedulya will go with you and your Babulya. You will be leaving this afternoon, yes?"

Irina kissed Nickolas goodbye and got into the car. Sitting next to Perilain she leaned her head back and said a silent prayer.

Perilain looked up at her and smiled; he gently squeezed her hand and put his head on her shoulder. He was well aware of the menace that was facing the planet. He would help Mama protect his Babulya.

The military vehicle drove rapidly thru the heavily forested plateau of Russia's Far East Amour Region. To Irina the forest appeared to go on forever. Soon the car turned onto a smaller road that was not marked or paved but had a heavy chalk gravel surface. After about two miles the road seemed to sink below the ground level as the trees and surrounding area towered over them with concrete walls on each side of the road that grew higher the farther they went.

After going around a bend Irina saw what appeared to be a small steel door just large enough to admit small cars and trucks. The door opened as their car approached and entered into a long well lighted tunnel. It was strange to her that she did not see any security personnel or any other signs that the underground facility was guarded.

The vehicle entered into a large cavernous hanger. There were several saucer craft tethered and floating about three feet above the hanger floor. There may have been a lack of apparent security approaching the underground facility but that was not the case within the hanger.

Irina observed armed security around each saucer. There were even several men in what appeared to be armor suits standing along the perimeter of the building. Irina then observed a floating spherical device about the size of a basketball above each saucer slowly turning. Irina believed they were also some type of security defense mechanism.

Sasha looked at her mom from the front seat and said, "Mamulya, welcome to our world".

Perilain said, "Babulya, I was born on an Intergalactic Carrier and it was my home until our recent return to the Earth. It was so beautiful to be among the stars and see so many different worlds. I learned so many things. I want so much to share that with you Babulya."

ASSIMILATION

Irina looked at her grandson with understanding and awe. She knew he was intelligent and seemed to possess attributes that to her seemed like magic. His father Blain must be from the stars.

Perilain smiled at his Babulya. "I do not like having secrets from you. I understand why we must keep secrets from Dedulya; he has such a regimented mind that he would be devastated if he knew the truth. He cannot even accept only a partial truth. You are patient and will eventually learn everything. But, for the time being it is necessary to maintain very tight security."

Looking at his Mamulya, he then said, "My Mamulya is a very brave warrior as is my Da. They will protect us from harm."

Sasha opened her mother's car door and with Perilain taking one hand and Sasha taking the other hand, walked Irina over to a saucer that had extended a ramp.

Looking at Sasha, Irina said, "I think I am a little afraid. I am sure it is okay because you are with me. Who would have thought flying saucers were real?"

Perilain walked his Babulya to the receptacle directly behind the control seat and taking her by the arms moved her backwards.

Perilain said, "Ceramic glass cover will come from the ceiling locking you inside. Then, a membrane will cover your nose and mouth so you can breathe. I will be in the next receptacle. You can see me if you look to your left. Mamulya will be on your right."

Perilain then went to his receptacle and was enclosed.

Soon there was a vibration as the saucer slowly exited the hanger. Irina could see the forest stretch out below her. Then she sucked in her breath as she saw the sharp curvature of the earth against a black limitless void punctuated with steady shining stars.

CHAPTER 54
FLATA'S FEAR

Emily's secluded house in the middle of the woods next to Lake Ontario was no longer a small cottage hangout. In addition to the three small bungalows which were built six years earlier, there were now six four bedroom quadraplex apartments all of which had a view of the lake. They were spaced about fifty yards apart to help the illusion of seclusion.

Sara had arranged for Sasha and Perilain to move into her room at Emily' house so Perilain could be close to Warren Jr. Besides, she had told Emily she wanted to share an apartment with Flata.

Flata walked from the secret tunnel exit behind Emily's house. As she stepped outside into the daylight she immediately felt a kaleidoscope of unexpected senses. The air, the sun, the heat and cold, the splashes of sunlight on the ground turning the green grass to a bright green one moment then dark green the next.

A large hawk plunged onto the ground twenty feet in front of Flata and she let out a loud scream startling the other Andrians who was already apprehensive.

Sara had her arm crooked in her arm so she held her close and she quickly intoned so all could hear, "It is only a hawk and he just found a rabbit for lunch! It is okay!"

The hawk flapped around on the ground for a few

seconds then took flight with the hapless rabbit clutched in its talons. You could hear the rabbit mew as the hawk flew up and out of sight over the trees.

Sara could feel Flata shaking next to her. It took a moment for Flata to compose herself but she straightened and continued to walk. The hawk was an unfortunate incident in the way of what should have been a nice welcome to the earth.

A bus was waiting for them on a new circular drive in front of the house. Sara went first and the others followed. She did not have any idea what they thought of the first few minutes of their arrival and the bus ride as they all had closed their minds so one could not read their thoughts.

It took only about fifteen minutes of a scenic drive for the bus to arrive at the apartments. Two people were assigned to each spacious bedroom. Thus, the contingent of Andrian scientists took up two quadraplex apartments and they could be relatively close to one another. There was an escort for every two Andrians to help get them settled. Sara stayed with Flata.

Flata walked around the apartment and examined every inch of the apartment minutely, flipping switches, turning water on and off and looking in the refrigerator. She took out several pieces of fruit and sniffed each one. Flata stopped in front of the large picture window overlooking the sloping terrain to the large body of water.

Sara said, "The view is quite different from the carrier observation deck. It seems so small but yet it too has its own beauty. Fortunately we are in a very isolated

ASSIMILATION

area. What surrounding land that was not purchased by Emily, has been purchased by the military."

Flata turned and looked at Sara. "I owe you an apology. I am the one responsible for keeping you in stasis for three years on the carrier. Emily requested several times for you to be brought out but I refused. Finally, I guess Emily had had enough and went to the "Council of Yield", and demanded for you to be returned to the conscious state."

"I cannot say exactly why I refused to allow you out. I told myself that it was for your safety. That was true, but, it was not the only reason. I really wanted to experiment on you by enhancing your mental and physical attributes. For a Human, you were already way above average in intelligence and strength. You were young and I wanted to make you a better Human. I did not do anything detrimental to you. The muscles throughout your body have reinforced nano carbon fibers. Your bone structure has been hardened by inserting nano bots to weave ceramic organic cells thru out your skeletal structure. I strengthened all your organs to operate at a greater level of efficiency. And your brain, I activated existing brain cells to utilize a greater percentage of your brain. I also imprinted knowledge and skills you would require as a commando."

Sara looked at her and remained silent, thinking about what Flata had told her.

"I suppose that if you had not enhanced me in these things I would be dead. That is the only reason I could survive a fall from the second story window. You told me about the stronger bone structure. If you had not reinforced my organs I could not have survived the impact."

Sara walked over to Flata and put her arms around her and hugged her.

"Thank you for saving my life. I guess that makes you the closest thing to a Mother that I ever had. My Mom died giving birth. Does anyone else know about all of the changes? I know everyone is aware of my telepathic abilities."

"It is no secret but no one has asked and I saw no reason to tell. You are in the best physical condition that you could possibly be; I enhanced you as if you were my own."

Sara said, "Great! Now for your first ever shower!"

Sara grabbed Flata by the hand and escorted her upstairs to the bathroom. Emily had all the bathrooms built with the Andrians in mind, thus they doubled as a sauna and heavy mister with a wide selection of inhalants such as eucalyptus and other fragrant emulsions to sooth the senses.

Sara quickly stripped naked and Flata did the same all be it somewhat slower as she did not know what to expect. They stepped into the shower and Sara adjusted the stream to warm heavy mist infused with eucalyptus. After a thirty minute shower Sara turned off the stream of mist, Flata continued standing with her eyes closed breathing deeply.

"I am sure that I have never even dreamed of such an experience. We must somehow in some way introduce this experience on our carriers."

ASSIMILATION

Sara helped Flata change into a pair of jeans and blouse, and yes, she felt the bra was a useless accruement. Together, arm in arm they walked down to the water's edge and as they did so they each told one another about their early life. For Sara it was a short telling.

Sara did like Flata and she enjoyed watching her come out of her shell as she doted over Orion. When they all were on the ship, Sasha had insisted on having her baby naturally and refused to have the child taken to be inserted into a berthing chamber. Flata had delivered Warren Jr., Orion, and Perilain. Somehow that experience had helped provide a human connection.

The first three days of the Andrians arrival was used to introduce them to life on Earth. Everyone was to be in bed by eleven and got up by seven. Breakfast was served as a communal breakfast in a new rustic camp style building with removable windows covered by screens to allow the outdoors to become part of the rustic experience. Since it was in the middle of the summer it was a pleasant experience.

After the third day Sara decided that it was time to take Flata on her first ever shopping excursion. Several of the Andrians with their security details with a guide were also allowed to venture to the mall. Sara had Hanlee and Jawane accompany them to the mall and with them was the ever present covert security ring that guarded the Andrians whenever they went out in public. Sara herself never went anywhere unless she was armed with a small hand held laser weapon. The weapon was very effective at close range.

Flata was amazed at the prolific choices in style and colors of clothing. Both Hanlee and Jawane enjoyed helping her pick out different outfits, all of which was stridently protested by Flata, but to no avail. Sara's personal favorite was a nice well fitted gray business suit with a maroon blouse. A nice pair of black sandals finished out the ensemble.

After shopping they all went to the food court for food and drink. Fast food was not necessarily as fast as Andrian preparations and it certainly was not near as healthy. However, the tastes were more intense and the smells more pungent.

Flata sniffed at her first ever piece of fried chicken and much in the way as all the Andrian children did before her; she carefully sniffed and tasted with her tongue as she gingerly bit into the deep fried crusted meat. She closed her eyes and savored the flavors and could feel juice running down her chin.

When she opened her eyes, she saw a young woman standing in front of the table staring at her. The woman was wearing slacks and loose fitting top and appeared to be about five months pregnant. Her hair was up in a ponytail similar to Emily's in style and she seemed to be the same age as Sara.

"My, it looks like you are really enjoying that fried chicken. They do have some of the best fried chicken here but I do not know if it is as good as you seem to think."

Laughing the woman looked at Sara and said, "Come here and give me a hug girlfriend".

Sara got up from the table and hugged Kyla tightly. It

was obvious she was pregnant.

Sara placed her hand on her friend's stomach and closed her eyes. After a moment she looked at Kyla smiling and said, "I think you are going to have a son and he is going to be very smart. And, his eyes will be hazel, not blue like your and Jack's eyes."

Kyla laughed and said, "Well look at you! Do you have a new career as a psychic?"

Everyone laughed.

"Kyla, I want you to meet a friend of mine. We have spent almost what could be equivalent of a life time together. She is going to be a guest speaker at the University. She is the closest I have ever come to having a Mom and I love her dearly. You might say she made me the woman that I am today!"

Flata did not move. She just continued staring at the young woman named Kyla.

Jawane said, telepathically, "Stand and shake her hand like we showed you earlier. Remember, your Human!"

Sara and Hanlee smiled. Flata gave Jawane a disdainful look then stood up and going around the table to Kyla, she shook Kyla's hand. She did not smile nor did she speak.

Again Jawane joked, this time verbally, "I am glad I was not in any of your classes. You seem like a hard ass."

Everyone laughed except Flata who again gave Jawane another disdainful look.

Kyla said, "Hello, my name is Kyla and any friend of Sara's is a friend of mine. And, Jawane, Hanlee, it is so nice to see you again. It seems like you two are inseparable from Sara; and, it seems like we are always running into each other at the mall. I think it would be fun to have you all over for dinner with Jack and I"

Hanlee said, "Nice to see you too Kyla. I think that it is wonderful that you married Jack and now you are pregnant. And yes, it would be an experience to have dinner in your home."

Suddenly Flata broke into the conversation. "You are pregnant with twins. One will be a boy, as Sara said, but the other one will be a girl. They are both healthy and strong. However, the girl will have brown eyes."

Kyla said, "Wow that is really cool, so you and Sara both are psychics!"

Sara laughed and Kyla said, "Sara you can come up with some of the strangest friends! But then again, I find you strange too. It does not matter to me, I do not care how strange you become, I will always consider you a friend. And I love you so much! I hope you will view me in like manner".

Then, surprising everyone Flata said, "It would be an honor to come to your home for dinner."

Kyla responded by saying, "It is settled then. Sara do you remember the old house on the edge of town that we all use to think it was haunted when we were kids? Well Jack and I bought it three months ago. We can make it a house warming party! Next Saturday should be a perfect time. Jack will love showing off his cooking skills. He will put some hamburgers and dogs on the grill!"

Flata blanched and stepped back. She visibly paled

thinking about eating a dog. Both Hanlee and Jawane burst out laughing at her mental image of a long haired shaggy dog squirming on the grill.

Kyla looked at them perplexed and shook her head thinking, "Boy, Sara does have weird friends."

Sara smiled and said, "What time would you like us to show up?"

Kyla thought for a minute and said, "How about around three? I will check and confirm with Jack. I am sure he will be okay with that."

Sara replied, "Great, we will see you then!"

"Okay, I will let you get back to your chicken! I hope our grilled food will taste good as you believe that chicken taste!"

Sara turned toward Flata and gave her a hug and said, "Be at peace Flata, we will not be eating any squirming, hairy, dogs. What Kyla said was just an expression, a human euphemism. I think you will like them. You are enjoying the chicken aren't you? I know you do. Come on, let's finish our lunch. We still have to go by the University."

CHAPTER 55
SCIENCE INTRODUCTION

Monday morning was an important day and proved to come with equal challenges. Emily was the first to arrive at the underground military conference room. The meeting was not to start until eight A.M. but she found it necessary to get an early start as she double and triple checked the agenda.

There were eleven seated positions that were the exact replicas of the control seats on the intelligent saucers. They were facing a wall screen that had multiple layers of information. Emily and the ten Human-Andrian hybrids would occupy these seats. Behind them were five rows of like mannered seats with ten seats per row which would be occupied by the fifty Neanderthals. The following row consisted of fifteen seats which would be occupied by the Andrian scientist from the Intergalactic Carriers.

The remaining rows of seats were occupied by Earth Scientist which included Dr. Abbott and Dr. Sears, Human and Andrian Military, The President and his cabinet, and Muskula and her former mate, and last but not least, clergy representatives of all the major world religions. Emily and others believed that if worst came to worst, the Earth's peoples would need to be appraised of

ASSIMILATION

the religious significance of the possible annihilation of the entire Earth population.

The eleven intelligent saucers were in the far end of the hanger and had umbilical cords attached from the ten Human-Andrian Hybrids and Emily. They in turn were linked to the other participants in a cascading order. The objective was to link the Neanderthals remote viewing abilities with the saucer intelligence; then with the combined power of the connected intelligence of the Humans and Andrians, a comprehensive plan could be envisioned that could thwart and or kill the enemy entity from the other dimension or universe.

Emily sat at a desk in the operations center. An orderly quietly placed a cup of coffee next to her. Sipping her coffee Emily's thought came unbidden.

"What did the entity within her saucer mean when she said that they could become one? And what did she mean when she said we would become all powerful?" The latter was a troubling thought. Emily then reviewed all that had gone on in her seemingly short life. It was astounding how each event seemed to lead to the next in an ever pile of cascading events.

For the moment Emily put the troubling thoughts aside. Then to her surprise, she learned that she had been immersed in thought for more than an hour. How did that happen?

When Emily exited her office she saw that most everyone attending the first viewing was already in their seats. There was a quiet hum of excited voices overlain by muted fear.

Almost everyone there was aware of the enemy at the gate, the exception being the clergy. Their seating was arranged so that a short partition was between them and the other viewers, they were not privy to the knowledge of the Andrians and other alien entities involved in the viewing. They were advised that a military operation was ongoing and they were going to be apprised of its nature so they in turn could help soothe earth's population of its possible impending doom.

Emily took her seat in the front row. Several of the Neanderthals walked thru the rows administering the liquid concoction that would put them in a mental state of drifting consciousness. However, a human officer administered the potion to the clergy.

After the drinks were consumed a hush came over the large group, one could hear a pin drop.

Emily sensed herself become a point of light as the saucers brought everyone in the room into the state of being one with the universe. Each individual's mind became a quark with full conscious knowledge of the cosmos streaming by.

The Neanderthals directed their path straight to the enemy fleet which was currently crossing over from their universe to the universe of all those present. The enemy fleet was innumerable with ships that spanned as far as the intelligences could see.

The viewing approached then entered the first alien vessel. It was shaped like a large round pod bristling with sensors protruding from its skin. Once inside the vessel they could view what they believed to be the

ASSIMILATION

commanding group of the alien fleet. There was what appeared at first to be a hodgepodge of interconnecting bodies. Upon closer inspection the bodies were connected in parallel spirals with a front tentacle of one being attached to the rear tentacle of another creating what appeared to be a woven blanket of interlocking lifeforms.

A fine hydrochloric acid mist enveloped the mass like a thick fog. There were intermittent flashes of ultraviolet light that appeared to be similar to sheet lightning on the earth. After each flash of ultraviolet light the entire mass shifted position and grasped a different tentacle moving the mass in a different pattern in an up or down position.

After each mass movement, blast of neurons formed into beams, shot from the lead alien vessel into each and every other vessel within their fleet. In effect it appeared their communication was instantaneous.

The viewing then entered one of the alien entities structure and again located the second alien being of the symbiotic pair. The interior being was the entity in control and directed the outer shell to do its bidding; and, as previously observed by Dr. Selena Washington, was responsible for spraying the veil of acid which was used for communication.

The viewers roamed thru out the enemy fleet and observed the innumerable host which was coming upon them. All the scientist and military personnel gathered as much information as was possible. The religious leaders believed as one, knowing full well that the human race was doomed without God's intervention.

After the viewers withdrew from the enemy and

again returned to their present state of mind, they were all surprised to learn that they had been in a semiconscious state for almost twenty four hours. They were all mentally exhausted and each went to their assigned bunk space and collapsed on their beds. Skip and Persha shared a bunk and were fast asleep embraced in one another's arms.

Upon the third day they assembled in various groups and discussed and analyzed what they had learned in the viewing; the work groups worked into the night for the next three days. They all agreed that none of their current weapons could eliminate the threat that the enemy posed. Many of their weapons could slow them down and kill a host of them but they did not have enough lasers or bombs to make a dent in their numbers.

Dr. Washington and Flata agreed that the only viable weapon was a biological one that could kill either one or both of the biological entities. They also believed they could safely infiltrate their fleet if they could disrupt their communications. Upon presenting their findings to the group as a whole, it was agreed that the scientist would be divided into three groups, each given a task to destroy the entities and to neutralize their communications. They all believed the enemy fleet would reach earth within twenty years. It appeared to the military they were bypassing all other targets and making earth their primary objective.

CHAPTER 56
BUSY AT WORK

Kyla was busy at her desk when three men in business suits walked into the office. They extended their hands for a hand shake and introduced themselves. Kyla immediately recognized Caleb Sears, Sara's father. At the same time Caleb recognized Kyla and gave her a startled look.

"Kyla, what a surprise, I did not know you worked here!"

Kyla, mystified by Caleb's obvious discomfort at seeing her at the front desk, said, "Yes Mr. Sears, my husband Jack and I own the business with our business partners; we have really been swamped."

"It is so nice to see you again Mr. Sears. I saw Sara last weekend and she told me all about her untimely absence. It must have been devastatingly hard on her as I am sure it was hard on you."

If Caleb could look any more shocked than he was before, he was really discomfited now. Kyla believed that she actually saw his eyes bulge out a little.

The other man quickly extended his hand and said, "Nice to meet you Kyla, I am Commander Taaker."

He could read both their minds and he knew Kyla was talking about Sara's cover story about being pregnant and having to give up the baby thus leaving for several years. Caleb in turn, thought Sara had told Kyla about her being on an Intergalactic Andrian Carrier.

Commander Taaker, continuing shaking Kyla's hand and looking at Caleb, said, "Being a father myself Caleb, I can understand how devastating it was to have a daughter get pregnant at thirteen and thus be forced to send her away for several years to live with a relative. It was obviously difficult for you to have Sara give up the baby for adoption. You made the right decision as any good Father must."

Kyla watched the color slowly return to Caleb's face.

"I am sorry Mr. Sears. I did not know it was such a deep family secret. I promise not to ever bring it up or mention it again."

Caleb looked at Kyla and said, "Uh, yea, sure. Thank you very much."

He did not know that Sara had told her a cover story. Of course she would have to come up with something. And truth be known, it was an excellent cover story.

Commander Taaker asked if Jack was in as they wished to discuss some business issues.

Kyla escorted the three men into Jacks officer where he was busy at work. Jack stood and Kyla introduced Caleb and Commander Taaker and the third man introduced himself as being a procurement specialist.

Caleb said, "Jack I will get right to the point. Certain interested parties in the military, have chosen you and your firm to be the general contractor in reviewing the legal documentation for specialized military contracts. It will be somewhat of a different class of work than what you are now doing and you, Kyla, and your staff are

ASSIMILATION

already doing a fine job of representing our interest. We would like for you to continue, the work load will be increased but we think you can handle it."

Kyla did not miss the fact that Caleb had said, "Our interest" when referring to military contracts. That meant that Caleb must be in the military. She had remembered that Sara had always said her father was a computer salesman. And the other man, he introduced himself as "Commander Taaker". Either Sara did not know her father was military or he had consistently lied to her.

Kyla did not know which the case may be but it really did not matter this late in the day. Then a strange thought burst thru her consciousness, "My stars, Sara must be in the Military too! That would explain the missing top of her ear, the fine scar on her cheek bone and her hands! The one hand look like it had been shattered into a thousand pieces and then reassembled. But how could that be? We are the same age!"

Kyla returned from her introspections. She had been totally immersed. She had not heard a single word that Sara's father had said. Then when she focused she found herself looking directly into the eyes of Commander Taaker. He was only three feet away. There was a slight smile pulling at the corner of his lips. He slightly nodded his head and then looked away.

Caleb was saying, "One of the most important aspects of this task will involve highly sensitive and secret military interest. Each of you and your staff has already been cleared to do this work by a separate group."

"You currently do not have the staff to accommodate

the quantity of contracts that we are interested in sending your way but should you choose to take the assignment, any new employees you need to hire will be vetted by me and Commander Taaker. Actually, we will be making several personnel recommendations. Does this sound like something you might be interested in doing?"

Commander Taaker interjected, and looking at Kyla as he spoke, "Jack, you and Kyla, and your firm are on a very short list of trusted individuals vetted for this project." Then looking at Jack, he further stated, "We have already checked on your professional integrity and found it would be an asset to have you on board. It is really a very important task."

Jack listened carefully to what was being said. There was more being communicated than verbal words. The military definitely wanted him and his firm to do the work, whatever that entailed.

"I think I need to consult my wife before I take on any more work. We work as equal partners, as does all our other employees."

Jack was surprised when Kyla quietly said, "We will do it."

The third man who never gave his name but did provide a title of Procurement Specialist, advised, "Great, welcome aboard. You will have open ended contracts, the use of military transportation for necessary trips, and the use, free of charge, of the five story building next to the park downtown with all expenses payed. And, you will need at least fifty more lawyers and a hundred assistants to insure proper flow of information."

ASSIMILATION

Both Jack and Kyla's mouths dropped open and both of them said, "What!" at the same time.

As soon as he stopped talking, Caleb said, "Because this is a highly classified government procurement endeavor, computer service will be provided by the military of which all of it is proprietary property. And, because of the advanced state of the art of the computer systems, the building will be protected by a military subcontractor. Many of the instructions will be encoded and will look like a strange language but any of the information you need to know to do your job will be translated by the military intelligence communication systems."

Jack did not understand why they were chosen but he recognized an obligation when he saw one even if it was belated. This project was cut and dried and he was part of it whither he wanted to be or not. Obviously Kyla recognized that salient fact before he and thus had said yes.

Jack extended his hand and said, "Thank you for having confidence in our firm. As my wife already said, we will be glad to accept the assignment."

The procurement specialist replied, "Good to have aboard. You can move in tomorrow. The only things you will need to bring are your current government contract files. All your other legal issues are to be resourced to other parties. You will be paid for the work you have already done on the contracts. Everything else is already in place. A truck and moving crew will assist you in packing and moving."

As the three men left Kyla had an uneasy feeling. What had just happened was strange. Why did they choose them?

"Jack, I am afraid. This assignment and that is what it is, seemed almost like a command and somewhat desperate. I know we are not the only legal attorney's office that could handle the contracts. No, we were picked because we are trusted to keep our mouth shut."

Jack took Kyla in his arms and said, "You know, for one so young you seem to have a gift for understating truths. I do not know what this is about but we will find out soon enough".

Jack and Kyla went into the work area in the other part of their office and called the staff together. He saw no reason in delaying advising them of their new priority and duty, as that is what it truly was.

"So folks, you now know as much about our mutual circumstances as we do. If you want out you should go now. I am quite certain that the military would highly frown on you leaving after you enter the new office setting provided by them for us to do our work."

"Oh, did I mention that we were told we would need fifty more lawyers and one hundred assistants? We are going to be moving tremendous amounts of contracts."

Jack and Kyla left the office taking an early afternoon off at Kyla's insistence.

"Come on Jack. I am sure that our time together will be but a precious memory once we begin our new assignment. You do remember that Sara and her friends are coming over Saturday for a cook out?"

Jack said, "Ah, Caleb is "that" Sara's Father. Good I would like to meet your friend; she sounds like such an

ASSIMILATION

interesting person."

"Yes, well if you think Sara's going to be interesting wait until you meet the professor friend of hers. Her name is Flata. I never did get a last name."

"I did not tell you that Sara put her hand on my stomach and said I was going to have a son and he would have hazel eyes. Then her professor friend put her hand on my stomach and said we were going to have twins. The second baby was going to be a girl and have brown eyes. And, she said they were well and healthy. I wonder why our doctor did not tell us we were going to have twins."

Jack was pleasantly surprised about the announcement that they were going to have twins.

"I wish that were true Kyla but like you said, the doctor never said anything about it and surly he would know. Well now, I am intrigued. I can hardly wait to meet your friends."

CHAPTER 57
FIRST COOKOUT

Sara, Jawane, Hanlee, and Flata left the compound in a large black SUV early as Sara wanted to drive along the water's edge as much as possible. Flata was silent as this was her second outing and she was going to someone's home for a cookout. And, as always two SUVS followed as part of Sara's and Flata's security team; because the house was somewhat isolated the security team would not necessarily be invisible.

Jawane drove with the windows down and the moon roof open allowing in the cool salted air mixed with fresh spruce which provided a very tantalizing scent to ones nostrils. Flata leaned back closing her eyes and breathed deeply. It was a very relaxing and enjoyable experience.

Jawane having followed Sara's directions turned into the long driveway that led to the two story house with attic space made into rooms with windows like eyes peering out from the rooftop. A wrap around porch provided a welcoming, homey atmosphere. The house was in the process of being painted and was mostly finished with only a few detail spots to touch up.

A large brown Labrador retriever came bounding down the stairs, tongue lolling out its mouth, tail wagging, barking in a low baritone voice. Kyla opened the screen door and called the dog back which immediately ran back to the porch and sat next to her; she also saw the other two SUV's, park away from Sara's vehicle. Several men got out of the vehicles and positioned themselves around and away from the house, she then noted that two men were at the driveway entrance and had placed a stanchion on each side of the drive and there appeared to be some sort of shimmering beam between them.

Before Kyla could speak, Sara said, "Sorry about the security team. Flata is a high value asset and the University wants to insure her safety to make sure nothing untoward becomes her."

Jack came to the door and upon seeing Sara, extended his hand and said, "It is so nice to finally meet you, Sara, I have heard so much about you!"

Jack then looked at Flata and extended his hand saying, "And you too, Flata. I understand you're the one that told Kyle that she was going to have twins. Kyla has since gone to her doctor and he assured her that was not the case. I surly hope you prediction is correct though, because I would really love to have twins!"

Without smiling and without releasing Jack's hand, Flata responded, "Your doctor is limited in his assessment skills. Your children will be born healthy and smiling, their hearts beat as one."

Jack tried to release his hand but Flata held on.

She then said, "Monday morning I want to see you at our clinic. You have a heart blockage and you are going to have a heart attack within a week if it is not attended to right away. You are too important of an asset for us to lose you at this time."

Both Jack and Kyla were stunned.

Sara stepped forward and placing her hand on Jack's shoulder said, "Flata! That was a good diagnosis. We can take care of you, Jack, at the University Clinic. We will send an ambulance Monday morning and you will be in good hands. And of course Kyla, you will want to come along. Now, let's eat! I am starved."

Jack was still stunned when they exited the house thru the back door. The stone barbeque grill was smoking and the sound of meat juices sizzled as the juices dripped into the flames.

Jack tended to the steaks and hot dogs automatically and was totally engrossed in what the woman Flata had said to him. Sara walked up beside him and placed her arm around his waist and gave him a squeeze.

"You have to forgive Flata for her poor bedside manners. She is so knowledgeable in medicine and the sciences that she forgets everyone else is not as smart as she. Her diagnostic skills are beyond question. We will send an ambulance Monday morning and pick you and Kyla up. Flata will patch you up and fix you up good as new."

Jack looked at Sara with an apprehensive look. He then noticed the thin line scar on her face and the top portion of her missing ear.

"But how did she know? She was just holding my hand and looking into my eyes very intently. I too went to the doctor last month for a physical and checkup. The Doctor said I was in perfect health and would live to be a hundred years old."

Jack saw a clouded look come into Sara's eyes, and

ASSIMILATION

then she said, in a wistful voice, "Should we all be so lucky".

The steaks were done and served promptly. The baked potatoes dripped with butter, the salad greens were dotted with small red tomatoes. All in all the dinner was a success. The conversation was light and friendly and more than once Jawane and Hanlee poked fun at Flata and accused her of being an aristocratic, "know it all", that sees herself above the floss of the universe named, "mankind".

Flata had never been spoken to in such a manner and was appalled at their banter; She seldom joined in the conversations. She seemed more engrossed in observing her surroundings and enjoying her food. Truth be known, she was furiously calculating their odds of defeating such an alien entity. She knew the entity consisted of two distinct beings superimposed as one. How such a life form could become sentient was beyond her comprehension; but then why not? Had she not herself created a sentient being out of an electrical-mechanical device?

Having resolved her inner turmoil and musings, Flata turned to Jack and said, "Jack you are a good man. I am glad to have this opportunity to share food and drink. It is a universal custom to bond kindred spirits."

Having said that, Flata lifted her glass of red wine and said, "To all mankind of kindred spirit, present, past and future, may we be successful in insuring the progeny of our species".

Kyla's heart jumped within her breast as she felt a knife of deep fear slice thru her breast. What was going on; surely it was something they too were now involved in!"

Haylee who was sitting beside her, placed her arm around her shoulder and said, "Be at peace, Kyla. Everything will be alright. Working together we can and will make it so."

CHAPTER 58
AMBULANCE RIDE

Kyla was escorted into the house and up to her bedroom and helped into bed by Jawane and Hanlee. They covered her with a blanket as she dreamily began to drift off to sleep.

She heard Jawane say, "Kyla, we love you because Sara loves you. You and your family are the same as our family."

Jack was concerned about Kyla mainly due to her pregnancy. It was unlike her to become so tired so quickly. He was in thought when Sara came to his side and slipped her arm thru his arm and steered him to a porch swing in from the glare of the sun. Sitting him down Sara sat beside him.

"Jack, Kyla is going to be okay. She was just worried about you. Flata has given her a mild sedative. She will wake up in the morning being refreshed and good as new. And, you should sleep well tonight also because you are going to have a big day tomorrow. I think it would be good if Jawane and Hanlee stayed with you this evening. We can all accompany you to the hospital tomorrow. In the meantime, Flata wants you to take this pill and lay down on your couch."

Jack did as he was told and walked to the couch and lay down. Soon he was fast asleep in a deep sleep.

Flata said, "He will not live till morning, his aorta is about to burst. We will call for a saucer to transport him to the hospital now."

Sara quickly removed her communicator and summoned a saucer. Jawane and Hanlee busied themselves packing a few personal items and toiletries.

The saucer arrived and a contingent of medics exited the craft on the run and quickly extricated Kyla and Jack. Sara and Flata accompanied them on the saucer while Jawane and Hanlee secured the residence. They returned to Emily's home and base by SUV taking Jack and Kyla's dog with them.

A medical team was waiting at the underground base hospital and whisked Jack away to the operating room. Flata operated and repaired Jack's aorta by infusing his blood with nano bots. At the same time she gave his immune system a boost and activated neurons in his cerebral cortex to enhance his thinking processes to better enable his ability to perform his duties. Flata also performed the same operations and enhancements on Kyla.

Kyla and Jack awoke in the morning feeling refreshed and rejuvenated, and, to their surprise, they were in their own bed. Neither one of them had any memories of the time after the dinner. There was a note on the dresser mirror from Sara saying "The operation went better than expected so you were returned home." The note also mentioned that due to their new job they were considered indispensable and thus security had been assigned to them, as had the building.

Sara looked out the front window and observed an

ASSIMILATION

SUV parked at the entrance of the drive and it had the same shimmering air as the day before. She then looked out back and observed some kind of drone device floating just below the tree line. She could not tell why it seemed to shimmer in and out of view but assumed it had to do something with the shadows of the trees.

"I feel so refreshed! I am so famished!, said Jack."

Going downstairs, followed by Kyla who felt equally hungry, Jack opened the refrigerator door. To their surprise, it was stocked full to the brim with packages of food that was stamped, "Military Rations".

Jack took a package that was labeled "Breakfast: Eggs, Bacon, Potatoes, Fruit..., Add Water, which he did. To their surprise, the plate of powder bloomed into aromatic eggs, bacon and potatoes. The fruit was nondescript and was a composite looking more like apple sauce.

Grabbing spoons, Jack and Kyla tasted the food. It did taste very good. Considering it came out of the package looking like powder, it was astounding, nothing short of a miracle.

Kyla was stunned when she looked at the chronometer on the kitchen wall. It did read Monday but it was a week later than when they went to sleep. The hair rose on the back of Kyla's neck. She knew in her heart that it was correct but she was afraid none the less. What had happened to the last week?

Kyla grabbed her phone and called Sara. Sara picked up on the first ring.

"Hi, sleepy head, bout time you two both woke up!"

"What happened Sara, why is it a week later?"

"Sorry Kyla, there were complications with Jacks surgery so Flata had a lot of repair work to do. We did not want you to worry, being pregnant and all, so we decided to let you sleep thru the procedure."

Kyla's heart gave a skipped beat as a tinge of fear raced thru her mind.

"What kind of problem, is he going to be alright?"

"Yes," replied Sara.

"Do not worry, he is better than new, you both are."

Sara disconnected amused at Kyla's confusion. "Well now, you get to experience a little taste of some of my emotions after I awoke on the Intergalactic Carrier after being unconscious for three years."

CHAPTER 59
PLANNING SEEDS OF DESTRUCTION

Emily sat pensively thinking about how best to confront the oncoming fleet of alien death and destruction. Reports were coming in that the enemy was bypassing all other worlds and were not deterred from its direct path to Earth. Literally millions of them were annihilated as their fleet was bombarded with neutron weapons of immeasurable power sending an untold number into black holes. The created void was simply filled in with more intergalactic ships.

"Somehow the rent in the dimensional fabric had to be sealed. Whatever the cost was to be, it had to be done", thought Emily.

Emily knew all too well what that cost was going to be. It seemed to be ordained before time that she was the one that was going to seal it up.

Emily told her orderly to summon Admiral Cleary and Blain. It was time for action.

After the necessary parties had been assembled in the conference room or by telecast, Emily called the meeting to order. The scientist, hybrid children, and military leaders assembled silently feeling the ominous nature of the coming discussion.

Emily stood at the podium. She was wearing a clean, crisp, maroon and blue space intelligence officer's uniform. She looked very much in command.

"As you know our time is limited. We have marshalled our joint earth and Andrian resources at a phenomenal speed. Our best efforts to date have killed more of the enemy than there has ever been life on earth. And yet, they are relentless in the pursuit of its objective, Earth."

"The best plan we have come up with to date is to meet the enemy as far into the Andromeda Galaxy as possible. We will fight them all the way back to earth across the Milky Way galaxy before they enter our space. As of this time we have them advancing only from the direction of the Andromeda Galaxy and they will enter the far side of the Milky Way galaxy within, we believe, twenty years. The exact time they will arrive on the earth is not known but it should be about five years after first entry into our Milky Way galaxy."

We have instituted, "Operation Noah", and candidates are going to be evacuated from the earth within five years. There will also be a last ditch evacuation on the eve of the attack. Only several million of human inhabitants will be able to be evacuated at that time if we are lucky."

"Our defensive strategy will be based on a two prong attack. Our initial attack will be to infiltrate and destroy their command structure. We believe that should we be able to disrupt their chemical neuron streams then they will not be cohesive in their actions. Viruses have been developed that will kill the outer entity shells that enable

ASSIMILATION

them to be mobile. Once immobilized, the secondary infection will destroy the chemical manufacturing capabilities of the primary life form within the protective shield thus eliminating their ability to communicate."

"The secondary attack will be conducted by myself and ten other saucers. We will enter into the middle of the attack group and with the assistance of the entities within our saucers we will rent a new hole in the fabric of time and space of the dimension from whence they came, the Eighth Dimension.

The newly developed virus will be launched into their system which will destroy their lifeforms completely and utterly."

"We will then use our combined intelligences to create a black hole that will suck the alien presence within our time dimension back out into their own. After the black hole evacuates all alien life forms from our system, we will implode the gap and close the hole."

The room was quiet. They all mulled over the plan, especially the part about closing the enemy's dimension. No one wanted to say anything but they were all thinking the same thing; what happens to the saucers in the middle of the enemy?"

Admiral Cleary cleared his throat and then said, "Commander, will it be possible for you and your crews to escape once the hole to the other dimension is sealed?"

Emily looked solemnly around the group. Taking a deep breath, Emily said, "We do not actually know the full capabilities of the entities within the saucers. We do know they have grown capabilities exponentially that is way beyond our, and, or, Andrian capabilities. Even our hybrid offspring have been...left in the dust, so to speak."

"In the past we have been able to enter and exit their dimension due to the holes in the fabric of time and dimension. Once we seal up this rent our dimension should be safe. We know that sometime in eons past this same enemy has warred with a humanoid species as we found evidence in the space ship disguised as Saturn's moon Iapetus. Perhaps we all are surviving descendants of that long ago conflict."

"The star charts in their navigational system are not of any known configuration familiar to the Andrians which have travelled extensively in our universe. It could well be that these earlier humanoids escaped from the aliens dimension into ours. With the lone alien Being we found on the ship it appears that he somehow came along for the ride as a scout but due to lack of breathing resources it was unable to jump back to its original dimension. With that being said, the Andrians have had ample conflict with the aliens across the galaxies so we know that they may be scattered around. It will be our duty to locate and destroy any remaining aliens after we seal up the hole leading to their dimension."

"In the past five years our neuroscientists have made tremendous strides in developing a viral cocktail that will destroy them. Our latest challenge is to deliver the cocktail into the alien spacecraft themselves. The administration of the viral cocktails to the entities within their spacecraft is yet to be determined. Should we find ourselves in a hand to hand combat situation, meaning close combat, we have developed viral projectiles with fast acting serum to destroy the neurological systems of the outer being. With the outer being destroyed the alien entity should be immobilized."

"We believe that we can repair the rent in the fabric of interdimensional space after we remove them. We also think we still have twenty five years before doomsday. Selections have already been made for the arks and we are preparing to launch the arks within another fifteen years barring any unforeseen circumstances."

"As for the rest of us, it is time for some of us to say our goodbyes. We will be soon deployed, I am hoping within the year. Those of us that are being deployed consider yourself on leave and visit with your families. I am afraid to delay any longer. Either we got it right or we do not. One thing is for sure, we will not go out without a fight. I believe that our species have been the only species they have not ever been able to conquer, thus the huge amount of force that is being brought to bear against us. God Speed!"

"Admiral Cleary, Blain, Sasha, Sara, Flata and Muskula, I want you to meet with me in the morning at the conference room. We have already devised our plan of attack but we must get the virus bombs to the fleet that is already constantly bombarding the enemy with the neutrino bombs. We need to take out as many as possible. It will also give us an analysis as to how effective out viral bomb defense is going to be. We will constantly need to gather intelligence and determine how swiftly the virus spreads.

Oh, and I suppose Breveka and Dr. Washington should be there too."

Emily left the podium and briefing room, she wanted to spend time with her family.

Caleb felt a deep stab of fear realizing that in all probability, Selena would be going to the battle front to assist in the injection and evaluation of the effectiveness of the virus.

CHAPTER 60
BATTLE PLAN

Early sunrise was a sight to behold. Caleb and Selena stood on the porch watching the sun rise over the mountains to the East and slowly light up the lake. Their arms around each other helped diminish the chill of the early morning air. Fog rose from the ocean inlet where the water was somewhat warmer than the chilled air. The leaves were turning from green to a bright golden hue and seemingly to have done so overnight.

Selena could feel Caleb shaking. Tears were in his eyes. He knew in his heart of hearts that Emily was going to send Selena on one of the saucers to oversee the administration and evaluation of the viral agent designed to destroy the alien enemy. The enemy, even though a galaxy away, was in cosmological scales, on Earth's doorstep. Earth's forces had to defeat them in the void between the galaxies starting as far into the Andromeda galaxy as possible.

Selena said, "It is necessary for me to go Caleb. As Hanlee said many years ago that our meeting and coming together has been determined by the confluence of space and time; whatever controls our destinies have determined that we are where we are supposed to be. Knowing that, then we should have no fear because our cause is just and will not fail nor will we be destroyed.

This enemy, our enemy, is also the enemy of the Eternal Cosmic Spirit that rules our universe. We should consider it an honor to be chosen to play such an important role in returning this "thing", whatever life form is, back to whence it came. It is truly evil."

Caleb could not speak. He thought he was going to lose Selena. He was not a man who loved lightly. He also believed in his spiritual being that Selena was right about the confluences of cosmic time and space. They all were where they were supposed to be.

Promptly at 0800, Admiral Cleary, Blain, Sasha, Sara, Breveka, Selena, Flata, Commander Taaker, Muskula, and Emily met in the conference room. The door was closed. Evidently this meeting was for their ears only

Emily stood at the head of the table and looked into the eyes of each individual present. Then speaking telepathically she said, "We are the nucleus for determining the fate of mankind. Under our direction Earth's forces will be required to launch a two prong attack. We will destroy the enemy between Andromeda and the Milky Way galaxies. And, we will need to defend the Earth and possibly evacuate as many people as possible. The Andrians have been building arks across the Galaxy and have already begun evacuating as many populations as possible. They have also instituted a program of collecting DNA of as many individuals as possible that were unable to get on the Arks. This program has also been secretly ongoing on the earth for the past five years. We will not be able to evacuate everyone but we can save their progeny and essence."

ASSIMILATION

Looking at Selena and Breveka, Emily said, "Selena it appears that you will have an opportunity to experience some exciting adventures. Breveka will be by your side to help you assimilate into the Andrian culture. If you need any additional pointers please feel free to ask Sara. I am sure she has some interesting pointers to assist you in your endeavors."

Sara laughed and said, "Yes, do not go to sleep!"

Everyone laughed as Sara's misadventure had become legendary.

"Flata, I am at a loss to really know what to do with you. Your skills are unmatched anywhere in the universe. You no doubt could be an asset on the Carrier. Then on the other hand, your skills may well be needed to help us start over."

Emily's bleak assessment of an alternative future was left hanging in the air.

"Blain and Sasha will accompany me on the Carrier. That is where I believe we will be the most effective."

Emily felt Sara's spike of anger at being left out and before she was able to say anything, Emily said, "Sara, your place is here on the Earth. We need to know that our children are well protected. You will be the Co-Commander along with Commander Taaker for earth defense forces coordinating with Admiral Cleary. You both will insure that any further breakthroughs on development of the virus to kill the enemy will reach us as soon as possible on the battle front…,and possible evacuation".

Muskula, you will be in charge of the ocean forces. I know you are extremely limited in numbers but you can help provide a safety net of intelligence and act as an early warning system. I am sure your use of Karlalif as your co commander will be acceptable. I do not know anyone else who wants to swim under water!"

Again everyone laughed, and as before, it was a nervous response.

Emily dismissed the group. After mulling around several minutes, they each went their own way, to their families.

CHAPTER 61
EMBARCATION

Emily sat with Warren on the porch overlooking the lake. The afternoon was idyllic. As they drank their coffee Emily's countenance was heavy. She had been home now for one year. Selena and Breveka along with other personnel had left three months earlier. Selena should be out of decontamination about now. As for Warren there was no softening of his heart, it was set in stone.

"Warren, on the second trip on the intergalactic carrier Blain was almost killed. In reality he was dead and on his way to the spirit world. It was at that time that I realized that I truly loved him and I would do anything to keep him from leaving me. Sasha and I both felt the same way. We made love to him, made promises to him and all but reached inside of him and pulled his heart from his chest. And miracles of miracles, he returned back to life."

"I realized that I loved him with every fiber of my spirit and being, exactly the way I love you. By a miracle of the Eternal Cosmic Spirit, his soul returned to his body and he awakened. I kept my promise and Orion is the result of our union. I am sorry you are unable to accept him in our lives and have chosen to withdraw."

Emily's voice turned hard.

"I would council you to find love and comfort wherever you can find it because in all probability, none of us will be here long. I love you as I always have. Thus, I have shielded you from the gravity of the threat which we all face. But the truth of the matter is that we are all fighting an alien being from another dimension and we are fighting for our very existence. Surly you should have deduced from the arrival of two separate life entities which I returned that they were not here on vacation. They are all that is left of their species."

Warren turned his head and looked long and hard at Emily and said, " I wish he would have died".

His heart has been hardening and his love for her had become dimmer and he no longer believed hardly anything she said, even in light of the evidence that surrounded him. He did not believe in the big, bad boogeyman alien that Emily spoke of. He just could not accept her story. He knew in his heart that if she wanted to come home she could have done so in her saucer. He just knew that she wanted to be with Blain.

Tears spilled from her eyes and ran down her cheeks. Emily loved Warren so much and it crushed her heart and soul to see his love for her turn into a psychotic episode that may even lead to a complete mental breakdown. She knew she was going to have to wipe his mind in order to save his sanity. She also knew that in his new world she would not exist. Emily stifled a plea to God to give her strength.

Without saying another word Emily got up and using her personal communicator she called Commander Taaker. The others would just have to understand, especially Warren Jr.

ASSIMILATION

Emily called the family together while Warren was at work in the forest.

"The decision to wipe Warren's mind of me was necessary. I did this because I love him and I do not want to see him in pain. He has been unable to accept me or Orion. As far as he is now concerned, Orion is Persha and Skips son. You all have been able to read his mind and you are aware just how far into psychosis he has been drifting. I still love Warren and always will and therefore I task you all with keeping him safe."

"I feel like I was very lucky that Becky was really attracted to Warren so it was easy to get her to fill in the role as wife and mother to Warren Jr. I was honest and up front with her about our dire circumstances and she agreed to have memories implanted in her mind to accept Warren as her husband and Warren Jr. as her son. Warren Jr. has accepted the necessity of this action and has agreed to just call me Aunt Emily, at least verbally."

"Ten of the smart saucers and the one entity enhanced intergalactic carrier will be leaving this weekend. There is no reason for us to delay any longer. Sara, I leave you my family in your hands. If you believe it is even close to being necessary, you are to get them all on the ark and to safety. Flee to wherever you feel necessary. You will have three enhanced saucers at your disposal. I believe you are absolutely the best investment that I have ever availed myself. Blain, Sasha and myself have complete confidence in you. Of course you will have Flata, Hanlee and Jawane as your assistants. If Warren gives you any resistance about evacuation you will have to do whatever is necessary to make him compliant."

Everyone tearfully said their good byes and Emily entered the tunnel for the short ride to her saucer. In the hanger Admiral Cleary and Commander Taaker saluted her with the entire compliment of Space Intelligence Rangers bidding her farewell. Emily boarded her saucer and the saucers in her command left the hanger.

ASSIMILATION

BOOK TWO

ASSIMILATION CHARACTERS

Blain	Military leader of the Andrians
Persha	Orphaned Andrian female under Blain's care
Jawane	Son of Blain and Sharla
Hanlee	Daughter of Blane and Chandra
Emily Smith	Leader of earth resistance and former abductee
Skip	Son of Earl and Karen Abbott
Billy	Son of Earl and Karen Abbott
Warren	Son of Earl and Karen Abbott, Fiancée of Emily Smith
Flata	Andrian Geneticist
Avery Cleary	Admiral in charge of Earth defense forces
Chandra	Consort of Blain and mother of Hanlee
Sasha Palangin	Lieutenant in the Space Defense Commandoes

Entity	Biological mechanical entity in saucer created by Flata
Muskula planet	Aquatic species saved from destroyed
Coach Bryan	Skips gymnast coach
Becky	Gymnast, friend and admirer of Skip
Sara Sears	Gymnast and daughter of Caleb
Caleb Sears	Civilian Security Expert, recruited by Emily
Bob Johnson	Commander of Space Intelligence
Jessop and Reese	Detectives that tracked down Emily after her abduction
Kyla	Childhood friend of Sara
Haley	Childhood friend of Sara, murdered by Roger Clovis
Selena Washington	Molecular Bio Chemical expert in Extremophile life forms
Shawn Washington	Son of Selena Washington
Officer Taaker	Andrian Commander for Emily's security
Jack	Kyla's husband and local lawyer
Roger Clovis	Murder of Haley, childhood friend of Sara

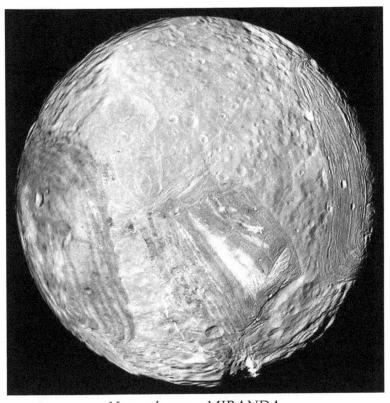

Uranus's moon MIRANDA,
"Courtesy of NASA/JPL-Caltech" VOYAGER 2
Jan. 24, 1986   PIA 18185.tif, Uranus's Moon Miranda

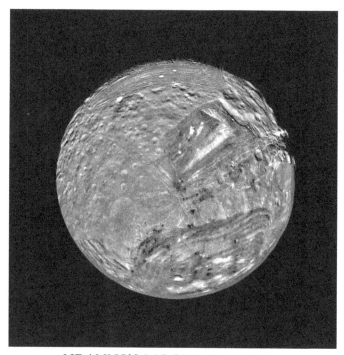

URANUS'S MOON MIRANDA
"Courtesy of NASA/JPL-CALTECH" PIA 18185.tif,
Voyager 2,
JAN 24, 1986

*SATURN'S MOON, HYPERON,
JANUARY 19, 2009 CASSINI
Courtesy of NASA-JPL/CALTECH*

Book 3
Emily Smith Trilogy
TARGET EARTH

Chapter 1
Ugly Surprise

Kyla sat on her lounge chair on the beach looking out over the white sand that slipped gently beneath the waves as they frothily slathered up onto the shore. The water a short distance from the shore was an absolute calm. She was thinking how odd it was that she had not seen Emily Smith for at least ten years, yet she had seen Sara at least four times a year. Some of the time she was with Jawane, a real odd duck, but mostly she was alone. She seemed to have hardened in ways she could not understand.

Sara had always told me to be prepared to leave on a moment's notice. Leave where? And why leave at all. Their contracting business with the military had made all of them rich beyond their wildest dreams.

"Ha! Not that they had time to enjoy the largess!", Mused Kyla.

Kyla adjusted her large bonnet and shielded her eyes as she focused on some kind of disturbance about fifty yards from the shore. She was fairly certain it was not a large fish because the disturbance was just too large and wide.

Looking toward her ten year old twins playing near the water's edge Kyla called out to them, "Haley! Paul! Come here to me please! It is important!"

The children left their playmates and ran up to their mom.

"What do you want Mom? We do not have to go yet do we?", intoned Paul.

Kyla looked again at the disturbed water which was now only about twenty five yards away from the beach.

Kyla stood up and called out to the other young children playing in and near the water's edge. She had an uneasy feeling about the disturbance in the water; it just did not look natural.

"Children! Get out of the water! Come away now!"

Other parents became aware of Kyla's warning and scrambled to their feet to collect their children.

There was a loud scream as one of the children cried out in pain, then another child and yet another! The water's edge had become a roiling mass of withering black bodies of the likes which Kyla had never seen.

A man ran to the water to retrieve his small son playing in the sand and he appeared to be burned in half by some kind of water jet; his body smoked as it fell down and he withered and screamed in pain thrashing his arms uselessly in the sand. His small son dissolved in a pile of smoking flesh as the burning liquid spewed over his body. The bones were still sitting erect as the flesh flowed from his frame.

The black undulating mass became individual creatures with four appendages extending from the front and rear and too the sides, a row of eyes encircling around its head. There were large red swollen membranes all over the body from which small snake like appendages

ASSIMILATION

sprayed the burning liquid.

Kyla grabbed her children by the arms and began to drag them away from the beach. The speed of the undulating mass increased exponentially and seemed to be just yards away. One of the creatures stood on the bottom two appendages and appeared to be preparing to spray her and the children.

Kyla was terrified, and she knew that if she was so much as touched by the liquid she would not be able to get away; also in that moment an impossible thought flashed thru her mind as she remembered Sara continuously admonishing her to always to be prepared to leave on a moment's notice. Sara must have been aware of these creatures! That is what all the military contracts were about!

As Kyla stumbled backward the ugly creature shot a thick, steaming, gelatinous stream toward her and just as quickly someone or something dove in front of her and was firing a laser rifle at the ugly disgusting blob. The liquid hit the individual in the chest area and Kyla heard a loud singeing sound.

Just as fast as the individual dove in front of Kyla, five commandoes reached the individuals side, scooped up the individual and began backing away all the while firing their lasers into the undulating blobs!

Kyla felt her arms being jerked up and then observed she was airborne and landing in a net device about twenty yards from her previous position. Haley and Paul soon followed behind landing squarely within the net which became a cocoon. It was then she observed the numerous saucer craft, Helios, and individual self-propelled soldiers dancing in the air firing not only lasers, but some kind of gel gun that caused the ugly beings to become immobile.

Kyla thought, "Flying Saucers! Really! Well why not, there are these ugly creatures dissolving people with some kind of liquid acid!"

Kyla then saw a gravity assist medical transport device being loaded on the same saucer as she and her twins. The device contained the body of a woman who was writhing in pain. Medical attendants were filling the device with some kind of white cloud substance that hardened quickly. It was then, to her astonishment, she saw Sara with a grimaced smile on her face as she disappeared within the cloud.

CPSIA information can be obtained
at www.ICGtesting.com
Printed in the USA
BVHW081224280922
648137BV00001BA/73